# NOWHERE TO HIDE

"**Holy. Hell.** I haven't finished a thriller this fast since *Gone Girl*."

★★★★★

"I am **freaking out!** Boy – did I not see that coming!"

★★★★★

"A fun, wild, suspenseful book that I **couldn't get enough of**."

★★★★★

"An **outstanding** thriller – impossible for me to put down!"

★★★★★

"I want to **read this story again** in case I missed anything the first time!"

★★★★★

"I am still thinking about it – the last sentence was a **jaw-dropper!**"

★★★★★

"Wow, **what a story!** The ending just blew me away."

★★★★★

"You'll definitely be left with your **jaw on the floor** and your head spinning."

★★★★★

After studying English at university, Nell Pattison became a teacher and specialised in Deaf education. She has been teaching in the Deaf community for fourteen years in both England and Scotland, working with students who use BSL, and began losing her hearing in her twenties. She lives in North Lincolnshire with her husband and son. Nell's first novel, *The Silent House*, was a *USA Today* bestseller.

## Also by Nell Pattison:

*The Silent House*
*Silent Night*
*The Silent Suspect*

# NOWHERE TO HIDE

## NELL PATTISON

avon.

Published by AVON
A division of HarperCollins*Publishers* Ltd
1 London Bridge Street
London SE1 9GF

www.harpercollins.co.uk

HarperCollins*Publishers*
1st Floor, Watermarque Building, Ringsend Road
Dublin 4, Ireland

A Paperback Original 2021

1

First published as *Hide* in Great Britain by HarperCollins*Publishers* 2021
This edition published in the United States by HarperCollins*Publishers* 2022

A catalogue copy of this book is available from the British Library.

ISBN: 978-0-00-848692-1

Typeset in Sabon LT Std by Palimpsest Book Production Limited,
Falkirk, Stirlingshire
Printed and Bound in the UK using
100% Renewable Electricity at CPI Group (UK) Ltd

MIX
Paper from
responsible sources
FSC™ C007454
www.fsc.org

*For my Grandma, Betty Hutchinson*
*1930—2021*

# Prologue

As I see their face turn in my direction, their eyes light on me and narrow. I feel a jolt of fear. Is this the killer? I have a horrible feeling I'm right, though I don't know why they did it, or why they're after me now. All I know is that I have to start running again.

The trees seem to press in on me as I leave the path, my head darting from left to right as I try to look for obstacles while still making progress. Every moment, I'm expecting to feel an impact as I'm shot, but nothing comes. Without sound, everything around me seems surreal – no pounding of my feet, no tearing of breath, no whistling of the wind around me. I don't feel like I'm making any progress, as if I'm trapped underwater and fighting my way through the depths.

My head whips round again, trying to get a look at my pursuer, but there's no sign of anyone. It's worse than if I'd been able to see them, because now they could be anywhere. They could be creeping up behind me, just out of sight, and I wouldn't be any the wiser.

I feel a whooshing sensation as something moves quickly past my face, but I can't stop to find out what it was. It might have been some more snow falling from a tree, or it could have been something thrown by the person chasing me, in an effort to slow me down.

My breathing is laboured now, exhausted as I am, both from the running and the fear. If I carry on like this, I'm going to collapse. Spotting a fallen tree up ahead, I scramble over it then duck down into its shadow. There's a small hollow there that has very little snow in it, and I curl up into the space, making myself as small as possible. I press myself to the ground, feeling for any vibrations caused by someone approaching. Please don't let them find me. Please. Let me stay hidden.

As my breathing and heart rate slow ever so slightly, I try to stay aware of what's around me. At first, I'm not sure I feel anything, but then there it is. The thud in the ground of someone running. I can't stay here; they'll find me.

Springing up, I take my chances and set off running again, not caring which direction I'm heading in. A low-hanging branch catches me with a glancing blow on the side of my face, making me gasp, but I don't stop, ducking when I see another one coming at me. This one snags on my rucksack, however, and I fight for a moment to try and untangle it. Fear grips my heart, and I shrug out of the bag and carry on running, not caring that I've left my belongings behind. Right now, the only thing I'm focused on is running.

I think I see a movement out of the corner of my eye, and I turn my head. Too late. A hand grabs my arm, forcing me around. I fall, my feet slipping on the snow as I try to break free from the grip, aware of the scream rising up inside me, feeling my body shake with it as I let it out into the night air.

# Chapter 1

## Lauren

'Emily!'

I pause for a moment after calling my sister's name, then have to hold back my impatience when I realise Emily probably can't hear me. Putting my cup of tea on the worktop, I go down the narrow corridor to the spare room and knock on the door.

'Emily, are you up?'

The door opens suddenly, setting me off balance for a moment, but I right myself and look my sister up and down.

'You're not ready yet. It's nearly twelve. We can't be late, not today.'

'Sorry, I lost track of time,' Emily explains. She clearly isn't as concerned about the time as I am, which riles me a little bit, but I bite back the response that's forming in my mind.

'Come on, you know what Morna will be like if we're late,' is all I say. If in doubt, I always project my own grumpiness onto someone else.

'I don't think that'll make a difference to her attitude,' Emily replies lightly, but turns back to her room and picks up her towel, before pushing past me towards the bathroom.

I watch my sister until the door closes, still struck by how eerie the likeness between us is. We're only a year apart in age, and even though Emily is younger than me, many people assume she's the elder sibling. I can't explain why that irritates me so much. It hardly matters.

Until April of this year, the two of us hadn't seen each other since I moved out at eighteen. So, that's nearly eleven years, I work out in my head. I'd never intended to lose touch with Emily, but I'd wanted to get as far away from my old life and the care system as possible, and that meant cutting ties until I was ready to reach out again. But time went on, and it never seemed like the right moment. In the end it was Emily who tracked me down and offered the hand of friendship, which I have been trying to accept over the last eight months, but with very little success.

It was a little awkward yesterday, and I can still feel some of that tension hanging around today. Emily had insisted it was important that we spend Christmas Day together, and I could see her point, so I reluctantly agreed. When it came to it, though, it was clear we would both have preferred to be doing what we usually did – Emily spending the day with friends in London, me either working or spending the day in my pyjamas with Netflix and junk food. It wasn't that bad, having company, really, I suppose. But we're still not fully relaxed with each other, and I'd felt like I needed to make a special effort. Maybe if I'd never been to Emily's place in London I would have felt differently, rather than feeling self-conscious about having her in my own tiny flat.

While Emily showers, I wander back through to my little living-dining-kitchen area and pick up the cup of tea I abandoned a few minutes ago. The pale purple mug is chipped in two separate places, and the glaze is wearing off the handle. I bought it as part of a cheap crockery set in a bargain store when I first got my own place. Most of the set has broken over the intervening years, and I've gradually bought other things, so my plates and bowls are now a mishmash of different colours and styles – whatever I could afford at the time. There was none of that when I went to stay with my sister a few weeks ago. Emily has a full matching set of patterned Royal Doulton tableware, including a gravy boat. The white and blue of the plates is an extension of the colour scheme of her flat. When I visited, I spent the entire time terrified of spilling something on the white sofa, or the pale blue rug that covers the hardwood floor in the living room. My sofa, in comparison, is a sagging purple affair with the fabric fraying around the edges. It came from a charity shop, as did the couple of tables and the multicoloured rag rug on the floor.

I know it probably sounds like I resent Emily's success, and maybe I do. I'm proud of the fact that I bought everything I own myself, with money I earned, and have made my home my own, but there's something about all the expensive and tasteful things Emily has that makes me more critical of my own belongings. Not that Emily has made any sign that she thinks my flat's beneath her, or anything like that. It's all in my head, I know. Still, I'm glad we've got it over with for this year, and we're going to spend today very firmly within my comfort zone. And who knows, maybe things will be different by next Christmas.

The sound of the shower is still drifting through the bathroom door and I check my watch again. There's no point shouting at Emily to hurry up: she will have taken her cochlear implant processors off when she went in, so won't be able to hear anything without them. Emily contracted meningitis when she was only a few days old, and it left her with no hearing in one ear and barely any in the other. She had implants in both ears when she was only a tiny baby, at a time when I was barely walking, so Emily's deafness is all the two of us have ever known. Within a few short years of that operation, we were placed in foster care.

A minute later, the door to the bathroom opens, and Emily emerges, brushing her hair. It's the same blonde as mine, but with expensive highlights added. Mine is all natural, from spending so much time outside, but it's always darker in the winter. Apart from that, it would be hard to tell us apart from the back, I think. My body is a bit more muscular than Emily's, which comes from a job that involves physical, outdoor work, and Emily's about half an inch taller, but at first glance these differences wouldn't really be noticeable. For a moment, I allow myself to wonder what it would be like to be Emily for a short time, to slip into her life and wear it like a coat.

Emily hooks a processor over her ear and attaches the transmitter to the left side of her head with the magnet. Picking up the other one, she does the same, then a moment later she frowns and removes it again.

'This one isn't working again. I keep telling them there's something wrong with it.'

'Did you charge it?' I ask. To be honest, I have no idea

how the technology works – I wasn't interested when we were kids and I haven't really thought about it again since.

'Yeah, it was charging overnight, but the light's not on now. I'll just have to make do with one today and let the hospital know it's not working.' Looking up at me, she grimaces. 'I'm sorry, I know you're in a hurry. I'll get a move on.'

'I just don't want to give Morna any more ammunition. You know what she's like.'

I click the kettle back on and offer Emily a cup of tea while she goes to the fridge and grabs some leftovers from yesterday. I hadn't planned for meals beyond Christmas dinner, so it's lucky that I overcatered and there's plenty of food left.

'Why doesn't she like you?' Emily asks.

I shrug, not wanting to start the uncomfortable task of analysing my relationship with Morna. 'She's a volunteer, I'm a paid employee. She doesn't like it when I get to tell her what to do.'

What I don't tell Emily is that Morna and I applied for the same job four years earlier, and I think Morna still hasn't got over the fact that she missed out on the position. It wasn't just the difference in our ages that made me the better candidate, although with Morna being in her sixties I can see why my boss hadn't been keen to employ someone who would probably retire within a couple of years. I was better qualified for the position, having taken a college course in wildlife conservation online while working two different jobs in order to afford rent and food. I worked bloody hard to get the job I desperately wanted, and I don't need someone like Morna constantly harping on at me.

'Is everyone going to be there today?' Emily asks, a forced casualness to her tone.

'Yes, including Ben,' I reply, trying really hard not to roll my eyes, though I think it comes across in my voice anyway.

Emily looks down at her plate and picks at a bit of leftover potato, then wipes her fingers delicately on a garish Santa napkin before she responds.

'I wasn't thinking about Ben. I was wondering if Alec would be there.'

A cold wave of nausea washes through me at the mention of Alec's name. I'm pretty sure he wouldn't miss today's walk if you paid him to stay away, because today is something a bit different. Today, the nature reserve is closed to the general public, but because I work there, I'm allowed to bring a small group of guests in, so it was an obvious venue for our little nature group's Boxing Day meet-up. I've been meeting up with them for over three years now, at least once a month, in different nature reserves, woods and beaches around Lincolnshire. The group was originally started by one of my former colleagues, but when she moved to Wales, I more or less took over responsibility for it. People have come and gone in that time, though only Alec and Ben have been part of the group longer than I have.

We all went out for drinks before Christmas, and it was a great evening until Alec ruined it. Anyone else would probably avoid the group for a while, or at least get in touch with us all to apologise, but there's been nothing from him on our group chat and I just know he'll be there. He won't be able to pass up the opportunity to try and show us all how clever he is, how knowledgeable about the birds and wildlife around the reserve. Our group doesn't have a leader, as such, but Alec is still convinced he's the one in charge, and the rest of us have a tacit agreement to either take it in turns pretending to listen to him, or change the subject to break the flow of his words. It works, most of the time, and we keep the peace, but I think things will change in a big way after what happened the other night.

I sigh and scrub a hand across my face. The headache is back, pulsating away in my temples, and I briefly wonder if it's the thought of Alec that brought it back.

'I don't know if he'll be there,' I tell Emily now. 'I can't see him staying away, unfortunately. I don't think he's socially aware enough to realise how he made everyone feel the other night.'

Our reactions were varied, I'd say, but Kai really surprised me with the vehemence of the way he tried to confront Alec. His temper might be something I need to keep an eye on today. When I planned this, all I'd wanted was for the seven of us to have a nice walk on Boxing Day, get some fresh air and maybe see a few birds. I don't want to find myself in charge of crowd control if someone takes Alec to task about the other night.

Honestly, I've considered saying something to Alec myself. What he came out with the other night . . . it rattled me, but I haven't yet decided the best way to go forward. It's dangerous, I know that much, and if I go about it the wrong way there could be serious repercussions. It has to be face to face, but should I try to speak to him alone, or completely ignore him and call his bluff? The wrong decision could be catastrophic.

Emily is shaking her head. 'I don't understand him, at all. I thought he was just a nice old man, but . . .'

I snort. 'He's not that old. He's only in his fifties.'

'Really? I thought he was older than that.'

'It's the way he dresses,' I reply, wondering if anyone has ever tried to give Alec a few pointers on dressing for the twenty-first century.

'Maybe so,' Emily concedes with a nod. 'Anyway, I'm not planning on going near him today if I can help it.'

I look at my watch again, anxious to change the subject. 'Are you nearly ready?'

'Sure, just let me get my boots.'

'Do you mind driving today?' I ask. I've been nervous about broaching the subject, so I've left it until as late as possible. 'I think my car has some sort of rattle on the engine, I need to get it booked in for a service.'

Emily hesitates, but then smiles. 'Fine. As long as you direct me. I don't know the way well enough yet.'

As my sister goes off to collect what she needs for the day, I stay in my seat and put my head in my hands. I normally look forward to these days out with the nature group. Emily started joining us when the two of us reconnected, in an effort to get to know me better, and I know I should be touched by the gesture, but it irritates me. This group was mine, my friends and my hobby; why did she have to come in and claim it for herself?

Checking Emily is still in her room, I go into my own bedroom and open my bedside drawer. There is a tin inside, which I open, moving aside a layer of papers until I find what's hidden beneath. I slip the penknife into my pocket, grab my rucksack, which is already packed, then go back into the living room to wait for my sister.

# Chapter 2

## Morna

There is something secretly thrilling about having the keys to the visitor centre and letting myself in when there is nobody else on the whole of the reserve. Well, apart from Alec, of course. I roll my eyes just at the thought of the man. His car was already in the car park when I arrived, and I actually felt a bit miffed that he'd beaten me to it. Of course, he would have gone in via the side gate. It's only about two hundred metres from the visitor centre, but it's there to allow rangers vehicle access to the paths across the reserve. Alec isn't supposed to have a key, but he's one of those men that seems to get everything he expects, simply because of the pompous way he speaks to people. Even I've found myself deferring to him, occasionally.

Anyway, at least he won't bother me for the next half hour or so if he's out with his scope. There might be something interesting out on the scrapes and he will be desperate to be the first one to spot it. I sigh, the sound echoing strangely off the glass doors as I let myself in.

13

Why can't he just wait? There's something lovely about a shared experience of wildlife, something special about being together in a group when someone spots something beautiful, or uncommon. But no, Alec always wants to find it by himself, then when all of the others arrive, he'll crow about what he's seen, puffing his chest out as if a sighting of a Great Grey Shrike is the sort of thing that elevates him above the rest of us.

It's midday, but the grey sky outside means the centre is gloomy with only the natural light that comes through the large windows facing out onto the reserve. Shaking my head and trying to rid myself of this negative mood, I turn on the lights in the entrance way and the café, then make my way through to the kitchen. I switch on the big urn, leaving it to heat up, so everyone will be able to have a hot drink when they arrive, as well as fill their flasks. Once that job is ticked off my mental list, I go back out to the car for the shopping bags that I left in the boot. A walk on Boxing Day should start with a full stomach, I'd decided that as soon as we'd planned this walk, so I've brought everything I think we might need for a satisfying lunch – muffins, bacon, and a selection of sauces. I expect everyone filled up on turkey and Christmas pudding yesterday, so they might not have eaten before they arrive, and it might be more like a late brunch. Emily is a vegetarian, so I spent some time looking at the range of fake meats, but in the end I decided that eggs were probably a safer bet than some sort of processed vegan 'bacon' that looks like it's made of playdough. I take the bags into the kitchen and lay everything out on the worktop, then root through the cupboards to find the equipment I'll need.

14

My head is deep in one of the metal cupboards when I hear the throaty rumble of an engine outside. Whatever the vehicle is, it sounds bigger than a car, and I don't know who it could be. Straightening up, I wipe my hands absentmindedly on a tea towel and walk back towards the entrance to the visitor centre. Here there is a large glass panel next to the door, from which I have a clear view of the majority of the car park, but the only vehicles I can see are my car and Alec's. I'm going to have to go outside and look. Pulling the door of the centre closed quietly behind me, I step out onto the decking at the front of the building, then begin to make my way down the path back towards the car park. Some instinct makes me move carefully, trying to avoid making a sound as I walk.

Rounding the corner, the rest of the car park comes into view, but there are no other vehicles there. Strange. I turn around a couple of times, in case I somehow missed it, but there's nothing. Only Alec's car, parked closest to the entrance, then mine a few spaces further down. It must have been a farm vehicle passing nearby, and I was wrong about where the sound was coming from. Something about it has rattled me, though.

The weather has been bitterly cold for the last week, and there's still ice on the ground, so I have to watch my footing as I walk back up the path. When I reach the door to the visitor centre, I notice it's standing ajar. Did I close it fully when I stepped outside, or did I fail to push it all the way? I can't be certain, but my heart increases its pace as I step across the threshold into the building. It's Boxing Day, and the whole reserve is closed for five days over the Christmas period. Lauren managed to get special permission from the director to open up and bring our little wildlife spotters group here today, so there's no reason for anyone else to be here. Surely anyone who shouldn't be here wouldn't just brazenly walk into the centre, even when it's deserted? But if someone has turned up at the reserve not knowing it's closed, and has found the door to the visitor centre open, it would stand to reason they might go inside.

'Hello?' I call as I step further into the entrance. 'Is there anyone there?'

Silence. I must have left the door open behind me, I think, giving a little self-deprecating laugh, though it sounds a bit strangled in the empty space. Come on, Morna, I tell myself. You're only sixty-seven. Too young to be losing your marbles just yet. Still, I take a deep breath to try and calm my nerves before going back through to the kitchen.

There's no sign of anyone having been in the café, and the door on the other side of the building, which leads out to the reserve, is still locked. In the kitchen, the first thing I do is pull up the metal serving hatch between the preparation area and the main part of the café – I want to see anyone else who arrives. I won't admit to being rattled, being there on my own, but I faff about nervously in the kitchen for a few moments, picking up pans and putting them back down again, before I actually light upon a useful task. Setting to, I start cutting the muffins and arranging them, ready to be grilled when the others arrive, as well as setting out pans for the bacon and eggs. I take the sauces and line them up on the counter, so we can all help ourselves – one thing I do know is never to get between a Northerner and their sauce preferences. I've brought brown sauce, ketchup, and a bottle of Henderson's relish: we're near enough to South Yorkshire that it's definitely a favourite amongst some locals, and as I'm from Sheffield myself I don't feel like any condiment tray is complete without it.

At one point, I think I hear a door closing, and I pause in the middle of what I'm doing, my hand hovering over a stack of coffee cups. There's no further sound, however, and I shake my head for what feels like the hundredth time, chastising myself for being so jumpy.

Everything is ready to go for when the others arrive, so I make myself a coffee and sit down at one of the large wooden tables in the café. I choose a seat facing the large window onto the reserve, and spend a few minutes just watching the sway of the trees, their bare branches scratching a sky the colour of dirty snow – not the crisp, pure white of a fresh fall, but the pale, murky brown of the slush that remains at the edges of the pavement after three days. Despite the image, I'm sure it's too warm for snow. I hope it doesn't rain, though. Even if we're all dressed for changeable weather, there's something about rain in December that always makes everyone miserable.

There's some movement out near the edge of the woods, and I move closer to the glass to get a better look. There's a pond just outside, on the other side of the decking, and we often get some interesting birds visiting. It's amazing to be able to sit and have a coffee, watching the wildlife as it goes about its business, seemingly unfazed by the presence of the visitor centre. The really shy ones won't come out here, we're not going to get a Bittern sighting from the café, but there are often Herons and Egrets

17

stalking the reeds at the edge of the pond, as well as a few different kinds of ducks.

Is that a bird, though? I peer into the treeline, where I think I've seen movement. It could be a deer, I suppose, though they don't usually come round this way. Grabbing my bag, I pull out my binoculars and take a closer look. A moment later, I realise I'm holding my breath. What's wrong with me today? True, I'm used to the centre having several members of staff in the kitchen or the shop, as well as a varying number of visitors to the reserve. I'd been looking forward to being here on my own this morning, but as it turns out, I'm not enjoying the atmosphere. With nobody else here, it strikes me just how isolated this place is. I know Alec is out there somewhere, but that thought isn't a particularly comforting one, either. Hopefully it won't be long until one of the others is here.

I sit back down, clutching my coffee, hoping the warmth from the mug will help me relax. There's no further sign of movement out in the trees, so it must have been a bird. Or maybe Alec, of course. Nothing to worry about. While I'm alone, I take the opportunity to pull out the photo I keep tucked into my purse. I gaze at it for a moment, lost in memory, then put it away again. It won't do to have someone else notice it, not after Alec . . . I catch my breath as a wave of anger rises up inside me. How could he have behaved so callously the other night? I'd thought he was better than that. My anger is a veneer, however, only finely covering the sick feeling of dread I've been experiencing in the pit of my stomach ever since I realised that he'd been talking about me. Of course, at the time I didn't dignify it with a response, and I haven't dared to contact him since. With any luck, he will have forgotten about it altogether, given how much he had to drink that night. If nobody else brings it up, perhaps we can all move on and pretend it never happened.

Remembering that night still chills me, though. He didn't look drunk when he fixed me with that piercing stare, teasing me and the others with what he might be about to say. No, I can't hope that it's all over. If I do that, and don't seize the opportunity myself, I will no longer have any control over the situation. Glancing over my shoulder to check nobody else has come in while I've been deep in thought, I pull out the photo once again, stroking it softly. Today is the day; I *will* do what I've been planning for a while now. It's going to be difficult, and scary, and might not go as smoothly as I hope, but it's the only thing to do now Alec has forced my hand. I look down at the photo and hope they will forgive me, in time.

# Chapter 3

## Alec

The door to the hide creaks as I open it, and I make a loud tutting noise. I'll have to mention it to Lauren when she arrives. It's no good letting the maintenance of the hides slacken, not when the slightest of sounds could scare off the birds out on the marshes. I'm sure I've told her before about the time when I was in the Western Isles, when I and a group of other keen birders had been waiting for a close sighting of some Blue-Winged Teal. A public footpath ran quite near the hide, and some idiot out for a ramble had left their phone on. It rang, loudly, just as the birds were coming in to land, and startled them so much they flew off. It was all I could do to keep a civil tongue in my head when the man walked past in full conversation, oblivious to the damage he'd done. Some people just have no respect for the environment and the living creatures around them.

This nature reserve is the biggest in Lincolnshire, and as such is one of my favourite places to spend a day.

There's such a wide variety of bird species, and always something interesting to see, no matter the time of year. It was developed from a mixture of disused agricultural land and clogged-up marshes, but soon became a haven for wildlife once some care and attention was put into the area. Of course, I've been visiting since before they had a fancy café and shop, before there were even public toilets, and I sometimes feel that too many people are encouraged to come here, but I suppose they have to make money somehow in order to pay their staff.

Setting my bag down with precision on one of the benches, I reach up and carefully open the hatch, securing it in place with the latch. This hide has solid wooden hatches with no glass in them, so the only light entering the hut comes from the opening I have just created. I settle myself on the bench then open my bag. I am very particular about the way I pack my bag, in order to be able to reach everything I need in the correct order. First, I remove my binoculars, placing them on the bench on my other side. They are my pride and joy, top of the range, and I always get the best view of the wildlife wherever I happen to be because of these beauties. The magnification level is superior to anything else on the market, and the seven-lens eyepiece gives a superb clarity of image. I've told the others in the nature group about the features several times, so I'm quite surprised that none of them have gone on to buy their own. Really, they're not capable of taking even a little bit of advice. As the most knowledgeable person in the group, and the de facto leader, I must confess to being a little disgruntled that they don't consider my expertise to be something worth acting on.

Next out of the bag is the new scope I bought myself for Christmas. I turn it over in my hands a couple of times, admiring the sleekness of it, before I set up my tripod and mount the scope. I spent hours poring over websites trying to choose the best one – both the dedicated birdwatching sites that I regularly frequent, and other sites devoted to digital cameras and stargazing. Many of the qualities desirable in a telescope are also useful for wildlife watching, and I didn't want to make a poor choice. In the end, I selected one, and I'm pleased with my choice. It has the largest diameter objective lens of all the scopes I've seen, and is made by one of the high-end brands. Some of my friends think it doesn't matter which brand you purchase, as long as it fulfils your requirements, but personally I feel there's something to be said for getting brands people know and recognise. A beginner is bound to have more respect for my expertise if they see the make of my equipment, I'm sure of it, and it's important to me to be able to pass on my wisdom to newcomers to birding.

There's a sudden flurry of activity out on the marshes in front of me, so I quickly adjust the settings on my new scope and set up my binoculars. A couple of months ago, Kai asked me why I use both pieces of equipment – I roll my eyes just remembering the exchange.

'They serve different purposes,' I replied, trying not to make my voice sound too patronising. It can be difficult, though, when people ask silly questions.

'How? They both give you a close-up view of the marshes. Why do you need to lug both around with you all day?' Kai had still looked perplexed, and not for the first time I wondered how serious the young man really was about observing wildlife in any form.

Sighing, I tapped the scope. 'This one is mounted on a tripod, so it's good for observing one particular patch of land or water. But if a bird takes flight and I want to track it, the binoculars are much better for that.'

'So why bother with the scope? You can watch a fixed point with binoculars, too. You know, you just stay still.' He'd given a shrug and wandered away, clearly not interested in the answer, and leaving me with my mouth open. Really, it was quite rude of him. Clearly Kai has never spent five hours sitting in one position waiting for a Sea Eagle to leave its nest so he can get a clear view of it in flight. If you try to hold your binoculars in one position for that long, you'll regret it.

Thinking of Kai sets a ripple of unease travelling through my stomach. The way the boy manhandled me the other evening had been uncalled for, though I do accept perhaps I was a little unwise. Emily was practically hysterical, silly girl. As if I did anything wrong; it was just a harmless touch to emphasise the importance of what I was saying to her. Young women today seem to think everything is about them, and I think I would be well within my rights to ask for an apology from her. If she hadn't started screeching and making a big deal out of it, I wouldn't have got angry and said those things. I only wanted to tell her, to warn her . . . Still, if she isn't interested, that's her problem, not mine.

Now I think about it, I didn't consider the potential impact of my words. Despite the fact that I might have had rather a few too many glasses of red wine, I still remember

24

the looks on all their faces as I stood there, before Kai hustled me outside. It was a few days ago, though, so hopefully they will have all got over it by now and won't try to bring it up again. That would just be embarrassing for everybody. After all, I have no intention of telling them all everything I know. That is, unless I think it will be worth my while. I only decided to say anything to Emily on the spur of the moment, and that was due to the alcohol. After the way she reacted, I don't think she deserves to know now, and she will have to suffer the consequences.

No, I'm satisfied that I didn't do anything wrong at the pub the other evening. What is it they call people who take offence at everything? Of course, I think, looking at the yellow-grey sky: snowflakes. If they have a problem with me, it's because they're snowflakes. Pushing that evening to the back of my mind, I open my bag once again and pull out my flask. When it came to packing for the day, I have made sure I'm prepared. It's not just my optical equipment that is top of the range, but also everything else that I carry. What's the use of having high-end binoculars if your flask leaks and tea gets into the mechanism? What if the lid of your sandwich box pops off and you get crumbs caught around the edge of the lenses? What if the strap of your bag breaks while you're walking, and you drop thousands of pounds of equipment in the mud? No, I always buy the best available when it comes to my outdoor pursuits, meaning not only do I always have a hot cup of tea, but I am content in the knowledge that my equipment is safe.

I check my watch. The others are due to arrive around one, giving us some time to catch up and share a drink and something to eat before setting out to the opposite end of the reserve. We are intending to catch the Starling murmuration, which will happen sometime between half past three and four this afternoon, I expect. The birds have been right down at the far end of the marshes for the last week, so it's necessary for us to walk the four or five miles to the furthest hide if we want to get the best view of the nightly display.

Murmurations are a beautiful sight, and something that I would happily watch on a daily basis, because they're never quite the same. The balletic movements of thousands of birds, all synchronised in a way only nature can choreograph. I do hope the others will be as respectful of the Starlings as the birds deserve, but unfortunately I've learnt recently that they're not all quite as dedicated to the beauties of the natural world as I am.

As I look across the marshes, I sweep my binoculars around from right to left, scanning to see what's out there. Plenty of Lapwings and Mallard, and Herring Gulls too. A Heron on the edge of the reeds, his head low. A strip of bright white catches my eye – a little Egret. Nothing too out of the ordinary, which is disappointing. I would dearly love to take a little titbit back for the others, a hint of something special they might see. As I continue to scan the reeds, I hear the tell-tale booming call of a Bittern, and my spirits rise slightly. Bittern are well known to frequent the reserve, but they're still rarely seen, and I expect at least a couple of the others have never seen one.

I catch sight of something moving, but it's not in the reeds, where I would expect to find a Bittern; there's something out beyond there, in the woods. Training my binoculars on the area, I can't see anything, so I switch to the scope, letting out another huff of indignation that Kai might think the two pieces of equipment do exactly the same job. A few moments of looking through the scope, and I sit up again, frowning. It looked like a person. Nobody else should be on the reserve right now. I know Morna had intended to arrive early and sort out the kitchen, but she wouldn't be wandering about on the edge of the woods, not on her own. But the reserve is closed to the public today, so who else can it be?

Making up my mind, I leave my scope where it is and step out of the hide, looking up and down the path before I set off to my right. The path skirts the edge of the marshes, then meets another path running along the edge of the woods. I won't have to go far to catch a glimpse of whoever it was. Of course, I'm wary of leaving the rest of my equipment in the hide, but as there's nobody else around, it should be perfectly safe.

I march up the path for a few metres, keeping my eyes on the woods ahead, occasionally stopping to look through my binoculars at the treeline. Even though the trees are bare of foliage, the forest still looks dense due to the sheer number of sycamore and beech trees that crowd up to the path. If someone walked only a few metres into the woodland here, I wouldn't be able to see them. But why would they be going into the woods that way? The path runs along the edge of the trees at this point, and anyone striking off the path would need a very good reason for doing so. There are all sorts of wildlife that could be disturbed, even at this time of year, and all visitors are asked to keep to the paths. Clearly whoever it is has no respect for the rules. Puffing out my chest, I continue walking.

As the path curves round to the right, there's a shortcut that dips into a hollow down to my left. I stand there for a moment, deciding which way to go, until I hear a sound that seems to come from the railway bridge. Making up my mind, I scramble down the bank into the hollow, then back up the other side, cutting out a good few metres of path. When I reach the top, I pause again, and for the first time I find myself thinking about who or what I might be following. Of course, it might not be a person at all, but a deer. There's a large herd of roe deer that roam the reserve, but that means you also get poachers. Could I have seen a poacher, thinking that nobody would be out on the reserve today, giving them free rein?

I shudder at the thought. Poachers will have shotguns, most likely. Maybe I saw a deer, or Morna having a quick walk, but if it was a poacher I don't want to interfere – let the police deal with criminals. I'm no have-a-go hero. Another sound comes from my left, an echo from under the railway bridge, and that makes up my mind for me. Turning around swiftly, I take the shortcut back over to the other path and head back to the hide, to my equipment and birds. I don't want to get involved.

# Chapter 4

## Ben

'Do you want to take a pack-up with you, love? I'll do you a couple of turkey sandwiches.'

'No thanks, Mum. Honestly, I'll be fine.'

I try not to wince as my mum fusses around me. I know she means well but that doesn't stop her from being embarrassing. I don't know why I let her talk me into staying over last night. Well, I do. I didn't want to leave her alone at any point on Christmas Day, not the first year since Dad left. I thought that if she had company for the whole day, maybe it would prevent her getting too maudlin. And I could stop her from getting drunk and calling Dad, which wouldn't have ended well for any of us.

In the end we had quite a nice day. There'd been a forced quality to Mum's smile several times during the day, but not as often as I'd expected. My brother turning up with the kids in tow definitely helped, because it focused her mind on the positives in her life. Jamie and I hadn't intended to take sides in the breakdown of our parents' marriage, but when Dad fucked off to Spain with his new girlfriend and told us he wouldn't be sending anything for Christmas, even for Jamie's kids, he made it a little more difficult to remain neutral.

I'd never tell Mum this, at least not for a few years, but I was glad to see the back of him. Dad was never abusive, or anything like that, but he was self-centred and had been making Mum miserable for years. Everything she did was for him, and the ungrateful bastard barely even noticed her. Well, good riddance. It's been less than six months, but I feel like Mum's already starting to get a bit of confidence back. It might be a while until I can convince her to date again, but we'll work on that. I don't want her to be alone.

'It's cold out there, love. You'll need something to keep you going,' she's saying, getting a loaf of bread out and cutting a couple of generous slices.

'Mum,' I begin, but then I realise there's no point arguing with her. Looking after me and Jamie gives her some pleasure, so I'm not going to deny her that. Besides, she makes amazing sandwiches, and even if I don't eat it while I'm on the reserve I'll have it to take home with me after-wards. Boxing Day isn't complete without a turkey sandwich. I settle myself on a stool at the breakfast bar and watch her as she busies herself with the food.

'Everyone going to be there today?' she asks casually.

'Yes, I think so,' I reply, not meeting her eye. I know what's coming.

'What about your girlfriend? About time you brought her here to meet me.'

I wince. 'I told you, Mum. She's not my girlfriend. She's just a friend.'

'Uh huh. So why are there so many photos of her on your phone?'

'You looked at my phone?' I can feel the colour flood my face, but Mum just laughs.

'Only over your shoulder when you were taking photos of the kids yesterday.' She leans over the breakfast bar and ruffles my hair, as if I'm twelve rather than thirty-two. 'I'm sorry, love. You know I'm only teasing you.'

I force a smile, knowing it's my own fault. Once Jamie and his brood had left yesterday, she started asking questions about my love life, obviously wondering if I have any plans to settle down and produce some more grandchildren for her, to keep up with my brother. Honestly, it's something I desperately want, but I never seem to have much luck with the women I meet. I can't tell Mum that, though. We're close, but not enough for me to open up to her about that sort of stuff.

'What's her name again?' she asks, even though I know she will have committed everything I've told her to memory.

'Emily,' I mutter. Why on earth did I tell Mum her real name? If I hadn't, then I could pretend I'd been talking about someone else entirely, and this fake woman could just fade away whenever the lie became too difficult to sustain. But in the spirit of pleasing Mum, I told her all about Emily. The problem was that I stretched the truth and mentioned that we might have been on a couple of dates, which of course we haven't, because idiot boy here hasn't managed to get up the courage to ask her out yet. I didn't think Mum needed to know that part, so last night after a couple of glasses of wine I embellished the truth a bit and spun a story that sounded like the start of a beautiful, lifelong

31

romance. It was only this morning that I realised the dangers of this – what if I do actually grow a pair and ask her out, and she accepts? When she eventually meets my mum, she'll think we've been dating for a lot longer than we have. Of course, I still need to ask her out in the first place.

It doesn't help that Lauren's making things awkward. She's the one I did find the courage to ask out, nearly a year ago. I made a new year's resolution to be more confident and conquer my fears in social situations, and talking to women I like had been a big part of it. Needless to say, she turned me down, in no uncertain terms, and the memory of it still stings. But then I met Emily . . .

Even thinking about her makes my face and neck heat up slightly, not to mention the sensations in other parts of my body. I got on well with her right from the start, but Lauren always seems to keep getting between us. Whenever I try to get Emily on her own, Lauren turns up. I know the pair of them are just getting to know each other again after however many years, but surely that shouldn't stop me also getting to know Emily? Maybe Lauren's jealous, and wants to keep Emily to herself. Anyway, I asked for Emily's number a couple of months ago and she was just about to give it to me when her sister turned up and distracted her. I haven't had the nerve to ask again. I keep hoping she'll remember and volunteer it, without me having to put myself out there.

Mum wraps up the turkey sandwich in some foil, then cuts a large piece of Christmas cake and wraps it up separately. Putting them in a bag, she goes to the fridge.

'Anything else you want to take, love? There's loads of food left here. That Michaela never eats much, does she?'

I roll my eyes behind Mum's back, knowing she's constantly trying to fatten up Jamie's wife. 'I thought she ate a perfectly normal amount of food for an adult,' I reply, not rising to it. 'It's the rest of us whose portions are off.'

'Well, if you can't eat as much as you want at Christmas, when can you? Christmas, and all-inclusive holidays,' she says with a grin.

'The sandwich and the cake are great, thanks Mum,' I say, getting off the stool and going to collect my stuff from the other room.

'You sure you won't stay another night?' she calls through to me.

'I'm only ten minutes away, you know that. Anyway, you'll want some peace and quiet tonight.' I know that might not be true, but I want a bit of space for a couple of days, before I go back to work. I don't get a lot of time off, working for a law firm, and I want to take advantage of some of it by going for a couple of walks by myself, and then spending the evening with a takeaway and a film. I could do the latter with Mum, but if I do things like that too often I know it won't be long until she suggests I move back in, and I definitely don't want to start down that slippery slope. Oh, she'd say it's so I can save some money, but I know her main reason would be that she wants some company. No, I'm better off going home after today's group walk, and trying to get Mum to go out and be a bit more sociable in the new year.

This gets me thinking about New Year's Eve. I know it's too late now to ask Emily out, that she'll probably already have plans. She lives in London after all, she's probably overrun with invitations at this time of year. A couple of friends have invited me over, but I know I'll be the only single person there, which is always awkward. All my friends have paired off, and I'm used to my third wheel status, but I really wish I could find myself a decent relationship.

I say goodbye to Mum, refusing yet another offer of extra food, and put my stuff in the boot of my car. I'm careful to avoid the other items I have stashed in there, which are well hidden under a blanket. It probably wouldn't be a good idea for Mum to see what I'm keeping in there, even if I could find a plausible explanation for what I'm doing with it.

Once I've finally shaken her off, I get in the car and head for the motorway. I could go across country, but just one junction will take half an hour off the journey, and I really don't want to be late today. Ideally, I'd like to be there before Emily and Lauren arrive.

As I drive, I find myself thinking about Lauren again. I just don't understand her. Okay, asking her out a second time was a bad idea. I knew she'd meant it when she said no the first time, but I obviously wasn't thinking straight. Yet in the last few months, her attitude has completely changed. Lauren's never been a particularly tactile friend, yet recently it feels like she's been taking every opportunity to have some physical contact with me, whether it's a light touch to the elbow or a hug goodbye. I'm not complaining, but I don't understand why there's been such a change in her.

Maybe it was because I took her side in one of her regular spats with Morna. The two of them never seem able to see eye to eye. I know part of it stems from Morna's belief that she should be doing Lauren's job, but secretly I think it's also because they're so similar in temperament and personality. Both women are passionate and also incredibly stubborn, so even when they agree there always seems to be *something* they end up arguing about. Not that it can even be called arguing most of the time; it's more like constant sniping. They both make little comments about the other when they're out of earshot too, in an attempt to get other people on side, but I have almost always tried to remain neutral. Admittedly, I do this by agreeing with both of them in private, which backfired once when they had a stand-off and tried to get me involved. I know I should have told them to let it go, that I didn't want to get involved, and that they needed to sort it out between themselves. But I didn't; instead I mumbled something and ended up siding with Lauren. So now she's being super friendly, which I would have welcomed if it hadn't been for Emily.

Emily. I feel a warmth spreading through me just thinking about her. Right, no more of this. Today's the day. I'm going to tell her how I feel. But just as I'm congratulating myself on my plan to take this step, I remember Alec, and the sly look on his face at the pub the other night, when he looked straight at me and slurred the words that had stopped all conversation for a few seconds. No, I can't speak to Emily until I get to the bottom of what the smug bastard meant.

# Chapter 5

## Emily

My phone rings while I'm finishing getting ready, and I glance at the door to the bedroom I'm using at Lauren's, feeling guilty but already knowing I'm going to answer it. If Scott is calling me on Boxing Day it must be important, and I can't risk anything going wrong with the app at this stage. I know Lauren's keen to get to the reserve, but we have plenty of time. My sister will just have to wait.

I connect my cochlear implant processor to my phone using Bluetooth, streaming the sound straight into the implant. Technology is a wonderful thing, and I marvel at it every day. Even though I work with assistive tech, I'm often still amazed at the things it can do, the things it can help people with, and how little it's used compared to the potential it has. My company is paving the way forward for disabled people to have access to the best assistive technology we can come up with, and I'm fuelled by a burning desire to make sure this app is just the beginning.

'Hi Scott,' I say, answering the call with a smile on my

face. I've found that people can hear the smile in my voice and respond better than if it wasn't there, even if the smile isn't genuine. Scott's one of those people who thinks he's more important than me simply because he's a couple of years older, and male. Don't get me wrong, I'm a staunch feminist, but I also know that fighting Scott and his shitty attitude won't make him see things any differently. Instead, I fake a smile, nod, and then do whatever the hell I want anyway. The trick is to do it in a way that ensures he can't take any of the credit. My ideas and innovations have all proven worthwhile in the last two years, so he just has to shut up and put up.

Scott actually asked me out last year, which took me aback. What on earth made him think I'd want to date him, with the way he spoke to me? Then again, I've made my share of poor choices in the past, going out with men who walked all over me then expected me to be grateful for their attention. I'm done with cocky men, now I've learnt to see past their charm to the ego behind.

We talk for ten minutes, and by the time I hang up I feel like I need a drink. My face hurts from trying to fake that smile. It wasn't an emergency at all, it could have waited a couple of days until we're back in the office, but that's another symptom of Scott's inflated sense of self-importance: if he thinks something needs doing, then it has to be done right away, preferably by someone else while he sits back and looks smug. I stood my ground and told him I'd get to it as soon as I'm back at work. For now, I'm going to enjoy the rest of my time off. True, this Christmas has been a bit more strained than usual, but that's the price I need to pay in order to reconnect with my sister. Maybe strained isn't the right word . . . It didn't feel very relaxed, certainly.

I still find myself wondering if it's worth it, all this effort for us to get to know each other again. If I hadn't reached out to Lauren earlier in the year, I don't think any sort of reconciliation would have happened. We were always very different as children, and that hasn't changed. I had a daydream that now we're adults we'd be able to find more common ground and repair our relationship, but after several months it's starting to dawn on me that perhaps there's a reason we never got on. As a teenager, Lauren was openly hostile towards me, which is very different from her attitude now, but spending time together still feels taxing. We always have to search around for conversation topics, having so little in common, and I've found that after a weekend with my sister I need a day to recharge, as if I've been working for two days straight.

When we first started talking again and Lauren told me about this nature group she was part of, I thought it would be a good opportunity for me to show an interest in Lauren's life. It wasn't exactly my idea of a fun day out – I'd much rather be sitting at home with a games console – but I didn't think it would be that bad. I'm not a particularly social person; I have a couple of colleagues I'd call friends, then another two or three people I've met through gaming, but I feel a lot more comfortable inter-acting with people from behind a screen. Still, I thought this experience would be good for me. As it turns out, I do quite enjoy group meet-ups now, because of Ben. He's really sweet and a bit shy, exactly the sort of man I need as an antidote to the flashy egotists I've dated before, but

I do wonder if he's ever going to get up the courage to ask me out. I would be very open to the idea, but I think if I make the first move he'll panic, like a deer caught in headlights, so I've been waiting for him to get around to it. The last thing I want to do is scare him off.

The others are all nice, too, even Morna. I can see why she doesn't get on with Lauren, because my sister always talks down to her. Just because she's only a volunteer at the reserve doesn't mean she doesn't know what she's talking about, and Lauren can be quite rude. Morna is quite a bit older, too, so she's got a lot of experience that Lauren never seems willing to take into account. I don't really want to get involved, so I try to ignore their arguments, as I rarely know what the hell they're talking about. Then I try to be friendly towards Morna when Lauren isn't watching.

Kai's an interesting one; I used to get the feeling he was no more interested in the birdwatching trips than I was, but I can't for the life of me figure out why he comes along every month. Maybe he fancies Lauren? Then again, his attitude does seem to have changed recently, and he asks a lot of questions of the others. Maybe he's just a beginner, like me.

Dan, I haven't figured out yet. He's only been coming to the group for a couple of months, and today's walk will be his third. On the couple of occasions we've chatted, I noticed he's one of those people who let you talk a lot about yourself. He gives you the space and waits for you to fill it with words, without actually contributing much about himself. He and Lauren seem to understand each other, though. I keep wondering if there's something going on between those two – she's so private I wouldn't put it past her to have a secret boyfriend.

From here, my mind drifts on to Alec and I feel as if a dark cloud has just settled above my head. Until last week I only thought of him as a harmless geek. I know plenty of them, through work and gaming – it's a category I'd put myself in, too. Alec is obsessed with birds and takes pride in showing off his life list – all of the bird species he's seen in his lifetime. He lives alone and spends his annual leave travelling abroad on special birdwatching trips. After he came back from the most recent one in September, he suggested the rest of us come round to his house one evening so he could present a slide show of all his photos. It was a pretty awkward moment, because all of us came up with some excuse as to why we couldn't go, and someone swiftly changed the subject. I felt pretty bad, seeing the hurt on Alec's face, but now I've had a glimpse of another side of him, that guilt has completely vanished.

It was less than a week ago, on the 20th December. The whole group planned to go out for a pub meal and a few drinks, a little nature group Christmas do. I hadn't been intending to go, as I was coming up for Christmas Day as well, but then I thought it would be an opportunity to spend a bit of time with Ben in a different environment, and maybe get some time to chat in private. Kai has a cousin who owns a pub, so he managed to get us a table reserved, at a time of year when everywhere is completely rammed. It was a slightly dingy place that could have done with a full refurbishment, but the food was good. Pubs can be difficult environments for deaf people; they're never designed for good acoustics. I struggled to follow the conversation, due to the amount of background noise, but I sat between Ben and Lauren so mostly spoke to the two of them until we all moved to the bar area for more drinks.

That's when everything started to go downhill. Alec came and settled himself next to me. I was sitting at one of those wooden bench seats, pulled up to a table, with one end against a wall, so I couldn't get away from him. Not that I had any reason to at first, other than how dull his conversation was likely to be. As I expected, he launched into a tale of his most recent birdwatching highlight, when he travelled down to Rutland Water at three in the morning to set up his equipment, because a type of vulture had been spotted that didn't usually land in the UK. I smiled and nodded in the right places, and when he finished his story, I hoped he would get up and corner someone else, leaving me to catch Ben's eye. But it wasn't to be.

Alec leaned back in his seat, and I noticed he was sweating slightly, beads of perspiration clinging to his hairline. He licked his lips nervously, then put a hand on my knee.

'Emily, I think there's something we need to talk about,' he began, but I cut him off straight away.

'Take your hand off my knee, please.' I was polite but firm. My philosophy is that everyone gets one chance. Alec, unfortunately, wasn't paying attention.

'I think you're beautiful,' he said, and that was when I noticed how slurred his words had become. 'You need to listen to me. Everyone thinks I'm just a bumbling idiot.

42

But I'm more than that, I'm smarter than any of them realise. You should listen to me. I could be good for you.'

'Take your hand off me,' I repeated, louder, making sure all politeness had gone from my voice. The volume of my words didn't penetrate the general background noise of the room, but I could see Kai looking over at us with a frown on his face.

Alec looked confused. 'There's no need to be rude, Emily. I'm trying to tell you something. Something I think you'll want to hear.'

At that point I physically pushed him away. What else was I supposed to do? I was stuck between the wall, the bench and the table, his warm, sweaty hand still gripping my thigh. The shove I gave him knocked him off balance and he looked at me askance. He was having trouble focusing, and I wondered just how much he'd had to drink.

'I know everyone's secrets,' he hissed at me then, leaning towards me and reaching out to put his hand on my shoulder to steady himself. I didn't want him to touch me again, so I twitched backwards, he missed and pitched forwards, banging his face against the table. The background noise died away as people turned to see what was happening.

'I told you to take your hands off me,' I repeated, more for the benefit of the rest of the room rather than Alec, who sat down again on the end of the bench, rubbing his chin.

'What the fuck is going on?' Kai asked, glaring down at Alec. 'You need to move.'

'I wasn't doing anything wrong,' Alec slurred.

'Clearly you were, or Emily wouldn't have to tell you to stop touching her.' Kai's eyes blazed, and I was surprised

43

at how swiftly his anger had risen once he'd realised what was happening.

'I only wanted to tell her about you. About all of you,' Alec replied, gesturing to the rest of our group with an exaggerated sweep of his hand. His voice was growing in volume as he got more worked up. 'You all think I'm an idiot, but I've got the measure of the lot of you. I know what sordid little secrets you're hiding. The crimes and the lies, I know them all.'

Alec stood up, swayed a little on his feet but remained upright. Even those in the bar who didn't know us had stopped to listen, eyes wide and mouths agape, drinks forgotten in their hands. My heart was racing, even though I didn't have a clue what Alec was talking about. Crimes? Lies? Who were his words aimed at?

He stumbled out from behind the bench, and was slowly turning, pointing his finger at all of the rest of them. Morna's face was deathly pale, and she clutched at her handbag; Ben looked affronted, and like he was considering saying something; Kai still looked furious, and he grabbed Alec roughly by the elbow.

'You need to go home and sober up,' he growled, steering Alec towards the door.

'That's right, throw me out, pretend none of you know what I'm talking about. Well, I'll show you. I'm not as big an idiot as you all think I am!'

He was still shouting and raving as Kai dragged him outside. A moment later, Dan came up to the table where I was still sitting.

'Are you okay?' he asked, his voice low and laced with concern.

I nodded. 'I thought he was just making a drunken pass at me. I don't know what the hell just happened.'

Dan looked over towards the door, a thoughtful expression on his face. 'Me neither. But I expect we'll find out sooner or later.'

Kai came back in and rejoined our group, and life gradually returned to the bar. I slid out from the bench and finished my drink before glancing over at Lauren to see if she was ready to go. During Alec's rant, I glanced at my sister, and I'd been surprised by the mix of emotions on Lauren's face – a combination of fear and something else. Could it have been glee?

Now, standing in my sister's spare room and preparing to see the rest of the group again, I try to remember the way Lauren had looked at Alec, wondering if I misinterpreted her expression. Whatever he meant, and whoever his words were aimed at, I know I want to do my best to avoid him today.

There's a knock at the door.

'Are you ready?' Lauren calls through the door. I look at my watch – it's gone half past twelve, and I know Lauren had hoped to be at the reserve by now. Grabbing my bag, I join my sister in the hall, apologising for the delay.

'It's okay,' Lauren replies with a shrug, leading the way out of the flat. As I pull the door shut behind me, I watch my sister retreating down the stairs and wonder if there is any truth in what Alec said. Is someone in the group hiding a dark secret? And could that someone be my own sister?

# Chapter 6

## Dan

'Morning Dan!'

I turn to see Lauren and Emily getting out of a car and stop to wait for them, raising a hand in greeting. 'Morning,' I reply, remembering to smile as I do so.

Ever since I lost Rachel, smiling is one of those things that doesn't come naturally anymore. The social contract has vanished from my memory, so when people speak to me, I have to stop and think about the appropriate response. Until Lauren spent some time working on my defences, I'd barely spoken to anyone in weeks.

My life has become a repetitive blur. I go to the supermarket, I eat, I sleep, and I walk. In all my waking hours, whatever the weather, I walk. If I keep moving, then I won't have to think about where everything in my life went wrong; I won't have to remember that Rachel isn't waiting for me at home, curled up on the sofa with a romance novel and a pair of fluffy socks.

It was one day when I was walking that I first saw

Lauren. I was doing a circuit of the reserve while she was out looking at a fence that needed repairing. On that particular occasion, I don't think I even made eye contact with her. We saw each other regularly after that, in passing, and eventually I remembered that I should look at her and nod, even say 'Hello'. One day, during a particularly heavy rain shower, I took shelter under the railway bridge, and she must have had the same thought. At the time I almost panicked at the idea of being forced to have a conversation, but I'm glad it happened. Meeting Lauren was a catalyst for change, I realise that now.

As I wait for the sisters to get their gear together, I cast my eye over the car and feel my breath catch in my throat.

'Nice car,' I murmur, though only Lauren hears me.

'It's Emily's,' she says with a nod at her sister. 'I told her she could drive us today, as she's the one with the fancy car.'

I nod, looking it over appreciatively. It's sleek, high-end, but still practical. The kind of car I might have bought myself, once. Not now.

Emily looks slightly embarrassed by Lauren's comment. 'When the app took off, I thought I deserved to have something nice. It was the first time I'd earned enough to buy anything more than a ten-year-old Fiesta,' she adds with a shrug.

I think it's strange, that she should buy herself a car that's so obviously a status symbol, yet be embarrassed by any mention of it. I walk round it once, until I've seen all I want, then come back to join them.

I find myself automatically turning to Lauren. I don't know Emily very well, having only met her on two of these monthly meetings, plus the outing to the pub last week. That was a complete disaster, but I'm glad it wasn't because of me. Just goes to show that you never really can tell what a person's like, and that first impressions can be very wrong. Still, I don't think I have anything to worry about from Alec. A lot of the others looked quite worried, or angry, but that's because I'm fairly sure everyone in this group has something to hide.

'Are we heading inside?' Lauren asks brightly, but despite her tone I can see there's some tension in her shoulders. She's told me all about her successful sister, how Emily has made an absolute fortune developing an app that helps deaf and disabled people to communicate. On the surface she seems thrilled for her, but I wonder if there's something else going on underneath. Lauren seems different when Emily's around, almost as if she has something to prove. Still, it's none of my business, I remind myself.

The three of us set off across the car park towards the visitor centre. I look up at the sky and frown. It has a murky yellow tinge to it that threatens snow, and I'm glad I packed well. Years of working offshore have taught me to be prepared for sudden changes in weather, and there was plenty of snow in the middle of the North Sea. If it snows today it won't make much of a difference to me, I can't imagine it will get too bad and I know the reserve well enough to think I can stay off the marshes. I think a couple of the others in the group might not feel the same about the snow, however.

As we walk, Lauren is talking. 'Alec's car,' she says, with a nod to the one closest to the visitor centre. 'Part of me hoped he wouldn't come today. Morna opened up, of course.'

She says this last part with a roll of her eyes. I'm well aware of the animosity between Morna and Lauren, though if I'm honest everything I've seen has been rather petty. A squabble for a little bit of power and influence, something so insignificant I wonder why they waste their energy on it.

Lauren and Emily walk onward, but I hang back, casting my eye around the car park. There are three other cars besides Emily's, which I take to be Ben's, Morna's and Alec's. I walked here. I walk everywhere now. If anyone is going to arrive late it will be Kai. I've spent the last two meetings of this group observing the others and while there's a lot I don't know about them, there are a couple of things I've picked up on, including Kai's seeming ambivalence towards the activities. There must be some reason why Kai comes every month, but I don't think it has anything to do with a love of wildlife. He's a physically strong bloke, that's plain for anyone to see, but they're the kind of muscles that come from the repetitive lifting of weights indoors, not hard graft outdoors. He doesn't have any of the outdoor gear, either, though that could just mean he's a beginner who doesn't understand what he needs, yet. Still, that's his own business.

In the visitor centre, we're greeted by the tantalising smell of frying bacon and fresh coffee, as well as the three people I had predicted would be there. Alec looks like he's just come in from the reserve; he's easily the most passionate birder among us, so he's probably already been halfway round the reserve to see what's out there today.

Morna bustles over, wiping her hands on a tea towel. 'Afternoon, you three. There are bacon butties, and the urns are full if you want to make a drink.'

Emily thanks her with a smile, but Lauren just nods, and I see Morna's face fall. She's obviously worked hard to prepare everything, so I add my thanks to Emily's and help myself to a roll stuffed with bacon, despite the fact that I don't have much appetite. Eating means I don't need to talk, however, so it's a good tactic when I find group interactions overwhelming. Before Lauren persuaded me to join this group, I hadn't been in a group of more than three people since I left my job, since Rachel . . .

No, I promised myself I wouldn't think about Rachel today. Today is about me, not about her. I need it in order to heal and move on, to finally draw a line under everything. If I think about her, and what she'd say to me right now, then I'll be lost. Focusing on the bacon roll in front of me, I chew slowly while trying to tune my racing mind back into the conversation that's going on around me. Alec is talking loudly about one of his birding holidays, as usual, though he seems slightly shriller today. He's probably hoping that none of us will bring up the scene in the pub, and so if he keeps talking and doesn't let anyone interrupt, we won't have the opportunity to take him to task.

Whatever the others might think, and his behaviour the other night notwithstanding, I quite like Alec. In the last few months, I've found the presence of nature soothing, and I've learnt a little about the wildlife around the reserve, but I'm still very much a newcomer. Half of the things Alec says don't make sense to me, when he names species I've never heard of, or talks about stringers or LBJs. Still, I've learnt a bit from him, when Alec has managed to get down off his high horse and deign to explain a couple of things to me. I think that once Alec realised I was willing to listen, that made all the difference. Until the other night in the pub, I'd thought Alec was pretty harmless, but there's obviously a different side to him. He's probably right about how the others treat him, but privately I think Alec brings it on himself with his superior attitude. If you make it so clear that you think you're better than those around you, it shouldn't really surprise you when they don't react kindly to that. And claiming to know everyone's secrets is hardly going to endear them to you.

Morna is trying to engage Emily in conversation but Lauren keeps interrupting her. From my experience of Lauren, she comes across as a pretty nice person, so I find myself wondering where her deep-seated dislike of Morna comes from. She never treats anyone else in the group with the disdain she turns on Morna. Perhaps that's one of Alec's secrets?

Ben jumps in and comes to Morna's rescue, asking Lauren a couple of questions about the day so Morna can focus on Emily. There's an observant guy, I think. I've noticed the way Ben watches the others in the group, though mostly Emily and Lauren. He really needs to get on and ask Emily out, though, before I do it for him, just to put Ben out of his misery. It's clear to all of us how he feels, clear to anyone with eyes, so if Emily doesn't already know I would be surprised.

'I thought I saw someone out on the reserve, earlier,' Morna is saying, and this catches my attention. The others seem to feel the same, because when she chips in with this bit of information they all stop what they're doing and look at her, then each other. Morna looks slightly embarrassed at the sudden attention, and I notice her glance out of the window that looks over the decking outside the café.

'I might have been wrong, though,' she continues, hastily backtracking. Is there something she's not saying? I didn't have her down as someone not happy to speak her mind, so there must be a reason for her holding back.

Lauren chews her lip for a moment. 'I'm sure it's nothing to worry about. I had hoped we'd have the reserve to ourselves, but there are always people who think they can just turn up and hop over a fence. I'll keep an eye out as we're going round, and report anything that doesn't seem right.'

Alec opens his mouth to say something, but then shuts it again, shaking his head. Does he know something too? I understand why he might be unwilling to say it out loud, given his outburst the other day. The conversation moves on, but I get the feeling that at least one member of the group isn't telling us all they know.

# Chapter 7

## Kai

Late, again. However hard I try to get up on time and make it there for the start of the meeting, I'm always late. I know it's becoming a running joke, but it's never intentional. There's always something that happens – my phone didn't charge overnight so my alarm didn't go off; my cousin rang me just as I was about to leave the house; I realised I needed petrol so had to divert on my way to the reserve. It really isn't my fault. Sometimes I swear I'm cursed.

Glancing around the car park, I can see that all the others are here – the Tesla must be Emily's, no way could Lauren afford a ride like that. Even though I'm late, I take a moment to admire the car, before jogging up the path to the visitor centre.

I'm about to push open the door and join the others when my phone rings. I pull it out of my pocket with a sigh and look at the name on the screen. Maybe I can just ignore it this time. But if I do that, I know the guy will just keep on calling me. I can see the others through the window, chatting and eating bacon butties, so I reckon I have a few minutes before they'll be getting impatient.

For a moment I think again about ignoring the call and turning my phone off. They can find a way of getting it done without me. Something about the image of the group sitting there, in the deserted café, chatting companionably, draws me to go inside. Recently, I've found myself wanting to feel more a part of the group, to get more involved and learn more about the wildlife we see. I felt a bit awkward at first, being the only black guy in a group of outdoorsy white people, but they made me feel at home in a way I never expected.

The call stops, then immediately starts again. I sigh, knowing nothing will change today. Nothing will ever fucking change. I'll answer the phone, and the distance between myself and the rest of the group will remain.

'Yeah?' I try to inject a note of gruff annoyance into my voice, which is the closest I'll get to rebellion. 'Fine. Yeah, just tell me what you need.'

The call lasts for another few minutes, with me occasionally responding but mostly listening to the person on the other end. After I hang up, I stay outside for a couple of minutes, wrestling with the thoughts that are racing through my mind. In the end, I kick part of the wooden decking in frustration, then step into the visitor centre.

Five minutes later, I'm sitting at the table with the rest of them, a mug of tea in front of me and a bacon roll slathered in ketchup in my hand. I'm sitting between Emily and Alec, and I know where the more interesting conversation lies between those two, so I turn to my left.

'Is that your Tesla in the car park?' I ask, my mouth still half full of bacon.

Emily gives me a slightly pained look, then I remember her deafness.

'Sorry,' I say, hastily swallowing. She told me once that she can never understand someone who talks with their mouth full, because it makes the shape of their lips all wrong, or something like that.

'It's okay,' she says, and I see she's tilting her head strangely. That's when I notice she doesn't have her bionic ear thing on the right side of her head like she usually does. She points to it and makes a face. 'I'm useless on that side today.'

I repeat the question about the car now I've finished my mouthful, and she nods.

'Yeah,' she replies, but then doesn't elaborate any further. I'm expecting her to start telling me all about the engine, or at least how it handles, but she doesn't seem interested in talking about it at all.

'Is it a good car?'

She nods again. 'I like it.'

'I'd love to drive one someday.'

She smiles. 'It's not much different to any other car. I wanted something high quality and that's what people I knew recommended. Now everyone asks me about it and I'm never sure what to say. It's a nice car.'

I nod. 'I saw your sticker, useful.'

I'm referring to the one with the little symbol of a stylised ear shape with a thick line through it, white on a blue background.

'It's to tell the emergency services that I'm deaf,' she explains. 'If I'm pulled over by the police, or if I'm in an accident, they should be able to see that, even if I'm not able to tell them myself for some reason.'

I nod again, satisfied with the explanation, but Emily continues talking.

'Do you know that's what "Baby On Board" signs are for? They were designed for parents to put in their cars when their children are travelling with them, so if they're in an accident the emergency services would know if they needed to be looking for a child. But they're pointless now, because people stick them in their car and leave them there, even if the child isn't in it.'

'Do you take the sticker off if someone else drives your car?'

She frowns at the question. 'Why would someone else drive my car?'

I shrug. 'I just wondered.'

She shakes her head. 'No, I'm the only one who drives it. But I suppose if someone else needed to drive it, I'd take it off, yes. I haven't ever needed to think about it.'

'Yeah, I wouldn't let anyone else drive my car either, not if I had one like yours,' I say with a chuckle.

Lauren and Dan have paused in their conversation and seem to be listening to what we're saying, Lauren giving me a strange look. I've always had the impression she doesn't like me, though I don't have a clue what I've done to deserve it. Maybe it's just because I don't think the sun shines out of her arse.

Morna turns to ask Emily something, and I find Alec leaning towards me.

'Did you get yourself some new bins like I recommended?' There's such an eager glow radiating from the older man's face, I suddenly feel a bit guilty; I've completely forgotten the conversation I had with Alec about the merits of different pairs of binoculars.

'I've not had the chance yet, mate,' I mumble.

Alec's face falls a bit. 'Oh, okay. Those sites I mentioned should be pretty useful. I can write them down for you, if you like.'

I nod, if only to get Alec to stop talking, but I should have realised that it wouldn't have the desired effect. Once Alec starts on a topic he's passionate about, it's hard to get him to change course.

'Of course, nothing beats actually trying them out your-self, so you know which pair is going to suit you. There could be half a dozen different models, all with the same spec, but until you actually pick them up and use them, feel them in your hand, you can't make a decision.' He leans over to his own bag and pulls out his binoculars. 'Take these, for instance. The price tag is steep, and prob-ably more than a relative beginner like you would want to pay, but they're worth every penny.'

I looked them up online after Alec showed them to me a couple of months ago, and the price isn't so much steep as astronomical. I know plenty of people who'd love to get their hands on a pair of binoculars worth a couple of grand, but only so they could flog them on.

'Have a look at the grip,' Alec is saying, lovingly turning the binoculars over and holding them towards me. I hesi-tate, unsure if Alec will let me handle them or if this is a look-don't-touch situation. I nod again in what I hope looks like an appreciative manner.

'It's ergonomic, fits smoothly into your hand so as not

to cause any unnecessary discomfort. If you're holding them for any length of time there's a real risk of hand or wrist strain.'

Resisting the urge to snigger, I nod once more. I get the feeling Alec wouldn't take kindly to me making a crude joke.

'Here, take them.'

Gingerly, I take the binoculars from Alec and hold them, wondering what exactly I'm expected to say. God help me if I drop and damage them. There's no way I'd be able to replace them, not with the money I owe to far more dangerous people than Alec.

I remain focused on handling the binoculars as carefully as I can, while Alec goes on about the balance of them, and how they are far superior to any other pair he's ever tried.

'That's why you need to try them, you see?' Alec points over his shoulder, to the area at the side of the visitor centre that's laid out as a shop. 'They run sessions here once a month, you know, where you can come and try them.' He nods out of the floor-to-ceiling window running along the length of the café. 'You can usually see a few different birds from here, and it gives you enough of an idea as to their performance. I'll meet you here one weekend if you like, and then I can give you some advice while you try some different ones.'

'Er, yeah, sure,' I reply, unable to think of a polite way to put him off. 'I'll have to check the dates, like. I do some work for my cousin most weekends, except when we're meeting up, that is.'

'Well, I'm sure we can work around it. If necessary, we can pick another day that suits you, and I'll demonstrate them for you myself.' Alec puffs out his chest and I know he's thinking of himself in that position of superior knowledge, telling me about the different pieces of equipment, maybe gathering a small crowd of other interested people around him as he talks. For a moment I want to laugh, but then I just feel a bit sorry for Alec. He probably doesn't have a lot else going on his life.

It strikes me that this whole thing, Alec letting me hold his precious binoculars, is some sort of peace offering. One of the reasons I had known I had to come today was because of what Alec said in the pub the other night. At one point, I was sure Alec looked right at me, and I'd thought the game was up. This conversation suggests to me that Alec doesn't know anything I don't want him to know. But then a thought strikes me – was it a test, rather than an offer of friendship? A cold sweat breaks out down my spine and I stand up from the table suddenly, making Alec jump.

'Sorry, need to pay a call before we go out onto the reserve.'

I dash down a side corridor and lock myself in the nearest toilet cubicle, bending over the sink and taking a deep breath before splashing my face with cold water. This is getting too risky. I can't keep it up. There's no way I want to risk going to jail, and I'm sure if Alec knows, that has to be the most likely outcome. He was drunk when he said those things, and his only motive is having some kind of power over the rest of us, that much was clear. Alec isn't the type to turn to blackmail. I should know. No, he just wants to be smug, and lord it over us, show off that he knows things about us that we'd rather

61

were kept secret. He wants people to think he's clever, and he probably hasn't thought beyond that. Hasn't thought of the possible consequences of putting us all on the spot like that.

As I'm there, I use the toilet then wash my hands thoroughly, splashing a bit more cool water on my face before rejoining the others. When I walk back into the café, it's clear the conversation has moved on, because all six of them are discussing something, and my absence doesn't seem to have been noted.

'Maybe you imagined it,' Lauren is saying.

Morna shakes her head. 'I didn't. There was someone there in the woods, I'm sure of it.'

'That's not what you said the first time,' Lauren replies drily.

Morna opens and closes her mouth a few times, looking like one of those novelty plastic singing fish that people thought were hilarious twenty years ago. As soon as I've had the thought, I feel bad. Morna takes a lot of shit from Lauren and I feel like I should defend her more.

Ben is clearly trying to keep the peace. 'Look, let's not argue about this. Does it really matter? We're here to have a day out, see the murmuration. It doesn't matter if someone else has slipped in the side gate.'

'You said there'd been poachers, after the deer,' Emily mentions to Lauren, her voice characterised by the slight nasal dullness often audible in the speech of a deaf person. I sometimes find myself staring at the implant things attached to the sides of her head, marvelling at the technology but also finding it a bit creepy. She explained to me once how they work, that an electrode was inserted into her cochlea to stimulate the nerve cells and send artificial messages to the brain, in the same way a functional inner ear would do. Until I met Emily, I admit I had a pretty blinkered view of what a deaf person would be like, and she's changed my perceptions completely.

As Emily speaks, I watch Lauren's face for a reaction, and she frowns, looking grave.

'It won't be poachers, not in broad daylight,' she replies.

'Course it won't,' I chip in, taking a seat. 'It must have been someone who didn't realise the reserve's closed today.'

Ben and Morna nod in response to this, and Dan appears to accept it as a likely explanation too. He never says much, so I'm not sure what he's thinking, but he doesn't seem inclined to argue.

'I expect you're right,' Emily says, though she glances at Lauren as if to check her sister agrees.

'They were probably coming in the hope of seeing some rare bird,' I say, nudging Alec. 'You were telling me about them, people who only care about ticking every bird off a list or something.'

'Twitchers,' Alec mutters.

'I thought all birdwatchers were twitchers?' Dan says.

Alec looks affronted. 'Absolutely not. Those of us who do it for the love of birds in general, who are happy to observe the more common birds just as much as the rarities, are birders. Twitchers are the ones who are only ever looking to the next big thing. They're the ones who will drive three hundred miles to get the briefest glimpse of a bird that doesn't normally frequent these shores, tick it off their list then say, "Right, what's next?"' Alec sniffs, to indicate his disdain for these people.

'Didn't you drive over to Leicestershire to see that vulture, though?' Ben asks, his face a picture of innocence. I remember the story, and press my lips together firmly to stop myself sniggering.

'That was different,' Alec snaps. 'Of course if there's a rare bird sighted not too far away then I'll go and see it if I can. But it's not the only thing I'm interested in.'

'Okay, so maybe it was a twitcher,' Lauren says, trying to regain control of the conversation. 'Let's just forget about it and concentrate on enjoying ourselves.' The expression on her face tells me she doesn't think that's going to be possible, however.

I nod along with the others, fervently hoping that none of them see anything out of the ordinary today whatsoever.

# Chapter 8

## Lauren

Everyone takes their plates to the serving hatch and passes them through to Morna, who's stacking the dishwasher.

'I'll come round and give you a hand.' Dan puts down his plate and turns, but Morna stops him.

'I'm fine, thank you. Maybe you could collect everything that's left on the table?'

I move to help him, but he shakes his head, so I sit down again. No point everyone trying to get involved. I'm going to be working hard enough for the rest of the day, keeping everyone organised. I know Alec has this idea in his head that he's the leader of the group, but I'm always the one who makes sure we stay together and decides which direction we're going in, and who chases them all up when we're ready to move on to a new hide or a new part of whichever reserve we're visiting. I'm the one who does the admin and the organisation, making sure we were able to use the reserve today, and arranging dates and times when we visit other sites.

To outsiders it probably sounds like we just have nice days out, but there's a lot more to it than that. I have to know where the nearest first aid kit is, aside from the basic one I keep in my day pack, as well as having a risk assessment for each outing. If anything happens to anyone in the group on one of these trips, there's no way I want to risk being held liable.

And then there's everyone else in the group and their mix of personalities. On a good day, we have fun and learn from each other. On a bad day, I can sometimes find myself fielding petty arguments, or having to get strict with Alec when he wants to separate off from the group to go hunting for a particular bird he's sure has just flown off to the next pond. Dan's first meeting was an especially fraught one, with Alec and Ben almost coming to blows over whether a wading bird they'd been looking at was a Black-Tailed Godwit or a Bar-Tailed Godwit, and I had been hard pushed to resist calling them both no-tailed halfwits. It's a miracle Dan actually came back the following month, after witnessing two grown men behaving like children over a bloody bird.

I'm passionate about wildlife and habitat conservation, of course I am, or I wouldn't have gone into this line of work. One of my first jobs was working in the café here: I needed work, and applied for everything, so I was serving tea and sandwiches here during the day then going straight to another job and cleaning offices at night. When I saw they were advertising an apprenticeship for under twenty-ones, I jumped at the opportunity. That led on to a college course, fitting studying around menial jobs, but it was worth it in the end.

I enjoy the thrill of seeing wild animals and birds in their natural habitats, but I can't ever imagine myself getting so worked up about what I'd seen that I ended up in a blazing row with someone else over it. It had surprised me that Ben had got involved, to be honest; I'd always thought he was a bit wet. We usually just let Alec go on about whatever it is on that particular day, nodding and smiling and then ignoring him. But Ben had clearly decided enough was enough, and he wasn't taking any of Alec's superior bullshit anymore. Or maybe there'd been something else running beneath the surface before then, and it only came out as an argument about a bird. I've considered asking Ben about it, but then everything appeared to be sorted between them the following month. It had better stay that way, though. I'm not putting up with that again.

Of course, everything has changed, now. We chatted as normal while we were sitting in the café, but the atmosphere was charged, and I know everyone was thinking the same thing. What had Alec been talking about? Who had he been referring to, and what were the secrets he claimed to know? It's something I've thought about countless times in the last few days, but just as nobody else seems ready to confront him, I've decided to bide my time. I'm pretty sure that if Alec knows anything about me that I don't want making public, it's nothing too serious, or he would have told someone by now. I shudder to think of the consequences of that happening, but then push the thought to the back of my mind. If that happens, I'll find a way to deal with the problem. I'm good at that.

Activity has stopped in the kitchen, and now everyone

is milling around, collecting rucksacks and coats, donning hats and gloves. Outside, the sky's still heavy, the yellow colour more pronounced than it was earlier. It's fresh, and very cold, and we're going to be out on the reserve until dark so it's important that we all layer up.

Morna clears her throat, and everyone turns to look at her.

'I just wanted to say, thank you everyone for coming today. I hope you all had a lovely Christmas, whatever you did, and it's lovely of you to come out today when you could have been spending time with your families.'

I honestly don't know what it is about Morna that bothers me so much, but just the fact that the woman has stood up to address the group as if she's in charge riles me. In theory, the two of us should get on really well – we have similar interests, and similar personalities in many ways – but there's just something about her that makes me want to throttle her.

I can tell that Morna is about to continue, so I step in.

'Right everyone, we're here to see the Starling murmuration. As you all know, it happens here every day through the winter, and has done for years, but it can move around. For the last few days they've been right at the far end of the reserve, so I hope you've put your comfiest boots on, because it's about four and a half miles to the best viewing point. They'll come to roost around four thirty, so we want to be in position by around three thirty. Is that okay for everyone?'

A wave of nods moves around the group, and Alec opens his mouth to speak but I continue before he gets the chance.

'Great. It's nearly two, so that should give us plenty of

time. Once we're up there, we can choose where we want to observe from. There are a couple of hides with good vantage points across that section of the marshes, looking out towards the woods where they've been roosting, but you might prefer to find a spot in the open.'

'Is it going to snow?' Emily asks, frowning at the sky outside. I nearly roll my eyes at my sister; I've noticed she seems to think that because I work outside a lot and I'm generally an outdoorsy person that I have some special insight into the weather.

'Not according to the forecast,' I reply with a tight smile, reminding myself that I need to keep putting in the effort to be nice to her. 'If it does, we'll keep an eye on the conditions and might need to make our way back here earlier than planned, but hopefully it'll hold off.'

I can see Dan, his frown matching Emily's, and I can tell from the look in his eyes that he disagrees with me, but he doesn't speak up. Dan's an enigma; it took me weeks to draw him out of himself enough that he'd have a conversation with me, and even longer for him to confide anything in me. He's been through a lot, I know, and there's plenty under the surface that he hasn't shared with me. By inviting him to this group, I'd hoped it would help his healing process, but I can't tell yet if it's working.

'Come on then,' Alec says with a grin. He's met with six blank stares, and I realise I'm right: nobody has forgotten about the incident in the pub. Alec no longer holds the respect of the others and it's clear that nobody is prepared to let him tell them what to do.

They all look back to me and I can't help but feel a bit of smugness. I nod towards the door.

'You lot go first, I need to lock up here.' I turn to Morna and hold my hand out, knowing full well that Morna will want to hold onto the key for the sense of importance it gives her. The others start to move past us, filing out onto the wooden decking. They'd normally be chatting, but everyone is strangely quiet today. Maybe it's the slightly eerie sky; maybe they all have other things on their minds.

'I'll lock up,' Morna tells me with a bright smile. 'I don't mind. I might pop back in later to check the dishwasher's finished.'

'Best not,' I reply. 'Nick left me in charge of the keys, so I'd better look after them from here.'

Morna's bright smile looks strained at the edges but she doesn't argue. I know I shouldn't have given Morna the keys in the first place, but she asked when we were in the pub the other night and I didn't see that there'd be a problem. It meant I didn't have to get here as early, which turned out to be a good thing with Emily holding us up so much, and I thought giving Morna a bit of leeway might make her less stroppy. It seems it hasn't made much difference, though, so I lock the front door of the visitor centre from the inside, then hold open the door that leads out to the reserve for Morna to leave, then lock up.

'Wait!' I turn. Kai is jogging back towards us from the path. 'Sorry, left my phone in the loo,' he says with a self-deprecating grin.

'Be quick,' I reply, unlocking the door again, then fold my arms and lean against the wall, watching Morna walk away to join the others. A minute later, Kai's back, and gives me a wink, which makes me smile despite myself.

We set off down the path into the reserve, the others

a few metres ahead of us and just disappearing into the trees. Alec is striding ahead, possibly conscious that none of the rest of us are interested in walking with him, or maybe he just wants to take the lead and be the first to spot the beginning of the murmuration. Emily and Ben are next, walking quite closely together, Ben turning his head as he speaks in order to make it easier for Emily to hear him. I feel a sharp, unexpected stab of jealousy at their closeness. Ben fancied me for months, actively pursued me, but as soon as my sister showed up, I was forgotten. Okay, I don't fancy Ben, and have no problem with him dating someone else, but not Emily. It's almost like this is yet another thing my sister has taken from me. There are thousands of men in the world that Emily could have her pick of, so why does it have to be Ben?

Behind them come Morna and Dan. Morna is chatting away, her head of cropped grey hair bobbing as she walks. Dan moves differently, almost gliding as he walks, and I'm suddenly struck by how attractive he is. Broad shoulders, muscled body, square jaw. He obviously takes care of himself, despite the difficulties he's faced, which gives me hope for him. Well, if my sister is going to cosy up with Ben, perhaps I should use this as an opportunity to get a bit closer to Dan. Though it might be a bit soon for him, of course.

'I'm looking forward to this,' Kai tells me, and I'm amused to see the way his face lights up like a small child's. 'I've never seen anything like this before.'

I smile. 'It's really impressive. I regularly see it at this time of year, when I'm at work, but it never gets old. It's always slightly different, and I love to watch it.'

'I was telling my cousin about it,' Kai begins, but then he stops, his voice tailing off.

'What is it?'

He shakes his head. 'It's nothing.'

'Tell me,' I say, resting a hand gently on Kai's arm. I don't know Kai that well, but I'm always happy to share my enthusiasm for wildlife.

He shrugs. 'He thought it was stupid, walking for miles just to watch a big group of birds flying around.'

'Hundreds of thousands of birds,' I point out, with a small smile. Kai's eyes widen slightly and I laugh. 'Ignore your cousin. There will always be people who don't care about the natural world, but for everyone with his attitude there will be someone like you, who's new to all this but sees the beauty in it.'

Kai nods, then glances over his shoulder at the visitor centre. I follow his gaze.

'What are you looking at?'

He shakes his head. 'Nothing.' He turns back to me with another bright smile, and we increase our pace to catch up with the others.

# Chapter 9

## Emily

Ben and I walk side by side, close enough that my hand occasionally brushes his. He doesn't move away, which I take as a good sign. Morna and Dan have caught up to us and I move to the side slightly to let them past. Dan smiles at me on the way past, and gives me a little nod, but Morna doesn't meet my eyes. That's strange; Morna's normally very friendly. What's happened?

The other two carry on ahead at a slightly faster pace, so only Lauren and Kai are behind me and Ben now. If I know my sister, it won't be long before they go past too. That suits me, because I want Ben all to myself today. On the way here, I started thinking about the idea of asking him out, but I'm still worried that I'll scare him and he'll back off. Perhaps I can flirt just enough to give him the confidence to say something, but I don't really feel comfortable doing that with my sister standing right behind me. 'Are you enjoying coming to this group?' Ben asks me. I smile at the way he makes sure he turns his head so I can hear him clearly, and so I can see his lip patterns as he speaks. With only one working processor, I made sure I was walking on his right, so my left side's nearest to him and I can hear him. I feel a bit off kilter, only having hearing on one side, but his consideration makes things easier and reassures me.

Before I have a chance to reply, sure enough, Lauren and Kai catch up and walk around us.

'Make sure you keep up,' Lauren says as she walks past. I only catch it because I'm looking at Lauren at the time. Why does my sister never pay attention to the things I ask her to do? If Ben can remember, then surely Lauren could put a bit of effort in. Kai just gives us a smile and a thumbs up as he walks past, jogging a little to keep up with Lauren's determined strides.

'I am enjoying it,' I say to Ben, returning to his question. 'I mean, outdoors stuff was never really my thing. I'm a techy person, and I'd rather be inside with a games console when I'm not working. But actually, there's definitely something about being out here in the woods that I'm starting to like.'

Ben nods. 'There are lots of health benefits to spending time in nature. There have been studies. Mental health and physical health.'

'Mmm, Lauren keeps telling me. I understand that. It's just never been something I've been interested in before.'

'Did you spend a lot of time outside together growing up?'

I shake my head, stifling a laugh at the very idea of it. 'We lived in a children's home. They didn't really spend a lot of time playing with us or organising outings. We were left to ourselves as much as they could get away with.'

I try to keep a light tone to my voice as I speak, but it's difficult. As much as possible, I try to avoid thinking about my childhood, characterised as it was by loneliness and isolation. Other children didn't know how to behave around me, and I missed their whispers and muttered conversations at nighttime after the lights were out, which was when their most important secrets were shared. I never crept into other girls' bedrooms to chat with them, and I know Lauren would sneak out without telling me. I also know that my sister regularly requested to be moved, to share a room with a different girl, but that request was never granted. Lauren's bitter resentment towards me was a tangible presence, a squat little troll that shared our space and wouldn't leave. It was only when we were teenagers and given our own rooms that the tension lifted, though our relationship was still strained.

'I'm sorry, I didn't realise. Weren't you ever fostered?'

I nod. 'A couple of times. But only when I was quite young, and both times the families said it was too much work, taking me for appointments all the time, doing speech and language games at home to try and help me develop.'

I notice him glance at my cochlear implant processor, and I shake my head. 'The media like to call them bionic ears, but they're not perfect. They don't give me the same experience of hearing as you have. When I take them off, or when one breaks,' I say with a wry smile, pointing to the right side of my head, 'then I'm profoundly deaf and can't hear anything. It took a lot of work and a long time before I was confident with language. Luckily, I had an amazing teacher of the deaf who worked with me all through primary school, so by the time I got to secondary I didn't feel as different from all the other kids.'

'I suppose I thought they were like a pair of glasses,' Ben says. 'You put them on and it makes everything clear again.'

'Unfortunately not. I mean, the technology nowadays is amazing, and I can do things now with my processors that I could never have done with the first ones I had, but it's still not the same as being hearing.'

We walk on in silence for a few moments, both of us deep in our own thoughts. The path winds between tall trees on either side, with a mixture of compacted earth and gravel underfoot. I can hear my own footsteps crunching as I walk, as well as the wind blowing through the trees. Ahead, there are voices but they're very faint. I can see the other five have stopped where the path comes out of the woods and opens out onto a wide clearing that's often a good place for spotting the deer that graze this land. Despite the breeze, the air feels strangely heavy, the sky darkening even though it isn't even two thirty yet. I shiver.

'Are you okay?' Ben asks, looking concerned.

'Yeah, I just don't like cold weather,' I reply with a laugh. 'I'll be okay, I have more layers in my bag.'

'You'll need them. If you think it's cold now, it's only going to get worse when it gets dark. Once the Starlings have roosted, there won't be much light left, so the walk back will be in the dark.'

'I've got a headtorch,' I reply, patting my coat pocket.

He chuckles. 'Is there anything you don't have?'

'Probably not. I like to be prepared. Well, the first time I came, I didn't have anything. I was wearing canvas trainers, and my feet were soaked and freezing by the time we'd finished. I didn't have any spare socks or shoes, and I was miserable, to be honest. And my coat was wool.'

Ben laughs, making me blush a little at the memory of my own cluelessness.

'I didn't really know what it would be like. I live in London, and when I go for a walk it's on a pavement at the side of a road. When it rains, I use an umbrella, and take an Uber if I can. Lauren laughed at me when I suggested we could get an Uber from her flat when we were going out for a meal; I didn't know you don't have them round here.'

'Too rural for something like that,' he replies with another laugh. 'Same for the companies that will deliver you a McDonald's. Not round here.'

'I would really struggle living without all of these things,' I say, now laughing myself. 'I like being able to get whatever I want in a short space of time, just by clicking an app. Sometimes I think it'd be nice to never have to go outside again!'

The others moved on as soon as they saw we were catching up, and now they're rounding a bend in the path that will take us under a railway bridge. The line runs through the reserve, but it's not a particularly busy one, so it's rare to see a train go past. We cross over a large drain that looks a little like a narrow canal, then follow the path as it winds up a small slope then under the brick arches of the bridge. As we pass underneath, Ben reaches out and brushes his hand over the moss that clings to the brick. I remember seeing him do this before, a few months ago, and wonder if it's just a habit he's picked up or if there's some meaning behind it.

We carry on up the slope, until the path levels out and we're back in another wooded area. Here, the path forks, and we take the right-hand branch, leading us out to the marshes. Within a few minutes, the space to our left opens up, and we find ourselves walking alongside a broad expanse of reeds and ponds, with woods in the distance on the other side, stretching round to the far end of the reed beds. Another section of woodland runs along the side of the path, and I know the railway line is hidden somewhere amongst the trees.

Further along the path there's a low wooden building: one of the bird hides. From here it's possible to look out over the marshes and observe the wide variety of birds that come to feed here, but I know that today we're going much further into the reserve.

Lauren turns and waves us forward, then points to the trees on the opposite side of the marshes, along at the far end.

'The Starlings have been roosting all the way over there, but it's impossible to know whether the murmuration will take place over this side, above the marshes, or over on the other side of the woods. If we carry on along here, we've got a greater chance of seeing them.'

She points to the path that continues into the distance, winding back into the woods as it goes.

'At the moment, we could stop at the large hide about a mile from the far end, but there's a chance we could miss a lot of the action if the birds are further round. So I think it would be better to push on. The two hides at that end of the reserve are smaller, and one of them won't even fit all of us in, but we can spread out.'

We continue as a group along the path, which goes in a straight line for about three quarters of a mile, before veering away from the marshes and back into the woodland for a while. Ben and I keep up with the others now, walking in companionable silence, though I make sure I stay close to Ben. I'm hoping that, if the two of us can find somewhere reasonably private to stand, perhaps the beauty of the birds' display coupled with the glow from our brisk walk in the cold will help to ignite something meaningful between us.

The sun is getting lower in the sky, the weak rays barely penetrating the trees in some places. I find some of the shadows a little disturbing, and twice think I see something moving out of the corner of my eye, but when I turn to look there's nothing. *It was probably a bird*, I tell myself. After all, the reserve is full of them.

There's a sharp bend in the path, then the seven of us emerge from the woods by the largest hide. It's an impressive octagonal structure and can easily fit a large group inside.

'I think it would be good to stay here,' Dan speaks up, nodding towards the hide. 'If the birds do come out over the marshes, we'll have a spectacular view from here, and even if they're over the woods we should still get a good glimpse.'

Lauren hesitates, then shrugs. 'Suit yourself. We'll all meet back here once they've roosted, before we head back to the visitor centre.'

Morna steps towards Dan. 'Think I'll stay here, too.'

Lauren opens her mouth as if to say something, then seems to change her mind, shrugs again and turns away to carry on walking up the path. Ben starts walking again too, so I fall in step beside him again.

We walk until the large hide is just a distant blob behind us. Alec stops at the next hide, a small one, and walks inside without saying a word to anyone. The remaining four of us look at each other with raised eyebrows, but nobody says anything. None of us want to be the one who brings up the incident the other night, in case it raises too many questions and leads to uncomfortable conversations.

Before we reach the very end of the reserve, Lauren stops by a patch of reeds that stick up above the rest.

'I'm going to stay here. Like I said, we'll meet back at the large hide once the Starlings have roosted.'

Kai looks like he's thinking of sticking with Lauren, but she's giving off a vibe that suggests she wants to be left alone, so he continues with Ben and me a little way along the path before picking his own spot. I'm glad he doesn't ask to join us, but he strikes me as pretty perceptive, so I think he's intentionally left me and Ben alone.

'Shall we go into the last hide?' I ask, pressing onward without waiting for an answer from Ben. When I reach the door, I push my way inside, then turn to hold the door open for Ben, but he isn't there.

'What's wrong?' He's standing outside on the path and hasn't moved towards the hide. Have I read this all wrong? Was I about to make a fool of myself?

'I'm sorry, Emily. I just need to . . .' His voice tails off and he points back over his shoulder. A moment later, he's gone.

# Chapter 10

## Ben

God, I'm a shit. Leaving Emily like that, when I could have gone and stood in the hide with her, maybe huddled up for warmth. It was the prime opportunity to ask her out, and I've blown it because I can't stop thinking about bloody Alec. If Alec knows as much as I think he does, there's no point me asking Emily out today, or ever. She won't want to have anything to do with me if Alec talks.

Alec went into the smallest hide, alone, so I reckon it'll be easy enough for me to go and talk to him and find out exactly what the hell he's intending to do. Then a thought strikes me and I freeze. What if I go prying, and Alec ignores me? What if he decides to tell the rest of the group while we're walking back to the visitor centre later today?

Ahead of me on the path, I can just make out a couple of other figures in the gloom. The light level is dropping faster than I anticipated, and I hesitate again. Turning towards the marshes, I spot the first handful of birds begin to take flight and wheel around in the sky. There's nothing particularly spectacular or graceful about the way they move, and I can tell it's just the start. I might have time, and it could be better for me to talk to Alec while everyone else is otherwise occupied.

I walk a little further up the path, keeping an eye out for Kai and Lauren as I go. I'm pretty sure Morna and Dan are safely ensconced in the biggest hide several hundred metres away along the edge of the marshes, and I know Emily is behind me. I feel another pang of guilt as I remember the look on her face when I turned round and left her alone in that hide. What the hell was I thinking? Here is a gorgeous woman who I'm pretty sure is interested in me, and an opportunity to spend a good few minutes alone with her, and instead I've chosen to wander around in the dark and confront Alec? Idiot.

Realising what a dickhead I am, I decide to walk back to the furthest hide, trying to put Alec from my mind. After all, if Alec was going to tell someone about me he would have done it by now, and if that had happened I would know about it. No, I'm just going to wait and see, and with any luck it'll turn out that Alec is what we've suspected all along, a slightly awkward middle-aged man who wanted a bit of attention when he'd had a few too many.

This is why I have no luck with women, I realise. I have no sense of when I should put them first. My mum always says I'm too nice, but if I'm that nice, how come women always make excuses when I ask them out? One of the guys I worked with teased me for ages about living with my mum, which is why I finally moved out last year, but that hasn't made much of a difference to my love life.

Turning, I'm about to start walking back to where I left Emily when something catches my eye. There's something moving just inside the woods that back onto the path. Something, or someone? I'm not sure. Trying to pretend I'm not feeling afraid, I pull my torch out of my pocket; it's already quite gloomy in the woods, and the torch itself is pretty heavy, it can double up as a weapon in a pinch.

Before I leave the path, I cast a glance over my shoulder at the marshes. More birds have joined the flock now, and their movements are beginning to ebb and flow in the characteristic movement of the murmuration. I really don't want to miss it, but I also feel the need to check out whatever it was I saw in the woods. Part of me has the idea that if I stumble upon a poacher and apprehend them, then I'll have something to impress Emily with when I drag myself back to her. It would be better than creeping back with my tail between my legs, apologising profusely for being so rude to her. It's actually one of my recurring fantasies, rescuing Emily from a dangerous situation, showing her a different side to myself, a side that I'm not even sure exists, in all honesty. I'd like to have the opportunity to prove myself in some way, though.

Stepping off the path, I move into the first line of trees, my torch not currently lit but hanging by my side. I pause for a moment, listening. There's the sound of the breeze moving the branches in the trees above my head, a soft susurration that's the constant background to walking here. There are rustles and creaks, as branches move or birds or animals scuttle through the undergrowth. Nothing I wouldn't expect to hear.

I push onwards, deeper into the woods, aware that I'm

missing the beginning of the display, the whole reason for this trip. This feels important, however; I want to find out what, or who, I saw a few minutes ago. Perhaps I imagined the figure, but if there's someone there who shouldn't be, I want to know what they're doing. If someone else has got onto the reserve who's just here for a walk, or some other innocent reason, then surely they'd be on the paths like everyone else.

For the next few minutes, I walk, concentrating on what I can see around me. As I penetrate further into the trees, I switch on my torch. What little light is left in the sky struggles to make it down here beneath the tangle of branches, bare though most of them are. I sweep the torch beam back and forth in front of me as I walk, looking for signs of human activity, but there's nothing obvious. I continue, finding myself deeper in the woods. I glance around, losing my bearings for a moment. At the far side of the woods I know there will be a deep ditch, then a steep bank up to the road, but it's almost impossible to get up there because of the mess of brambles and other undergrowth around it, even if you manage to find your way through the woods. Once you're in among the trees, it's hard to tell which direction is which.

My heart is racing, and I'm feeling spooked by my surroundings. It occurs to me that none of the others know I've come this way, so if I get lost they won't have any idea where I am. Pulling out my phone, I check for reception but there's none – I should have known to expect that. I've been visiting this reserve for years, but suddenly realising that I could be lost in the woods without any means of contacting anyone else, while it's getting dark, freaks me out a little.

Standing still for a moment, I take a deep breath and try to think logically. I've walked in more or less a straight line, so if I turn around by 180 degrees, I'll be facing back the way I came. This plan calms me for a moment, until another part of my mind pipes up: I've turned a few times, looking into the trees, so how can I be certain that I've gone in a straight line?

Cursing my own idiocy, I turn around. The trees do look thinner that way, suggesting that if I carry on walking I'll find myself back at the path, looking over the open marshes. I decide I might as well risk it, because standing in one place isn't going to get me back to a place I recognise. I start walking again, using the torch to check for roots or fallen branches that I could fall over. A broken ankle is the last thing I need after I've got myself lost in the woods.

I can't believe how much of an idiot I've been recently. Berating myself in my head, I trudge onward, listing all the stupid things I've done: talking to my mum about Emily; not contacting Alec to have it out with him before today; leaving Emily on her own in that hide just to go on this fool's errand; and now getting lost in the woods just because I thought I might have seen something. Since the moment I stepped off the path I've seen no sign of anyone at all, let alone someone who shouldn't be here. I realise I'm muttering to myself and press my lips tightly together to stop it from happening again.

A sudden clattering noise above my head startles me and draws my attention upward. It was a Crow taking flight, that's all. Nothing more sinister. Shaking my head at how jumpy I am, I continue walking, but my attention is no longer on the path in front of me and I stumble, falling to the ground and smacking my knee on a root that's sticking out.

'Shit,' I mutter, pulling myself back up to sitting and brushing leaf mulch off my face. I feel the knee I landed on gingerly, but it doesn't seem too bad, so I get back onto my feet.

'Is someone there?' A voice comes from quite nearby, making me jump once again. I peer through the trees, grabbing my torch from where it fell when I stumbled. There's someone walking towards me, but a quick flash of the torch beam shows it's only Kai.

'Ben, mate, what the fuck are you doing?' Kai's tone is light, but I can hear a slight edge to his words.

'Thought I saw something,' I mutter in response. 'Lauren said there might be poachers, so I thought I'd better take a look.'

'Whatever,' Kai replies. 'You're missing everything.' He nods back over his shoulder to indicate he means the murmuration.

I don't reply, but start moving again, pushing past Kai and walking in the direction he came from. Kai follows me, and we walk in silence for a moment until I have a thought that makes me stop.

'Hang on. What were you doing in here?'

'Saw you, didn't I?' Kai replies with a nonchalant shrug. 'Wondered what you were up to.'

'How could you have seen me through the trees? It's getting dark, you can barely see anything in here.'

'I got good eyes.'

The two of us eyeball each other for a moment, and I'm wondering if I can call Kai's bluff, but I decide against it. It's too risky, until I've found out how much Alec knows and who else he's told. Kai was the one who dragged Alec out of the pub the other night; what if he said more once he was outside? What if Alec told Kai what he saw?

Because now I'm prepared to admit it to myself; I'm positive that Alec was talking about me the other night, about my secret. He knows, and I can't undo that, so I'm going to have to do something about it.

Kai's watching me, his eyes narrowed, and I feel a stab of fear. If Kai knows, will he keep it to himself? I'm not sure. The two of us are from very different backgrounds, and I have a feeling it might be possible to buy Kai's silence, but not until I've worked out just how much he knows. Offering him a bribe when he might not even know anything could backfire spectacularly, highlighting my own weakness.

Breaking the stalemate, I turn and carry on walking, not saying another word to Kai. When we come out onto the path, I realise we're quite a bit further along from where I entered the woods, not far from the hide where Alec has taken up his post to watch the Starlings. It's a sign. I need to do what I set out to do this morning.

I turn to Kai. 'Are you going back to watch the birds?'

Kai nods slowly. 'Sure. You?'

'Yeah. Might go further up.' I point past the smallest hide, back the way we came earlier, in the opposite direction from where Kai had been standing.

I wait for Kai to get the hint, and eventually he turns and starts to walk away down the path, glancing over his shoulder at me a couple of times. I don't move again until Kai has rounded a slight bend in the path and is out of sight.

# Chapter 11

## Alec

I close the door of the hide behind me, pushing it roughly so it shuts with a bang. There is a flap of startled wings outside one of the hide windows, and I force myself to freeze. I can't let my emotions get the better of me, not if it means I end up disturbing the wildlife. That's when I realise one of the shutters has been left open, and my mind goes straight back to the group of rude, ungrateful deviants I have found myself in the company of. Really, they have been very unpleasant to me today, which isn't what I deserve. Granted, I behaved a little unwisely the other evening, but given that I'm far more knowledgeable than any of the others when it comes to the wildlife around us, I would have still expected them to defer to me today. Nevertheless, now I'm alone in a hide, and none of them have seen fit to join me, to gain the benefit of my wisdom and understanding of the spectacle they are about to witness. I've seen Starling murmurations the world over, including one in Israel, and one with over three million birds in Rome. The one this evening should be a couple of hundred thousand, impressive to a novice perhaps but nothing to an experienced birder like myself.

Settling myself on one of the benches, once again I go through the ritual of setting up my tripod and scope, then get out my binoculars and scan the marshes in front of me. No sign of any Starlings yet; a few waterfowl of various kinds still out amongst the reeds. For a moment I watch a Heron stalking away, and a couple of Water Rails. I hold my binoculars lovingly, almost caressing them, still feeling the sting that Kai ignored my advice. Perhaps the price tag was too steep for him, but quality like that doesn't come cheap, and with the antics that young man has been up to I bet that Kai can afford them. Though he would probably prefer to spend his money on something more frivolous. I have no idea what would interest a man in his twenties, not these days, and definitely not one of Kai's sort.

The sisters could be a bit more respectful, too. Lauren's the one who works here, so of course she has taken charge of the logistics of the day, but that doesn't mean she can't recognise someone else's experience. She actually sneered at me when I claimed to know their secrets; perhaps she thinks there's nothing worth sharing, but I'm sure each of the sisters would be interested to know what the other one has been saying about her behind her back. Do they think that people in this group never talk to each other? I have no interest in gossip, of course, but I can't help what I overhear.

Some birds are starting to gather now, and I use their position to alter the focus of my scope. Binoculars will be better for watching the murmuration, or even just the naked eye, because seeing it from a greater distance sometimes helps you to get the full perspective of how special it is. Scientists have studied the birds so many times, all over the world, trying to understand just how and why they do what they do every evening through the autumn and winter. The movement is incredible – each bird responding to the movements of those in its immediate vicinity, meaning the whole flock swirls and undulates in the sky as if they're performing an elaborately choreographed dance. They never crash into each other, each of them so attuned to the other birds nearby. It's magical, really, and such a wondrous example of the ways nature can escape our understanding.

It's thought that they do it to avoid predators, to ensure their roosting site is safe for the night. It's harder for a bird of prey to pick off a Starling in flight when they're in such a large group, constantly moving in directions that can't be predicted. I once saw a Marsh Harrier fly through a murmuration, probably trying to get its claws into a juvenile, but it failed and gave up quite quickly. The murmuration doesn't behave like thousands of individual birds; it is more like one cohesive, fluid organism, and I am still in awe every time I see one.

I find myself wondering how Dan will find the experience. As a newcomer to the group, I've done my best to try and befriend him, but Dan seems quite closed off. I won't take that personally, of course. I know a couple of other men who have worked offshore, and they seem to be good at compartmentalising, probably because of the way they work, having weeks at a time away from their families, doing nothing other than working and sleeping. There's something else that Dan isn't telling us, I know that, but the man's entitled to his privacy.

Morna, on the other hand, has every reason to be ashamed of herself for keeping the secret she holds. I discovered it only recently, when she let her guard down after our last meeting. Maybe I shouldn't have been snooping, but the fact remains that she's keeping something to herself that really should be out in the open. Of course, I wouldn't dream of telling anyone else, but if she's not going to do it then I might have to put a little bit of pressure on her. She's the only one who hasn't been outright rude to me today, I feel, so perhaps she's coming around to my way of thinking. Honesty is always the best policy, however long it is since you made the mistake. Because it's clear that this was a mistake on Morna's part, something she chose but then has come to regret, and I can't find fault with her for that. We all have those moments we wish we could relive and do differently.

My binoculars drift out along the edge of the marshes. I watch as Lauren, Kai, Ben and Emily all walk away from the hide and separate out along the path to watch the murmuration. Lauren spends some time scanning the whole of the marshes with her binoculars, then turns and watches the woods for a while. Is she keeping an eye out for whoever I saw earlier, or is she up to something? I do think she's right to be wary, but I also don't understand why this piece of land has become such a prime target. There must be other places with deer and birds' nests that are more accessible. Unless you have someone on the inside, I remind myself. These people think they can pull the wool over my eyes, but I know what's going on. Well, something like poaching is a matter for the police. No more taunting the group with what I know; I realise that was petty. I've already reported something I've discovered, and other things . . . well, I will have to decide. Out above the marshes, I see the first Starlings begin to come together. It's amazing how it happens. One minute there's a handful of birds in the air, no particular pattern to their movements, then suddenly they come together and it begins. Small at first, before other birds arrive and join the dance, the numbers swelling until there are thousands of them, undulating across the sky, as if they're painting a picture against the clouds that melts within seconds, only to reform in a different way.

As I sit back to enjoy the spectacle, a movement catches my eye. What the hell is Ben doing, wandering back this way? I would have thought he'd be snuggled up in a hide with Emily; the boy can barely keep his tongue inside his mouth when he's looking at her. Of all the secrets I know about this group, Ben's is the one that most surprised me. Such a nice young man, everyone else thinks. Polite, respectful. Well, what I know about him would certainly make everyone think again.

I watch Ben for a few minutes, until he disappears into the trees. Perhaps this would be a good time for me to follow him and find out what he's up to. After all, if he's doing something that could jeopardise the safety of the group, someone really needs to be aware of it. Standing up, I open the door of the hide and peer out into the woods. It's starting to get dark, and the woods look particularly sinister. No, I think, shutting the door and retreating to the wooden bench once more. No, I won't follow Ben right now. Whatever he's up to, it can wait. Why should I miss out on the murmuration just because of someone else, someone with already questionable habits?

I sit there for another ten minutes, watching as the number of birds increases and swells the size of the flock, swaying and dipping through the sky. At times they're packed so tightly together it looks like a huge dark ball of energy hanging above the trees, then suddenly they separate slightly, spreading further across the sky. As each bird responds to the movements of those around it, the murmuration dips low across the marshes, becoming harder to see with the trees looming large in the background, but then moments later they are rising again to be silhouetted against the fast-waning daylight. I am mesmerised, as always.

It takes me a few moments to realise that something feels wrong. There's a prickle on the back of my neck that tells me I should have been paying more attention to my surroundings, but I've been sucked in in the way I always am when I'm watching birds. Many times, I've found myself rushing to get back to the entrance of a reserve before the car park is locked, because time has run away with me while I've had my binoculars glued to my face. Tearing my gaze away from the murmuration for a moment, I sit up straighter and listen. Some faint bird calls from the marshes, but nothing unexpected for this time of night. I scan the paths leading up to the hide, or as much as I can see of them, in both directions, but there's nothing untoward. Something isn't right, though.

Turning around, I notice the door is standing ajar. Did I neglect to shut it properly when I got up earlier? Maybe, though that's very unlikely. I stand up and cross to the door, my eyes struggling to accustom to the gloom inside the hide after staring out into the sky for ten minutes.

A scraping sound. There's someone standing just outside the hide! I pull the door open wider, blinking rapidly to try and make out the shape. They're raising their arm, and there's something in their hands. Something long.

'Hey!' I say, trying to put as much authority into my voice as possible. 'What do you think you're doing?'

It all happens at once. I take a step forward just as the other person does the same, the sudden movement catching me off balance. There's a rush of noise and light, a brief moment of terror, then nothing more.

# Chapter 12

## Emily

Even with only one implant processor, I hear the blast. I've been cycling through a range of emotions as I've been sitting here, alone in the hide, watching the majesty of the Starlings' display as it takes place over the marshes. Ben left me here, without even a backward glance; at first the rejection hurt, and I felt stupid for ever thinking something might happen between us. But since that faded, I've mostly been feeling angry with him for doing that to me. Regardless of whether anything romantic might blossom between us, it was rude of him to suggest he'd stay with me then leave all of a sudden. What was it that made him change his mind so abruptly?

The noise puts all these thoughts out of my mind, however. It echoes around the reserve, the sound bouncing off the trees and sending birds into panicked flight. I jump up off my seat and peer out of the hide windows, but I can't see anything much other than the marshes. I run to the door, but hesitate before pulling it open. The noise was difficult to identify, but whatever it was sent a jolt of fear through me. Is it safe to leave the hide, or should I stay where I am?

I stay there for a moment, frozen by indecision, but then a thought strikes me. The noise clearly wasn't anything good. If there's someone dangerous out there, someone who shouldn't be on the reserve, I don't want to be trapped inside a little wooden shed. Throwing open the door, I look around me. To my left, the path curves around the end of the marshes, leading up to the woods on the other side of the water. It disappears into the reed beds, and I can't see any further than that. It's gloomy, with little light left in the sky, and it takes a moment for my eyes to adjust. Looking the other way, I see the path that leads back the way we came, and I hear raised voices. Making a decision, I step out onto the path.

'Emily!'

I turn to see Kai coming towards me. It looks like he's coming from the reeds, but that's a dangerous shortcut to take if you don't know the reserve well, especially with the light rapidly waning. Lauren's drummed it into me to stick to the paths at all times, because the ground can be deceptive – what looks like a solid surface beneath your feet could be marsh, and there's a possibility you could get stuck. With little phone reception around here, it's important not to do anything that could put yourself at unnecessary risk.

'What happened? What was that noise?' I call to Kai as soon as he's close enough for me to hear his reply.

'Shotgun,' Kai replies, and a ripple of fear runs through me. He looks tense, almost ill, and I wonder if there's something he isn't telling me.

'Where did it come from?'

He gestures back along the path. 'Somewhere along there. Stay here, it might not be safe.'

I ignore him, closing the door to the hide behind me and slinging my bag onto my back. Kai is trotting along the path, so I jog to keep up with him. He realises I'm following him and shakes his head at me, telling me to stay back, but I won't be put off.

Kai stops and I walk into the back of him. He turns around and gives me a hard look.

'I mean it, Emily. It might be dangerous. None of our group were carrying a shotgun, so there must be someone else here.'

'Poachers?' I say, remembering that muttered refrain that has been following us all day.

Kai flinches, then nods.

'Well, I don't want to be on my own in a hide if there's someone wandering around the reserve with a shotgun,' I reply, folding my arms. 'I'll go and find Alec, or Lauren.'

Kai mutters something, but he's turned away from me and I can't hear him clearly or read his lips in the gloom. I grab him by the shoulder and pull him round to face me.

'Say that again, I didn't catch it.'

'I don't know where Lauren is,' he says, glancing to the side. 'I thought she'd gone into the reed beds along here, but I can't see her now.'

'Where would she have gone?' I feel a pang of concern for my sister. 'We need to head back to the big hide and see what the hell is going on,' I tell him, trying to appear confident despite the fear growing in my heart. 'That's where we're supposed to be meeting up.'

Kai points over his shoulder. 'I'm going to have a look in the woods, try and figure out where that shot came from.'

I grab his arm and shake my head. 'No, we need to stick together.' What I don't say is that I don't want to be alone out here. The sky is almost dark now, and the clouds are heavy, not allowing us any glimpse of the moon or stars. Even though I've walked around this reserve a few times before today, I have never really paid much attention to my surroundings, and I certainly wouldn't be able to get my bearings in the dark. Having only one working processor is making me nervous, too, because it affects how well I can hear things around me, as well as meaning I can't tell what direction any sound is coming from.

For a moment, Kai looks like he's going to argue with me, but in the end, he gives a reluctant shrug, shoves his hands in his pockets and sets off back towards the large hide.

As we walk along the path, I can't hear any more sounds of people – no movement, no voices. Where are the others? Why aren't they outside, trying to figure out where that noise came from? If it hadn't been for Kai's presence, and his confidence that he knows it was the report from a shotgun, I might have started to think I imagined it.

'Where is everyone?' I mutter to myself. Kai turns and frowns at me, and I repeat the question louder.

'I don't know. That's what worries me.'

'Maybe they didn't think there was anything wrong?' I suggest.

'Yeah, maybe.' Kai's tone of voice doesn't fill me with confidence.

100

We continue on for another few metres, then Kai holds out a hand to stop me.

'This is where I was standing,' he tells me. 'Lauren was a bit further up, I thought. I didn't notice her leave, though.'

I walk a bit further up the path, looking for signs of where my sister might be, but after a few moments I shake my head. Who am I kidding? I have no idea where to start or what to look for; any changes to the path or the reeds where Lauren was standing would mean nothing to me. I would barely know the difference between an animal track and a bike track. Give me some intricate but problematic code and I'll be able to find the bug in no time at all, but in the natural world I am well out of my depth.

Staring around me in desperation, I wonder where Lauren could have gone. The logical explanation is that she followed the sound of the shotgun blast to try and find its source, just as Kai was intending to do.

'Could she have gone looking for poachers?' I ask him now.

He frowns. 'Maybe, but I'm sure I would have seen her. I moved away from where I was standing as soon as I heard the noise.'

Kai shifts uneasily as he speaks, and I get the feeling he's not telling me the truth. Has he seen Lauren and he's refusing to say where she's gone? But why would he do that? Unless something has happened to my sister . . .

I back away from Kai and return to the path, keeping my eyes on him the whole time in case he moves towards me. It's not too far to the hide Alec went in to watch the murmuration, so I find myself hoping he's still there. I don't make any sudden movements, but keep increasing the gap between myself and Kai, not wanting to take any risks.

'What's wrong?' he asks. I only just catch the words drifting on the cold evening air and suddenly feel very vulnerable with two of my senses impaired.

'Nothing,' I say, continuing to move away from him, shaking my head.

'Seriously, Emily, what's wrong? Have you seen something?'

'Where's Lauren?' I blurt out. 'How could you not have seen her move?'

Kai stops and stares at me, his expression incredulous. 'I have no idea where she went. Emily, seriously. I'm sorry, I . . .' He grimaces. 'Look, I just dashed into the woods for a minute, you know . . .' His voice tails off.

'Why?'

He comes closer to me. 'Do I have to spell it out?'

It dawns on me what he's trying to say and I feel a bit embarrassed, essentially confronting him about his need to urinate. But is he telling me the truth? I continue to move away from him, but now I'm willing to risk turning my back on him.

'I'm going to go and find the others,' I tell Kai over my shoulder. 'Maybe one of them knows what the sound was.'

Kai catches up and walks next to me, thankfully picking the side that still has a processor. I keep to the edge of the path and he seems to respect the distance I'm keeping between us, not coming too close.

'It might not have even been on the reserve,' he tells me, though it sounds like he's trying to convince himself just as much as he is me. 'There's plenty of farmland beyond the boundary of the nature reserve, you know. It could have been a farmer after a fox.'

'I thought you weren't allowed to kill foxes anymore?'

Kai gives me a look that's a little amused, a little condescending. 'You can't hunt them down with dogs while riding a horse anymore, though people still do. Nobody's fooled just because they call it trail hunting. But farmers can still kill vermin on their land, no laws against that.'

I try not to look surprised; I don't like showing my ignorance. 'With guns?'

Kai laughs. 'Yeah, how else?'

I shrug. 'I don't know. Traps?'

'Traps aren't as humane. Someone who's a good shot can make a clean kill, avoid any suffering. Traps are slow and painful.'

'But I thought guns were illegal?'

He laughs again. 'Most are, but if you have a licence for a shotgun, it's fine. You need a reason to have it, but if you've got land then it's pretty normal round here to have one.'

I realise just how little I know about life in the country. Despite having grown up here, I moved to London when I was seventeen and got my first job, or rather jobs, because I had to work every hour I could in order to afford the rent on my mouldy bedsit. It was a combination of hard work and luck that got me my first job with a tech company, after I applied for one of their apprenticeships straight out of school, but I couldn't live on those wages. I cleaned offices in the evenings until I managed to work my way up to a position with decent pay. From the moment I left the children's home and took a train to King's Cross,

I assimilated myself to city life and did my best to forget what I experienced before London became my home.

The two of us approach the hide where we last saw Alec, and I notice the door is slightly ajar. Kai puts out an arm to stop me again, and my gaze is drawn downward. I gasp at the sight of a foot in the doorway, clearly attached to a person who is lying on the floor of the hide.

'Who is it?' I ask, but Kai glares at me to be quiet.

'Is there anyone in there?' he calls out, but no sound comes in response.

Kai walks forward slowly, leaning over and gently pushing open the door of the hide. It is pitch black inside, so he pulls out a torch and switches it on, the beam playing over the wooden walls. I hang back, not sure I want to see who it is or what has happened to them.

I hear a gasp, and Kai steps back, his lips pressed tightly together.

'Oh God,' I hear him say. 'Oh fucking hell.'

'Is it Alec?' I ask, and he nods. Just one sharp nod, but it's enough.

'Don't go in there.'

I hold up my palms to show I have no intention of doing so.

'Is he . . .?'

Kai nods.

'Are you sure?'

He takes a deep breath. 'With a wound like that, there's no doubt. Alec's dead. He's been shot in the chest.'

# Chapter 13

## Kai

My head's reeling. From the moment I heard that blast I knew something was wrong, something serious, but I didn't expect this. As I pushed open the door to the hide, my nostrils were hit by a coppery smell, with an undertone of shit. I've never seen a dead body before, something I lie about regularly to my cousin and his mates.

Shit. What the fuck am I supposed to do now? Alec is just lying here on the floor of the hide, one foot propped up against the door, the other sprawled further away from his body than looks natural. It must be the way he fell. Alec's chest is a gory mess; actually, I don't even want to think of the thing on the floor as Alec. If I just think of it as 'the body', maybe I can cope with this without passing out.

I know enough about shotguns to recognise the sound I heard, as well as the damage done to . . . the body. It was a close-range shot, so the pellets didn't have the chance to spread very far apart, leaving a ragged, gaping hole torn in his chest. Its chest, I correct myself. Think it, not he.

'Kai, what are we going to do?' Emily's voice brings me out of my own thoughts and back into the present moment. 'How the hell did this happen?'

I turn back to her, swallowing the bile that rises in my throat. Shaking my head, I try to think. What now?

'We need to find the others,' I say, unsure what good that will do but knowing it's better than doing nothing. 'We need to make sure everyone else is okay, and that they know what's happened.'

'But what the hell are we supposed to tell them?' Emily leans forward, as if she's trying to catch a glimpse of Alec's body, but I stop her. I go to move Alec's foot so I can shut the door, but Emily cries out.

'Don't touch anything! There could be evidence.'

'What? Right now I don't give a fuck about evidence, I just want to forget what I've seen and get out of here.' I don't mean to get so angry with her, but I'm shit scared and that's how it comes out.

Emily takes a step back and glances over her shoulder. 'Did he kill himself?'

I haven't considered that she might come to that conclusion, and I know I'm an idiot for not thinking of it myself. A close-range shotgun wound could be suicide, surely? I sweep the beam of my torch across the floor of the hide, careful to avoid looking at the body, but there's no sign of a shotgun.

I turn back to Emily. 'I don't think so. I can't see the gun, and I think it would be at the wrong angle.' We're getting beyond my level of knowledge here, but I'm pretty

106

sure nobody's arms are long enough to shoot themselves in the chest with a shotgun. Besides, the gun would have fallen next to him, or on top of him, and there's nothing there. I look again at the angle of the body, the way Alec has fallen. I'm no expert, but to me it seems as if Alec was still standing inside the hide when he was shot. So that means whoever killed Alec was either just outside the door or in the hide with him.

I don't share this insight with Emily, not until I can figure out what it means. None of our group followed Alec into this hide when we walked round earlier, but that doesn't mean someone didn't join him later. Or could it have been someone else? I glance over my shoulder towards the woods, aware that Emily is watching me. I desperately need to get some phone reception, then I can find out if anyone I know can shed some light on what's happened here.

Emily shivers. 'We need to get back to the other hide and tell everyone what's happened,' she says. I think we should stay with the body, just in case I can find anything else out, but I really don't like the idea of staying here alone. Not that I'm prepared to admit to that if anyone asks.

The two of us step away from the hide and hurry along the path to the next one. On the way, we're both startled by someone stepping out of the reed beds to our right.

'Lauren!' I'm relieved to see her but my heart is thundering out of my chest. You need to get a grip, I tell myself. 'Where the hell have you been?'

'Trying to find out where that shotgun blast came from,' she snaps. I can see a mixture of fear and anger in her eyes, and I wonder how she got all the way over here from where she was originally standing.

Emily speaks before I get the chance. 'It's Alec. Someone shot him.'

There's a moment of silence as Lauren takes this in, only disturbed by a flutter of wings out on the other side of the marshes. I'm suddenly aware of how isolated we are right now. I know a few people who are handy with shotguns, and they'd have no problem picking us off, being as exposed as we are. Without another word, I touch both sisters lightly on the arm and nod at the path.

'We need to keep moving, find the others.'

'Wait,' Lauren says, jerking her arm away from my hand. 'What the hell are you talking about?'

I swallow, not wanting to think about the body in the hide behind us. 'We went to find Alec and he was lying there in the hide, dead. He's been shot in the chest.'

'What?'

I repeat what I said, and she shakes her head.

'No, that can't be right.'

Lauren moves to push past me, but I stop her firmly. 'You don't want to go and see that.'

'How do I know you're telling me the truth?' she snaps.

I look at Emily, who appears to be as stunned as I am by Lauren's outburst.

'Why the fuck would we lie about something like that, Lauren?' I ask.

She shakes her head, backing away slightly. 'I'm sorry, you're right. But maybe you made a mistake.'

'There's no way I was mistaken. He's definitely dead.' I want to describe the scene just to make her squirm after she doubted me, but I'm aware of Emily next to me and feel an unexplained urge to protect her from the worst of it.

'I assumed that shot was poachers. Why would someone kill Alec?' Lauren is looking past me towards the hide, so I step aside with a shrug. If she wants to go and have a look, it's her choice. I've warned her.

At that moment, we see a torch beam sweeping its way along the path towards us. I shield my eyes from the beam and see Morna and Dan coming in our direction.

'Shotgun?' Dan asks, his piercing gaze meeting mine. I nod. Why is he looking at me to confirm what he heard, rather than one of the others?

'They've just told me Alec's been shot,' Lauren butts in, a note of hysteria in her voice. 'He's dead. I was just going to go and see for myself.'

Dan frowns and looks towards the hide where Alec's body lies. 'I'll go.'

The others all seem happy for Dan to take the lead, so he strides off in that direction, looking about him as he goes.

While he's gone, the four of us who are left find it difficult to meet each other's eyes. Morna seems to be frozen with the shock, while Emily and Lauren both shift from foot to foot anxiously. Funny how siblings who rarely see each other still have similar mannerisms, I think.

Lauren's head suddenly snaps round. 'Where's Ben?'

In the tension, I haven't realised there's still one person missing from our group.

'Last time I saw him, he was walking to the furthest hide with Emily.'

For a moment, Emily looks like she's been caught in headlights.

'Well?' Lauren demands. 'Where is he?'

'I . . . I don't know,' Emily replies, looking as if she's almost on the verge of tears under the ferocity of Lauren's glare. 'He told me he had something he needed to do. He came back up this way, but I don't know where he went.'

For a moment the sisters seem to be in a stand-off, until Lauren steps forward and gives Emily a look that's partly sympathetic, partly accusing. 'You do realise Ben could have done this?'

There's a pause, then Morna, Emily and I all speak at once.

'No way!'

'I really don't think . . .'

'How could you even think that?'

Emily is staring at her sister, tears in her eyes, but Lauren just shrugs.

'There has to be another explanation,' Emily says, turning to Morna, who nods.

'Let's just wait for Dan to get back before we jump to any conclusions,' I say, hoping to be the voice of reason, but I don't know if any of the three women even hear me.

It seems an age before Dan comes into view again in the gloom. He walks purposefully, and his expression is grim. His face looks pale and drawn in the torchlight, which sends eerie shadows across his features as he moves.

When Dan reaches us, he points along the path. 'Let's get back to the large hide.'

'We need to find Ben,' Lauren insists.

'He knows where we're convening,' Dan says. 'I feel like we'd be safer under cover at the moment.'

His words hit home the seriousness of the situation,

110

and the whole group follow him without saying a word. I try not to make it obvious as I scan the woods that meet the path, as well as casting my gaze out over the marshes, but I soon realise both Dan and Lauren are doing the same thing. Morna walks with her eyes down, Emily with hers fixed ahead on the largest hide. There's no sign of anyone else on the reserve, and no sign of Ben either. As we keep being reminded, nobody else is here today.

The five of us go into the hide and Lauren automatically reaches for the electric light. Dan darts over to close the two shutters that have been left open, preventing some of the light from being seen from the outside. I don't think it'll make much difference, however. If there is someone out there waiting for us with a shotgun, they'll have been keeping an eye on us for the last ten minutes. Out on the marshes there's no cover, except for the hides, and the shutters won't keep the light out.

Emily is blinking in the bright light inside the hide, the only one on the reserve that's fitted with electricity. She looks over at me, then looks away again as soon as our gazes meet. Does she know where Ben is?

'What in God's name happened out there?' Lauren demands. She looks furious, but I know that anger is masking her fear.

Dan takes a deep breath, and the softness of his words when he speaks doesn't lessen their impact.

'Looking at where he fell, I'd say Alec was shot by someone who was standing right in front of him. To me, that suggests it was someone he trusted.'

Morna lets out a gasp, and Emily sits down heavily on one of the benches.

'Ben isn't here,' Dan continues, looking pointedly at the rest of us in turn. 'Perhaps we shouldn't jump to any conclusions, but I think the best thing to do right now is for the rest of us to get to a place of safety as quickly as possible.'

There's a pained silence before Emily speaks up.

'Wait, you actually think Ben did this? No, he couldn't have.'

Dan holds up a hand. 'I have no idea what happened. All I know is that someone we were all a bit pissed off at is now dead, and there is someone out there with a shotgun.'

Lauren opens her mouth as if to speak, then shuts it again. I don't trust myself to speak. Should I share what I know with the rest of them? No, it won't do anyone any good, and it might put me in a dangerous position. I keep my mouth shut, while everyone around me starts to argue, but they all fall silent when the door opens and Ben stumbles in, covered in blood.

# Chapter 14

## Lauren

The blood is darker than I expect, contrasting with his skin that looks so pale in the electric light in the hide. There's a trickle of it running down the side of his face, and as he steps further in, he stretches out a hand that is also covered. Instinctively, I step back. I don't want him to touch me, don't want him anywhere near me.

Emily, of course, rushes forward, taking him by the elbow and guiding him to one of the bench seats.

'Ben! Are you okay? What happened?'

He shakes his head, but it's slow and laboured, as if he's trying to clear water out of his ears.

'I . . . I don't know.'

Dan steps forward and gently moves Emily out of the way, then starts to check Ben over for injuries. I know I shouldn't be scared of him – there are five of us and one of him, and if he shot Alec, he's ditched the gun – but I am still tensed and ready to run.

None of us speak while Dan deals with Ben. When he

reaches the back of his head, Ben winces and pulls away from him.

'Turn around, I need to look at it.' Dan's tone of voice doesn't allow for arguments, and Ben doesn't look like he's in any fit state to resist. He does as Dan says, and I open the front pocket of my rucksack to remove the first aid kit. Even if Ben did kill Alec, I don't want us leaving a second dead body in the woods.

Dan takes it from me with a nod, then gets his torch and shines it on Ben's wound.

'I don't think there's anything in there, but a doctor will need to check. I'll dress it for now, stem the bleeding.' He works as he talks, quietly explaining to Ben what he's doing while he does it. Ben just sits there, docile, almost dazed.

Morna steps forward. 'What happened? What did you do to Alec?' There's a note of hysteria in her voice.

Ben looks confused. 'Alec? I didn't . . . I went to talk to him. I don't know what happened.' There's a pause while he waits for Dan to finish tending to his head wound. 'I just remember someone running towards me and knocking me over. Then I was lying on the ground. Pain in my head. I got up and ran away, but I ended up in the woods. Must've lost my bearings.' His speech has the blurry quality of someone who's just woken up.

'If you were outside the hide where Alec was shot, why didn't Emily and I see you there when we came past?' Kai demands. He's got a good point.

'What?' Ben stares at Kai. 'Alec was shot?'

Dan nods at Ben's shoulder. 'You might have been, too.'

'That doesn't answer my question,' Kai says.

'I don't know. Like I said, I wandered into the woods.

Then I saw lights, came here. I don't know anything about Alec.'

'You told Emily you had something to do,' I snap at him. 'You were going to speak to Alec, weren't you, about the other night? What did he know about you, Ben?'

Ben looks aghast, staring at me then at Emily, his expression turns to one of pleading. 'No, no, I wouldn't do anything like that. Honestly, Em, you have to believe me. I wouldn't hurt him. I wanted to talk to him, but I didn't get there. There was . . . I don't know what it was, a noise, an explosion, something. There was someone in a dark coat. I didn't see who it was, though. I think I hit my head.'

Emily reaches for Ben's hand and I can't stop myself from tutting. Of course she would automatically believe him. Well, I'm not going to be that gullible. I think Morna agrees with me, because her body is tensed as if she wants to grab Emily and pull her away from him.

Looking around, I notice that all of us are wearing dark coats. That's a convenient detail for Ben to drop in: on the face of it, it sounds like an important piece of information, but really it means absolutely nothing.

'Will someone explain what the hell is going on?' Ben says, and I can hear fear in his voice. But is it the same fear we're all experiencing, or fear of what he's done?

Emily sits next to him and explains in a soft voice what we all heard, and what we found in the smallest hide. I shudder at the thought of it, and I'm glad I didn't go to look. Ben looks like he's going to be sick.

Dan's finished seeing to Ben's head wound, so I pull Dan to the side, and Kai follows.

'What do you think?' I ask Dan.

He chews his bottom lip in thought for a moment. 'It looks like he's hit his head on the ground, like he says. There was dirt around the wound, and a few bits of grass and dead leaves in his hair. It isn't deep, just a bad graze really, but head wounds bleed like mad, and losing a lot of blood could easily make him confused. So he might be telling the truth.'

'But he might not,' I say.

'He might not,' he agrees. 'He could have inflicted that injury himself, but it's the less likely explanation, in my opinion.'

Kai frowns. 'So you're saying there could be someone else out there, in the woods? Someone else shot Alec?'

Dan spreads his palms wide. 'Unless you think one of the rest of us did it.'

There is a pause as this sinks in, and I notice Morna has joined us.

'You think he's telling the truth?' She looks aghast. 'So who the hell killed Alec? Are you telling me there's someone just wandering around in the woods with a bloody shotgun?'

'That's not what we're saying,' Kai begins, at the same time as I say, 'It's possible, I suppose.' We look at each other, and I can see he's worried, but I honestly don't know what the hell to think.

'Look, we were all pissed off with Alec. Weren't we?' The others reluctantly nod. 'But were any of us really that angry that we'd kill him? I know it looks suspicious, Ben turning up like this, but Dan says he's probably telling the truth, and I'm willing to trust his judgement.'

'You mean you wouldn't have believed Ben's story otherwise?' Emily's voice comes from behind me, and I see her staring at me, her arms crossed. 'Great friendship and leadership you're showing, here.'

I bite back the retort that springs to mind. There's no sense arguing with her about this right now. The important thing is that we're all safe, and we need to get away from here to contact the police, which is what I tell her.

'Wait,' Kai said. 'I don't buy it, that Ben wanders in here covered in blood, not knowing what happened. Don't you think it's pretty convenient?'

'What's that supposed to mean?' Emily snaps.

Kai glances over at Ben, who is still sitting on the other side of the hide, his head leaning on the wooden wall behind him, eyes closed. I see what he means.

'Well, aren't we missing something here? If Ben went up to the hide, wanting to talk to Alec, then found himself outside the hide when he was shot . . .'

'Surely he saw who shot him,' I finish, understanding what he's getting at. 'That's a very good point. If he wants us to believe he didn't do it, surely he'll be able to tell us that.'

Dan nods his agreement. 'Let's see what he says.'

I go over to Ben and crouch down in front of him. 'Tell us what you saw.'

He looks confused and shakes his head. 'I already told you, I don't remember.'

'You said you were going to talk to Alec. So you went to the hide. What next?'

Ben sighs. 'I don't know. Like I said, there was something big, an explosion or something, and someone ran past me. Then the next thing I knew, I was lying on the ground, every bit of me hurt. I didn't get up for a couple of minutes,

I was too shaken. Then I did, and I must have wandered into the woods. I don't remember thinking anything, just that I had to get away from where I was.' He looks over at Emily and gives a little apologetic shrug, which pisses me off. I'm the one who asked him the question, not her.

'Well, did you see who it was?'

'No. I don't know.'

'Ben, do you understand how important this is? Someone killed Alec. You're telling us that it wasn't you, so we need some evidence in order to believe you.' Regardless of what Dan said about his injury, doubt is starting to creep into my mind. He'd said it was possible that Ben inflicted it on himself, and I try to picture it.

'Of course it wasn't me! For fuck's sake, Lauren, do you actually believe I could kill someone?' I see anger join the fear in his eyes and I take a step back. Okay, he doesn't have a gun right now, but that doesn't mean he isn't dangerous.

I step back, then turn to the others. 'Don't you see? If Ben was there, and he's telling the truth, he must have seen who shot Alec. He should be able to tell us who it was, but he can't. I don't believe him.'

Emily lets out a disgusted noise, but I ignore her. She can think what she wants.

'How could it be him?' she asks. 'He's injured! He'd hardly have had time to shoot Alec, bash himself over the head to make it look genuine, then escape into the woods before Kai and I found Alec's body. We would have seen him.'

'He could have done it before going in there to shoot Alec, then run into the woods afterwards.' I'm not going to let her put me off. Ben isn't safe. We can't trust him.

'And where would he get a gun from?'

I think for a moment. 'I don't know where he got it from originally, but he could have stashed it in the woods earlier today. He's had plenty of opportunity. In fact, that's probably who Morna thought she saw out here earlier. Ben might have come over the fence, somewhere round the side of the reserve, hidden a shotgun somewhere he knew he could retrieve it later, then come and sat with us in the café as if nothing was different about today.' As I say it, I feel a shiver down the back of my spine.

Dan and Kai are both nodding, and I can see that they're both thinking about my explanation of today's events.

'I don't know how you can believe someone you know, one of your friends, is a killer,' Emily says, her voice heavy with emotion. She turns to Morna. 'You believe him, don't you? He can't have done it.'

Morna looks torn. 'I don't know what to believe, Emily. Of course I don't want to believe Ben killed Alec, but what's the alternative explanation? That there's a madman on the loose on the reserve, who shot Alec at random? That's even harder to believe.'

Emily's eyes narrow. 'It could have been someone else in this room.'

The silence that follows is almost painful.

'Ben's the one who came here injured, telling us a story about confronting Alec,' I point out, trying to keep the impatience from my voice.

'So? If he's telling the truth, any one of you could have shot Alec, then come back here to meet us and ask what was going on. If Ben could have got onto the reserve earlier today and stashed a gun, so could any of us.'

119

I want to point out she and I have been together all the time for the last two days, but I don't think it's the right moment. Morna looks at Emily, then back at the rest of us, and I can see the panic starting to form in her mind as her expression changes. I don't want to give the idea room in my mind, to be honest. If I start to think that any of us could be Alec's killer, that's going to cause the sort of fear I don't think I can cope with, so I shut down the thought straight away. It was Ben. I'm sure of it. It was Ben.

# Chapter 15

## Morna

'Right now, it doesn't matter who believes what. Let the police sort that out. We all need to stick together and get back to the visitor centre as quickly as possible. I'll lead the way, because I know the reserve better than anyone else,' Lauren is saying. She's standing in the middle of the hide, one hand on her hip, the other hand gesticulating firmly at the windows of the hide as if she were already directing us. Part of me can't help but admire the young woman for her confidence and assertiveness, but that's soon overtaken by that creeping dislike of the superior way she speaks to other people.

Kai and Dan are nodding, seemingly happy to agree with Lauren, but I can see dissent brewing in Emily's eyes. I feel the same – on this occasion, I don't think Lauren automatically knows best.

'What about the road?' I blurt out. 'From here, it's a shorter distance across country to get to the main road than it is to get back to the visitor centre. It's maybe only a couple of miles, as opposed to more than five in the other direction.'

Lauren gives me an incredulous look. 'What? Why would we go that way? It may be a shorter distance, but it's not exactly easy terrain to cross. First we'd have to find the low fences in the dark, because most of the reserve has a fence that's way too high for any of us to climb, to keep people off the railway line. It's only a small section that backs onto farmland that has a low fence. Once you're on the other side there's thick foliage and ditches to get through. Then what would we do when we got to the road? Walk all the way back to the car park so we can leave?' She rolls her eyes and turns away from me, and I feel my face heat up. How dare she? Rude and dismissive of anyone she disagrees with, Lauren instantly reminds me of my daughter.

'Don't speak to me like that,' I snap, and Lauren turns back to me with her eyebrows raised. She's not used to me fighting back. 'Ben might not be the one who killed Alec. We don't know for certain. So how do we know that there isn't someone out there, waiting for us? They'll be expecting us to go back to the visitor centre, and on the paths around here we'll be like sitting ducks, waiting to be picked off one by one.' I'm aware of the pitch of my voice rising, but now I've started speaking I can't keep my fear from showing itself. 'If we go towards the road we'll be under cover for a good proportion of the time, and then we can flag down a passing car and get help. We have no mobile reception out here, so we can't contact the police.' I point back towards the hide where Alec's body still lies. 'One of our friends is dead. Yes, perhaps

122

he wound us all up last week in the pub, but we all know he was talking crap and was harmless. He was a lonely bird geek, nothing more! Someone has brutally murdered him, and we don't know if they're coming for the rest of us next.' My voice breaks at the end of this sentence and I silently curse myself. How can I expect the others to take me seriously if I can't come across as calm and self-assured? My emotions have always got the better of me, my entire life, but I thought I'd learnt to keep them in check recently.

'Morna, why do you think someone else is out there? I know you don't want to believe Ben did it, but there's nothing to suggest the rest of us are in any danger,' Lauren says, her tone of voice soothing but still patronising in a way that makes my blood boil. If only Lauren knew, then maybe she'd have a bit of respect. Probably not, now I think about it. It would probably just make her opinion of me worse.

'We don't know it was Ben,' Emily snaps, glaring at her sister. Ben himself is leaning against the wall with his eyes closed again, and I don't know if he's listening or even awake. He might have passed out due to blood loss.

There's a heavy pause as the others avoid Emily's gaze. It's common knowledge that Ben and Emily are sweet on each other, so it's understandable that she doesn't want to believe it. She's made her point now, and I don't think she's going to convince anyone else. I don't even know what I believe, but I know I don't think I'll feel safe until I'm away from here, and my affection for Emily means I want to trust her judgement of him.

'Emily, I know it's a shock, but do we really have to keep having the same argument? Alec pissed us all off the other day, and we thought he was just exaggerating, but maybe he really did know something serious about Ben.'

Emily shakes her head. 'No. The person who killed Alec hurt Ben too. We need to get him to safety too, not just ourselves, and he's the one who's most in danger. If he remembers who he saw, they're going to want him dead too. You're all standing here slagging him off and figuring out how to help yourselves rather than how we can help him.'

She glares at each of us in turn. Dan nods his head slowly before speaking.

'Emily's right, we can't jump to conclusions. However, I also don't think we can go racing across a nature reserve at night, when we don't know what happened. It's better if we get away from here as quickly as possible and call the police, then they can figure out what happened. That's their job, not ours.'

Emily looks like she's going to respond, but then her shoulders sag and she folds her arms, turning away and looking out of the window of the hide. Dan looks back to Lauren with a nod, telling her to continue.

'Okay, so we'll head back towards the visitor centre. Once we're there, we can contact the emergency services, and those of you who want to go home can do so. There's no sense all of us waiting around here for the police.'

'Won't we need to give statements?' Kai asks, picking at the skin next to his thumbnail. It looks like a nervous habit, and I really want to step in and stop him before he draws blood.

Lauren shrugs. 'I don't have a clue. Probably, but I have all your phone numbers, I'm sure they can arrange that.

That doesn't matter right now, what matters is getting away from here.'

'I don't like just leaving Alec like that,' Emily says. She's turned around and rejoined the conversation, an anxious frown on her face. 'It doesn't seem right.'

'Well, if you want to volunteer to sit in the woods with only a dead body for company for the next three hours, be my guest,' Lauren snaps.

Tension crackles between the sisters, and again I want to step in, but I know any interference from me will just antagonise Lauren and make the situation worse. Thankfully, Dan has clearly had the same thought.

'Emily, again, you're right, but we don't really have any other option. We're all scared and confused, and there's no clear path that's the right thing to do.'

'Look, let's just get going,' Lauren says, her expression sullen. It seems she doesn't like Dan repeatedly agreeing with Emily, even if his diplomacy is helping to calm the situation.

Kai steps towards the door, but I hesitate. I know what I'm about to do is bound to cause another argument, but I refuse to back down on this one.

'No. I know you think you're right, and I'm not going to change your mind on that one, but I'm not going back to the visitor centre along exposed paths, when we don't know who might be out there waiting for us. I'm going across country to the road, and when I get there, I'll flag someone down who can help us.'

'For Christ's sake, Morna. That's a bloody stupid idea,' Lauren hisses. 'If you get lost out here, I'm the one who's going to be held responsible, so I'm making the decision about where we go.'

'Stop behaving as if you have some sort of authority over us,' I snap back. 'We are all adults here, and in this situation we're all capable of judging the right path for ourselves.'

'Are you suggesting we should split up?' Dan asks, looking between me and Lauren. 'Because that doesn't sound like a great idea to me. We're safer if we're all together.'

'Listen to Dan,' Lauren says to Morna, with a nod in his direction, that patronising note back in her voice. 'He knows what he's talking about. He's used to working in dangerous situations, so perhaps we should listen to him.'

'I'm not saying we should split up, I'm saying you need to think about listening to someone else's opinion first before assuming you're going to get the final say.'

Lauren mutters something under her breath then sighs deeply. 'I'm the one who knows this reserve better than any of you. I think that qualifies me to make an informed decision.'

I shake my head but don't say anything else, waiting to see if any of the others want to share an opinion.

'I think Morna's right,' Emily says, surprising me, and I feel a surge of affection for her. 'I know Ben didn't do this, and I think if there is someone still out there, they'll expect us to go back to the visitor centre. They might even be waiting there for us. Going across country will mean we can call for help sooner than if we went the other way.'

'Fine,' Lauren spits. 'You're right, I'm not actually responsible for you. Kai and Dan can back me up, that I told you this was the safest way to go but you refused. Do whatever the fuck you want, I can't stop you.'

I'm taken aback by the venom in Lauren's eyes and words as she glares between me and Emily, but I fight down my emotions and don't let it get to me. I won't be bullied into changing my mind.

Lauren is grabbing her bag, pulling an extra jumper out and layering up under her coat. 'I'd ask which way you two were thinking of going, but that's a fucking joke, because you'll get lost in about five minutes. You'll probably go round in circles for hours, and the police will have to come and rescue you as well as figure out what the hell happened to Alec.'

As she speaks, the pitch of her voice rises, and it suddenly dawns on me how scared Lauren is; all of this attitude is masking her fear, but how can I get through to her and make her see that we're all scared, and we all just want to get away from here? I step forward and put a hand on Lauren's arm, but she pulls away sharply as if she's been scalded. Not looking up, she continues putting items back into her bag and redressing herself in her layers.

She looks at the others. 'It's going to be pretty cold out there. We've wasted time arguing about this, it's completely dark now and the temperature will have dropped. If you've got other layers, you might want to think about putting them on, and snacks will come in handy too.'

Dan nods his agreement. 'I'm not clear what we've decided, though. Are we actually going to split up? Because that doesn't seem like a sensible course of action to me.' He looks between me and Lauren.

'I don't want us to split up,' I say quickly, hoping to get my point across before Lauren can interrupt me. 'I agree that we're safer together. But I'm not prepared to expose myself on this path. It runs around the edge of the marshes for at least a mile, and in that time we'll be easily visible, which isn't a risk I'm willing to take.'

'Well it looks like we're splitting up, then,' Lauren snaps, 'because I'm equally unwilling to strike out across country without any sort of navigation equipment or means of calling for help just because Morna's been watching too many shitty horror films.'

I can see how wide Kai's eyes are as he looks between the two of us, clearly not planning on picking a side. Dan is frowning, thinking, while Lauren finishes sorting out her bag and flings it onto her back with a violent movement that nearly makes her lose her balance.

'Lauren, can you see the road from here?' Emily suddenly asks, breaking the painful silence.

'No, you're facing completely the wrong way, which proves my point about how stupid it is to go away from the path,' Lauren replies, her mouth twisting into a sneer. I wonder if it's just her fear making her speak so harshly to her own sister, or if she's always like this in private. Surely Emily wouldn't have continued visiting if Lauren was such a bitch to her all the time, would she?

'The visitor centre, then? Or the car park?'

'No, we're miles away, and the woodland between here and there is too dense. Why?'

Emily points out of the window she's been standing next to while we've been arguing. 'Then what's that light, out in the woods?'

# Chapter 16

## Emily

As far as I'm concerned, the argument is pointless. I don't care what any of them think, I know Ben is innocent, but none of the others seem to agree with me. How can they have jumped to such a conclusion so quickly? The Ben I know could never hurt someone, let alone kill them in cold blood, and even though the others have known him longer than I have, I know it's not true. It can't be. So I stand and look out of the window while Morna and Lauren fight, trying to decide what I want to do, and formulating my own plan.

We missed the end of the Starling murmuration, as the birds all came in to roost, but perhaps the gunshot disturbed them all anyway. My eyes haven't been on the sky since it happened, all thoughts of nature pushed away by the primal instinct to survive. I think about going back to the hide where Alec's body is still lying and looking for signs that Ben was there. When he told me he had something to do, I did wonder if it had something to do with Alec's behaviour at the pub the other evening. Perhaps he wanted to confront him, either about what Alec said, or about his behaviour towards me, but to then shoot him? Hell no. What on earth could Alec know about someone that led them to such extremes? He was a harmless middle-aged geek, not some sort of gangster.

The first glimpse I get of the light is so brief, I think I must have imagined it. After all, we're in the middle of nowhere out here. It's another minute or so until I see it again. It's moving, with a sort of sweeping motion, as if someone's standing still and moving their torch, rather than walking in a straight line. I wait for the third time it appears before trying to attract anyone's attention, but by then there's a bitter argument raging between Lauren and Morna.

My sister's attitude has become awful on this trip, and I have no idea why. It's true that things were a bit awkward between us yesterday, and with hindsight maybe we weren't ready to spend Christmas Day together, but I also didn't expect Lauren to speak to me like that in front of other people. I'm taken aback, to the extent that I don't know what to say or how to react. For a moment I feel like I've been transported right back to our teenage years, to the few occasions on which Lauren would deign to speak to me, but I'd kind of assumed we'd moved past that by now. Has she been hiding her true feelings this whole time, or have fear and frustration turned her into a person she hasn't been for a long time? This isn't the time to try and find the answer, but once we're away from here and safe, and once I've helped clear Ben's name, I'm not going to let it drop. When we were younger, I never defended myself and just took everything Lauren threw at me, but I have certainly changed a lot in the last ten years, even if my sister hasn't.

'What are you talking about?' Lauren snaps, when I manage to interrupt the row and point out the lights. 'There shouldn't be any lights out there.'

Lauren comes to the window, subtly inserting herself into my personal space, forcing me to take a step back. Kai approaches from the other side.

'Where did you see it?' he asks.

'Out in the woods,' I reply, pointing in the direction I saw the brief flashes coming from.

'There's nothing there now,' Lauren replies, turning round with a shake of her head. 'You must have imagined it.'

I grit my teeth but don't rise to the bait. Now it's Dan's turn to approach, and he and Kai watch out of the window for a moment. Morna hangs back, leaning against a wall with her arms wrapped tightly around herself. I can tell that she's terrified, and I don't blame her. Something horrific happened this evening, and I'm worried that we haven't seen the end of it yet. My gaze falls on Ben, and he's so pale, I'm really worried about his injury. Could it be more serious than Dan thinks? We need to get him to a hospital as soon as possible.

I turn back to the window and see another burst of light that sweeps between the trees.

'There,' I say triumphantly. 'I knew I hadn't imagined it.'

Of course, Lauren isn't looking, so she turns to check with Dan, who nods. Thank God he saw it and they won't all insist I'm seeing things.

'There was something out there,' Dan says, looking at me. 'I can't tell how far away it was, though. It might be something beyond the woods. Perhaps someone working on the railway line.' He turns to Kai, who shrugs.

'I didn't see anything,' he says.

'Seriously?' I ask, cross that the two people who were looking in the right direction aren't backing me up on my concerns. 'You were looking right at it, Kai.'

He shrugs again. 'Maybe I blinked at the wrong time.'

Sighing with frustration, I step back from the window. 'Well Dan saw it. There's a light out there, somewhere over towards the woods. Something or someone who shouldn't be there. Do you still want to go that way?'

'Emily, stop being so melodramatic,' Lauren says with a withering look.

'What the hell? Someone from our group is dead, Lauren! Don't you understand that? He's been murdered, it's not like he had a heart attack or something! Someone killed him, and we don't know who, or where they are now. We don't know why they killed him, or whether they want to hurt any of the rest of us. Even if you think it's someone already in this hide, we have no proof, no evidence that we're safe. How the hell can you accuse me of being melodramatic, when you're behaving as if one of us has fallen over and sprained an ankle? This isn't some minor inconvenience, it's bloody serious.' I take a deep breath to try and calm my racing heart, glaring at each of the group in turn. How can they be arguing over this? The more time we waste hanging around here, the longer it will take for us to be able to contact the police and actually get some help.

Morna comes to stand beside me. 'I agree with Emily,' she says. 'We need to start taking this seriously and get out of here, get help. I know you don't agree with me about the best route to take, but right now I don't care. I'm leaving.'

Nodding, I turn to Morna. 'I'll come with you. I don't want to go out along that path either, especially since I saw that light.' I have a vision of someone waiting in the woods, shotgun at the ready, watching us approach along the path. It would be so easy to pick one of us off without the attacker ever being seen, and the thought of it makes me shudder. Remembering the blast we all heard earlier, then seeing Alec's feet sticking out of the door to the hide . . . I fight down a rising feeling of panic. If I don't think about it too much, I can focus on getting away from here and being safe. I'm grateful Kai stopped me from going into the hide and seeing Alec's body, because that's an image I definitely don't want in my mind right now.

Lauren is looking at both of us with one eyebrow raised. She seems to be thinking, then she throws her hands up in the air in a gesture of defeat.

'Fine, do what you want. I'll be sure to tell the police I tried to stop you, when they have to come out and rescue you, too.'

'You can't just accept that we think differently from you, can you?' I snap, finally having had enough of my sister's attitude. 'You have to keep pointing out that you think you know better, rubbing it in and gaslighting us as if we're not rational adults, perfectly capable of judging the situation and making our own decision. You don't know everything, Lauren.'

133

'And you're not cleverer than everyone else in the room just because you made money off some shitty little app,' Lauren barks back.

Dan and Kai are fiddling with their backpacks, but each of them freezes, and Morna gives a little gasp. Even Ben opens his eyes. I swallow, feeling my whole body begin to shake with a combination of anger and humiliation. After all this time trying to rebuild a relationship with my sister, the sister who always treated me appallingly when we were kids, I never expected such a vicious reaction from Lauren.

I turn to Morna. 'Let's go,' I say, keeping my voice low in order to stop the tremor in it becoming audible.

'Are you sure?' the older woman asks, her eyes searching my face. 'Do you have everything?'

'Yes.'

Morna nods. 'Come on.'

I know I would benefit from donning an extra layer before we leave the large hide, but I don't want to wait here any longer and potentially expose myself to more of Lauren's vitriol.

'Wait,' Lauren says, clearly struggling with what she's about to say. 'Look, I'm sorry, okay? This situation is very stressful, and I feel responsible for everyone because this is where I work. I don't want us to split up.'

Taking a deep breath, I look up at Lauren. 'Unless we can agree on what to do next, I don't think there's any other option.'

Lauren pauses, her jaw clenched tightly, then gives a sharp nod. 'Fine.'

She goes back over to Dan and Kai and lowers her voice so Morna and I can't hear them.

'Are we waiting? Are we all going towards the road now?' Morna asks.

I shrug, watching the other three as they talk. Whatever they're saying, they don't seem to agree, so I use the time to get another jumper out of my bag and shrug into it before replacing my coat, scarf and hat.

'We need to see if Ben has any more layers, too. It's going to be hard enough helping him without him getting hypothermia.'

Morna stares at me when I say this, and I realise she hasn't thought about Ben.

'I'm not leaving him here,' I tell her. 'I need to make sure he's safe.'

She doesn't say anything, so I start rooting through Ben's bag, finding a thicker pair of gloves and another jumper. I help him to pull them on, and I'm pleased how cooperative he is – I was worried he was only semi-conscious. By the time I've finished, the other three seem to have reached some sort of reluctant agreement.

'What's happening?' I ask, my arms folded. I know I look defensive, perhaps even confrontational, but one grudging apology from Lauren doesn't make up for all of the years of mistreatment. I tried to start with a blank slate when we reconnected, but Lauren's shitty attitude today has reversed all of that, and I find myself wondering why I wasted all my time coming up here, trying to build a relationship. At least I met Ben, I remind myself, but this is swiftly followed by a pang of fear about what the police might think. But Ben isn't stupid, and even if he wanted to hurt Alec, I don't think he would have done it with a large group of people around, making it so clear

135

that he's the prime suspect. Besides, where the hell would Ben have got a shotgun from? He hates hunting, and he certainly doesn't own any farmland.

Lauren, Dan and Kai are sorting out their backpacks and preparing to leave.

'Morna, Emily, if you're determined to go across country and try to reach the road, then I'll come with you. I still don't think we should split up, but if you're determined to go that way, I think I can be of use,' Dan says, and I find myself sagging slightly with relief. Dan is the biggest and toughest looking man in the group, and years of working offshore have given him the ability to keep a clear head in a dangerous situation. Knowing he'll be with us already makes me feel a bit safer. Between the four of us, hopefully we'll find a way to the road and get help as quickly as possible, and Dan can help us if Ben is struggling.

'We're still heading back to the visitor centre,' Lauren says, tilting her head towards Kai. 'I don't want us to split up either, but I also can't countenance leaving the paths. It's too dangerous.'

Of course, she has to have the last word. I don't care anymore, so I turn towards the door, not waiting for Morna and Dan to follow me. I go to help Ben up from the bench, but Kai puts out a hand to stop me.

'No, Ben comes with me and Lauren.'

From the look on my sister's face, I can see that they have planned this. She assumes she can get me to follow her by using Ben against me, and my blood boils with anger.

'Absolutely not. How do I know you're actually going to check he's okay?'

Lauren's jaw is clenched and I can see she's resisting

rolling her eyes at me. 'This one is non-negotiable. We've discussed it, and there's no way Kai and I are letting Ben out of our sight. Fine, we don't know what happened, but on the off chance that he killed Alec, we're going to take him with us to the visitor centre to wait for the police.'

'Emily,' Dan says, stepping forward and laying a hand on my arm. 'The route we're going to be taking is mostly cross-country, without paths, and there might well be fences we have to climb, difficult terrain to negotiate. Ben's in no fit state to do that.'

He's right, and after a moment, I nod. So do I go with Ben, and put up with Lauren's smugness that she was right all along, or do I carry on with Morna? I realise I can't help Ben right now, so I have to help myself.

'Fine. Ben goes with you, and I'm sticking with Morna and Dan. But if anything happens to him, I'll make sure you're held responsible.'

This time Lauren does roll her eyes, while turning her back on me, and I reach for the door. Before I open it, Dan tells me to wait, then he turns off the light inside the hide, plunging us all into pitch blackness that makes my breath catch in my throat.

I pull open the door and step outside, giving myself a moment to let my eyes adjust to the darkness. Something brushes against my face and I raise a hand quickly, then look up. It's snowing.

# Chapter 17

## Lauren

I stride along the path away from the hide without a backward glance, keeping my head down slightly, out of the wind that has sprung up in the last half hour, trusting Kai to hustle Ben out with us. This is a stupid plan, completely ridiculous. What the hell are they thinking?

Staying mad at the three who have set off towards the road helps to take my mind off my own fear. I'm trying to fully convince myself of what happened, that Ben killed Alec in order to hide some sordid secret, but there's something else nagging at the back of my mind. But surely, that idea doesn't make any sense. I should have known there was something not right about Ben, the way he kept hanging around me like a sick puppy, then suddenly switched his attention to Emily in the blink of an eye.

The snow is only very light, for now, and I hope we'll be back under cover before it gets any worse. Even under heavy snow I'm fairly confident I can keep us on the paths and away from the marshes, but it will be a hell of a lot harder. In snow, everything looks different, including the familiar landmarks I know so well around the reserve, and one wrong move could mean one of us falling into the marshes. They're not deep, so there isn't really a risk of drowning, but being soaked to the skin in these temperatures, when we're trying to move quickly and get help, could prove dangerous. There's the risk of hypothermia if one of us is stuck in wet clothes for too long, as well as the added difficulty in movement. No, I desperately don't want the snow to get any worse.

Behind me, I can hear the crunch of gravel as Kai does his best to keep Ben moving. I doubt we'll be able to keep up much of a pace, not with Ben having lost so much blood. He's probably already struggling. Well, tough; I'm not hanging around waiting for him, not now. Whatever I might have said to the others, I don't have any desire to be exposed on the paths either; I just know that the visitor centre is the closest safe place for us to be. Maybe I'll be proven wrong, but there is no way I'm trying to get out of the other end of the reserve. Even in my job there are only certain points off the paths that I'm familiar with, and they're areas of particular interest for conservation or development. I don't know the ground at all between the last point on the path and the boundary of the reserve, just that the fence next to the railway line stretches around most of it. Then, once you've found a fence you can actually get over, there's farmland to cross, which carries its own risks. No, I want to stick with what I know.

'Lauren, slow down a bit,' Kai calls. I ignore him at first, but then I become aware that the sound of him and Ben walking behind me has got quieter, so I stop and turn.

Kai is a few metres behind me, holding onto Ben's elbow. They're still walking but Ben is holding one side of his abdomen and breathing heavily.

'What's wrong?' I try not to snap at him, but fail. Staying still is threatening to put me into panic mode, which I can't afford.

'Stitch,' he pants, drawing level with me. 'I can't move this fast.'

'He's lost a lot of blood,' Kai points out. 'We need to be careful, take it slowly so he doesn't faint or anything.'

He's looking at me like I should know better, which only serves to make me angry. I take a deep breath and count to ten in my head. Or at least, I try. I only get to seven before impatience gets the better of me.

'Kai, we're trying to get to the visitor centre and call the police because one of our friends has been murdered,' I say quietly, doing my best to keep a calm tone. 'We have to move quickly whether you like it or not.'

'And you always say the rule is that the group moves at the pace of the slowest member,' he points out. His tone is light-hearted, but I know he's having a dig at me. 'Right now, Ben is going to struggle to keep this up for more than half a mile, and we have several miles to cover.'

'This is a slightly different situation,' I respond drily.

'Not really. In an emergency, it's even more vital that we stick together.'

There's a pause while I glare at him, then he sighs. 'Look, Lauren, I know we're not like bezzy mates or anything, but we need to cooperate now. We're doing this together whether you like it or not. Now get your head out of your arse and talk to me. What's the plan?'

Ben is looking between the two of us, taking deep breaths but wisely not getting involved. I feel my anger fizzing at the way Kai spoke to me, but then suddenly let out a laugh. He's right.

'Fine. The path goes back through the woods from here, for about two miles, maybe three,' I say, pointing ahead of us into the trees. 'Then we come to the dip in the ground that gives us a shortcut between the two paths. If we can get to the railway bridge, then we can stop and check for signal.'

'I thought there wasn't any signal in the reserve at all?' he asks, rubbing his hands together as he stands still for a moment and gets his breath back.

'Sometimes there's a patchy bit near the railway line, but it dips in and out,' Ben chips in. 'It's not strong enough for us to rely on.'

I glare at him, but he's right.

Kai stretches, then looks around. 'Doesn't the railway line run along the edge of the woods?' He points in that direction then sweeps his arm around to indicate the way the line travels. I nod. 'Then why don't we go straight to the line then follow its route through the reserve, checking for signal as we go? That way we'll still make progress in the direction of the visitor centre but there's a greater chance we'll pick up enough bars to call the police along the way.'

I stop and think about it for a moment, pulling up my mental map of the reserve. 'It's an idea, but I'm worried we'd get lost in the woods trying to find the railway line. It's not as simple as just walking in a straight line, not once you're off the path. You step to the side to go round a tree, and you've actually changed direction ever so

142

slightly. There's a big tangle of brambles you can't get past, so you turn back and take a different route, and once again you're off course. Before you know it, you've gone in a circle.' I shake my head. 'Plus, it'll be more difficult for Ben. Dan was right, it's going to be hard enough to get him anywhere sticking to the paths, which are easy to walk on. Going through the woods will be much more difficult. It's too risky. We might waste loads of time and not get any further.'

'Fine. Whatever,' Kai says, disgruntled because I've shot down his idea. I roll my eyes but don't apologise. It's not my responsibility to pander to the male ego.

'Ready to move again?' I ask him, and he nods. We both look at Ben, who winces when he moves his arm, but he nods too. Good, because I'm not standing here any longer if I don't need to. The three of us start moving again, and I'm surprised to feel an ache deep in my knee joints. It's the weather, must be. Standing still in cold, damp woodland isn't good for anyone.

We walk in silence, trudging along the path through the woods at a moderate speed. I keep checking over my shoulder to make sure Ben's keeping up, and to his credit he doesn't complain. Part of me starts to wonder why he's being so compliant, if he did kill Alec. Is it because he realises he can't escape, at least until we're near the car park? Or is it because he didn't actually do it? I stop this thought before it has a chance to develop any further, because the alternative is too frightening.

It's as we're passing through a particularly dense clump of sycamore that I think I see something. I stop, and Ben bumps into the back of me, clearly not expecting it.

'What is it?' he whispers. At least he has the sense to realise something might be wrong. Kai brings up the rear and I can see from his body language that he's tense, alert.

'Shit,' I mutter, as it comes again. There was a light in the woods after all. It's too late to apologise to Emily, not that I have ever felt inclined to say sorry to my sister, but it looks like she was right.

'Did you see that?' I whisper to Kai. His face looks blank, so I point in the direction it came from and wait. Sure enough, a few moments later, there's another light.

'What is it?' I say, more to myself than to Kai. I step forward, so I'm standing between two large trees next to the path. Listening intently, I strain for any sounds that might be carried towards us on the wind, but I think it's blowing in the wrong direction.

Behind me, Kai scuffs his toe on the path. 'Maybe it's nothing,' he says. I turn and peer at him in the dark; he looks scared.

'It's not nothing. There's someone out there.'

'Maybe it's not someone we want to go looking for,' Kai says darkly, and I hesitate. He's right. In my stress and anger at Emily and Morna I've almost forgotten that there's a murderer somewhere on the reserve tonight. Until now, I was convinced he was standing right next to me, but what if I'm wrong? What if . . .?

There's something about the light that I feel drawn to. Something tells me that if I find its source, perhaps some questions will be answered. Stepping a bit further into the trees, I pull my torch out of my bag. Up to now I haven't used it, my own knowledge of the reserve and what little moonlight there is being enough to guide me, but now I want the security of it.

Kai grabs my wrist. 'What the hell do you think you're doing?'

'If I shine my light back at them, maybe they'll come this way,' I say.

'Yeah, exactly. Why the hell would we want that to happen?'

'Look, if it was a stranger who killed Alec, why would they be hanging around in the woods waving a torch around?' I ask. 'Surely they'd be long gone by now. So it must be someone else. Maybe someone who can help us.'

'What if Alec wasn't their target?' Kai replies. 'What if they're going after the rest of us?'

'Don't be so ridiculous, why would anyone want to hurt us?'

'Because we walked through the woods waving a bloody great light at them instead of minding our own business and getting the hell out of here.' Even in the darkness I can see the anger and fear flashing in his eyes. 'Seriously, Lauren, you gave Morna and your sister a fucking lecture about not looking after their own safety, and now you want to wander off the path to follow some light?'

After a pause, I nod. 'You're right. I'm sorry. I just want to know who it is. It's part of my job to help keep the reserve secure. It might be poachers, and while there won't be any birds' eggs right now for them to steal, there's still plenty of deer.'

He pulls a face. 'I get that, but right now we need to keep ourselves safe. We have to take priority over the animals.' He speaks slowly, as if I'm stupid, but I know it's not worth arguing with him. I hold my hands up and step back onto the path, where Ben is leaning against a tree. The snow is starting to settle where the ground is exposed, which worries me. Kai gets hold of Ben's elbow and we set off again, but I keep my eye on where I saw the light so I can try and pinpoint its location.

'Do you think we might have been wrong?' Kai asks quietly, and I'm glad he can't see my face as I process his question. I know he's talking about Ben, and whether or not he killed Alec.

'I have no idea, Kai,' I whisper, though Ben can probably still hear me, stumbling along a little way behind us. 'I thought I knew Ben well enough to confidently say he couldn't have done this, but do we ever really know other people?' I know my answer sounds vague and a bit snobby, but what else can I say? 'I think he was really pissed off at Alec the other night, but that could be because he had his hands all over Emily.'

'Yeah, he's got a real thing for her, hasn't he?'

I nod. 'Yeah, I think so.'

We walk in silence for a moment, before Kai speaks again, still keeping his voice low.

'He was in the woods, you know. Around the time the Starlings started to take flight.'

'Who? Ben?' I slow my pace a little so Kai is now walking next to me.

'Yeah. I don't know what he was doing in there, but he looked pretty angry that I'd seen him.'

We both glance back. Ben is still keeping up with us, but really we should be making sure he's in sight at all times. I think about what Kai said. If someone in our

146

group shot Alec, they must have had the shotgun hidden somewhere nearby, somewhere they knew they could access it and creep up on Alec. But that suggests it was premeditated. I was thinking of it as a spontaneous act, but it can't have been. Something tells me it's not as simple as that, however, and I continue to think about Kai's words as we walk through the woods. Part of me would actually be relieved if it was Ben, and not someone else in the group. What I really want to know is what Alec knew about each of the others that made them all so edgy earlier today. If I find out the answers to that question, I'm sure I'll know the truth about his death.

# Chapter 18

## Dan

I stop and put out a hand, covering the beam of Emily's torch.

'You can't use that,' I tell her with a sharp shake of my head. 'It's not safe.'

She lets out a frustrated sound and turns it off. 'Well, you're going to have to gain some deaf awareness pretty damn quick, because now I'm really going to struggle to understand what either of you are saying.'

I can hear the fear in Emily's voice, something I'm used to picking up on in other people. However hard they try to hide it, their voices always betray them somehow. Whether it's by a change in pitch or volume, or the words they speak, I always know if someone is afraid as soon as they've spoken a few words to me. And she should be afraid. I made sure none of the others went into the hide and saw the state of Alec's body, but Kai had already given them a fairly graphic description by the time I got there. A shotgun isn't kind at close range.

'Morna, you know the reserve better than me,' I say, making sure I speak clearly to help Emily. 'Are you happy to take the lead? Then I'll bring up the rear and Emily can go in the middle.'

The two women look at me and nod their assent to the plan. I know they'll both feel safer if I'm at the back of the group, and this way I can keep an eye on both of them. Right now, I don't feel like I can trust anyone.

A snowflake lands on my cheek and I brush it off. We're going to be quite exposed here if it starts coming down heavily, so we'll have to be careful. There's also the matter of leaving footprints, but I don't want to worry about that right now. Suddenly, an image of my wife rises up in my mind, her beautiful smile stopping me in my tracks. I can picture her perfectly, rubbing the round swell of her belly and laughing at one of my ridiculous name suggestions. The memory almost has me on my knees, but I shake it off. She loved snow, that's what triggered it. She was like a child every time she saw even a small flurry, wanting to go outside and run around in it. I miss that lightness of her spirit more than anything.

I can't lose myself down that rabbit hole, not now. The three of us are about to walk past the hide where Alec's body is; I feel a strange urge to put my head round the door and check the man's still there, that I haven't imagined this whole nightmare scenario. I hold back, though, keeping my head down as I approach. Ahead of me, I notice Morna sneak a sideways glance at the hide, whereas Emily keeps her gaze averted and doesn't turn to look. Interesting reactions. After only a couple of sessions with this group I'm only just beginning to get to know them, so before today I wasn't sure how any of them would react in an emergency situation. Though the events so far this evening have taught me a lot.

Morna turns to look at me and Emily. 'We need to go off the path here,' she says, pointing a little further ahead, then off to the right-hand side. 'If we carry on along the path, we'll be moving further away from the road and end up looping back on ourselves. It's a circular path all around the main section of marshes, but there are also some marshes a bit further ahead, between the path and the road.'

'What happens if we walk into the marshes by mistake?' Emily asks.

'We get wet feet,' I reply, with a wry smile, but Morna clearly doesn't appreciate my joke.

'The marshes are not to be treated lightly,' she replies, drawing herself up a little. 'It could be very dangerous if we go too far in that direction. That's why we need to leave the path now and not risk it further along.'

Emily turns to look into the darkness of the woods to the side of us, and I can see the hesitation in her body. Is she already regretting agreeing to come this way? Does she want to be with Ben? Though after the way she and Lauren fought back there, I'm not surprised she doesn't want to be with her sister right now. There's plenty I know about those two and their history that Lauren has shared with me, and I wonder why either of them even attempted to repair their relationship. After tonight, perhaps it's lost forever.

I'm glad of the dark as we walk past the hide, because neither Morna nor Emily have a chance of seeing what I spotted when I came to look in here earlier: a small amount of blood around a metre away on the path. I assume it was from Ben's injury, but I also know that in any emergency situation you can't rely on assumptions. If it had been up to me, I would have gone out alone and found Ben while the rest of them waited in the hide; then perhaps I could have found a way to make him tell me what happened, find out what he saw. I'm pretty sure he must have stumbled straight into the woods after Alec was shot, from what he said. So it's unlikely he knows who he saw. Unless he wasn't actually stunned by the blow to his head. I didn't have him down as a particularly good actor, but then Alec muttered something to me about Ben and his extra-curricular activities once, which makes me think perhaps there's a lot more to Ben than any of the others realise. In which case, he could well have been keeping something from us when we were back in the hide. We should never have split up, I think, trying not to get angry at myself for letting this happen. I should have made sure we all stuck together, then I could keep my eye on all of them.

If Ben knows something, but kept it a secret, his motivation for doing that is important. Is his aim to get help, for the group and for himself, and not distract us with further accusations? Or is it simply to get away from the reserve as quickly as possible, to put as much distance between himself and Alec's lifeless body as he can? Will he talk to Lauren and Kai while they're walking, or will he stay quiet until he has a chance to speak to the police? I have no way of knowing what he did, what he knows, or what he's planning to do, and that makes me uneasy, even though he, Lauren and Kai are walking in a completely different direction from us.

'How well do you know Ben?' I ask Emily, increasing my pace briefly in order to draw alongside her.

She turns to me, a frown just visible on her face in the darkness. 'What did you say?'

I repeat my question, but she shakes her head. 'Come round to the other side. I can't hear clearly on this side, and I can't turn my head right round towards you while we're walking.'

Realising that she's referring to her hearing aid things, I move round to her other side and ask the question for a third time.

'I know him well enough to know he wouldn't hurt anyone,' she says firmly. 'There must be some other explanation.'

I think about this before replying. 'What other explanation would you suggest?'

'Maybe Ben saw who it was and he's too scared to say anything,' she replies. 'Maybe whoever killed Alec is another person in our group, and he doesn't want them to know he saw their face.'

'Okay,' I reply, thinking through what she said. 'If you think Ben saw the person who killed Alec, why do you think he'd keep it to himself? Wouldn't it be better to tell us what he saw, then we all know the truth? He didn't implicate anyone else, just said it wasn't him. At least not that I heard.' I wonder if he could have muttered something to Emily when she was sitting next to him, but I don't think she would have kept that to herself.

There's a pause as Emily thinks about my question. 'He

might have been too scared, or he might genuinely be confused as to what happened. He hit his head when he fell over.'

'Surely he still would have told us a bit more, suggested who it might be that he saw? Unless he's waiting for some reason?'

Emily gives a frustrated sigh. 'I don't know, Dan. Why are you pushing this?'

'I'm trying to figure out what alternatives there are to Ben having killed Alec,' I say softly. 'I want to know if you really think, deep down, that anything else could have happened.'

'I don't know,' she says, and this time her voice is much smaller, more like a frightened child than the confident woman I've seen earlier in the day. I can feel her confidence in her own theory slipping away as we speak.

Ahead of us, Morna is clearly listening in, but hasn't offered her own theory. Her pace has slowed slightly, so we're only just picking our way through the first layer of trees along the edge of the path. It seems she's not quite as confident in our route as she made out, which doesn't surprise me. As long as we cover a decent amount of ground and don't end up walking in circles, I'm sure we'll be fine.

'There's another question I've got, Emily, and you might not like it,' I continue, and I see Morna tense slightly as I speak. 'In your version of events, Ben isn't the one who shot Alec. If you don't think he did it, then who could it have been?'

'Poachers,' Morna butts in before Emily has a chance to speak, no hesitation before she speaks. 'Lauren keeps banging on about them, and they'll have guns. Alec surprised one of them, they shot him, knocked Ben out, and then ran before we had a chance to catch them.'

'Any poachers out on the reserve tonight will be after deer, and the deer don't tend to come out as far as the marshes,' Emily points out. Morna frowns, clearly taken aback that Emily has picked up on this piece of information.

'Well, they must have been down here for a reason,' she replies, stubbornly sticking to her theory.

'Even if a poacher found themselves in a bird hide with Alec, for some unknown reason, why would they shoot him?' I'm conscious that I'm starting to push a little too hard, and make a mental note to back off a bit. I don't want to wind Morna or Emily up to the extent that either of them become hysterical or cause any trouble.

'I don't know who it might have been,' Emily says, frustration heavy in her voice now. 'I don't know, okay? I don't want to think it was anyone in this group, but that's the most obvious explanation. I just don't believe Ben could hurt someone.'

There's a long pause as the three of us trudge onward. I don't speak, waiting for one of the two women to say something first.

'It could be someone else in the group, though, couldn't it?' Emily asks, her voice so soft I almost miss what she says.

'How could it have been?' Morna asks. 'Did you see anyone with a gun right after it happened? We were all there, Emily. Someone who had just killed a man wouldn't be hanging around and chatting calmly.' She shakes her head slowly. 'I'm sorry, if it wasn't poachers, you're going to have to accept it was Ben.'

There's a quiver in Emily's voice when she next speaks, as if she's close to tears. 'But why? How could he do something like that?'

'Maybe Alec wasn't exaggerating when he said he knew secrets about everyone,' Morna replies, a tremor in her own voice now that makes me think Alec knew something about her that she didn't want anyone revealing. 'Maybe whatever he knew about Ben was something he was desperate to keep quiet.'

I'm not prepared for Emily to stop dead in front of me, so I nearly trip over her. Grabbing a tree for support, I turn to see her crouching on the ground, her head in her hands. She looks up at Morna.

'Could I have been wrong about him?'

I reach over and squeeze her shoulder. 'Sometimes the people we think are completely harmless are the ones who end up ruining lives.'

Emily looks up at me sharply and when our eyes meet I wonder if she knows what I'm thinking, but then the moment passes. Morna puts her arms around Emily and encourages her to get up and keep going, and the three of us move on.

# Chapter 19

## Kai

The snow is falling more heavily now, though under the cover of the trees it's not having much of an impact yet. I know we'll soon be out of the woods, the path curving back to the edge of the marshes again. Ahead of us, I can see where the trees start to thin out, and the section of the path I can see is already white over.

'Are you going to be able to keep us on the path if it's covered in snow?' I ask Lauren, trying to keep my voice light and casual. Any suggestion of criticism and I know she'll jump down my throat. She never would have been my first choice of companion today, emergency situation or not, but there's no way I would have let her go back this way on her own. When we were discussing it, the two of us and Dan, I insisted on accompanying her. From the look on her face, she assumed I was trying to be chivalrous, and suggesting that she needed protecting, and I'm happy to let her think that even if it does bring out her attitude.

She snorts in response to my question. 'It runs along the edge of the marshes in a straight line from here, then it's pretty obvious where it cuts through the trees again. Even someone who didn't know the reserve well should be able to do it.'

'Okay, I was just asking,' I say. Part of me wants to hurry her up so I don't have to hang around with her any longer than necessary, but Ben can't move quickly. He's already flagging, so I'm worried we might have to stop to let him rest soon. It suits me, though, because I don't want to get back to the visitor centre too soon.

I pull out my phone and check it again, holding it at various angles in the hope of connecting to a weak signal. For the first time, a bar flashes up, and I have to stop myself letting out a noise of triumph. Quickly opening up the text app, I type out a message and press send, but by the time I've done that the signal has disappeared again, and a little red cross appears next to the message.

'Shit,' I mutter to myself. Lauren turns to look at me, frowning at the phone in my hand. 'I thought I had a signal,' I explain.

'I've told you, it drops in and out all along here, but it's never strong enough to allow you to make a phone call.'

'You should be able to text the police, or something,' I grumble. 'What if you can't call?'

'There's an emergency text service for deaf people,' Lauren says, turning back and continuing to walk. 'Emily told me about it a few months ago.'

'We should have asked her to send a text, then, before we split up,' I say. 'Then if her phone finds any signal along the way it should send any messages that are queued.'

158

Lauren grunts and I have to resist sticking two fingers up behind her back.

'You're welcome to turn around and go and find her,' she says, not looking around to see my reaction to her words. 'I'm quite happy to do this on my own.'

'And what would happen to you if I left you alone with Ben, and he started feeling better?' I ask. 'Wouldn't you rather have a bit of back-up?'

Lauren stops dead and I nearly walk into the back of her, Ben still stumbling along beside us. She gives me a searching look for a moment, before glancing over at Ben, who has shown no reaction to what I've said.

'You think I need protecting from him?'

I shrug. 'Two against one, it's got to be better odds than if you were on your own.'

'Maybe,' she replies enigmatically. I suddenly have a vision of her with a shotgun slung over her shoulder, striding confidently through the woods, and I pause. As Lauren continues ahead, Ben trudging behind her, I find myself starting to wonder if everything is as it seems. I let a little distance grow between us before I start walking again, and in a moment I find myself leaving the cover of the trees.

To the left, the woods continue, lining the path as it stretches away ahead of me, now a white ribbon as the snow continues to fall. To the right, I know a wide space is beginning to open up, but even with the light reflecting off the snow I can't see much. The marshes scare me a little in the dark, though I'd never admit it. I know the water isn't particularly deep at any point, but I don't want to end up blundering in there and getting tangled in the reeds. Focusing on Lauren, I follow her footprints in the snow as I make my way along the path.

A few metres away, on the edge of the marshes, is another hide. None of us went in there this evening, but Lauren stops by the door anyway. I'm glad of this – any opportunity to stall her is welcome, but right now I'm most worried about Ben. He looks like he's ready to drop, and what if he ends up being unable to walk? We can't exactly leave him here – if he killed Alec, it's our responsibility to get him to the police, and if he didn't then we need to look after him. I'm happy to let her think I'm only concerned about Ben, though. I know I can't let Lauren get back to the visitor centre before I've had a chance to send my message, but if I can't get any signal then I'll just have to hold her back as much as I can. She'll be pissed off at me, but I might not notice the difference from the usual Lauren.

'What's up?' I ask. She's standing by the hide, one hand on the door, and Ben has leant against the wall.

'I was trying to work out what must have happened to Alec,' she replies, then looks at Ben. 'Were you inside the hide with him?'

Ben shakes his head. 'No,' he says slowly. 'I was outside. I didn't make it to the door.'

'If it wasn't Ben, why would someone else have been in the hide with Alec?'

I shrug. 'They might not have been in there with him. Maybe someone stood in the doorway and shot him. I don't know.' I finish up with another shrug.

'I want to check something, too.'

'What?'

She hesitates before replying. 'This hide is identical to the one Alec was in. There are a few the same, dotted around the reserve. They were built at the same time, to the same blueprint.'

I nod. I knew this already, having had a few confusing moments on previous visits to the reserve when I'd forgotten which hide I'd been in then lost my bearings once I'd stepped out onto the path again.

'So?'

Lauren cocks her head on one side. 'I just want to check something out.'

Without another word, she opens the door to the hide and disappears inside. Ben follows her in, muttering something about being able to sit down. I hesitate for a moment; this is a good opportunity to stall Lauren, by keeping her here at the hide for a while, but I have no idea what she's doing. After seeing Alec's body I have no interest in going inside another hide for a long time, but standing outside alone is already giving me the creeps. I shiver as a fat snowflake lands on my neck and slides down inside my scarf. That makes up my mind, and I push open the door to follow Lauren and Ben into the hide.

At first, I can't see them, so I have to step inside and allow my eyes to adjust to the gloom. Ben is slumped on one of the benches, wedged into a corner. When I still haven't spotted Lauren I feel a surge of panic, until I realise she's lying flat on the floor in front of the benches.

'What the hell are you doing down there?' I ask, but she doesn't reply. Shuffling along on her stomach, she's tapping different sections of floor. A moment later, she pulls out her torch and shines it up underneath the ledge that sits under the window hatches. I wait, knowing that if I let her take her time in here, there's less chance of us getting back to the visitor centre earlier than we had originally planned.

I just know what my cousin will say when he sees that shiny new Tesla sitting in the car park. Looking at it earlier, I'd seen an answer to all my problems, all those debts that keep on growing, no matter how much I pay off. Boosting cars isn't my thing, but I knew telling Ant there's a Tesla in the car park while its owner is off walking in the woods a couple of miles away gave him an opportunity too good for him to pass up.

'I'm looking for hiding spaces,' Lauren eventually says, getting up off the floor and startling me out of my thoughts.

'No way could a person hide in one of these,' I say. 'It's way too small.'

'I didn't mean for a person,' she replies with a withering look. 'You could definitely hide a shotgun in there, tucked away between the benches. Unless someone was looking for it, I doubt they'd notice it.'

I try to follow her train of thought. 'You think someone hid a shotgun in the hide, then came back for it and used it to kill Alec?'

She shrugs. 'It's a possibility. I mean, Ben didn't have it on him when he arrived today, did he? Or anyone else,' she adds, when Ben frowns at her. 'One of us would have noticed a shotgun poking out of someone's rucksack.'

I shake my head. I'm happy for Lauren to keep thinking that Ben killed Alec, so I don't say anything that might contradict her, even though I'm worried there's another explanation.

'So he hid it in there earlier?'

Lauren nods. 'Or even yesterday, or the day before. Nobody would have been in there for a couple of days, or if they did, it would have just been a passing check by a warden. I did it myself the day before Christmas Eve, and I know I only stuck my head in there to check nobody was hanging around, and maybe pick up any lost property. I didn't search every corner.'

I think about it for a moment. 'But how could he have been sure that Alec would go in that hide, and that he'd be alone? One of us could have easily gone with him.'

'After his outburst the other night? You felt the atmosphere earlier. There was no way any of us wanted to be stuck in a hide with him.' She folds her arms, as if adding some final punctuation to her sentence.

'That doesn't answer my first question, though. Alec could have picked a spot outside, or one of the other hides. There was no guarantee he'd be in that particular hide, meaning it was a risky place to hide the weapon.'

'Are either of you going to bother asking me about any of this?' Ben asks, his voice angrier than I'm expecting. 'You're just talking about me as if I'm not here. I keep telling you, I didn't kill Alec.'

Lauren turns away from both of us, and I feel her anger as she speaks. 'Look, Ben, we have no idea what to think. Right now, we just want to get to a safe place, then we can figure out who did what. As for you, Kai, I don't know what the hell goes through the mind of someone planning a murder, do I? I just thought it was something worth considering, something we can tell the police when we finally get in touch with them.'

I hold my hands up in apology, but she's already on her way back out of the hide. Ben groans and gets up, stumbling slightly as he sets off again, and I can see from the way he's moving that his muscles are getting stiff. I follow them both, and Ben and I watch as Lauren builds up speed until she's striding up the snow-covered path, her footprints blurring as she slides slightly with each step.

'Come on, mate, we need to keep up,' I tell Ben, who grimaces but increases his pace.

Catching up to her, I put a hand on Lauren's shoulder, then step back when I see how her eyes blaze.

'What?'

'Sorry,' I say automatically. 'It wasn't a bad idea.'

She lets out a quick huff.

'I know it's scary, and you're worried about your sister,' I continue, but then stop when Lauren lets out a bark of laughter.

'You don't know anything. Come on, we need to get a move on.' With that she turns away from me again and resumes her high-speed walk, leaving me almost jogging to keep up. I've got my hand on Ben's arm, trying to guide him along the snowy path, half supporting him as he struggles. As I focus my energy on following her and keeping us both upright, I wonder what the hell I said to make her so angry.

# Chapter 20

## Emily

The snow's getting heavier, and I keep having to wipe flakes from my face. The ones that melt on contact with my skin leave trails of water that run down towards my neckline, invading my clothes and making me feel miserable. I want to stop and put on another layer of clothing, maybe look for some shelter from the weather, but I know Morna won't countenance anything that might slow us down.

Morna and Dan are walking ahead of me, having given up their attempts to include me in their conversation. I understand that it's difficult, and it's more important that we get to a place of safety, but I hate being put in this position. Occasional snatches of conversation drift back to me, and at one point I get the impression from their body language that they're disagreeing about something, but I have no idea what they're saying. At one point I stride ahead and try to insert myself between them, Dan taking the hint for a few hundred yards, but he eventually draws level with me again and asks Morna a question, pulling himself back in front of me.

I'm suddenly reminded of a school trip, when I was about thirteen. I always struggled to make friends, but the teenage years were already proving to be a nightmare. Growing up deaf meant I sometimes missed social cues, or parts of conversation that then became talking points for every group of kids. Nobody was close enough to me to fill me in on what I missed, and as hormones started to do their worst on me and the kids around me, I found myself becoming more isolated. On this trip I'd been left without anyone to sit next to on the bus, so our ageing geography teacher had occupied the aisle seat next to me. I spent an hour looking out of the window, trying to avoid the awkward stilted conversation Miss Higgins tried to instigate. When we arrived, I hoped it would be different: the class were put into groups of four, and I felt I'd always got on well with the two girls and the boy I was placed with.

We arrived in Hornsea, prepped for a day of looking at coastal erosion and bombarding locals and tourists with questions about their visit that day. It started when we were handing out the questionnaires, and one of the girls in my group only brought back three clipboards, claiming she thought I wouldn't want one as I couldn't hear people's answers. Lacking the confidence to speak up for myself, I shrank into my hoodie and said nothing. I trailed round after the other three for the rest of the morning, but it got worse when it came to lunchtime.

'Give us a fiver and we'll get your chips for you,' the lad and one of the girls said to me and the other girl. It was well known that the two of them fancied each other, so I assumed they wanted some time together. I handed over the money, wondering just how long it would be until I got my lunch. Within a couple of minutes of those two leaving, another group from our class wandered past, and the other girl from my group joined them, leaving me sitting on a bench on the sea front.

I stayed there for about forty-five minutes, watching people walk past, families with young children or people walking their dogs. The tide was in, and the waves were crashing up against the sea wall. It was pretty impressive, and I wanted to go up the promenade and have a closer look, but I was worried the other members of my group wouldn't find me. Of course, they'd only find me if they were looking for me. I was naive to think they even cared.

If it had ended there, if I'd found my group by myself without any outside interference, I could have coped with the abandonment and the hunger (because of course, the young couple had snuck off and never returned with any food for me). But that wasn't to be. By the time I realised I would have to try and get the group back together myself, Miss Higgins had spotted me and made a beeline for me. When she realised I was on my own, she marched along the sea front until she found the scattered members of my group, and berated them for leaving me on my own. The worst part was that Miss Higgins loudly counselled the other three that they should be more sensitive to their classmates with special needs. I could have run away at that point, and from then on my school experience made me wish I had. Now, pushed to the back behind Morna and Dan, scared and confused, I feel much the same as I did when I was thirteen.

It's completely dark now, and in such an isolated spot, with only one working cochlear implant processor, I start to feel my anxiety increase. Being deprived of hearing on one side is bad enough, but now I can barely see more than a couple of metres in front of me.

Taking a deep breath, I stop. The snow continues to swirl around me and I shiver, but I can't seem to find the energy to get my legs moving again. It's like my brain is unwilling to send the signal. Dan glances over his shoulder and notices I'm not keeping up.

'Everything okay?' he calls. The snow produces a strange acoustic effect, meaning I can hear him quite clearly now he's facing me. This helps me to relax a little, but I stay where I am.

'Yeah, just catching my breath,' I say. It's too difficult to put my true feelings into words: I feel completely out of my depth, stunned by Alec's death then thrown into this situation with two people I barely know and whose deaf awareness is woefully lacking. Then there's my confusion and guilt about Ben – I don't believe he did it, I don't. Whatever they say, I won't believe it. I never should have let Lauren and Kai take him the other way, or I should have swallowed my pride and gone with them.

Dan walks back a little, towards me.

'Sorry, we shouldn't be pushing on ahead. I said I'd stay at the back, but I get ahead of myself sometimes.'

I nod, grateful that he's at least recognised part of the problem. 'I don't know where the hell we are, or if we're getting any closer to the road. I hope you or Morna have a better sense of direction than me.' I give him a wry

168

smile, hoping it will raise my own spirits and take some of the terror out of my words.

Dan doesn't answer straight away, and I catch my breath as another wave of fear washes over me. He's not sure; I can tell he's not sure, and he's possibly regretting following Morna in the first place.

'We've come in more or less a straight line,' he says, looking up at the sky for a moment, then looking down as a large snowflake lands in his eye. As he rubs it away, I see a flash of anger cross his face, but it's gone an instant later. Is it the weather that's got him so worked up, or something else?

'At some point we'll come to the boundary of the nature reserve, even if we've gone off track slightly,' he continues. 'It should be marked, then we'll know we're not far from the road. Once we're out of the woods, it's open country between us and the road, so hopefully we'll be able to see it soon.'

I look around me at the trees, their bare branches doing little to keep us sheltered from the snow, now it's falling thick and fast. Ahead of us, Morna is standing with her arms wrapped closely around herself, watching us. She hasn't made any move to come and speak to us, or to find out what's wrong. I find myself wondering if Morna's still confident in the path she's chosen. Whatever happens now, we have to keep going, because we certainly can't go back into the reserve. Between the snow and a murderer, I feel a sudden panic that I've been wasting time.

'Come on,' I say, shrugging my rucksack into a more comfortable position on my back then striding past Dan. 'We'd better get moving again.'

'Emily,' Dan begins, and I turn to look at him. He shakes his head. 'Nothing. You're right.'

'What were you going to say?'

'It doesn't matter.'

We look at each other for a moment, before Dan looks away. I decide it's not worth the argument, so I turn away again and catch up with Morna before Dan has a chance to overtake me again.

'Which way?' I ask. Ahead of us, the trees are thinning out, but that means the path is less obvious, particularly with the layer of snow that's now building up.

Morna looks at me for a moment, then shakes her head. 'I don't know.' She speaks so softly that her words are almost lost to the air, despite me standing so close to her.

Swallowing my own fear, I give Morna a sharp look. 'What do you mean, you don't know?'

'I think it's this way,' she says, indicating a space between the trees that will mean we veer slightly to the left. 'Yes, yes it must be.'

Without another glance at me or Dan, Morna starts walking in the direction she indicated. She still has her arms wrapped round herself, but when she stumbles she drops them so they hang by her sides, her hands balled into fists. For a moment, I'm struck by the familiarity of the posture, but the thought is pushed out of my head as Morna stops again. She looks to her left, then her right, then does a full turn, stopping when she's looking ahead again.

'Morna?' Dan calls from behind me. 'Is everything okay?'

I marvel at how calm his voice is. In his position, I'd be running forward and shaking Morna, which is exactly what I'm tempted to do right now.

170

'Yes. It's fine. Of course it's fine. We must be nearly there. It can't be far now.' Morna barks out these sentences, then sets off again without making eye contact with either me or Dan. With a feeling of foreboding in the pit of my stomach, I continue to follow, scanning as I go for any signs that we might be near to the boundary of the nature reserve. Even if we don't come out of the woods at the point we intended, presumably we can just follow the boundary for a while, if that's what we need to do.

Just then, I hear a strange noise, a sort of ragged rasping, and I glance around to try and locate the source of the sound. A moment later, I realise it's coming from Morna, who's scrabbling at the scarf around her own neck, gasping for breath. I rush forward to support her as she sinks to the ground.

'She's having a panic attack,' I tell Dan as he grabs Morna's arm. 'Morna, look at me,' I say, gently taking hold of her chin and turning her face so she makes eye contact with me. 'Listen to me, and do exactly what I say. Breathe in through your nose, and out through your mouth. Slowly. With me. In through your nose,' I repeat slowly, leaving a pause so Morna can slow her breathing, 'then out through your mouth.'

I stay by Morna's side, talking her through the steps to bring her breathing back to normal, then put my arms around her as she cries.

'I'm sorry, I feel so stupid,' she says, burying her face in my shoulder.

'It's okay. You're stressed and scared.'

'I've let you down. I'm so sorry.'

I make soothing noises until I feel her start to relax

171

slightly. Throughout Morna's panic attack, Dan has stood at the side watching us, then once he realises Morna is okay he walks away. When he comes back a moment later, his face is grave.

'There's a problem.'

Morna nods, and I wonder what they've both seen that I haven't. My gaze follows the direction of Dan's pointing finger through the trees to our right, and I see what made Morna panic. We've found the boundary of the reserve, but it's marked by a four-metre-high fence. There's no way out.

# Chapter 21

## Lauren

'Oh, shit!'

I turn at the sound of slithering and snapping branches, which come from behind me. I've just descended into a hollow in the trees that provides a shortcut between two of the paths, and I was careful to pick my way slowly down the slope. There are rough steps cut into the bank, but they're covered with snow now and it's difficult to tell exactly where each step ends. Kai insisted he would be able to help Ben down, but it seems he underestimated the difficulty of it.

The two of them are lying in a heap at the bottom of the slope, but Ben soon picks himself up and dusts the snow off his legs. Kai's moving and the swearing has died down quickly, so he must be okay. Not for the first time, I consider leaving the two of them behind and carrying on across the clearing, but I know we have to stick together.

'You okay?' I ask, approaching Kai. I keep my voice low to try and avoid it carrying too far. If there is someone else on the reserve, someone we don't want following us, it won't do to advertise our location by making too much noise.

Kai grimaces. He's sitting up, and I can see where he's fallen from the path he's made in the snow, along with a few broken branches.

'I don't know. My ankle bloody hurts.'

I bend down, but he's wearing thick socks and walking boots, so there's no way I can take a look at his ankle. I have basic first aid training for my job, but I don't really know what I'm looking for.

'Can you stand?' I hold out a hand to help him up, which he takes, leaning on a tree stump next to him for support.

'Agh, no,' he cries out, putting weight on his left foot. 'Shit, that hurts.' He sits down again with a thump.

Frustration rises up in me and I take a deep breath, trying to quell my anger. 'Come on, let's try again. You didn't even get upright. Put your weight on your other foot, and get upright.'

Kai doesn't look convinced, but I brace myself to take more of his weight as he tries again. Once he's on his feet, after a few more pained noises, he nods at me.

'Okay, I'm standing. What now?'

'Just take a minute to get your balance, then gently try putting more weight on your left foot.'

I'm holding onto his shoulders, doing my best to be reassuring, when really I want to shout at him to get over it and keep moving. Ben's no use; he's sunk down onto a fallen tree and his head is drooping. There's no way I can rely on him to help support Kai when he can barely stand up by himself. If it comes to it, I have no qualms about leaving the pair of them here while I go on alone, but I know if anything happens to either of them there'll be a lot of questions, both from my friends and colleagues.

Kai's looking down at the ground and I wonder what he's thinking. Is he as scared as I am? I don't want to admit to my fear and give it any opportunity to mess with my head, but I can't deny it's there.

Leaning on me, Kai starts to put more weight on the ankle he's injured, but after a few seconds he winces and shifts back.

'I can't. I think I've broken it.'

I feel a fleeting moment of panic.

'Come on, try again,' I say, hoping my voice sounds encouraging rather than authoritarian. 'I'm sure it won't be broken, you didn't fall that hard.'

Looking unsure, he tries again, but shakes his head a moment later.

'It's no good.' He looks around the clearing, then at Ben, who still hasn't moved. 'What the hell do we do now?'

I take a deep breath. 'I know it hurts, Kai, but this isn't an everyday situation. We need to move. We can't stay here. You're just going to have to suck it up and push through the pain.'

'What, "man up" you mean?' he spits. Glowering at me, he sits down again in the snow with a thump, then winces again. 'Just give me a few minutes, okay? I can't go anywhere right now.'

Backing off, I move away to give him some space, and to take some for myself. Kai is six foot and broad shouldered, so there's no way I can carry him. If Ben wasn't injured, we'd probably be able to lift Kai between us, but I can't rely on him to help me now. Kai could lean on me for support, but getting up the opposite bank like that will be a nightmare if he's not willing to at least give it a try. Why has he given up so easily? I want to go back there and shake him, tell him he's being ridiculous, that it's only a twisted ankle and he'll just have to get over it. Instead, I look around to see if there's anything practical I can do.

The opposite bank has slightly clearer steps cut into it, so it might be easier to get up, as long as Kai can put some weight on his bad ankle for long enough to get up each one. So I have to find a way to convince him he can do it.

'Let me have a look at your ankle,' I say, striding back over to where he's sitting. He gingerly removes his boot then his sock, shivering as the cold air hits his skin.

I bend down and have a look at it. I can see a bit of swelling, but not too much, which is reassuring. I straighten up and pull my rucksack off my back, then dig through it until I find a spare pair of socks. I then fill one sock with snow and hand it to Kai.

'Use this as an ice pack. It'll help the swelling and hopefully numb the pain a little.'

He looks dubious, but presses the sock to his ankle anyway. The snow inside it is already starting to melt, leaving little wet trails down his foot, but it's the best we can do in our current environment. I'm quite pleased with myself for thinking of it, and Kai's lack of enthusiasm annoys me.

'Ice it for a few minutes,' I tell him. 'Then we'll see if

we can strap it up. I've got a small first aid kit with a couple of bandages in, so I can use those to brace it. Then hopefully you can put enough weight on it to get you up the other side.'

Kai eyes the route out of the hollow with a concerned expression, but then nods.

'You're right, we need to get moving. Sorry I snapped at you.'

I shrug. 'You're in pain.'

'I know, but you're only trying to help me. Thank you.'

I smile then, glad that he's coming round. More flies with honey than vinegar, I tell myself. It's something I was never very good at when I was younger, opting for shouting at people when they didn't do what I wanted rather than trying to talk them round. Who knew that being stuck in a crisis situation would lead to this personal growth? I smile at the irony of it, then go back over to the steps on the other side.

To my surprise, I find Ben joining me. He comes to stand next to me, but I take a step away from him. I still don't trust him, even though he's injured.

'Can I help? Sorry, I just felt really dizzy after we fell.'

With a jolt I remember that Ben fell just as far as Kai, yet I didn't check him for further injuries. Until we know for certain what happened, I need to treat him a bit better, I think. If it turns out that he didn't kill Alec, I don't want to be the one who let him get sick, or worse, because I wasn't willing to help him.

'Are you okay now?'

He nods. 'Just needed a minute. I'm okay.'

While Kai keeps the snowy sock pressed against his

ankle, Ben and I do our best to sweep some of the snow clear of the steps. It's still coming down, but not too heavily at this point, and these steps are more sheltered than the ones Kai fell down. After a few minutes, we've cleared enough so the edge of each step is easy to see.

'How are you doing?' I ask Kai, and he nods.

'Yeah, I reckon that's helped.'

'Good.' I pull a small microfibre towel out of my bag and hand it to him. 'Dry off before I bandage you up. We don't want it turning to ice in your boot and giving you frostbite.'

'Not ideal,' he agrees, towelling off his foot and ankle. My spare sock that started off holding snow is now just a soggy mess, so I wring it out and shove it into a side pocket of my bag. As I do, my fingers brush against my knife, and the feel of it gives me courage.

'Right, can you put your foot up on my knee?'

Kai manoeuvres himself into position without complaint, despite the pained look on his face. I pull off my gloves and get one of the bandages out of my kit, trying to remember the best way to do this. I've done it once, on one of my colleagues as part of my training assessment, but that was a couple of years ago now. Should I start with the foot, or further up his leg? I seem to remember it's the foot, so I start to wrap the bandage, gently pulling it tight as I go. Ben stands to the side, watching carefully, but not offering any help. The bandage isn't a particularly long one, but I manage to get it wrapped around Kai's foot and ankle a few times before I reach the end of it. The pin is the trickiest part, because my hands are so cold, and I stab Kai in the leg a couple of times before I manage to get it through the bandage and clipped together again. I make a note to replace it in my kit with an adhesive bandage.

'There,' I say, sitting back. It's not the neatest job, and he might have some trouble getting his boot on again, but it's done.

'Thanks,' he replies, grabbing his sock and slipping it over his foot. 'At least it'll keep me a bit warmer,' he jokes as he loosens his laces in order to widen the boot and get his foot back in. Ben comes over to help him, bracing himself against the tree stump.

Once Kai has his boot on and laced up, we repeat our earlier attempt to get him upright. This time, Ben helps too, so Kai manages to put a lot more weight on his left foot, though he still needs to lean on one of us. Half shuffling and half hopping, the three of us make our way across the clearing to the steps in the opposite bank.

'I don't know if I can do this,' Kai says, and I can see the apprehension on his face as he looks at the slope.

'Don't think about the whole thing,' I say. 'Just think about the first step. Once we've done that one, we can think about the second one, but right now there's only one step we need to get up.'

'Okay,' he replies. 'Okay, I can do that.'

I'm surprised by Kai's reaction to pain. I was sure he was the sort of bloke to tough it out, to pretend he was completely fine even if one of his limbs was hanging off. But there's something very vulnerable about him now, which I have mixed feelings about. On the one hand, I'm glad he feels safe enough with me to show that side of himself, but on the other I can't shake my frustration at the inconvenience of it. I'd hoped to be at the visitor centre by now, and now I'm faced with trying to get two injured men there. To top it all, Kai's slowing us down even further with his fear.

'I'm going to get on the first step, then you can use me to lean on as you step up. Ben can come up behind us, and help if you need it, too,' I tell them, grateful that the steps are wide enough for both me and Kai to stand together comfortably. Ben nods his agreement, though I'm not sure what use he'll be.

I do as I said, and Kai reaches up to grip my shoulder as he lifts his right foot off the ground. Crying out in pain, he slumps back again.

'I can't do it.'

'You can. Try the other foot. If you put your bad foot on the step, you can push off with your good foot, then use me to lean on until you're up onto the step.'

This time he manages it, panting slightly with the pain and effort. He looks up, and I can tell he's counting the rest of the steps.

'Don't do that. We only need to worry about the next step, okay?'

We continue like this for what feels like hours, me slightly ahead to help him up, Ben behind to support him when he needs it, but it's really only about ten minutes, until we're nearly at the top of the bank and back onto the path. I look at the top step and realise it's a narrow one, and we might not fit both of us on it.

'Do you think you can do the last one by yourself?' I ask, but the way Kai's eyes widen tells me that plan won't work. I climb up to the path and lean forward, hoping I

180

can help him up that way, but as soon as he tries to use me for support, I feel myself being pulled forward.

'No, that won't work.' I look down at Kai, swaying slightly two steps down from the path, then at Ben.

'Can you help him up, give him a boost?'

Ben looks pale, but I see him angling his body towards Kai so he can help to support him without them both tumbling back down to the bottom.

'Sure. I'll try,' he says, and I feel a wave of relief that I'm not on my own with Kai, even if Ben might be a murderer.

'I'll manage,' Kai says, a look of determination suddenly fixing itself on his face. 'I got this far, I can do the last bit.'

He flings himself forward slightly, obviously hoping to jump up the step, and lands on the top step with his face on the path. Ben scrabbles up behind him, putting himself directly behind Kai in case he slips backwards again, stopping him from tumbling back down into the clearing. Between Kai crawling, Ben pushing from behind and me pulling him, we get Kai onto the path, where he rolls over onto his back and looks up at the canopy of trees above him.

He laughs. 'Right, just another couple of miles back to the visitor centre.'

Ben and I laugh too; what else can we do?

'Come on, let's get you up,' I say, crouching down to help him, Ben on the other side of Kai. With a few more winces and muffled cries of pain, Kai's back on his feet, and the three of us set off slowly along the path, Kai leaning on me.

At least if anyone is following us, they don't want to kill us, I tell myself. Sitting in that clearing was the perfect opportunity, anyone with a shotgun could have picked us off like rabbits. But the other alternative is that the murderer has been with us all along, and that's not a thought I want to entertain right now.

# Chapter 22

## Morna

It's okay, we'll just walk along the boundary fence until we come to a gap. That's what Dan said, and that's what I keep repeating in my head as we continue. I'm still at the front, in some sort of pretence that I know where we're going, with Emily behind me and Dan at the back. The panic attack scared me nearly as much as the situation we currently find ourselves in, and it's all I can do to keep my breathing regular.

Why did I insist on coming this way? At least if we'd all stuck together then we'd have some safety in numbers. As it is, I feel isolated and vulnerable. We're easy targets here, having a fence on one side and the woods on the other.

I'm sure it can't be far until we get to the low fence. I came out to the edges of the reserve with one of the wardens last summer, and the huge fence hadn't run this far then. How far does it go? Lauren said we might run into it, but I ignored her, because I thought we'd be well

183

beyond this section by now. I put my hand out to touch the fence, but then stop. What's that noise?

'Are you okay?' Emily asks me. The girl's closer behind me than I realised and I jump.

'I thought I heard something,' I say, looking past Emily to where Dan has stopped behind us.

'We need to keep moving,' Dan says.

'I heard something,' I repeat. I move away from the fence and back towards the trees. Is there someone there? Stopping, I hold my breath, but that makes my blood pound so loudly in my ears that there's no chance of me hearing anything.

There it is again. A cracking noise, like someone stepping on a fallen branch.

'There's someone following us,' I say, my voice coming out as a cracked whisper.

Dan frowns. 'That was just the snow sliding off a branch,' he says, his matter-of-fact tone doing nothing to reassure me. I know he's getting fed up with me, I can read it in his body language, but I'm not going to back down.

'No, I'm sure it wasn't. There's someone moving out there, and they're following us.' I can't keep the panic from my voice.

'Maybe it was a deer,' Emily suggests. 'They're all over the reserve, aren't they? It's probably just an animal.'

I know Emily means well, but this refusal to believe me just makes me angry.

'For God's sake, why are you two behaving as if there's nothing wrong? Someone we know just killed a man, and now he might be after us, too! How do we know he hasn't got away from the others and turned round, followed us through the woods?' This idea hasn't even occurred to me until now, but once the idea is planted in my mind it immediately begins to take root. 'Emily, of all people you should be most scared about Ben following us!'

'Why me?' she asks, confusion on her face.

'Because he's obsessed with you!' I don't mean to shout, and clap my hand over my mouth when I realise just how loud my words are.

Emily has gone pale, and she and Dan glance at each other.

'Look, Morna, we know Ben's got a thing for Emily, but surely that means he'd want her safe, doesn't it? If he's out there in the woods, he won't want to hurt her, or us because we're with her. Anyway, if he has any sense he'll still be with Lauren and Kai. We have no reason to believe he's not.'

I take a moment to absorb Dan's words, but I'm not convinced. I know Dan would have preferred it if we'd all stuck together so he could keep an eye on Ben – he'd said so himself – so maybe he'll be pleased if Ben catches up with us, then the two of them can have it out. This might all be an act to throw me off, make me think I'm imagining things when all the time Ben's following us, shotgun loaded, just waiting for his opportunity.

'No, I don't believe that,' I say, making sure I keep my voice quiet this time. 'Ben's in love with Emily, that's obvious, but what makes you assume he wants to keep her safe? Love can turn to violence faster than you might realise.' I fold my arms, as much to stop myself from shaking as to make my point.

'Hang on, will you stop talking about this as if I'm not here?' Emily says. 'Ben might like me, but not enough for it to be relevant.'

I exchange a glance with Dan; I'm not sure if Emily's in denial or if she genuinely doesn't know what Ben's like. But then I've seen it before, when he was besotted with Lauren before Emily came along. At one point I was worried where his obsession would lead, but then he backed off and turned his attention to the younger sister. It all seems to be happening again, though, and I wonder if that was what Alec had been talking about in the pub the other night. He tried to talk to me about Ben the week before, when I was here volunteering and he'd been out birdwatching. When Alec was on his way out, he asked me some pointed questions about Ben and his interest in both Emily and Lauren, which I brushed off at the time. But maybe Alec noticed something none of the rest of us did. After all, whatever else I could say about him, he was certainly observant. Just bad luck for him that he seems to have taken that as a way to manipulate us and try to get one over on us, rather than sitting down and talking to us about his concerns. So just what did he know about Ben, and how did it connect to Lauren and Emily? And was it really worth killing over?

I shiver at the thought, aware that Dan and Emily are both watching me.

'There's nobody there, Morna,' Emily says softly, stepping forward and putting her hand gently on my arm. Looking her in the eyes, I'm suddenly reminded so clearly of my daughter, so much so that it takes my breath away. I have to stop myself from throwing my arms around her, reminding myself that the young woman standing in front of me isn't Sarah.

With a shrug, I turn away from the other two and start walking, following the fence once again. If they don't believe me, there isn't much I can do. I'm stuck in the position of wanting to be proved right, but also wanting to be wrong. If Ben really is following us, I know we have no way of defending ourselves. Maybe Alec found something out about Ben, about the depth of his obsession with Emily, and perhaps Ben killed him for it. So now he could be coming for Emily, wanting to declare his love. Or does he mean her harm? The more I think about it, the more convinced I am that Ben won't want to leave without her, meaning that my job, and Dan's, should be to protect her.

There's another crack from behind us, and I turn. Emily and Dan are following me, though they're now walking next to each other rather than in single file. Have they been talking about me? I turn to look further behind and see movement.

I suck in my breath. 'He's there!' I hiss.

Rather than turn round to look behind them, Dan and Emily just look at each other, which makes me see red.

'Why the hell won't you two believe me? I saw someone!'

Another movement; is it just a shadow on the snow, or is it someone coming towards us? Ben will have a shotgun with him; if he's given Kai and Lauren the slip, he will have looped back round to wherever he dumped the gun, so he didn't leave any evidence behind. And if he's coming for Emily the quickest way to get her would be to pick off me and Dan. Without us here, Emily will be alone and Ben can take her wherever he wants.

As soon as this thought rises in my mind, I'm convinced that's Ben's plan, and if anyone could read my thoughts I'm sure they'd be convinced too. There's another movement in my peripheral vision, and I whip round, half expecting to see Ben emerge from the undergrowth. He doesn't, but the constant stress has triggered my fight-or-flight mode. I run.

The ground's slippery and uneven underfoot, so I slide and stumble as I go, but I don't care. I have to move, to get away from there as fast as I can. Vaguely aware of someone calling my name, I pick up speed to put more distance between myself and the person I'm convinced is following us.

A line of trees looms ahead of me and I dart off to the side in order to follow them, turning further into the woods as I go. I no longer care about following the fence, in fact actively want to get away from it. If I'm deep in the woods, I'll be harder to find. The snow hasn't penetrated much in the densest areas of trees, so it will be more difficult to track me.

All of these thoughts flow through my mind as I run, but they're eventually overtaken by the panic, so before long I have no conscious purpose in my mind other than running. My breathing is becoming laboured, unused as I am to this level of physical exertion, and I slow down a little in order to catch my breath. As I do, I hear the clear sound of running feet behind me, tipping me over the edge into full-blown panic.

No, not again! I fight to catch my breath, wheezing as each lungful seems to do nothing for me, snatching at the next breath until I'm dizzy and fall to my knees. The edges of my vision go fuzzy as the panic attack threatens to overwhelm me. What was it Emily told me to do? I can't remember. There's someone next to me. Is it Ben? Is he going to kill me?

'Morna. Morna, it's me, Dan. Remember what Emily told you? Breathe in through your nose and out through your mouth.'

Dan, not Ben. Not Ben. I'm safe. He's right, that's what Emily said, and it worked last time. I focus on my breathing and manage to get it under control, but the adrenaline is still coursing through my body and I realise I'm shaking.

'We're going to die,' I murmur. 'It's all ruined. I just wanted to tell them.'

'Morna? It's okay, you're not going to die. It's a panic attack, and it feels scary, but you're going to be fine.'

Dan's voice is deep and calm, and it helps. As my breathing returns to normal, I sit up and look at him, aware that there are tears streaming down my face.

'I'm so scared,' I say, my voice barely audible.

Dan nods. 'I know. I understand. But if we let the fear take over, we won't be able to get away from here. Do you think you can stand up?'

I take a slow breath, then nod. Dan holds out a hand to help me up, which I take gratefully. Once we're both on our feet again, he reaches out and squeezes my shoulders.

'I need you to keep it together, okay?'

I nod, sniffing and trying to stop myself from trembling.

'What did you mean, when you said it was all ruined?'

I look up at him, and see sincere concern in his eyes. 'Have you ever made such a huge mistake, it took you so long to figure out how to fix it, that by then it was too late?'

189

A shadow crosses his face, a look that makes his features change completely, but then it is gone.

'I don't know. But perhaps, I know what you mean.'

'I just wanted to try and make it right,' I say, looking down at my feet again, then taking a deep breath to try and hold back the sob that's threatening to burst out of me. I take my bag off my back and rummage through it, looking for something to wipe my face, but I can't find a towel and have to settle for a spare T-shirt. As I straighten up, I glance around. Dan is standing next to me, watching me carefully as if I were a rare bird he might frighten away at any minute.

'Dan?' I say, unable to keep the fear from my voice now. 'Where's Emily?'

# Chapter 23

## Ben

The pain has faded to a dull throb by now, probably because it's so bloody cold. With my good arm, I'm helping to support Kai as he limps along, but we're making such slow progress even I'm starting to get frustrated. His ankle hadn't looked that bad to me, and a couple of times I'm sure he's put weight on it without a problem. I think he even limped on the wrong foot at one point. But if he's making it out to be worse than it is, I honestly can't think why. If any of us wanted to cause a distraction it would be me.

I don't think it's quite sunk in that Alec's dead, let alone that the others think I killed him. Apart from Emily. God, I wish I'd stood up for myself and gone with her, but I wasn't with it at all. I just remember feeling dizzy and sick, everyone arguing around me until I couldn't make out what any of them were saying. Of course, half the time they were talking about me, but I found I didn't care what they were saying.

As we've been walking, I've been racking my brains trying to remember what happened, but now I'm worried that I've pushed it too far and I'm creating memories where there weren't any to begin with. I know I left Emily behind, bastard that I am, and went to talk to Alec. At the time, it seemed like the best plan, because I couldn't make a move on Emily without being sure of how much Alec knew. If I hadn't bothered, none of this would have happened. Well, Alec still might be dead, but nobody would suspect me and we'd probably all be together still.

I remember the shotgun blast; I didn't know that's what it was at the time, but from what I've found out since it seems pretty obvious. I remember the pain exploding in my head as I hit the ground. That's when it becomes blurry, and I'm not sure what I really remember, and what my wishful thinking has conjured up since. Did I see someone standing just outside the hide, shotgun in hand? Did I see them run away, knocking me over as they made a bid for freedom? Maybe. Or maybe I didn't. One thing is certain, and that's the unshakeable fact that I didn't kill Alec. I was going to talk to him, that's all. Even if I'd wanted to intimidate Alec, physical threats wouldn't have done any good. I would have played him at his own game, found one of his own secrets to hold against him. So that means it must have been one of the others in this group. But who?

I don't think it can have been Morna. Not that I believe she's incapable of murder – on the contrary, I think she definitely has it in her, but she would never shoot someone. She'd poison them, slowly. I think back to the row of sauces she lined up in the café this morning, just for seven of us, and I realise that would be perfect. Find out which sauce a person likes best, slip something in there, and any strange taste would be disguised by the strength of the flavour of whichever condiment they'd picked. Yes, I could definitely see Morna killing someone. Just not like this.

I skip over Emily. She wouldn't have done this, and I don't think she could have physically got back to the hide, either. I know I was lost in the woods for a bit, but that still didn't give her much time. So, Lauren. I chew this over for a moment. Definitely a possibility. Alec could well have known something about her, and I think she's determined enough to stop at nothing to keep him quiet. So I keep her in mind as a possibility.

Dan, also a strong possibility, but the whole scenario seems too clumsy for someone who's as cool-headed as he is. I could see him creeping up behind someone and slitting their throat silently, without leaving a trace. Okay, maybe that's a bit dramatic, but Alec's death seems too chaotic for someone like him. Besides, we barely know Dan. Alec would have had to work pretty damn hard to find out any secrets just from meeting him on a couple of occasions. I barely know anything about him, and what I do know is more from Lauren prompting him than from Dan himself.

So, that leaves Kai. For me, Kai is the most obvious suspect. He's been behaving weirdly all day. I saw him arrive, out of the window down the corridor by the loos, and he didn't come inside for ages. He was talking to someone on the phone, and whatever the conversation was, he clearly wasn't happy about it. Then he dashed back inside just after we left, claiming he'd left his phone, even though I saw it sticking out of his pocket. And, of course, he was wandering around in the woods when we were all getting ready to watch the murmuration. Okay, so was I, but I had a good reason. And now here we are, trying to get back to the visitor centre, and Kai is the one slowing us down. Now that I'm starting to feel a bit better, I want to push the pace on, but his laboured limping is holding us back.

'Come on Kai,' Lauren says, as if she's read my mind. 'You can move a bit faster now. Try to get a rhythm while you're moving.'

'I'm doing my best,' he grumbles, but she's right. Rather than trying to walk a bit more normally, Kai is taking two steps then stopping each time. We're only just in sight of the railway bridge, and it's taken us forever to get this far.

'She's right,' I chip in. 'You keep stopping, when you could put your other foot down and keep going. It's not as bad as you're making out.'

I shouldn't have goaded him. He has his arm round my back for support, but now he shifts his weight so he's leaning more on me, and reaches his hand across my back, knocking me on the side of the head as he does so. I cry out and jump away from him, pulling away so he falls to the ground.

'Shit. What the fuck did you do that for?' he snaps at me.

'Me? You know full well you just smacked me right on my fucking head injury.'

Kai and I glare at each other, and I'm glad I've got the advantage of standing while he struggles to get up. Eventually, he's on his feet again, and he's taller than me so I take a step back. Lauren sighs and folds her arms.

'You two need to stop pissing around. Can we carry on now?'

Kai shoves me, hard, and I stumble backwards but stay on my feet. 'No,' he says. 'I don't think we can.'

'What's the problem?' I ask, trying to keep my voice level, while at the same time clenching my jaw.

'My problem is you dropping me on the ground, you wanker. What the hell are you trying to do?'

'Prove that you can walk without help,' I snap. 'You're not limping like you've hurt yourself, you're limping like a bad actor.'

Kai lunges for me then, and a moment later I'm on the ground, pain radiating out from the wound in my shoulder. I swear at him again, and he kicks me.

'Kai, what the fuck?' Lauren shouts. 'We need to get out of here, we don't have time for the two of you to start fighting like little boys.'

I see Kai round on her, but I pull myself up off the floor and smack him across the side of the head. I've misjudged the punch, so it ends up as more of a slap, but it still knocks him off balance and leaves him reeling.

'We're trying to help you, for fuck's sake!' Spit flies out of Kai's mouth as he yells at me. 'We could have left you out there for the police to find, or just made you fend for yourself, but we brought you with us so we can get you to a hospital. Whatever you've done, we thought you deserved that. Looks like we were wrong.'

'Whatever I've done? You can't get it through your thick skull, can you? I. Didn't. Kill. Alec.' I emphasise each word with a prod in his chest, and now we're nose to nose, snarling at each other like feral dogs. 'I should be the one worrying about the rest of you. All I know is that I didn't kill him, so one of you must have done it, and from where I'm standing, you look like the most promising candidate.'

Kai's eyes narrow and his lip curls. 'Yeah nice try, take the focus off yourself by blaming someone else. I saw the way you looked at Alec the other night in the pub when he said those things. Maybe looks can't kill, but the shotgun certainly did the trick. Well, what you don't know is that Alec told me a couple of things when I dragged him outside and put him in a taxi. He started muttering all sorts of dirty little secrets.' He gives me a nasty grin, and I launch myself at him.

'Stop it, right now!' Lauren is trying to get herself in between us, but we're both a lot bigger than her, so she's fighting a losing battle. One of Kai's punches lands on my ear, and I manage to get him in the gut, before Lauren cries out and I realise Kai has caught her by mistake. We back off from each other, Kai with his hands in the air.

'Shit. Lauren. I'm sorry.' He steps forward to try and placate her, but she shoots him such a dirty look he's stopped in his tracks. Wiping a hand across her mouth, I can see her lip is bleeding.

'The pair of you are pathetic,' she spits. 'I find it hard to believe either of you would have the balls to murder Alec,' she continues, and I see Kai bristle, but he doesn't say a word. Lauren gets a bottle of water out of her bag, takes a swig, swills her mouth out, then spits. A patch of snow darkens, the gloom making the red look black, but the bleeding seems to be stopping already, thankfully. I feel deeply ashamed of myself; not for fighting with Kai,

196

but for not backing off when Lauren got involved. She's hurt now because of me, because of us, and we have to shoulder the responsibility for that.

'For the record, right now I don't give a shit which of you killed Alec. If it was one of you, you'd better not fucking try to go for me, or I will make sure there is hell to pay.' The bravado in her words doesn't hide the tremor in her voice. 'Right now, I just want to get out of here, so if you've finished, I'm leaving. Hell, stay here and keep kicking the shit out of each other if you like, but I'm not getting involved again.'

With that, she shoulders her rucksack again and marches off into the darkness. Kai and I don't look at each other. We've both dropped our bags, so we scramble to pick them up again and follow her. There's a bit of a stand-off when neither of us wants to go first and have the other walking behind us, so we settle for walking side by side, leaving a couple of arms' lengths between us. Kai is still limping, but I notice that it's less pronounced than it was before, when Lauren and I were helping him. I want to point this out, have the last word, but right now I know the safest thing is to keep my mouth shut.

A little way up the path, Lauren has stopped to wait for us. She says nothing as we approach, just nods, turns around and sets off again; Kai and I follow behind like chastised dogs.

# Chapter 24

## Emily

Morna runs off before Dan or I realise what's happening. We both stay exactly where we are for a moment, thinking she'll stop or turn around after a moment, but she doesn't. As she disappears into the trees, Dan swears quietly under his breath and takes off after her. He calls something back to me over his shoulder, but I have no idea what he said. It might have been 'Stay there,' or it might have been 'Keep up.' Either way, I find myself frozen by indecision. Should I follow them? Dan should be able to catch up with Morna without too much difficulty, as long as he can keep her in sight. So will they want to come back to this spot by the fence, or continue on from where they are?

I shiver as I realise just how alone I am. I have no idea where this fence will lead if I continue to follow it, and for all I know I could just be skirting the boundary of the reserve if I carry on walking. But staying where I am doesn't feel like a sensible option – after all, whoever killed Alec is still out there somewhere.

I remain unconvinced that Ben is the murderer. I know all the evidence points towards him, but it feels too convenient. Of course, it's possible that an outsider came onto the reserve and hurt Alec, but somehow that doesn't feel at all plausible to me either. After all, who else knew we were here? If there are poachers on the land, they would have no cause to go near the bird hides. No, I'm convinced that one of our group killed Alec, and I don't think it was Ben. So the question remains – who was it? I know who I suspect.

Making a decision, I start to follow the tracks Dan and Morna have made in the snow. I saw the general direction they went in, so it hopefully won't be too long until I catch up with them. A little way ahead, they moved away from the fence and back into the woods, which was when they disappeared from my sight, so I head that way.

There are a few sounds around me as I move, but I can't identify them. It's hard not to start getting scared of every single sound, but I'm aware it might be my own passage through the trees that is making them. A cochlear implant doesn't replicate sound exactly – I don't have any frame of reference, having no memorable experience of full hearing, but I know I don't hear the same way that hearing people do. If I'd spent some time in the woods with someone familiar to the area, I could have asked them what different sounds were, but I don't have the luxury of time right now. I'll just have to trust in my instinct that right now I have to keep moving.

For a few minutes I follow the tracks without a problem, as the clouds part and the snow around me reflects the moonlight that filters between the trees. Morna's boots have left scuff marks rather than footprints, but Dan's strides were more controlled, meaning his tracks are a bit clearer. I feel a small sense of pride in myself for being able to follow them this way, without panicking, and I relax a little as I continue to walk. They were both running, but I know it's more sensible for me to walk in order to catch up with them. Once Dan has caught up to Morna I'm fairly sure they'll stop, giving me a chance to find them.

A gust of wind blows up, scattering a few twigs and blowing the snow into my face. I stop for a moment to wipe the flakes from my eyelashes, then realise that the snow underfoot is becoming sparser as the trees around me crowd together. Despite the lack of leaves on their branches, the density of the tree cover is preventing the snow from falling to the ground. The trail I'm following is starting to fade.

Okay, don't panic. Dan and Morna can't have got very far. Morna is fit from walking around the reserve, but she's not a runner, and the after-effects of her earlier panic attack will prevent her from being able to run too far, I'm sure. So hopefully, if I keep moving in the same direction, the two of them will be visible again very soon.

I keep checking the ground as I walk, looking for any signs of their footprints, but there's nothing. There are still quite a few patches of snow, but none of them bear any marks made by Morna or Dan. Does that mean I've made a wrong turn, and they didn't come this way? Wanting to be certain, I retrace my steps until I come to the last footprint I saw. The angle of Dan's foot suggests he veered off to the left a little, so I change my direction slightly and continue again, praising myself for keeping a cool head as I go.

A moment later, I think I hear voices. I stop, listening carefully. Speech sounds are always difficult ones at a distance – I can't be certain it was someone speaking, it could have just been the wind. I set off again, glancing around to make sure I'm checking everywhere for any signs of Dan or Morna, but I don't see any more footprints or any indication they went this way between the trees.

I feel my heart rate increase and there's a shakiness to my gait as I walk, so I stop and take a drink of water, determined not to let myself panic. Either I've gone the wrong way, or I just haven't gone far enough yet. Both Dan and Morna are wearing dark jackets and trousers, and there's very little light filtering through the trees, so I won't see them until I'm reasonably close. Staying here isn't an option, because there's no way they'll find me if they come looking for me, so that leaves two choices: keep going this way, or retrace my steps for a second time. If I retrace my steps, there's no guarantee I'll find the right direction next time, so that makes up my mind for me. I'm going to continue the way I'm going, whether or not that leads me to Morna and Dan. Eventually I'll find a path, or the fence, then I can find a way out of the reserve by myself.

The thought of being alone on an isolated nature reserve in the middle of the night is one I push away quickly. I live in London and will sometimes walk alone after dark, though not often, and I've learnt some techniques for coping with my fear. The terrain here is completely different, but the sense of threat is the same, so I look around to try and find something to focus on. Unfortunately, the landscape all looks the same to me at this moment in time, and turning around does little other than confuse me. Which direction was I walking in to begin with? There are no clear footprints that I can see, and all of the trees look the same. I can't see the fence, or anywhere the trees thin out that might lead back to a path, so I have no way of knowing if I've turned a full 360 degrees or have altered my heading slightly.

'Shit,' I mutter under my breath, hoping speaking it aloud will give me some confidence, but my own voice sounds so alien to me in this environment it actually makes me shrink a little with fear.

'Come on.' I take a deep breath and walk forward. As I've already decided that staying still will do me no good, I have to keep moving. It's time to admit I'm lost; there's no sign of Dan or Morna, or anything that looks familiar, so I'll just have to walk until I find something or someone, and hope that anyone I come across doesn't mean me harm.

This thought brings Ben into my mind again, and I find myself going over everything that happened earlier today, before the Starling murmuration. Ben had seemed a little distracted, but I assumed that had been to do with me. I actually laugh at my own ego now, but I'd had high hopes for today, where Ben was concerned. When we were in the pub just before Christmas, I was convinced he was about to ask me out, until Alec ruined the whole evening, so I'd thought it was only natural that he'd try again at the next opportunity. But maybe that was all in my head, and there had been something else preying on his mind today. Something to do with what Alec had said in the pub . . .

Ben certainly had the opportunity, as nobody saw him during the murmuration after he left me in the end hide on my own. I can't really judge whether or not he had motive without talking to him or Alec, and that's not going to be possible. But did any of the others have the same opportunity?

I think back to where everyone was when Alec was killed. Morna and Dan were in the same hide, so it can't have been either of them. That's one of the reasons I felt safest going in a group with them. That left Lauren and Kai. Could one of them have killed Alec? I struggle with my relationship with my sister, and if I'm honest I'm learning that I don't actually like Lauren, but that doesn't mean she's a murderer. We're two people with very different personalities, who had a shared experience growing up that pushed us apart rather than drawing us together. It isn't unusual, and I'll be the first one to admit Lauren has tried to push aside her old dislike of me. That has nothing to do with Alec, and I can't imagine why Lauren would have any problem with him, other than him being slightly annoying. Lauren's issues come from people she sees as a threat to her position, like Morna, or people she can't forgive for some perceived slight. I'm well aware that I fit into the latter category, but by now Lauren should have got over her belief that I got all the attention because I'm deaf, and that I'm the reason we never lasted with a foster family. The adults in that situation were the problem, not me.

So that leaves Kai. I don't know him very well, but he's always seemed nice. Perhaps he was a little on edge earlier today, but am I just thinking that with the benefit of hindsight? Of course, he was the one to escort Alec out of the pub after his outburst, so there's no way of knowing what went on between the two of them when they were outside. Did Alec know something about Kai, something that Kai would do anything to prevent people knowing? I don't know, and that's the worst of it. There's no way I want to think that any of these people could be guilty of murder. In fact, I'd rather believe it of Lauren than any of the others, which says a lot about our relationship and how much work we still need to do. Not that I feel inclined to do that work now, not after today.

Taking another opportunity to glance around, I feel another jolt of fear shoot through me. My shoulders are so tense I can feel a pain stretching right across my back and up my neck, so I stop for a moment and try to stretch it out. Moving my head from side to side, I try to get rid of some of the ache in my neck by loosening the muscles, and as I do I find myself looking through the trees. I realise that there are fewer of them in one direction, so I change heading slightly to see why they're thinning out. A moment later, I find myself stepping forward into water, then jump back quickly to avoid it seeping into my boots. The woods come right up to the edge of the marshes.

I think back to the map of the reserve, but can't for the life of me figure out where I've ended up. The path skirts the main scrapes, but I know there are other, smaller, marshes dotted around the edges of the reserve. I assumed that when I found my way out of the trees there would be a path I could follow, but now I'm trapped between the woods, where I have no sense of direction, and marshes, which I can't cross safely.

Fighting the rising feeling that my heart is trying to block my throat, and the tears of fear that prick my eyes, I take a few deep breaths. I'm well and truly lost.

# Chapter 25

## Lauren

Kai grimaces and rubs his ankle as I pause for a rest. He's definitely been taking more of his own weight on it since we started walking again, and I wonder if there's something in what Ben said. Still, it's taken the three of us nearly fifteen minutes to get along the path that winds under the railway bridge and past the canal. We've just crossed over the canal again, following a brief argument about which is the best route to take from here: one leads to the visitor centre but takes a circuitous route, whereas the other is a long straight path coming out near the overflow car park and the side gate, about two hundred metres from the main entrance. To both of our surprise, Kai managed to convince me that the latter is the better path to take, because we'll have a better view of anyone ahead of or behind us, and it's slightly shorter in distance.

'Why don't we stop at the education block?' he suggests now, and I think he's probably longing for somewhere to sit down that isn't a rock or a tree stump.

My attempts at strapping up his ankle were pretty successful, but I suppose he still needs to take the weight off it for a few minutes. I'm not happy about it, though, and neither is Ben.

He stops in the middle of gingerly touching his head wound and looks at Kai. 'The education block?'

'Yeah,' Kai replies, nodding at the stretch of trees next to us, knowing the building is concealed behind them a little way ahead.

Suddenly, a thought strikes me and I smack myself on the head. 'Why the hell didn't I think of that? There's a phone in there!'

'Great, you can try the phone while I sit down,' he replies, turning in the direction of the building, obviously prepared to hobble for another few minutes if there's a chair at the end of it.

'We can't stop for long,' I caution. 'Just until I can get through to the police. Then we still need to make it back to the main entrance, so I can direct them to the hide once they arrive.' There's a triumphant glow on my face, and I'll admit I'm pleased that we're going to be the ones to raise the alarm. One thing I love is being proved right, and I don't care how that makes me sound.

Ben follows us without a comment, but I can tell there's something on his mind. Maybe he doesn't think we should be stopping here, but after the stress these two have put me through, I think I've earned the right to make the decisions. Besides, there's a phone here. That's all we need right now.

I move over to help Kai and we walk the distance to the education block in silence. It's a bit awkward, him relying on me physically, but I'm at least convinced it is actually hurting him. I know Ben thinks Kai is faking, but he's been putting it on for a while now if he is. Kai himself has been quite dramatic, convinced he must have shattered his ankle into several pieces, but I'm pretty sure it's just a sprain. He can go to a hospital and get it X-rayed if he really wants to waste half a day in an A&E waiting room, but a couple of days at home with his foot up is all he really needs.

When we reach the education block, I pull out a bunch of keys. 'Bloody good job I brought all my work keys with me,' I say, unlocking the door and letting us in. There's an alarm system but I swiftly deactivate it by punching in a six-digit code, and as soon as the console stops flashing Kai finds a chair and plonks himself down in it. He lets out a deep sigh as he takes the weight off his feet; I wouldn't be surprised if his right leg's now hurting from doing more work than it's used to, and when added to the pain in his left ankle he's probably exhausted. Now that we're here, with a phone, and I'm not feeling the pressure to get to the visitor centre, I feel bad for pushing him so hard.

Ben goes straight towards the loo, and while that's also on my list of things to do, I'm going for the phone first. The door to the office is unlocked, which makes me tut out loud. I'll have to report that to my boss. The thought of going in to work tomorrow seems so strange, the idea of being back here on a normal day, with people going about their business as usual. Will we even be able to open? Part of the reserve is a crime scene, so I expect we'll need to stay closed until the police have finished doing whatever they need to do. I feel a pang of guilt, despite the fact that none of this is my fault. A small voice at the back of my mind begs to differ, but I silence it quickly.

Going into the office, I permit myself the luxury of sitting in the comfy chair next to the desk. As soon as I sit down, I know it's a mistake, because I won't want to get up again. I sink back into it for a moment, feeling every ache and pain in my muscles from the tension and physical exertion of this awful day. Picking up the phone, I listen for the dial tone, but it doesn't come. I try dialling 999, but there's still no sound on the end of the phone. I check it's plugged in – it has power, because there's a little light on the base, and the battery symbol is showing full. The cable for the phone line is also plugged into the wall, but it's not working. Shit.

I go back through to the other room, where the two men are sitting in silence, deep in thought.

'The bloody phone isn't working,' I growl, glaring at them as if it's their fault.

'How come?' Ben asks.

'If I knew that, I might know how to fix it,' I snap. 'There's no dial tone, nothing.'

'Is it plugged in?'

I can't believe Kai even asks me that. 'Of course it's fucking plugged in, smartarse. Do you honestly think I wouldn't have checked? I can dial the numbers, but there's no sound when I do.'

'Shit.' Kai rests his elbows on his knees. 'What the hell do we do now?'

'Back to the original plan,' I reply, grabbing my bag, which I flung down in the corner when we arrived. Hoisting it onto my back, I look back at the two of them. 'Are you up to this?'

Ben stands, stretching himself out. 'Yeah. Let's get on with it.'

We both look at Kai. He swallows. I get the feeling the idea of trying to walk another mile and a half on that ankle fills him with dread, but he also doesn't fancy sitting here on his own until someone comes to help him. He probably doesn't want to leave me alone with Ben, either.

'Yeah, I can do it,' he says, looking out of the window. As he does, I catch a flash of movement. I look at Kai, and can tell from the frown on his face that he saw it too.

'What was that?'

'I don't know,' he replies. 'Maybe we'd be better off staying here for a bit. Keep checking the phone, in case it starts working again.'

I curl my lip at that suggestion. 'I know you're getting comfy here, but we're supposed to be trying to get somewhere we can call the police. Nothing is going to happen if we just sit here, nobody is going to know anything's wrong.'

'True, but if someone's out there, maybe we should wait a few minutes. We don't want to bump into them, not knowing who it was.' Ben makes a good point, but I'm surprised that he's sided with Kai in this instance.

'You two do what you want. I'm going to go out and see what it was,' I say, shouldering my rucksack again. 'You stay here. I'll be back in ten minutes.'

'Hang on,' Kai says, clearly hoping to stall me. 'What are you going to do if you see someone?'

'That depends who I see,' I reply with a shrug. 'I'm not

going to approach anyone who's brandishing a shotgun, don't worry. I'm not that stupid.'

'I just don't think it's safe,' he replies.

'Of course it's not safe, Kai,' I hiss, and at that point even I can hear the fear in my voice. 'How can anywhere on this reserve be safe right now?' The pitch of my words rises at the end until my voice cracks and I turn away. I don't want either of them seeing how scared I am, but I think it's too late now.

'I don't want anything to happen to you,' Kai says carefully. 'If there's someone out there, we should wait until they've had a chance to move on.' He looks over at Ben, who nods his agreement. 'Then we can go in the opposite direction and get the hell out of here.'

'No,' I say defiantly, refusing to just sit still and wait for something to happen. 'I want to know who the hell it is, and what they think they're doing here, on my reserve.' I'm not sure what my expression is, but it stops Kai from arguing. 'I'm going out there. Wait here.'

'Wait, Lauren. Please.' Ben steps forward and holds out a hand, but doesn't actually touch me. 'I understand you want to check, but we need to stick together. The phone might be out because of the weather, but it might have been done deliberately.'

As he mentions the weather, all three of us turn to look at the window. The snow seems to be getting heavier. It's been coming down steadily but the flakes have only been small; now they're getting larger and with each passing moment it's getting harder to see out of the window.

'Why don't we use this time to see if there's anything in here that could be useful?' Ben suggests. He nods at

Kai. 'If he's going to be of any use, he needs something to help him walk.'

I sigh, frustrated at feeling like we're doing nothing, but I know what he's saying makes sense. Going back into the office, I open the cupboards in there but can't find anything long or strong enough. In the main room there are another two cupboards. Ben and Kai look like they're about to break into them, but I hurriedly find my keys and unlock the doors. The last thing I need is to have to explain any damage we've caused. I don't get involved in the education activities; it's not my area of expertise, so I have no idea what's stored in these cupboards. Inside the first one we draw a blank: it's full of worksheets and school trip activities. The second one is much better, however, with various pieces of equipment that are used around the reserve for education purposes. Ben roots around at the back for a while, then emerges clutching a bundle of nets for pond dipping. They're just the right height for Kai, but one on its own bends under his weight. Another trip to the office locates some electrical tape, and soon Kai has a walking stick constructed from three nets lashed together. It's not perfect, but it'll do, and the three of us give each other nods of satisfaction at a job well done.

'Come on,' I say, grabbing my bag again. 'Let's get going before the snow gets any worse.'

Kai grimaces and looks out of the window. 'Can we wait a few minutes? I'm knackered from trying to get this sorted.' He nods at the stick we've made.

I sigh. 'Seriously? I don't want to delay any longer.'

'If we rest for a bit longer, we might be able to get further,' he says, but I can see that Ben is on my side this time.

213

'Come on, we need to get moving again,' he says. 'The snow isn't going to get any better.'

Kai grumbles, but he knows he's lost this one. I fling open the front door, only to have a blast of freezing cold air blow snow right into my face. I get the feeling the rest of this journey is going to be arduous, but we have no other option now. The snow has already covered up our tracks from when we arrived, but at least the path from here is just a straight line. I set off, Ben following me. Taking a deep breath and gritting his teeth, Kai leans on his makeshift walking stick and joins us.

# Chapter 26

## Dan

'Where is she?' Morna asks for what feels like the hundredth time. Her voice is starting to put my teeth on edge, but I take a slow breath and do my best to stay calm.

'Morna, try not to worry. She's here somewhere, and she's sensible enough to have a plan.'

'A plan? What sort of plan?'

'When she realised she couldn't see us, she will have either continued walking along the boundary fence, or she would have followed our footprints to see if she could find us. Either way, we need to go back the way we came to see if we can find her.'

Morna is silent for the next few minutes as we walk, which I'm grateful for. I don't want her to know just how worried I am that we might not find Emily. When I agreed to come with them, when they insisted on making for the road, I thought it would be a pretty straightforward if tedious task. Now I wonder if I should have put my foot down, insisted we all stuck together and went to the visitor centre. My leadership skills seem to have faded away in the last few months, but then so much of who I was vanished along with Rachel.

I wonder what she'd say if she could see me now. Of course, if that were possible, I wouldn't be here. It was only after her death that I took to walking the paths of the nature reserve, trying to cope with the gaping hole she left in my life. She and the little life inside her. The house is exactly as it was the day I got back, apart from the closed doors. I've been sleeping in the spare bedroom, and won't even look at the door to the room I used to share with Rachel, or the one to the nursery. At some point I know I will have to face it, go in there and dismantle the cot, take down the Winnie-the-Pooh pictures we selected the day after the first scan, before I went back offshore. I missed so much of her pregnancy when I was working away for weeks on end, but I didn't think it would matter, because I'd be there to see our child grow up. But that won't happen now, all because of the selfish actions of a complete stranger.

'I think we should be going back towards the fence,' Morna says, stopping next to me. 'I can't see that she would just wander off into the woods.'

'I didn't say she'd wander off,' I say, amazed at the calm in my own voice. 'I said she'd be coming to look for us. Wherever she's gone, there will have been a purpose behind it.'

'She's young, young people don't think the same way as we do.'

I turn to look at her. 'She's twenty-eight. She's hardly a kid who's just left school. What's your problem with her anyway?'

Morna looks shocked at this question. 'Problem? I don't have a problem with Emily. She's a lovely girl. Why would you ask that?'

'Because you're talking about her as if she's stupid.'

Morna opens her mouth to reply, frowns, then closes it again. Shaking her head, she starts walking again. 'Okay, I see your point. That wasn't my intention. I'm just worried about her.'

There's a pause, but I know Morna is gearing up to say something else, so I keep my mouth shut and let her fill the silence.

'I shouldn't have pushed to come this way. I'm sorry. And I shouldn't have let Emily come with me.'

'As we've just discussed, she's an adult who can make her own choices,' I reply, not pointing out that she clearly had no problem with me also joining them.

'I've put her in danger. And that's the last thing I wanted!'

I stop. 'Look, Morna, why don't I go on ahead and look for Emily? I can probably follow her tracks more easily on my own, then I can bring her back here. You'll have to wait right here, though.'

I see the terrified look on her face and know she's not going to agree to it as soon as she speaks.

'No! You can't leave me on my own! Anyway,' she sniffs, 'it's my fault we got split up in the first place. I don't want to be responsible for all three of us ending up alone.'

I know there's no way Morna will want to be alone in the woods, not when she's convinced Ben is stalking us, but I'd thought it was worth a try in order to find Emily faster. Morna has been imagining her sightings of Ben, I know that much. If there'd been any sign of anyone else in the woods, I would have picked up on it, and I would have been after them like a shot. I've been keeping my eyes open for anything unusual while we've been walking, but there's been nothing.

'Okay, if you don't want to stay by yourself, I understand,' I tell Morna soothingly. 'But right now I need to be able to concentrate if we're going to find her.'

She nods, understanding that I'm asking her to be quiet, then hangs her head. I don't want to feel responsible for her emotions but I'm finding it quite difficult right now.

'What did you mean earlier when you said everything was ruined?' She didn't give me an answer the first time I asked, but I wonder if she might be inclined to open up a bit more now she's calmed down. Movement helps, too. I've had some of the most meaningful conversations of my life while I've been either walking or working.

'I . . .' she begins, but then stops. I hear a deep sigh. 'I thought today would be perfect, just the seven of us having a nice walk, bonding over the Starlings. Despite what happened at the pub, I thought we were really starting to form a nice little group. But then this happened, and nothing is going to be the same again.'

There's something very precise about this little speech, almost practised, that makes me wonder if she's being completely honest with me, but I have to take her words at face value. I remember the first time I met Morna, on one of my walks around the reserve. It was around the time I started chatting with Lauren, after several weeks of seeing her regularly and forcing myself not to avoid eye contact altogether. She's the one who brought me out of the worst of the dark cloud that hovered over me, and inadvertently showed me there's another way to deal with my problems.

Anyway, Morna had presumably heard about me from Lauren, and she spotted me one day on one of my walks. I like to walk alone, and while I would generally stop and speak to Lauren if I saw her, we rarely walked together. Morna wanted to walk with me, however, and she chattered away chirpily the whole time. It had nearly been enough to prevent me coming back here at all, no matter how much I was coming to value my friendship with Lauren. I ended up blocking her out, which hadn't mattered most of the time, because Morna often talks without needing a response from her audience. That was the first time I met her, and the first time I realised that I've developed huge reserves of patience along with other coping strategies.

That's why now I'm not sure if I believe what she's saying. I've never known her to talk in such a measured, considered way before. Normally she opens her mouth and whatever she's thinking comes out, without much thought for the impact of her words on the people around her. So what could she have meant, and what is she hiding? Is it something to do with Alec and his outburst at the pub?

It was a strange evening. I was reluctant to accept the invitation, but I knew it was important that I try to bond with these people. It was a conversation with Lauren that made my mind up, just a few days earlier. After that, I knew I had to go; in fact had even felt compelled to. It wasn't my usual sort of thing, and I didn't touch a drop of alcohol all night, but I still found it strangely enjoyable in a way I know I'd struggle to describe to someone else.

When Alec started ranting, however, I was more interested in observing the reactions of the rest of the group.

I wasn't worried about Alec's pronouncements. I knew there was nothing untoward that Alec could possibly know about me, because there's nothing for him to know. All the bad stuff I wouldn't want others to find out is all in my head, and there's no way for Alec to have seen in there. No, I wasn't worried. But a few of the others had looked scared, which interested me. Not the person I'd expected to, though. When Kai took Alec outside, I realised I should have volunteered to do it; it could have been useful for me to find out more, so I knew just how much Alec suspected about each of the other members of the group.

Morna and I arrive back at the spot near the fence where we last saw Emily, but there's no sign of her.

'Where is she?' Morna asks, her voice squeaky with fear and panic.

'I'm sure she won't have gone far,' I say, trying to be reassuring, even though I'm as concerned as Morna is about Emily's whereabouts. Bloody Morna, running off like that. What the hell was she thinking?

Backtracking slightly, I scan the ground for footprints that might indicate where Emily has gone. The areas where the snow has made it through the tree cover are starting to pile up again, obscuring most of our prints, and those that aren't refilling with snow have been walked over by the two of us just now. I should have been looking more carefully, I know, but I was distracted by Morna, and by memories of Alec's outburst.

'No, Dan, that's not good enough!' Morna's eyes are wide and she's looking from side to side so quickly I know she can't possibly be taking in any useful information. 'We need to find her! What if something happens to her? It'll be our fault, we were supposed to be sticking together!'

'Maybe you should have thought about that before you ran away from us,' I snap. 'If I hadn't run after you, Emily would have still been with me.'

'It's not my fault! I saw Ben. I saw him. He had a shotgun. He had . . .'

I see Morna's eyes flicker and I reach out to grab her by the shoulders, worried she's going to faint. When she shakes her head and sags into me, I tense.

'Look, this isn't getting us anywhere. We'll make our way back to the path, like we said. That way we're more likely to find her.'

'But what if she followed the fence?'

'Then she'll probably get out of here quicker than us. I don't think she did, though.' I point towards where a set of footprints passes where we're standing. 'Those are her prints, and I can't see any going the other way.'

A lot of that is guesswork, but Morna doesn't know that. I can't explain that I just know Emily won't have gone that way; I've spent a lot of time observing the members of this group when we've been out, and I feel like I could predict the way that most of them would think. Though this whole situation has shown that I've certainly been wrong about at least one of them.

'Come on,' I say, hoping I've managed to inject some brightness into my tone of voice. 'Let's go this way.'

I set off, keeping my pace relatively slow to ensure Morna is keeping up, but fast enough that we're still making progress. A moment later, however, an explosive boom shatters the silence of the woods, and we both freeze. Morna drops to the floor, covering her head, and I need to stop myself from joining her.

'What was it? Who's there?'

I can hear the terror in her voice, followed by a horrible retching sound. She's trying not to be sick with the fear.

For a few moments I hold my breath, wondering if the sound will come again, but there's nothing. Which direction did it come from?

'It was a shotgun,' I tell Morna, keeping my voice as steady as I can, knowing there's no point in lying to her. Someone is in these woods, and they've just fired a shot. But who, and why? Is there someone following us, someone I completely overlooked? I look over at Morna, and she's still crouching on the ground, her arms raised over her head.

'Come on, we need to move. Now, Morna.' It's difficult not to let my impatience show, but we don't have time to waste on our own fear. After hearing the blast I know just how important it is that we find Emily as soon as possible.

# Chapter 27

## Kai

There's no sign of anyone out on the path, and the snow is coming down so heavily that I'm worried we won't be able to make it much further through the reserve. As we trudge through the snow, I wonder why Lauren felt the need to come out after whoever it was. There's a murderer around here somewhere, and the most important thing right now is protecting ourselves from them, not confronting them.

I shiver, knowing that trying to walk through this depth of snow isn't doing me any good, and it's probably no better for Ben. I'd really like to call it quits, turn round and follow my own trail through the snow back to the education block. I know that Lauren won't go for that, though, so I don't even bother suggesting it. Maybe I can hang back and slip away, but Ben's behind me. He's still watching me suspiciously, ever since our fight back there. I shouldn't have laid into him the way I did, and I feel so bad for splitting Lauren's lip, but I didn't like him suggesting I'm faking it. Yes, I wanted to try and stall Lauren, but I wasn't going to pretend to break my ankle.

What a nightmare this whole thing is. Poor Alec. It's all a complete bloody mess. I think back to the night in the pub, when I dragged Alec out and shoved him into a taxi.

'Nobody ever listens to me,' he slurred, resisting my attempts to get him moving faster. 'They should.'

'Yeah, you're right, but they're not going to listen when you're pissed and raving, are they mate?'

I'd been happy to be the one turfing him out, hoping to find out exactly what Alec had been talking about.

'You all think nobody knows, and that the others are all sweet and innocent, but I know it all. Ben and his camera, oh don't think I haven't seen some of the shots he's been taking. Morna and that photo she keeps in her purse. Have you seen it? She keeps it hidden, but I've seen it and I know who's in it. As for your little extra-curricular activities . . .' Here Alec had paused to vomit in the bushes, much to my disgust. He'd barely been able to get his mouth around the words 'extra-curricular', but I got the gist. A taxi appeared at that point, however, and Alec stumbled towards it before I had the opportunity to find out exactly how much he knew.

See, if only people knew why I do what I do, I think at least some of the group would look on me a little more kindly. Alec was one of those black and white people though – you're good or bad, and that's the end of it. I'd been hoping to talk to him today, explain my side of the story, but of course that never happened.

I think about what he said to me about Ben, and I

224

suddenly wonder if I have some leverage here. I slow my pace slightly so he's walking alongside me.

'What was it you wanted to talk to Alec about, then?' I ask, keeping my voice quite light, like it's just a chat between mates.

Ben pauses. 'His behaviour towards Emily.'

I nod. 'Right. So, nothing to do with the dirt he had on you?'

Lauren turns at this, and I realise she's been listening in. She narrows her eyes at Ben. 'So, Alec knew something about you? A secret? And you thought that's what he was threatening to tell everyone. That's why you wanted to talk to him, wasn't it? Nothing to do with Emily.'

Ben opens and closes his mouth a couple of times, stuck for an answer, but I don't want to give him a chance to think of another excuse.

'What was it?' I ask, getting straight to the point.

'It doesn't matter now,' Ben replies, trying to keep his voice nonchalant, obviously hoping we won't push it. I understand how he feels, to be honest. While I'm horrified that Alec is dead, it won't do me any harm if my secret died with Alec, and I expect Ben feels the same. It means I actually have a chance to sort everything out, put a stop to it once and for all. There's no sense dragging it all up unnecessarily. For me, anyway. I still want to dig and find out what Ben's been up to.

'How can you expect us to believe you didn't kill him, if you won't tell us what he knew about you?' I ask with a shrug. I look at Lauren, who nods her agreement.

'For all we know you cooked up a story about wanting to talk to Alec in case something happened and one of us saw you by the hide,' she adds. 'If you want us to believe you, you need to tell us what Alec knew about you.'

Ben tips his head back and looks up at the canopy of trees, as if inspiration might come from above. Eventually, he must realise that nothing but the truth will do, and his shoulders sag as he looks back at us.

'He saw me taking a photo of Emily,' he says quietly. 'When she wasn't looking.'

Lauren makes a tutting noise. 'Seriously? Creep.'

'Look, I like her, okay? We were here the other month; she was standing looking out over the marshes and she just looked . . .' He swallows. 'She looked beautiful. I just wanted to take a picture of her.'

'Then you could look at her when you were home alone at night?' Lauren replies scathingly. Ben's face reddens.

'I know it sounds really creepy, but it wasn't. Alec saw me, though, and he kept making all these pointed comments about it. He was making it out to be something a lot worse than it was. I wanted to talk to him today to tell him I wasn't a creep, that I was going to ask Emily out.' He shakes his head, clearly annoyed at himself for opening up so much, but I'm not done yet.

'Show us, then.'

'What?'

'Show us the picture,' I say.

Ben pulls his phone out of his pocket and scrolls through the images until he finds the one he was talking about. I wonder if that day had been the start of his adoration of Emily, but I know he's not going to tell me anything as personal as that. He holds up the screen and I step forward to look at it, then nod.

'She looks pretty fine, you're right.'

Lauren shoots me a dirty look, but I shrug. 'He might be telling the truth.'

'Whatever.'

She turns around and continues marching ahead. After a few minutes we come to an open area, and Lauren pauses in her headlong stride. Without the snow, she knows this reserve like the back of her hand, but right now the blanket of white is enough to mess with anyone's sense of direction. I don't know it well enough to help, unfortunately. Is this where the path splits off into several smaller ones? Or is this just the open grassy area leading down to the scrapes? Lauren swivels her head around a few times, and I realise she's trying to get her bearings, when there's a rustle in the bushes off to the side.

For a moment I can't breathe. The others have frozen, so I know they heard it too. It was probably a fox, I tell myself. It's nighttime, there'll be plenty of animal activity around here. The rustling continues, however, and I find myself stepping backwards, away from the source of the sound. Before we have a chance to discuss it, or investigate, a thundering boom echoes out around the reserve.

'Shotgun,' I say immediately, recognising the sound. Lauren turns to me, her eyes wide, and I think until this moment she hadn't really thought there might be anyone else out there. Unless it's someone in the other group? But I don't want to think about that possibility, either.

'Quick, we need to keep moving,' Ben snaps, and the three of us press forward. The sound came from behind us, so we're all happy enough to keep moving in the same direction. We need to stick together and stay calm, though. If any of us loses it at this point it could be disastrous.

We round a corner, and there it is ahead of us, the visitor centre that we've been so keen to get back to. In daylight it looks quite sleek and modern, but in the darkness, after what we've experienced, it looks almost malevolent. I find myself slowing down, not actually wanting to approach it, which is ridiculous after we've made it this far.

The three of us approach the building in silence. My feet are heavy, and these last few steps almost feel like an anticlimax, walking up to the door and going inside. But, as it turns out, we're not going to do that. Ben comes to a halt, sticking his arm out to stop us walking past him. I've seen it too, but Lauren isn't paying attention. She's deep in thought when I grab her arm, and before she has a chance to react, I put a hand over her mouth. She fights for a second, before she realises I'm being as gentle as I can – I'm trying to keep her quiet, not hurt her. Relaxing, she stops struggling and looks at me; I point further up the path, to where a snow-covered walkway leads up to the visitor centre. There, we can clearly see footprints in the snow. They're fresh, and they can't have been made by anyone from our group; if one of them had passed us, we would have seen them.

'What do we do?' Ben's whisper is almost inaudible. Lauren glances around at the tree cover. I know what she's thinking, but there isn't much, except a moderate stand of holly a few metres to our right. It's not huge, but it could probably hide us in these conditions.

'Come on,' she mouths, moving towards the holly bush.

She walks quietly, lifting her knees high, making large strides in order to try and avoid unnecessary noise, though to my ears she might as well have yelled out our names and set off a flare for good measure.

It's a tight squeeze, but the three of us get behind the bush and wait for a moment. There's a sound off towards the visitor centre, and we hear one of the doors creak. I can tell the other two are holding their breath, the same as me. There are footsteps, but they're moving further away from us, and when their sound dies away I dare to breathe again.

'What now?' I ask, keeping my voice as quiet as possible. There are people in the visitor centre, and I know the three of us can't just walk in there and expect to be safe. But somewhere behind us is someone with a shotgun. Which do we take our chances with?

The side gate is only a couple of hundred metres away, but I want to avoid going that way if we can. I don't know who might be there, or what they might be up to. We could probably get around the visitor centre to the car park, but what can we do then? There's no way we'll be able to drive out in this weather, none of us has a 4x4, and there's still no phone reception there.

I poke my head out from the bush just in time to see a shadow pass across the huge window facing out onto the reserve. If we go round the building, they'll see us. We'll be sitting ducks.

'There's someone inside.'

Lauren copies me, wanting to see for herself, and I see her go pale as she realises I'm telling the truth.

'We'll try the side gate,' she suggests, but I shake my head.

'There's not enough cover going that way. They'll see us, and that's probably how they got in.' She doesn't know this is more than an educated guess.

'Can we make it back to the education block?' Ben mutters. 'We can lock ourselves in there, lie low.'

Lauren takes a deep breath, then lets it out slowly, and I wonder just how panicked she is right now. 'Yes, I think that's the best option right now. But once we're there, I don't know if it'll be safe. We should never have split up.'

I've been thinking the same thing, but voicing it out loud won't help anyone. There's a painful throb from my injured ankle, and I just want to sit down somewhere and stay there for a while. She has a point though; we can't stay behind a bush until it's safe to leave, because we have no idea when that will be. At least inside the education block we can try to get warm, barricade the door with something, make it safe.

'Kai, how fast can you move?' There's a look of determination on Lauren's face, and I try to conceal my grimace.

'Maybe a fast walk, but nothing more than that.'

She nods, possibly not happy but at least satisfied that I'm taking this seriously.

'Come on then,' she says, her jaw set. 'Let's move.'

And with that, the three of us break cover and set off back the way we came, retracing our steps. I try not to feel a sense of despair at having come so close to safety only to have it snatched away.

I noticed Lauren give me a strange look before we set off. Does she know? Has she suspected all along? Maybe that's why she was happy for me to go with her, because she wanted to keep me in sight. I wouldn't be surprised.

Perhaps when the police arrive, she'll hand me over, and I know she'd be justified.

Because I'm the one who let these people in. Earlier today, I went round to the side entrance of the reserve and cut the padlock on the gates, to let my cousin and his mates onto the land at the best point for finding deer, the only point where they could get their van onto one of the paths. At this time of year deer is about all they'll get, but at other times it's birds' eggs they're after, too. I've never actually got involved. I'm not up for killing anything, but I know I'm an accomplice all the same. I'm the one who finds out where the nests are, or where the deer are likely to be sleeping. It's not something I'm proud of, but I know now I'm in too deep to find any way out.

It started to get really bad when my dad turned up, asking for money. I was already in debt, but I'm a soft idiot, so I gave him some, but apparently it wasn't enough. My cousin said he knew a bloke who did loans. That was my first mistake. Because the loan wasn't in my dad's name, it was in mine, and pretty soon I found myself being chased by a pretty fucking vicious loan shark.

I'm not suggesting I'm an angel who got in with the wrong crowd. I was a bit of a bad lad, never engaged at school – smart enough, but 'lacked motivation' according to my teachers, and I ended up in trouble. Being black didn't help; I was suspended for things some of the white boys in my class would have got away with. My feelings of discontent festered until they grew into anger. Anger at the system, mostly, so I left school with no GCSEs. I tried college, doing a couple of practical courses, but I didn't do as well as I could have done because my own mouth got in the way. My mum managed to keep me out of the worst sort of trouble, because I knew she relied on me, but that's where my self-restraint ended.

So I ended up mostly working casual jobs, never knowing from month to month where the money might be coming from. But I'm sensible and started saving it up. One of my mates died when he was twenty-two, of cancer, and that gave me a bit of a wakeup call about how short life is. By then it was too late, though, and I'd already started giving my dad money. It got to the stage where I didn't know what to do, and I turned to my cousin, who offered me a way out. He'd pay off my debt, if I did a few jobs for him. It sounded so good, so easy. Too easy. I assumed he meant labouring work, maybe a bit of driving, but it soon turned out to be something different. If it comes down to any arrests, I'm not even sure what I'm guilty of; but there's no way I could say I'm innocent.

I'd been sneaking onto the reserve for a few months when I first found out about the nature group. There used to be a way in near the railway line, before they added new fences during the summer. Hopping the old fence during the day last spring, I was walking round the paths when I bumped into them. They were all looking up, and I realised they were looking at the same nest I'd been looking for: Ospreys. They were new to this area the previous year, and everyone was desperate to see if they'd come back. I found out all of this by looking online, gathering all the information that my cousin asked for. I stood there with this group, craning up at the huge mass of twigs and foliage that formed the messy nest, and marvelled at it. One thing I have never admitted to my cousin is that I had started to become interested in the wildlife I was researching, and actually seeing the Osprey nest for myself gave me a thrill I wasn't expecting.

'They're going to have to protect this site,' Alec had said that day. 'Close off the path, maybe set up a viewing camera.'

Lauren had nodded her agreement. 'Absolutely, we've already got plans in place. We need to keep them safe.'

After that, Alec introduced himself to me and we got talking, which led to me joining them the following month. That was the first time I lied to my cousin, telling him I couldn't find the nest. By the time I went back the following week, it was well protected, and I knew there was no chance of any of them getting to the eggs. And I'd been relieved.

So now I'm here, in the snow, knowing my cousin and a couple of his mates are probably out trying to bag some deer nearby. I told them about Emily's car, in the hope they'd focus on that instead. The fact that we just saw someone inside the visitor centre suggests they've gone to have a look at it, but I'd bet the second shotgun blast came from them too. I think they've split up, hoping to come away with deer and a Tesla – they've hit the jackpot tonight.

One thing I know is that none of them killed Alec. For a start, they wouldn't have come onto the reserve until it was fully dark, and Alec was killed at dusk. Secondly, they know the reserve pretty well by now, and they keep away from the hides. No, it was one of our own who killed Alec, I'm sure of that.

# Chapter 28

## Emily

Head down, I keep walking. What's important right now isn't where I'm going, but that I keep moving. If I stay in one place, it's more dangerous. The snow is coming down heavily now, and I'm worried that if I stop I'll never get going again, and then hypothermia will set in.

I pause briefly to check my bag in case there's another item of clothing in there that I've forgotten about, but I'm already wearing every layer that I've brought with me. There's one bar of chocolate left in the side pocket, but I'm determined to save that. After all, I don't know how long I'm going to be wandering around out here.

When I found the marshes I realised I must have been going in the opposite direction to the one I intended, and made the decision to turn around, thinking that I'd find my way back to a path more easily. I was wrong, and now I'm still trudging through the woods, my energy fast dissipating. The problem is that it all looks the same – trees, snow, more trees, as far as I can see in every direction. Every time I turn my head I'm concerned that I've been walking in circles. Part of my brain tells me it's the stress and fear making everything seem worse than it is, but that doesn't really help.

My new goal is to find the perimeter fence again and try to follow it back round, in the hope that it will eventually lead me back to the visitor centre. Wherever Morna and Dan are, they're probably still looking for the low section of the fence, intending to make for the road, but I've changed my mind on that. In this weather, the chances of us finding a car travelling along the road are slim, so there'll be nobody to help us, and we'd be miles away from our own vehicles. No, I've realised that Lauren's plan was the better one all along, despite the risk from whoever killed Alec. And if we'd all stuck together, that risk would have been reduced, because it would have meant we had safety in numbers.

No point worrying about that now, I tell myself briskly. Right now, I need to keep moving. Just keep moving. I repeat it to myself like a mantra, and I find I end up walking in time to the words. Even though I've been coming to these sessions once a month with Lauren, I'm not particularly fit, and I'm certainly not used to spending a lot of time walking on uneven ground in the snow, so I'm really starting to feel fatigue dragging at my limbs. It would be so easy to stop and sit down somewhere, rest for a little while, but I can't let the cold settle into my bones, or I won't be able to move at all.

I plod on, still repeating my mantra. For a while I don't even look up, just watch my own boots as they hit the snow underfoot. It's only when I think I see a movement out of the corner of my eye that I look up, and my breath catches in my throat – I've found the fence. It stretches away from me in both directions, but now I'm next to it again I at least have something to follow, to be certain I'm not walking in circles, and now I have a chance of finding the visitor centre. The sight of it spurs me on, and I stride confidently for the next few minutes. Occasionally I have to move away from the fence briefly, in order to walk around a stand of trees, but I keep it in sight at all times.

I come to a fallen tree, and decide to scramble over it rather than go around. The time it would take isn't worth wasting, and now I'm feeling confident again I want to get out of here as quickly as possible. Even if the snow means we're unable to drive away from the reserve just yet, in the visitor centre we'll be able to call the police, as well as warm ourselves up.

Deep in thought, I don't notice the rumble that's coming up through the ground, the vibrations that would normally warn me of an approaching train. It bursts into my line of sight on the other side of the fence, racing past me with a rush of air that leaves me unable to draw breath for a moment, my heart pounding. I grip the fence for support as the train flashes past, and as I look up the light from the carriages illuminates part of the woods ahead of me.

What's that? I squint at the form that has been lit up, then take a step back. Is it a person? I'm sure it is. There's someone in the woods, not far ahead of me. Without stopping to think, I turn and run.

Going back the way I came, I see the fallen tree and divert this time, running along the length of the trunk until I come to the remains of the branches, heaped with snow. Scrambling partly over and partly through them, I can feel my breath coming in ragged gasps. Who was it? I don't have the time to stop and find out.

Despite the pain in my tired legs, I run, dodging round trees and jumping over rocks. The snow is slippery underfoot and I slide a couple of times, but manage to right myself quite quickly and keep going. Behind me there's a huge explosive sound, and I recognise it as a shotgun blast, just like the one I heard when Alec was killed. Turning my head, I try to work out where the sound came from, but then suddenly I'm on the floor, snow in my face, rolling down a bank until I come to a stop when my body slams sideways into a tree trunk.

I close my eyes. All the air has been knocked from my lungs, so I fight to fill them again before thinking about the pain in my body. I know there are ditches near the path in some places around the reserve, and I must have fallen headlong into one. Is anything broken? There's a sharp pain in one of my wrists; I must have used that hand to break my fall and landed on it hard, but I can still move it. Other than that, I just feel a bit battered. Pulling myself to my feet, I groan slightly at the stiffness that's already setting into my muscles, then freeze. It's not because I hear something. In fact, it's because I hear nothing. Not my own voice when I should have just made a sound, nor the crunch of my boots on the snow as I hauled myself to my feet. My hands go to my head and confirm what I already know: I've lost my cochlear implant processor.

My fear ramps up several notches at the realisation that I'm alone in the woods in the dark and the cold with nothing to help me hear. Whatever people like to say about cochlear implants being 'bionic ears', as soon as you remove the processor I'm back to being profoundly deaf. Having one of my senses ripped away like that, especially when I also can't see very well, means a cold fist of fear squeezes tightly at my heart. What the hell am I going to do?

I look up the bank of the ditch that I've fallen into, a clear path in the snow showing where I slid down. Getting down on my hands and knees, I start digging through the snow around the flattened section, pausing any time my fingers meet something hard. I throw away several rocks before ripping off my gloves and rooting further into the snow, moving up the bank as I search, all the while trying to stay alert to any movement in my peripheral vision. Because now, it would be so easy for someone to creep up on me in the dark, when I have no way of hearing them coming. Perhaps they won't know that, but it won't take them long to realise I'm an easy target.

Where is it? Shit. Shit, shit, shit. I can barely keep the panic at bay now, and I want to curl up in a ball at the bottom of the ditch and wail. There's a small part of me that still has some self-preservation instincts left, though, so I take some deep breaths and keep searching.

When I get to the top of the bank, I can see the tree root that tripped me up and sent me hurtling down there in the first place. I'm sure my processor didn't drop off while I was running, because surely I would have noticed, so that means it has to be in the ditch. Pausing for a moment, I consider my options. I can stay here and hope to find my processor, then pray it's still working before I continue trying to get to the main entrance of the reserve. But that carries a risk that I won't find it at all, and I will have delayed my escape for nothing. Or I can accept that I might not find it, take the risk and carry on running, in silence.

The idea of running without any access to sound makes my whole body convulse with fear, but I know it's the better option. If there's a killer in these woods, it won't matter if I can hear or not when they catch up with me. I scan my surroundings, climbing back up the bank and peering into the woods. It's so dark I can't see far, but in the furthest reaches of my vision I think I can see a figure moving among the trees. Swallowing hard, I turn around again and run.

It's a horrible sensation, my feet pounding the hard forest floor sending vibrations through my body, but no sound reaching me. I left the boundary fence behind when I ran, but I know the ditches are near the path, so as soon as I see the trees opening out slightly, I head in that direction. A moment later, I see a small wooden hut on my left – it's one of the bird hides, so despite the thick layer of snow I must have found a path. Slowing slightly, I clutch my side, a stitch threatening to halt my progress altogether.

Breathing heavily, I lean against the wooden wall of the hide and wait for the pain to subside. I don't know how long I can keep this up, but if I move quickly, hopefully I'll find one of the others. At this point in time I don't care who it is; I just know I'll feel safer with someone else, someone who can listen for the sounds of someone approaching.

Looking back along the path, I can see my tracks clearly in the snow. The depth of the snow on the path is going to severely slow down my progress – I don't know if I'll even be able to walk that fast in it, let alone run. Also, the footprints are like a beacon, standing out against the fresh white. It'd be easy for someone to follow me if they wanted. Should I try to obscure them?

A sudden movement to my right makes me jump and sets my heart racing, but when I turn in that direction I can't see anything. Perhaps it was only some snow falling off a branch, but I can't be certain. At least standing with my back to something solid makes me feel like nobody can creep up on me. I pull out my phone and check for signal, just in case, but there's nothing. It's hard to resist the temptation to use my torch, but Dan was right, it would be like putting a flashing sign above my head to show someone where I am. It wouldn't matter if he or Morna found me, but it would if it was someone else.

Trying my best to push through my fear, I move to the edge of the path where the ground is more uneven and the snow cover less pristine, then start moving again.

# Chapter 29

## Morna

Which way? Haven't we come this way already? That stand of trees looks familiar, but then they all look the same in the snow. Shouldn't we have reached the path by now?

I look up at the trees and feel the starkness of the branches closing in on me, the bare trunks leering as I pass. No, I tell myself. I cannot have another panic attack. There's too much at stake. I reach into my inside pocket, past the layers of clothing I'm now wearing, and pull out the photo I always carry. Dan is striding ahead, but I don't care. I slow down to pull off my gloves. Despite the layers, my fingers are so cold I struggle to grasp it.

I hold the crumpled photo in my trembling palm and gaze down at it, briefly lost in the past. They didn't deserve what I did, the selfish decision I made.

I had the opportunity to change things, to start again and right my own wrongs, but I was too wrapped up in myself and my own life. Things could have been so different, should have been, and it's my fault that they weren't. Maybe it's too late now to start again, to try and put things right, but I know I have to try. It's as if I've been given a second chance, and I don't want to mess it up.

'Morna? What are you doing?' I can hear the irritation in Dan's voice, but I don't care. I'm exhausted, from fear and from running in snow, because I've had to jog to keep up with Dan at some points. It's as if I'm becoming numb to the danger, now. There's someone in the woods, we know that, we heard the gunshot, but I don't care as much as I did before. If they want to kill me, they probably would have done it by now. Alec had been their target, and now Alec's dead.

I didn't witness Alec's death; I didn't even hear the shotgun – I had wanted to immerse myself completely in the visual experience of the Starling murmuration, so I'd put my headphones in with some white noise playing, so nothing else could distract me. It was such a beautiful experience, I was so present in the moment, so lost in the visual spectacle, that I had been quite angry with Dan for tapping me on the shoulder and pulling me out of it. It took me several moments to process what he was saying, that there'd been a shotgun blast and he wanted to go and see where it had come from. Why was he bothered? The reserve backs onto farmland on two sides, so it had probably been a farmer after a fox. It was only when I heard the raised voices of the others out on the path that I realised it must have been something else, something closer to where we were.

Alec hadn't been able to keep his nose out of other people's business. I made the mistake of leaving my handbag unattended once, on a really busy day during the summer when I was helping out in the café kitchen. I thought I'd left it hidden away in a corner, but of course Alec found it. He had a nose for things like that. Or perhaps he'd been watching me and had seen where I put it, with the express purpose of having a look inside my purse and finding that photo. He'd caught a glimpse of it once and asked me about it regularly after that. I rebuffed him with a bland response every time. In hindsight, I realise that probably made him even more intrigued and determined to find out why I kept it so close to me, both literally and figuratively.

'We need to get moving,' Dan says, after retracing some of his steps. He doesn't come too close, which I'm glad of. He's the sort of man who could be physically intimidating without realising it, but he's respectful of personal space. I sigh deeply, then put the photo away and pull my gloves back on.

'I can't do this,' I say, my voice cracking. 'I can't keep wandering round in circles, not knowing where the hell we're going. I want to just sit here and wait for someone to find me.'

'Even if that's someone who means you harm?' Dan asks. There's no harshness to his tone, but his words make me flinch all the same.

'Nobody means us harm. Ben killed Alec, and now he's probably already back at the visitor centre with the others. I don't know why I convinced myself that he was behind us, that he'd got away. I've been under a lot of stress lately.'

Dan turns away from me for a moment, and I wonder if he's trying to stop himself from getting angry with me.

When he turns back, there's a tight smile on his face that looks forced.

'Look, we're nearly back at the path,' he says, pointing away from where we're standing to an area of thinner tree cover. 'It's not much further at all. Then we can find somewhere safe for you to wait, if that's what you want to do.'

I think about it for a moment. It's certainly an option, and at least if I were in a hide, I'd feel safer. I'd be able to see out, but nobody could see in. That sort of security sounds good to me right now.

'What will you do?'

'I'll keep looking for Emily. And whoever fired that gun,' he says quietly, a note of determination in his voice. That makes sense. Dan isn't the sort of person to run from a fight.

'Will you tell the others where I am, if you find them? *When* you find them,' I correct myself. We won't be lost on this nature reserve forever, but right now I'm happy to sit and wait. Dan or Lauren can tell the police where I am, and they can come and find me. Then I'll know I'm safe. Whatever has happened tonight, there will still be a sunrise and things will be better in the morning.

'Of course,' Dan says, and I think he's starting to get irritated now. 'Come on, we need to keep moving. The longer we stop, the harder it is to keep your muscles warm and keep going.'

I nod and stretch my arms out behind me, then pull my bag onto my back. It feels heavier than it did this morning, despite the fact that I'm wearing all of the extra layers I packed, and have drunk most of my water. When I start walking again, pain shoots through each foot and I wince, but Dan has already turned away and doesn't notice.

As we walk, I can tell he wants to speed up, but he's doing his best to go at my pace. I'm grateful for that, but also annoyed at myself. I pride myself on my fitness; I'm sixty-seven, and I'm in better shape than many of my friends who are ten or twenty years younger. Some of the other, younger volunteers struggle to keep up with me when we're walking around the reserve, but now I feel like my body is betraying me. It's the cold, I tell myself. I'm not used to this much walking in such low temperatures, and in snow. Most of my walking is on paths, not on the uneven terrain of the woods, with the added obstacle of a layer of fresh snow.

'What?' Dan stops and turns to look at me. I didn't realise I was thinking out loud, muttering to myself as I walk. I shake my head.

'Nothing. Sorry.'

He gives me a strange look before carrying on again. I want to talk to him, to start some conversation just to pass the time, to make this walk easier, but I don't know where to begin. He's such a private person, keeps things so close, that until tonight I didn't feel like I knew him at all. How a person behaves in a crisis tells you a lot about them, but even so, I feel almost as if Dan is playing a role, showing himself to be the person everyone expects him to be.

A couple of times I open my mouth to say something, then stop. How can I ask him a personal question now, here? No, I'll have to make my own distractions.

Suddenly, Dan stops dead. I do the same, getting a bit closer to him first. Safety in numbers, I keep telling myself.

'What is it?'

Suddenly I think of Emily. How did I forget about Emily? In the stress and confusion she's completely gone out of my mind. Where is she? Is she okay?

'Is it Emily?' I whisper to Dan, if only to prove to myself that I care. He shakes his head.

'No, I think it was just some snow falling off a branch.'

I didn't hear anything myself, but I trust Dan's senses more than my own right now.

'Maybe I should stick with you, at least until we find her.'

'Are you sure?' he asks. 'Maybe it would be better for you to wait in a hide, like we said.' Behind his words I hear the meaning he doesn't speak: he can move faster without me. I'm slowing him down, putting him off. If he has to keep an eye on me, as well as trying to find Emily, then it will be harder work.

I bite my lip. 'Fine,' I say eventually. We start walking again, and soon the line of trees comes to an end and the vast expanse of the marshes stretches out in front of us. Just to our right is the largest hide, its strange geometrical shape standing out against the dark sky.

'We're back here,' I murmur. Exactly where we started. In several hours, all we've succeeded in doing is going in one big circle. We haven't achieved anything, and we've lost one member of our trio along the way. I find myself letting out a hollow laugh, then have to clamp a hand over my mouth to stop it escalating, hysteria rising inside me and threatening to overtake me.

Dan opens the door to the hide. 'Come on,' he says. 'Let's try and warm up for a minute.'

Inside the hide conditions aren't much better than outside, but just being surrounded by the walls and ceiling help to dampen some of my heightened emotions. It's as if I've been suddenly cocooned, enveloped in some semblance of safety.

I put my bag down and sit down on one of the benches, stretching out my arms and legs, reaching down to my ankles and massaging them, then moving my hands back up my calves, working on the muscles as I go. It's important to try and stay warm inside the hide; it has electric lights, but no form of heating. Neither I nor Dan move to switch the lights on, however, knowing there's no sense in advertising our presence.

Dan paces up and down the hide for a few moments, then sits down on a bench briefly, before resuming his pacing again. He's obviously keen to get going again.

'You can go,' I tell him gently. 'I'll be fine. Hopefully Emily will come back here and find me, if you don't find her in the woods.'

Dan nods. 'Okay. If she does come back, turn on the lights. That way I'll know I don't have to keep looking for her.'

I'm not sure of the wisdom of this plan, especially as Dan could be deep in the woods or away across the other side of the reserve if or when that happens, but I don't contradict him. With one last nod at me, he steps outside the hide and shuts the door. I sit on a bench and turn to look out at the marshes, wondering if I'll be able to see anything. A thump outside the door makes me jump, and I almost regret my decision, but when no other sound comes I relax. Accepting that I've failed, I sit and wait for someone to come and find me, whoever that might be.

# Chapter 30

## Lauren

'What the fuck are we going to do now?'

I'm not really asking the question, I just need to let out some of my frustration. The three of us have made it back to the education block: Kai is slumped in a chair, massaging his ankle; Ben is standing by the window, looking out at the snow; and I'm pacing. Even though my muscles are begging me to stop moving, to rest, I can't bring myself to. I need action.

'We can stay here, at least until morning,' Kai suggests. I know he probably doesn't want to move any more on his injury, but the idea of sitting in here for hours with the two of them, doing nothing, makes me want to scream.

'But if nobody knows we're here, we could be waiting a long time,' Ben points out.

'Yeah, but it'll be safer to move in daylight.'

Ben nods, accepting that Kai has a point.

'We're not staying here,' I snap. 'We're going to have to go a different way, back into the reserve.'

'There's someone out there with a shotgun, Lauren,' Ben says, and I don't like the patronising tone of his voice.

'You don't get a say in the decision-making. For all we know, you're a murderer.' I can't help myself. The dig just slips out. Something about the fear I'm feeling is making me cruel.

Ben shakes his head. 'I'm not. I promise, Lauren.' He stops and turns to face me, then takes my arm and leads me over to the other side of the room, away from Kai. 'Look, you can search me, tie me up if you want. I'm no threat to you.'

I don't want to admit it, but his confession about taking photos of Emily stung. It's true, I've always thought Ben was a bit odd, but there was a point earlier this year when I started to think I shouldn't have brushed him off so easily. He's always seemed pleasant, respectful, and when we're on these days out we've often had a laugh together. I resolved to give Ben a chance, and say yes the next time he asked me out – he did it that often, it didn't cross my mind that he wouldn't ask again. But then he met Emily. Beautiful, perfect Emily. Ben didn't care that she made my life a misery when we were kids, all he saw were her big eyes and flawless skin. Before I knew it, he was hanging on my sister's every word, and I could see him falling in love with her before my very eyes. Emily takes everything from me.

When we went into care, I was four and Emily had just turned three. I'm not sure how much my sister remembers about our home life before that, if anything, but I know everything had always been about Emily. Emily had 'special needs' so took all our mum's attention, but then she couldn't cope. There was someone else occasionally, an older woman. Maybe a grandmother, but she could have been a neighbour, or even a social worker. Whoever she was, our mum always cried after she left, and usually got drunk and locked herself in her bedroom. I remember a couple of occasions when I climbed up to look in the kitchen cupboards, getting myself and Emily cereal or biscuits when we were hungry. Emily always complained bitterly, making strange noises, pointing at the cupboards or the cooker. Her deafness meant she didn't speak until she was a bit older, and I could never understand what she wanted from me. Even then, Emily was so demanding.

When we went to the home, I remember being told that it was just for a little while, because our mummy needed some help to get better. I didn't even realise she'd been poorly. As an adult, I can look back and see the signs of addiction and mental illness written all over our mother's chaotic life, but at the time I didn't know any better. It was supposed to be a temporary placement, then from there we went to a foster home, but I didn't like these new people who were looking after us. They were supposed to be helping Emily to speak, but they never bothered. People came to the house and talked to Emily, but they were never interested in me.

I know I shouldn't have let childish bitterness follow me into adulthood, but it's not a rational part of my brain that controls that thinking. For our entire childhood, social services insisted that we shouldn't be separated, yet they couldn't find a foster family willing to take on two girls because one of us was deaf. I sometimes wonder if our mum would have coped better if Emily hadn't been ill and lost her hearing, or if she hadn't been born at all.

Would we have still ended up in care? Would my life have been different? At one point there'd been the suggestion of us going to live with another family member, but nothing ever came of it. I've often thought about trying to find out more information about our birth family, but in the end I decided against it. If we have family who didn't want to help us when we were young, I have no interest in getting to know them now.

Ben's still looking at me. He gives me a look exactly like a kicked puppy. 'I wanted to talk to Alec, check he wasn't going to make a big thing about what he'd seen. I really like Emily and I didn't want her getting the wrong impression.'

'Well why didn't you ask her out, like a normal person?' I ask. 'Instead of taking photos of her and keeping them on your phone. I don't believe for one minute that that's the only photo. Alec was a nosy gossip, but he liked things a bit juicier than that.' I should know. There's plenty he might know about me that I don't want to share with the rest of the group.

Ben doesn't answer my question, so I make a disgusted noise in the back of my throat and turn back to Kai.

'How soon do you think you can get moving again?'

He grimaces. 'If we have to get going, then I'll be ready whenever you want. But look, Lauren.' There's pleading in his eyes. 'We're safe in here. We can stay warm. There's a kettle in the office, we can make a hot drink and hunker down here for a while. If we take a chance, the snow might stop, then it'll be easier for us to continue.'

I think about his suggestion for a moment. I can't say the idea of a cup of tea, or maybe a hot chocolate, doesn't fill me with longing right now, but I also feel like sitting still is giving up.

'You know what, that's a really good idea,' Ben says, and without waiting for either of us to reply he leaves the room. I can hear him filling the kettle and switching it on. It'll only take a few minutes to make tea, I suppose, and we could still be arguing about what to do by then.

'I know you want to keep moving, but we have to look after ourselves, too,' Kai says, and I wonder how he's suddenly become the voice of reason. 'We need to warm up a bit, and it's important to keep our fluids up, too.'

'Alright, Dr Kai. You sound like someone off those cheesy morning programmes on the telly.'

He laughs. 'You know I'm talking sense, though. I can see how much you want a cup of tea.'

To my surprise, I find myself laughing too. How can I laugh, with everything that's happened? Still, it feels good.

The moment passes quickly, however, and the two of us lapse into silence. I walk over to the window and stare out at the snow. It's not coming down as heavily now, thankfully, but it's thick on the ground, which will make our passage more difficult. We might have to go the long way round the little hollow where Kai hurt his ankle. I don't want to risk any of us getting injured again, we're going slow enough as it is.

'I still think we should try to find the others,' I say, turning back to Kai. 'Right now, I want everyone else where I can see them. We never should have split up in the first place, and the snow has just made everything impossible. I doubt they made it very far, in this weather, so hopefully we can find them.'

'They could be anywhere by now, though. They might already be at the road, flagging down a lorry.'

I shake my head. 'I don't think so. Don't ask me how, but I think they're all still on the reserve.' There's only one small section where they could have got over the fence, and even if they found it, the snow is so thick the fields beyond will be a nightmare to get through.

Kai looks sceptical, but I know I have one more ace to play.

'Or do you want to go back to the visitor centre and try your luck with your poacher friends?'

Kai looks stunned, but I can see something behind his expression: could it be relief? That doesn't make any sense to me, and as he hangs his head in his hands I wonder if I've got everything correct. I've been keeping my eye on Kai this evening, knowing he's one of the people most likely to have a shotgun stashed somewhere on the reserve, yet at times he's seemed as scared as me. I don't know how to read him at all.

'Lauren, I can explain.'

'I'm not the one you need to explain anything to,' I say drily. 'Save it for the police.' I haven't reported him before now because I didn't have any proof, only rumour. But after tonight, I can hopefully put a stop to what they've been doing.

'But you are,' he says. 'I think you're the only one who'll give me the opportunity to tell you the truth, show you my perspective.'

I shrug and turn back to the window, not interested in his excuses. Squinting, I look down at the snow that's lying several centimetres deep along the path, and I see something strange. There's a set of footprints out there, leading away from the building and back towards the marshes.

'Kai, did you see anyone go past the window?'

'No, honestly. I don't know where they are.'

'That's not what I'm saying. Look.' I beckon him over, and he joins me at the window, giving a sharp intake of breath when he sees the footprints. The falling snow is only just starting to fill them, meaning they haven't been there for very long at all.

We look at each other, then I realise that it's awfully quiet in here. The kettle stopped boiling and clicked itself off several minutes ago, but there are none of the tell-tale sounds of someone making a cup of tea – the clink of spoons in mugs, the pouring of water. I dash through to the office, but there's no sign of Ben, then I turn round and pull the front door to the building open. Sure enough, the footprints lead away from here. I go back in, grabbing my bag and motioning to Kai to do the same.

'How could we be so bloody stupid? We've kept him in sight the whole time, then when we let our guard down, he does a runner!'

'What?' He looks confused.

'Ben. He's gone!'

# Chapter 31

## Emily

I'm just running, running, running, with no care for the noise I might be making. I can't hear it, so I don't worry about it. The snow whips against my face, and I brush it out of my eyebrows every so often. There are flakes sticking to my eyelashes, but I blink them away. All that matters now is running.

As I run, I think. I think about my sister's shocking attitude, and how twitchy she was all through Christmas Day. I think of the look she gave Alec in the pub the other night, that seemed to be a look of pure loathing. There always was a vicious side to her. All the little pranks played on me in the children's home where we lived, they were all so very personal. At the time I didn't suspect that Lauren was behind them, believing with childish naivety that my sister loved me and cared about me.

Now, forced to cope without one of my senses, I'm reminded of the time my cochlear implant processors went missing overnight. I left them by my bed to charge, same as I did every night, but when I woke up in the morning, they were gone. Of course, I reported it immediately to the staff, who gathered all the children (or inmates, as we referred to ourselves) and asked for them to be returned. At least, that's what I think they said, because I couldn't hear the conversation.

That was the first day I realised my sister had a cruel streak. While the staff were speaking, I sat at the side of the room, enveloped in my own lonely silence, watching the expressions and body language of the others. They ranged in age from seven to fourteen at that time. I was eleven, and Lauren had just turned thirteen. When my eyes landed on my sister, I could see that Lauren was watching me with a satisfied smirk on her face. She mouthed something: *You're so stupid.* Taken aback, I didn't know what to do. What had my sister done with my processors? Why would she take them from me?

It took two days for new processors to arrive from the hospital, and in that time, I felt lost in a way I never had before. Everything I thought I knew, about my life and my sister, had crumbled. I begged the cochlear implant team to give me a spare set of processors, in case it happened again, but they refused due to the cost. They told me I had to get better at looking after them, which stung. It wasn't my fault.

From that day on, I saw Lauren in a different light. Maybe she changed, or maybe I had never noticed before, but little jibes started appearing in conversations. Lauren would be hanging around with other kids and deliberately turn her back on me, or raise her voice if she wanted it to be known they were talking about me. I hoped the attitude would wear off after a while, but it never did. When we parted company after Lauren turned eighteen, we didn't speak to each other again until I got back in touch, hoping to rebuild our relationship as adults.

What I've never told Lauren is how lonely I am, as a young adult living alone in London. Yes, I have money now, but what I really want – the only thing I've ever wanted – is family and friends. I've been in the process of finding out more about our family, and have traced our roots back here. Christmas Day would have been the perfect time to share it with Lauren, but everything had felt so awkward that I kept my mouth shut. And perhaps Lauren isn't the first person I should speak to, after all.

When I managed to get the records from social services, I was surprised to see there was so much I was allowed to read. It was an eye-opener: our mother had only been fifteen when Lauren was born, seventeen when she had me. By that time, she was living in a council flat, alone. There's no mention of who our father is, or even if we have the same father. I suppose DNA testing would help us to find out, but I've never been brave enough to broach the subject with Lauren. Not that it really matters; we're the closest each of us has to any sort of family.

After my birth, our mother suffered from severe post-natal depression, and became addicted to prescription painkillers. She was given support, but nowhere near enough, by the sounds of the reports that were filed. I required a lot of medical attention as a newborn, and then contracted meningitis. It had been touch and go – I hadn't known how close I came to death as a baby until I read those notes, and it took me several weeks to build up the emotional strength to keep reading. The meningitis left me profoundly deaf in both ears, and I had the operation for bilateral cochlear implants as soon as it was safe to do so. Later reports from the social workers show that our mother claimed she was pressured into making the decision, but that she hadn't wanted to give me the implants. The social worker noted that she didn't believe that I, her baby daughter, was deaf and wanted to 'give her a chance to heal' first. I did my own research and discovered that wouldn't have happened, that the damage done to the cochleas by meningitis is irreversible, but my mother had only been a child herself. She was thrust into adulthood, and motherhood, before she was ready, and suddenly she had two small children, one of whom was severely unwell. I have no memory of my mother, but I feel a lot of pity and compassion for her.

The reports became more regular, after that. Social workers came and went, but they all had concerns about the way our mother was caring for her two daughters. We were rarely clean, didn't appear to be well fed, and I was showing very delayed communication skills, even more than would be expected due to my deafness. The team from the cochlear implant centre even wrote a report stating their concerns that nobody was making the effort to communicate properly with me, and as such I wouldn't develop age-appropriate language skills. It looks like that was one of the things that tipped the balance, but we weren't removed from our mother's care until the social worker arrived to find Lauren and me sitting in the living room, both filthy, eating raw fish fingers that Lauren had found in the freezer. Our mother had passed out in her bedroom after an overdose.

A couple of years of court proceedings followed, but in the end, our mother gave up on trying to get her children back, and she died a year later of another overdose. It was all so desperately sad, I haven't been able to hate her, even though it's because of her that we ended up in the care system. No, it's the other family members that I want to speak to, want to grill. I want to know why nobody ever tried to get custody of the two of us. Most of all I want to speak to our grandmother, someone who could have taken us in if she'd been willing. It was in the file; the social workers asked her to consider it, and they went as far as doing a full home inspection to check it was suitable. But she pulled out at the last minute, leaving us in a children's home. I've been preparing myself for this for weeks, to look the woman in the eye and ask how she could have done that to us.

I think Morna knows. I've seen it in her eyes, whenever she looks at me and Lauren. She knows we're her grand-daughters. It's almost been like a dance, seeing which of us would say something first, but perhaps Morna's avoiding it, knowing how angry the two of us will be. And oh, I am so angry, but it's nothing compared to how Lauren will feel when she finds out, I know that for certain.

Lost in my thoughts, I realise I've slowed down. Brought back to my current predicament, I turn around and see someone coming towards me along the path. Too late, I realise I should have stuck to the woods rather than running so openly, where my tracks can be followed and I can be seen across the marshes.

As I see their face turn in my direction, their eyes light on me and narrow. I feel a jolt of recognition, swiftly followed by a burst of fear. Is this the killer? Is this who murdered Alec in cold blood? I have a horrible feeling I'm right, though I don't know why they did it, or why they're after me now. All I know is that I have to start running again.

The trees seem to press in on me as I leave the path, my head darting from left to right as I try to look for obstacles while still making progress. Every moment, I'm expecting to feel an impact as I'm shot, but nothing comes. Without sound, everything around me seems surreal – no pounding of my feet, no tearing of breath, no whistling of the wind around me. I don't feel like I'm making any progress, as if I'm trapped underwater and fighting my way through the depths.

My head whips around again, trying to get a look at my pursuer, but there's no sign of anyone. It's worse than if I'd been able to see them, because now they could be anywhere. They could be creeping up behind me, just out of sight, and I wouldn't be any the wiser.

I feel a whooshing sensation as something moves quickly past my face, but I can't stop to find out what it was. It might have been some more snow falling from a tree, or it could have been something thrown by the person chasing me, in an effort to slow me down.

My breathing is laboured now, exhausted as I am, both from the running and the fear. If I carry on like this, I'm going to collapse. Spotting a fallen tree up ahead, I scramble over it then duck down into its shadow. There's a little hollow there that has very little snow in it, and I curl up into the space, making myself as small as possible. I press myself to the ground, feeling for any vibrations caused by someone approaching. Please don't let them find me. Please. Let me stay hidden.

As my breathing and heart rate slow ever so slightly, I try to stay aware of what's around me. At first, I'm not sure I feel anything, but then there it is. The thud in the ground of someone running. I can't stay here; they'll find me.

Springing up, I take my chances and set off running again, not caring which direction I'm heading in. A low-hanging branch catches me a glancing blow on the side of my face, making me gasp, but I don't stop, ducking when I see another one coming at me. This one snags on my rucksack, however, and I fight for a moment to try and untangle it. Fear grips my heart, and I shrug out of the bag and carry on running, not caring that I've left my belongings behind. Right now, the only thing I'm focused on is running.

I think I see a movement, out of the corner of my eye, and I turn my head. Too late. A hand grabs my arm, forcing me around. I fall, my feet slipping on the snow as I try to break free from the grip, aware of the scream rising up inside me, feeling my body shake with it as I let it out into the night air.

# Chapter 32

## Ben

I don't get very far before I hear my name being shouted from behind me. I should have known they'd notice I'd gone, but I wanted to be a bit further away before they came after me. Resigning myself to it, I stop in the middle of the path and wait for Kai and Lauren to catch up.

Lauren throws herself at me, her open palm making contact with my head and sending a sharp bolt of pain running through me.

'Shit! What was that for?'

'You fucking bastard! We've trusted you, this whole time, then you try to give us the slip!'

'I want to find Emily! You said you think the others are still on the reserve. I never should have left her.'

Kai is glaring at me, so he probably assumes I was trying to lose them in the dark, the same as Lauren. I thought by now I'd managed to convince them I didn't kill Alec, but it looks like I was wrong.

'The pair of you are despicable,' Lauren spits, and I

notice that Kai seems to be bearing the same brunt of her hatred as me. What happened in the ten minutes since I left the education block?

'Well, whatever you think of us, you're stuck with us now,' Kai says, and I can see all the fight has gone out of him. 'We might as well get on with it, then we can find the others, somehow call the police, then you can shop every single one of us for whatever crimes you think we've committed.'

I feel like I've stumbled into the middle of an argument between them, and I have no idea where it started, but now isn't the time to ask.

'That's all I was trying to do,' I insist. 'I want to find the others. Kai was stalling, and I thought he'd win you over,' I say with a nod at Lauren. 'So I thought I'd get a head start.'

Lauren's lip curls, but she nods. 'I'm walking at the back, so neither of you can disappear.'

I look between the two of them, still wondering what I've missed, but knowing if I ask I'll feel the wrath of both of them. I realise I'm not feeling quite as cold; it looks like the snow has finally stopped falling.

We set off along the path again and all we can hear is the sound of our own footsteps crunching in the thick layer coating the path. The marks where we walked earlier are either completely covered by fresh snow, or starting to freeze over, and I slip a couple of times.

'I think I can find us a different route out of the reserve. There's only one other point that has a fence we can get over, and if we go back along the path towards the hides we'll be going in the same direction as the others. If they found the right point, they'll be near the road by now. If they didn't, hopefully we'll find them. Now it's stopped snowing the visibility will be easier.' Lauren looks up, to where the moon is emerging from behind a cloud, bathing everywhere around us in an eerie silver light.

'They're probably long gone,' Kai mutters. 'The police might be on their way by now. If we sit inside, we can wait it out.'

Lauren spins around and glares at him. 'And what if you're wrong? What if one of the others dies out here tonight as well? Will you be able to live with yourself?' She turns around and carries on walking, and a moment later Kai prods me in the back to tell me to follow her.

I get it, I do. She's the one who works here so she takes it personally that something bad has happened while she's in charge. She made such a big thing about us being allowed onto the reserve on Boxing Day, when it's closed to the general public, as if we should all be grateful she'd done it for us. If Alec and Lauren ever came to blows it was because each of them saw themselves as the person in charge. Alec had been coming here for years, long before Lauren started working here, so he thought he knew far more than she ever could. Probably her being a woman hadn't helped. Alec was that sort of bloke, unfortunately.

Thinking about him gives me a small pang of regret, knowing he's dead. I didn't really believe it at first. Seeing Lauren and Kai now has been an eye opener. They're scared, that's obvious, and it's coming out in different ways. I just hope neither of them take it out on me again.

There's a sharp pain in my head and I suck in my breath between my teeth. Dan put some sort of antiseptic on it that stung like a bastard, but any numbing effects it had have worn off by now. It had better bloody work. If there's an infection in it and I'm stuck out here much longer I don't really want to think about what might happen. I blame myself – if I hadn't been so hell bent on getting Alec on his own earlier, it wouldn't have happened. I should have just gone with Emily, asked her out like I intended, and then maybe I would be with her right now instead of these two, sandwiched between them like a prisoner.

My steps falter slightly and I stumble on a rock that's hidden beneath the snow.

'Guys, can I just have a minute?' I ask. I feel a bit dizzy, like everything has slowed down for a moment. Kai puts a hand on my back, but Lauren doesn't alter her pace. 'Seriously, I feel like crap.'

Lauren huffs and turns to look at me. 'We can't stop for long,' she snaps. 'You need to try and keep moving.'

'I'll try, just walk a bit slower,' I say.

'Come on, I'll give you a hand,' Kai says, slinging my arm over his shoulder. I'm not sure that's going to help, considering he's injured too, but taking a bit of the weight off my own feet keeps me going for a bit longer.

When we reach the railway bridge, I look up at the brickwork overhead, then stumble backwards as this move-ment makes me lose my balance. I catch Kai unawares and we both fall onto our arses, letting out grunts of pain. He gets straight up again and puts out a hand to help me, but in front of us Lauren keeps moving.

'What's her problem?' I mutter to Kai, but all I get in return is a raised eyebrow.

It's another few minutes until we reach the shortcut between the two paths, the one that goes down a steep dip, where Kai fell earlier. We can't see the steps under the snow, and Lauren stands at the top of the bank, looking at it with a critical eye.

'I don't know if it's safest to try and find the steps or just take a leap and scramble down.'

'Can't we go round?' I ask.

She shakes her head. 'It'll take too long.'

Kai steps away from me and joins her. 'If you take it slowly you should be okay to get down. Probably safer to go down where you know it's just a slope than take the risk with the steps. If you miss a step in this, you could break an ankle.' They both glance at me, and I know they're thinking they've got enough dead weight as it is without Lauren getting hurt too.

I look down the bank and swallow hard. It's steeper than I remember, and this dizziness has completely thrown my balance. My head is throbbing and the wound feels hot, as if the dressing Dan put on it is squeezing it too tightly. I'm just going to have to slide down on my arse and hope for the best.

Lauren and Kai are looking at each other. 'Go on then,' she says to him, nodding to the slope. He wants to protest, I can tell, but he knows as well as I do that there's no arguing with Lauren when she's in this mood.

Swearing quietly, Kai crouches down, then swings a leg over the edge. He's going down on his back, his feet scrabbling beneath him. About halfway down his top half gains more momentum than he's expecting and he starts to fall faster, catching himself just before he hits the bottom. He groans, but we can both tell he's okay, and a moment later he struggles to his feet.

271

I step forward, assuming Lauren will want me to go next, but she's already turned around and is starting her descent. She's going the opposite way from Kai, so she's facing the bank, which makes a lot more sense to me. Her jaw clenched tightly, she scrambles and slides down to the bottom.

Now it's my turn, and I glance to the side, where I know the steps begin. Maybe it would be better to try and find them, I think, but then I remember what Kai said. Missing a step in the snow could be a lot more dangerous than just sliding down a bank. But if I go backwards, like Lauren did, I won't be able to see where I'm going. Still, hers looked the easiest way, so I turn around and copy her.

It's going well until I hit a tree root part of the way down. It's probably what tripped Kai up too, I realise, as I'm thrown off balance and land hard on my left shoulder, letting out a cry of pain as I do. It's agony, and it bursts through me as I lie there, face down in the snow. A moment later Kai is there, helping me up again, but I shake my head. I can't move for a moment.

'Come on,' Lauren barks. 'We don't have time for this.'

'Give him a break, he's got a bloody head wound and he's just wrenched his shoulder.'

'Oh, come on. Dan said it was only a graze.'

'That doesn't mean it doesn't hurt. And he's lost a lot of blood, don't forget that.'

I listen to the two of them arguing for a moment, glad of the chance to stop moving, until I feel the cold start to seep through my trousers. They're supposedly water-proof, but they certainly haven't done much to keep me warm over the last couple of hours.

I sit up and look at them, Lauren standing with her arms folded, Kai inspecting the bank on the other side.

'The steps are clearer over here,' he says, sweeping some snow from a couple with his hand. 'I think if we're careful we can get up them.'

Before Lauren has a chance to respond, Kai is starting up the steps, sweeping snow off as he goes. I can tell he's trying to make it easier for me so that I don't slow everything down too much more, and I'm grateful, even if his main motivation is to keep Lauren sweet. I benefit from it regardless, and that's what matters to me.

This time, Lauren stays behind in the hollow while I climb the steps. They're cut into the bank at an angle, so I'm forced to lean on my left arm to keep my balance, which makes me wince every time. I'm worried I injured my shoulder when I fell, but I know Lauren won't want to stop so I can check. When I'm halfway up I hear a forced sigh from below, and I know Lauren has got too impatient and is following me up. I hope I don't fall on her, though at least she'd make for a softer landing than the stony ground below.

At last, all three of us are at the top. I'm considering chancing another rest before I faint, when a terrible sound rips through the air. We all turn and stare in the direction it's coming from before looking back at each other. I can see fear in Kai's eyes, but it's nothing to that in Lauren's. The scream stops as abruptly as it began. She inhales sharply then says just one word.

'Emily.'

A moment later, Lauren is running.

# Chapter 33

## Dan

'What the hell are you doing? I'm trying to help you!' I struggle with Emily as she writhes in my arms, deftly avoiding a swift kick she aims at my ankles. I know I'm a lot stronger than her, but I don't want to hurt her. That's not why I was following her.

Why won't she listen to me? I'd been behind her for a good ten or fifteen minutes before I finally caught up to her, and all that time I'd been calling out to her. It's only when I glance at her now that I realise she doesn't have those things stuck to the side of her head, the bits of her hearing aids. She told me once that they're held on with magnets, that there's a piece of metal inside each side of her skull, and she always sets off metal detectors at airports so has to carry a special medical card. Well, they're not there now, neither of them. Does that mean she can't hear me?

I'm still struggling with her, trying to wrestle her into a sitting position, but now I try to turn her around so she can see my face. The fear in her eyes is so obvious it takes me aback for a moment, but when she sees me she is still at last.

'Can you hear me?' I ask, and I see a frown cross her face, but she doesn't answer me. I point to my ears, and she shakes her head. That explains it. I wonder how scared she must have been, running around a nature reserve in the middle of the night, not being able to hear anything.

'I want to help you.' I point to myself, then to her as I say it, but she doesn't seem to understand me. Or maybe she doesn't believe me. She's smart, I know that, and I know she won't know who to trust. So it's important I get her to trust me, or we're going to be right back where we started earlier this evening.

'Come with me.' I try to indicate this one with gestures as well, and she nods slowly. I let my grip on her relax and she turns, looking at me with such a penetrating gaze I feel like she can see exactly what I'm thinking. Which is why I'm completely unprepared when, a moment later, she shoves me over and starts running again.

'Shit.' I'm on my backside in the snow and she's on the move again, but at least she's going in the direction I want her to, back towards where Morna is waiting in the big hide. If I can keep Emily moving in that direction, eventually I'll be able to catch her again.

She moves faster than I expect, so as soon as I'm on my feet I need to get going again if I'm going to catch her. From here there's only one way she can go, so I sprint after her, keeping an eye out for any potential obstacles. Hopefully she'll stay on the path, which will make my job a bit easier, but if she's trying to lose me, I'm expecting she'll dart back into the woods.

Running through snow on a night like this makes me think of Rachel, and try as I might, I can't stop my mind from going there. We met when we were out running, when I was between offshore trips. It was one evening in early March, and we'd had some beautiful weather that week, but then suddenly the temperature had plummeted again and we'd been forecast snow. I didn't believe it, so I set off on my evening run anyway. There wasn't a lot that could mess with my routine back then, and I wanted to get my miles in.

It was on my way home that I saw her, running ahead of me. She slipped and slid on a patch of ice, but then righted herself and carried on. There was something about the grace of her movements that caught my eye, and I found myself thinking about her as I ran. She was still ahead of me when I reached the same patch of ice, but being a clumsy brute I went down heavier than a felled oak.

She must have heard, because she turned around and came back to see if I was okay. Whenever we told the story to friends and family, how we met, we painted it as the hero rescuing the damsel in distress. Nobody expected the punchline, that I was the one who needed the help. She got me up off the floor and helped me limp home, making sure I was inside and comfortable before finishing her run. I offered to make her a drink, help her warm up, but she refused. She still had another couple of miles to do and she didn't want to get too comfy, she told me. When I offered her my phone number, I hadn't expected her to take it, but she did, with a laugh.

It took her a week to call me. That was the longest week of my life, and I'm not ashamed to admit it. I couldn't stop thinking about her, and I didn't even care that my mates were giving me shit about falling while I was out running. All I wanted was to hear her voice again, see her face and that beautiful smile. When she finally called, I couldn't believe my luck.

The whole of my relationship with Rachel was like that. I couldn't believe how lucky I was that she'd picked me. She was everything I could ever want in a woman – smart, funny, independent, beautiful. She didn't hang off my every word, but challenged me when I said something she disagreed with. When she was wrong, she was quick to apologise, and I found myself behaving the same way, so the communication in our relationship was the best I've ever experienced.

Those memories are like a punch to the gut right now, out here in the snow. Knowing that someone I've spent time with in this group was the one who killed her, who drove so recklessly through the streets one night that they didn't even notice a heavily pregnant woman crossing the road. A woman who had nipped out for a McDonald's milkshake at a stupid time of night, because she was craving them, and her husband was on an oil rig, hundreds of miles away instead of being at home with her, catering to her every whim. I'm furious at the person who killed her and got away with it, but that doesn't compare to the rage I feel at myself for not being there with her, for not finding a way to get home and be with her. It should have been me going out that night, looking for the one food she was craving, bringing it home for her. She shouldn't have had to do it all by herself. She'd been to scans and midwife appointments alone, had even spent a night in hospital alone, and then she died alone. And it was my fault.

I stop, squeezing my eyes shut and trying to force thoughts of Rachel from my mind. I have to hold it together, at least until I finish what I've started. Right now, the important thing is to find Emily and get her into that hide with Morna. Then I can find Ben, Lauren and Kai. They'll be around here too, I'm sure. There's no indication that they've managed to alert the police, no sirens wailing or helicopter hovering overhead. I should never have let everyone split up in the first place. I'm used to asserting my authority at work, so I should have put it to better use here. It was the shock, seeing Alec's body lying there. It threw me for a moment.

Setting off again, I realise I've lost sight of Emily. This is the worst thing that could have happened. I jog a little way up the path, looking for Emily's footprints in the snow. It's stopped snowing, so it's difficult to see the difference between her most recent prints and the ones I made earlier, but with a bit of effort I think I can see which are hers. Hopefully she's just gone round this next corner, rather than ducking back into the woods.

A moment later, something slams into my midriff and I fall to my knees, completely winded. I look up, and Emily is standing there, her eyes blazing, a dead branch in her hands. It's huge, and I'm momentarily impressed that she can even lift it, let alone swing it.

'Why are you chasing me?' she asks, and her voice sounds strange, different from usual. I remember that she can't hear anything, which must be disconcerting, if you can't even hear what you're saying.

I shake my head and hold my hands up in a gesture that I hope shows her that I don't want to hurt her. She glares at me.

'Leave me alone. I don't want your help.' She turns away, but then thinks better of it and throws the branch back at me. It doesn't make the impact she's hoping for, but the bruise it leaves on my leg will certainly sting for a few minutes. Heading into the woods, she's running again, and I watch her go, knowing she'll reach the boundary fence at some point. She won't be able to keep going forever, and I hope my stamina is still as good as it used to be.

I can still see her between the trees, so I walk along the path, keeping an eye on her as she goes. This is what I'm good at, and I know I can keep it up longer than she can. Why won't she just let me help her? I know fear can do strange things to people, but I don't look any more threatening than I did earlier. Something must have happened for her to stop trusting me, but I can't think what it might be.

A moment later I glance up and she's gone. Wise to her moves after last time, I look around for signs that she's crept back around to hit me again, but I don't think she'd do that twice. It was a very risky move, and she can't guarantee she'll get away with it again. Leaving the path, I strike out into the woods, looking for her tracks as I go. She wasn't moving particularly quietly, but now I stop and listen I can't hear anything that sounds like she's making progress through the woods. So, she's stopped, which means all I have to do is find out where she is.

Easier said than done, I tell myself ten minutes later,

when I still can't find any sign of her in the woods. This is one of the densest parts, so the snow cover on the ground is quite sparse – it couldn't make it through the canopy, and a lot of it is resting on the branches above my head. I'm suddenly wary, knowing what might happen if that weight of snow suddenly falls on me, or worse, brings a branch down with it. I turn back to the path and make my way back there, accepting defeat for now.

As I walk, I glance across the marshes towards the hide where Morna is now waiting, and I see a light flashing from the windows. I told her to turn on the lights in there if Emily made it back, but this looks like it's coming from a torch. I watch for a while longer, seeing a system of flashes that reminds me of Morse code. What the hell is she doing? Picking up speed, I start running back along the path, before the stupid cow ruins everything.

# Chapter 34

## Kai

Lauren sets off running before I can even process what's happened. I turn to look at Ben.

'Was that Emily?'

He shrugs, but I can see he looks worried. 'It might have been. I'm sure Lauren knows. She's her sister after all.'

'Right. We need to go after her.'

'Hang on,' Ben says, grabbing my arm. 'Why? If someone's screaming, my instinct is to run away, not towards.'

I glower at him. Fucking coward. He was the one who wanted to find Emily, but as soon as we think she's in immediate danger, he wants to run. 'Fine, you stay here. I'm going to see what the hell has happened to Emily to make her scream like that.'

Ben blushes, and I realise he hadn't even thought of it like that. Some boyfriend he'd make. 'You're right, I'm sorry. I'll come with you.'

As soon as he says this, I realise maybe I would be better off going on my own. Even though it's his head he's hurt, not his leg, he's moving pretty slowly. He's probably weak from the blood loss, which leaves me in a really shit position. Do I leave him behind because he'll slow me down, knowing he might end up dying here in the snow, or do we go together, knowing we probably won't catch up with Lauren?

In the end, he makes the decision for me, setting off along the path in the direction Lauren took. I join him, and we walk in silence for a few minutes. I know I have to go at Ben's pace, letting him set the speed, but I'm itching to go faster. It was clear to me back in the education block that Lauren knew more than she'd been letting on about me and the poaching. Maybe Alec had told her, and she was just biding her time to do something about it. I've been worried that Alec found out about it a few weeks ago, when he'd been birdwatching and I'd been prowling around looking for another way for the guys to get into the reserve. We'd used a few different routes by then, and I thought it was important to keep mixing it up, in case the staff got wise to it. I saw him, but I can't be sure he'd seen me, and he never came out and said anything directly. When I dragged him out of the pub the other day he wasn't making much sense, but I was scared the game was up. I tried to convince my cousin that we needed to change our plan. There's no way I want to go to prison, and if there's someone who can make that happen I don't want to be around them. He was having none of it, though. So what was I supposed to do? I found myself stuck between Alec's drunken threats and the people I have to answer to, and though I'm scared of both I knew Alec was less likely to break my fingers. I turned up today fervently hoping that Alec didn't see anything untoward that day, and hadn't been talking about me, though the odd look he gave me this morning gave me cause to doubt that. I was so glad when he went off into that hide on his own earlier.

As we walk, I can tell Ben is building up to saying something. He keeps taking these weird deep breaths, then shaking his head and letting it out again.

'Just spit it out, will you mate?'

He looks at me and he reminds me of the deer my cousin got, the one time he took me out lamping with him.

'There's obviously something on your mind,' I tell him, and he swallows.

'It's about the shotgun,' he says, and I narrow my eyes.

'What shotgun?'

'The one that someone had, the person who killed Alec?'

I stop and stare at him. 'What about it?'

'I wasn't exactly telling you the truth.'

'The truth about what? Are you telling me you killed Alec?' I back away from him, feeling a mixture of anger and fear igniting my flight response.

'No! No, that's not what I'm saying. I mean, I know where the shotgun is.'

I stare at him for a moment, incredulous.

'Go on.'

'When I got near the hide and the gun went off, I fell over. Hit my head on the ground,' he says, pointing to the back of his skull. I nod, knowing all this, though I hadn't paid much attention to the extent of the injury. Now I look, there's a sizeable egg on his head, hidden by his hair. No wonder he's been feeling woozy, I think.

'Someone jumped over me and ran away from the hide,' he continues. 'They dropped the shotgun as they ran.'

I pause for a minute, trying to take in what he's telling me. 'You're saying whoever killed Alec dropped the shotgun they used? Then, I assume, you picked it up and took it with you?'

Ben shrugs. 'I thought it was better for me to have it, for self-defence, than to just leave it lying there. But then I heard the rest of you in the hide, so I dropped it again.'

'Why did you do that? You could have shown it to us. We could have kept it to protect ourselves!'

'Because I didn't know which one of you killed him, did I?'

There's a long silence between the two of us as we take it all in. Someone in our group killed Alec, and none of us knows who it was. What other secrets have we all been hiding?

'So you took the shotgun, then what? Dropped it in the snow?'

'I hid it when I saw you. I knew you wouldn't trust me if you saw me with a shotgun. You'd just assume I'd killed Alec.'

I look him up and down. 'I'm still not convinced you didn't. But right now, you're in a worse state than me, so I reckon I'm safe enough. But we need to get back to the hide and find the shotgun, before someone else does.'

Ben doesn't look relieved by my pronouncement, but we both carry on walking along the path. I can't see any sign of Lauren, or Emily, but there are footprints in the snow that look reasonably fresh.

'We might as well follow these for a bit,' I say, pointing

them out, and Ben agrees. I think he'd agree with anything I say right now, if it means I'm more likely to believe his story.

'What's the deal with you and Emily, anyway?' I ask, thinking that time might go quicker if we get chatting. I picked the wrong topic, though, because Ben shuts down.

'Nothing.'

'Alright, I was just asking.'

The silence that follows is awkward, and I'm just about to try something else, when I think I see something. Putting out my hand, I stop Ben in his tracks, and nod in the direction I've been looking.

'Do you see that?'

Ben shakes his head, but then a moment later freezes.

'A light.'

'Yeah. Where's it coming from?'

He frowns. 'It must be one of the hides.'

We're looking out across the marshes, and I know he must be right. There's someone inside one of the hides, and they're flashing a torch or something.

'Do you think it means something?' I ask Ben, and he watches for a bit longer.

'I think it's SOS in Morse code. You know, dots and dashes.'

I watch again. 'So the short flashes are dots and the long ones are dashes?'

Ben nods, and I watch again. 'Six dots, three dashes.'

'No, it's three dots, three dashes, then three more dots. S-O-S.' I must be looking completely blank, so he tries to explain. Something about each letter having a unique corresponding pattern of dots and dashes. 'S is three dots,

O is three dashes. Do you remember that alert everyone used to have on their mobiles for a text arriving? That's Morse code for SMS.'

I shake my head. 'I'm a bit too young to remember that, mate.' He rolls his eyes at me, but it's true. My cousin got the first iPhone when I was about nine, and I don't really remember what phones were like before that.

'Whatever,' Ben says. 'That means SOS. Which means someone is in trouble.'

'In one of the hides?'

He shrugs. 'I think that's where it's coming from.'

We keep walking, but I'm thinking about this and I'm not happy. 'What if it's a trap?'

'Why would it be a trap?'

It's my turn to shrug. 'I don't know. I just have a feeling something's not right. Why would someone be signalling to us from inside a hide?'

'Even if it is a trap, I think we've got to go and see.' Ben sounds a lot more confident than I feel. He's right, though. I know I won't forgive myself if something happens to one of the others while we're out here.

There's something about this group that gets me emotional sometimes. I know I don't deserve them, with the way I've behaved. But what they don't realise is that even if I didn't join them with the best of intentions, I've since realised that here is finally something I'm interested in. I haven't told anyone, but I've even been looking at college courses I can do, things like conservation and environment studies. Lauren's job looks ace, and I've been talking to Morna about what she does for volunteering. But I think if I want to do that, I'm going to have to move away. Pay off my debts, cut ties with my cousin, and my bloodsucking dad. I don't want to lose the friends I've made here, though.

I think about the look Lauren gave me when she said something about my 'poacher friends'. She knows, and I don't doubt she'll tell all the others, then they'll hate me. They won't understand how it happened, why it happened. All they'll see is someone who joined their group to try and make some money out of the animals and birds on this reserve. And that makes me sad.

Ben seems weighed down by his own thoughts too, and we don't speak as we walk. I notice he's starting to slow down, then suddenly he sways and grabs onto me. I slip my arm across his back to support him, then guide him over to a tree where he can lean a moment to rest.

'You need to give me some warning when you're going to do that,' I tell him, only half joking. 'If you keel over, I don't think I can carry you.'

Ben gives me a weak smile. 'Sorry. It just sort of washed over me, you know?'

I wonder again if he has a concussion from when he fell. The last thing we need is to be going further into the reserve, away from the only route in for the emergency services, but now we've come this far I don't really think we can go back. I just have to hope he's okay and can make it to the hide.

'Do you have any water?' he asks me, and I wonder how long it is since he had anything to eat. I dig a chocolate bar out of my bag and hand it over along with my water bottle, and he wolfs it down gratefully. I could do with some energy myself, but I figure he needs it more than I do. My ankle is only giving me the odd twinge now, and I feel a bit embarrassed about making such a big deal of it earlier. The colour of Ben's skin is not a healthy one, I can see that even by the weak light of the moon over the marshes.

'Think you can carry on?' I ask him, and he looks doubtful, but then nods his head firmly. 'You sure? We can rest longer if you need.'

We take another couple of minutes, and in that time we see the light flashing again. I think I hear a shout in the distance, but it could have come from anywhere. There are no more screams, and I can't hear anyone running either. That's almost more unnerving than if I could hear some big fight going on in the trees. Where's Lauren? Has she found Emily? What if something's happened to both of them?

'Come on, I'm ready,' Ben says, and he stands, swaying slightly until he gets his balance. I take his arm and swing it over my shoulders again, and he doesn't protest. What a pair we make, I think, as we carry on along the path, all the time fervently hoping that the person we're running from doesn't turn out to be the one we're now walking towards.

# Chapter 35

## Lauren

Whatever issues I have with my sister, I don't even hesitate when I hear her scream. Something has happened to her, and I need to know what, and who's responsible. For several minutes I run headlong along the path, not caring who might hear me or see me, until I realise I can't hear any other sounds coming from the woods. I ran in the direction of the scream when I first heard it, but now I have no idea where Emily might be.

'Emily!' I call her name, but my voice sounds hoarse. It comes out as little more than a whisper, and I don't try again. I don't want anyone else finding me.

It was definitely her screaming, I'm certain. We shared a room for years as kids, and she had nightmares. I'll always be able to identify her voice. Is she hurt? I shiver as I think about it.

Slowing down, I maintain a gentle jog along the path, keeping my eyes on the woods as much as possible as I run. The snow slows me down a lot, and I know I would have been able to cover this ground much faster if the weather hadn't turned on us. Still, now the moon is out, it makes it a little easier to see, because the light reflects off the snow.

Hang on. There's another light. I stop for a moment and look out over the marshes. It's coming from the large hide. Someone's in there. I feel my heart beating rapidly, and I realise I'm scared of who it is, and why they're signalling. Could it be something to do with Kai?

Alec told me about his suspicions that Kai was connected to the poachers a couple of weeks ago, though he had no evidence. It's under investigation, which is why I haven't confronted Kai about it, but for now my boss wants me to keep an eye on him in case he does anything that causes suspicion. That's easier said than done, because I can't imagine him wandering off in the middle of a group walk, pretending to be having a piss behind a tree when he's actually hunting deer. No, my suspicions are that Kai doesn't actually do any of the poaching himself. He's definitely in on it, though. It was risky, taking him to task like that earlier, but the look on his face told me all I needed to know.

Right now, though, it doesn't matter. I don't think whatever's happening here tonight is anything to do with poachers. I'm starting to think it might be my fault, or at least that it might be a result of something I set in motion. I just hadn't expected . . . No, I can't think about it that way. Right now, what matters is finding my sister.

I slow down, because running is just too difficult in snow, and it's thicker on this part of the path. It only comes up to my ankles, but that's enough right now. My shoes are waterproof, but I feel the snow start to seep into my socks, where it comes up over the tops. Ugh, that's the last thing I need. Having wet feet in this kind of environment could be really problematic – blisters, certainly, but also greater chance of me getting frostbite. Is there anything in my bag that can help? I don't think so, but glancing to my right I realise there's a lot less snow just a little way into the woods. I leave the path and start walking between the trees.

It's still not easy going, because I don't have a smooth, straight path, and I keep needing to walk around trees or clumps of rocks. As I walk, I keep the path visible on my left, so I don't get lost. That's not always as easy as it sounds; there's something about walking in the woods that can make you lose your bearings quite easily, if you're not careful. Still, I keep checking in regularly to make sure I can still see the marshes easily between the trees.

The light from the largest hide seems to have stopped, or at least I haven't seen it for a few minutes. I pause, looking out in that direction, and there it is again. A rhythmic series of flashes – what does it mean? I've never learnt any sort of signalling code, but it's clear whoever is making the light is trying to communicate something. But is it someone who needs help, or someone trying to entice us in? I have to take the risk that I might be walking into danger.

I keep walking for a while, always on the lookout for signs of anyone else in the woods. Emily must be around here somewhere. She doesn't know the woods, barely knows her way around the reserve using the paths, so I'm sure she's lost. How can I find her, though, when I want to stay as quiet as possible? There are some scuffed tracks on the path, but they could have been made by any of us,

I think. But then I look closely – some of the footprints were made recently, after it stopped snowing, because no snow has filled them. That means someone else was going along here, in the same direction as me, not long ago.

The shiver that runs down my back is nothing to do with the sub-zero temperature. I could turn around and go back, now. I've lost Kai and Ben, and I could loop back around behind them without them ever knowing. Then I could get to the visitor centre, sneak past whoever is in there, and get away from here as quickly as possible. That's if I can get my car out of the car park.

Even as I think of it, I know I'm not going to do it. If Ben is the one who killed Alec, then Kai is in danger. If it was one of the others, I'm probably the one who's in danger. But we need to end this, once and for all.

Turning a corner, I can no longer see the largest hide across the marshes, and I know it won't come back into sight until I'm quite close to it. Stopping, I pick up a decent-sized rock from the ground, wiping the snow off it and clutching it in my fist. My mind goes to the knife at the bottom of my bag, but I don't want to stop to dig it out. The rock might not be much of a weapon, but it's the best option right now. I can feel myself trembling slightly with nerves, but I press on.

Suddenly, there's a movement. Someone is on the path, not far ahead. I stop, holding my breath. I can't see who it is, so I take a risk and step out onto the path.

'Dan?' Of all the people in the group for me to bump into, I'm glad it's him. I feel safe with him, knowing he can't have been the one to kill Alec – he was in a hide with Morna at the time, and there's no way she would protect someone if she thought they'd committed murder. Plus, he barely knew Alec; there was no time for him to have built up any sort of grudge against him.

Dan turns and peers at me through the darkness.

'Lauren? What are you doing here? I thought you and the other two would be at the visitor centre by now.'

'Kai hurt himself, then we saw someone inside the visitor centre. Poachers. It wasn't safe, so we turned around.'

'What about Ben?' There's a sharpness to his tone. 'Where is he? We need to make sure we know where he is at all times.'

'He's with Kai.' I don't tell him that I ran away from both of them when I heard Emily scream. 'Where are Morna and Emily?' I ask, realising that he, too, is alone.

He tells me a story about Morna having a panic attack and disappearing into the woods, then the pair of them losing Emily when he went after Morna.

'I'm sorry, Lauren. I feel really bad. I was supposed to be the one keeping them safe.'

'Did you hear a scream, not long ago? I'm sure it was Emily. We need to find her.'

He hesitates, then glances into the woods, over my shoulder. Is there something behind me? I don't look, keeping my eyes on him, willing him to answer me.

'I did, but I didn't know who it was. I've been looking for her, but I haven't found her yet.'

I nod, unsure of what to say. This whole evening seems completely surreal, and I know now that we should never have split up. The best thing is to get everyone back together again, and I tell him as much.

He nods. 'I left Morna in the big hide, the funny-shaped

one,' he says, nodding vaguely in its direction. 'She was getting so worked up, I thought I'd be better looking for Emily on my own. The plan was to find her, get her back to the hide, then wait for help to arrive. If we can't get out, the rest of you had better come that way too.' There's a dark look on his face. 'I said from the start that we needed to stay together, rather than go running off in different directions. Now look where it's got us.'

I feel my face burn, interpreting that as a dig at me. He's right, though, and I can't argue with him. Then I remember the light.

'So that's Morna, back there, shining a light out of the windows?'

His eyes widen slightly. 'I think so. I was on my way back to check on her. Make sure she's okay.'

'I'll come with you.'

He looks like he's about to tell me not to, but he was the one who just said we should all congregate in the same place seeing as none of us has managed to get out of the reserve. I start walking, and a moment later he follows me. As we walk, I tell him about the poachers, and also about Alec reporting his belief that Kai was part of their gang. I don't understand the dynamic there – we're pretty sure he's involved, yet he seems to be scared of them. He's obviously made an effort to stop us finding out about them, but it doesn't feel like he's doing it in order to avoid getting in trouble with the police. And I overheard Kai talking to Alec about the wildlife the other week, and Kai genuinely seemed like he wanted to learn. It's something I want to get to the bottom of, but now isn't the time.

'Why do you think Morna's flashing her torch out of

the window?' I ask now, hoping that keeping the conversation going will make me feel a little less scared.

Dan takes a moment before he answers. 'I don't know. That's what worries me. I told her to turn the lights on if Emily turned up at the hide, or anyone else, so then I knew she wasn't alone, but like you say, this looks more like a torch. Which makes me wonder if it is Morna, or if someone else has found her there.'

'Who?' I ask. Ben and Kai are together, and I know they're further back around the path than we are. I heard Emily scream in the woods, but there's always a chance she was further away than I thought. Snow does strange things to acoustics in outdoor environments. But why would Emily pose a threat to Morna? I can't imagine my sister scaring anyone. But then, I remind myself, how well do I really know her?

We round a corner and we can see the hide in front of us. Dan slows down slightly and I tense. I realise I'm still holding the rock I picked up earlier, and I wrap my fingers around it a little more tightly now. The door is around the side, so we pick our way through the snow.

A banging noise startles me and I jump. Someone is banging on the inside of the door.

'Help! Let me out! Is anyone there?'

Now I can see the door, I realise there's a thick branch wedged under it, with snow deliberately piled up around it, to prevent anyone who's inside from opening the door.

'What the hell?' I say, more to myself than to Dan. Dropping the rock, I start using my hands to dig away the snow, but before I make much progress pain blooms from the back of my skull and everything goes black.

# Chapter 36

## Morna

There's someone outside. I can hear them.

I stop hammering on the door and back away slightly, listening. A voice – it sounds like Lauren, I think. There's a scrabbling sound, then a thud, then nothing more.

Holding my breath, I back away from the door again, slowly. I don't want my feet to make a sound, but the floorboards creak treacherously beneath me.

When Dan left me in here, I was fine to begin with. Of course, I jumped at every sound, every suggestion of movement outside the window, but I felt like I was in the safest place possible. Then I started to feel claustrophobic, and decided I would step outside for a moment, check there was no sign of anyone else nearby. That was when I discovered I couldn't get the door open. The snow was coming down quite heavily, but I didn't think it would have drifted enough to block the door.

Now I can hear something else coming from outside. A scraping noise, followed by a hollow thunk, and the

299

door opens. Dan is silhouetted in the doorway, and his bulk makes me bite back a cry. He's holding Lauren under the arms and dragging her into the hide.

'Dan?' I ask quietly. 'What happened? What happened to Lauren?'

He turns to look at me, and the expression on his face silences me. I daren't even breathe as he pulls her further into the hide then shuts the door behind him.

I rush over to help Lauren, to check she's okay, but Dan puts himself between me and her, glaring at me until I take a step back.

'She hit her head.'

I get the feeling this isn't the full story, but I don't want to question him right now. He looks different, like he was wearing a mask earlier that he's no longer bothered about maintaining.

Dan looks back at the door, then runs his fingers over the wood. 'No good,' he says, shaking his head, then shrugs his bag off his shoulders and opens it up. A moment later, he pulls out a length of rope, and I feel an iron fist constrict around my chest. What the hell is he doing? Dan is the one who's been keeping me safe all evening, me and Emily. Oh God, where is Emily?

'Morna, if you fight with me now, it's just going to make everything more difficult for both of us. Do you understand that?'

I try to swallow, but my throat is dry and has a lump in it the size of a golf ball. 'I understand,' I say, though it comes out as more of a croak. I try again. 'I understand.'

He sniffs, then nods at one of the benches. 'Go and sit down.'

I do as he says, shuffling backwards rather than risking turning away from him. I don't believe his story about what happened to Lauren, and I don't trust him not to do something similar to me while my back is turned.

Sitting down, I wait patiently while he comes around behind me and ties my wrists together. He does it tightly, pulling the knots so my shoulders are tugged back, giving me a shooting pain up to my neck from both sides.

'Do I need to do your feet, too?'

I shake my head, meekly. I don't want him to think I'm going to try any heroics – it's the last thing on my mind. I just want him to finish what he's doing, and go, but my curiosity gets the better of me.

'Dan. Why are you doing this?' I keep my voice as soft as I can manage it. He looks up at me in surprise.

'An eye for an eye, Morna.'

With that, he leaves me and crosses over to Lauren. She's still unconscious, but I can see her chest rising and falling so at least I know she's alive. I can't see any blood, so hopefully he didn't hit her that hard. Dan rolls Lauren onto her side, wrenches her arms behind her back and ties her wrists, too.

'She's not even conscious, you don't need to do that.'

He narrows his eyes at me. 'And what if she comes to before I get back? No, I need to know you're both exactly where I left you. No more of this idiocy, running round a nature reserve in the snow in the middle of the night. This ends here.'

He stands up, leaving Lauren lying on her side, then leaves the hide. After the door bangs shut, I hear the scrape of him pushing something up against the door, trapping

Lauren and me inside. The sound of my own blood rushing in my ears is enough to drown out any noise he makes as he walks away, and I start to feel a bit light-headed, so I shuffle back a bit on the bench to make sure I'm balanced and lean forward, putting my head between my knees. I remember the way Emily told me to breathe, determined not to have another panic attack. Fainting won't do me any good, either.

How can it have been Dan? That's the one thing that keeps going round in my mind. He and I were in the same hide, he can't have killed Alec. But then I remember my headphones, and the white noise I turned up while I stood and looked out of the hatch. He must have crept out when I was busy watching the Starlings, then ran straight back after he shot Alec, knowing I wouldn't have heard it. It was a risky move on his part, but it obviously worked. I didn't suspect him, not for a moment. The one person I was sure I could trust is the one I should have been running from.

But why would Dan hurt Alec? Had Alec managed to find out something about Dan in the short space of time they'd known each other? Lauren had told me something about Dan having a recent tragedy he needed time to get over, but that was all she shared. Could it be connected? What did he mean by 'an eye for an eye'? If he wanted revenge for something Alec had done, I don't understand why he's behaving like this. Alec is already dead.

On the other side of the hide, Lauren begins to stir. I hold my breath, waiting to see if she'll say anything, but she only groans and keeps her eyes shut. It's another minute or two before her eyelids flicker, and she squints at me across the hide. My eyes are accustomed to the gloom in here so I can see her quite clearly, but she might be struggling to make me out.

'Morna?'

'Lauren, are you okay?'

She tries to move, then realises her wrists are tied and she swears. 'What happened? I was with Dan, looking for Emily. I heard her scream.'

I inhale sharply at this. Earlier I'd heard a sound across the marshes, but I wasn't sure what it was. Please let Emily be okay, I pray to any God who might be listening. Please, let her stay hidden from Dan.

'My head hurts.'

'I think Dan hit you,' I tell her. 'I'm tied up too. I'm sorry, I can't really do much to help you.'

I watch as she rolls onto her back, then manages to sit up. She shuffles backwards on her bum until she's leaning against the wall of the hide, then she lets out a sigh.

'Dan. How can it have been him? What did I miss?'

'I've just been asking myself the same thing.'

She turns to me with a calculating stare. 'You never said he left the hide. You said you were together when Alec was shot.'

I hang my head and explain about the headphones. I expect her to berate me, but she just sighs again.

'My head really hurts.'

'I have some painkillers in my bag, but they're no use if neither of us can get them out.' It's lying on the floor next to Lauren, so she shuffles over and turns her back to the bag, her fingers scrabbling at the zips. Her bonds are too tight, however, and she soon gives up, and slumps back against the wall, frustrated.

'What the hell are we going to do?'

I shrug. 'What can we do? I don't know how we can get away from here. We might just have to hope that one of the others has managed to call the police.'

She shakes her head. 'Doubt it, Kai and Ben are too busy bickering, and we couldn't get to the visitor centre.' I want to ask what happened, but she doesn't seem to be in the mood to talk.

'Lauren, I'm so sorry,' I begin, but she rolls her eyes at me.

'Morna, this isn't the time. We were all in the wrong here, none of us realised it was Dan. How could we?'

'I'm not talking about that,' I say, but I know my voice is so quiet she hasn't heard me. I want to come out with it; I want to tell her that I'm her grandmother, that I made the colossal mistake of thinking that my tearaway daughter needed to learn to stand on her own two feet without help from me. Then, when it all went so horribly, tragically wrong, I couldn't bear the thought of taking the two girls in, not after Sarah died. My husband left when Sarah was thirteen, and neither of us heard from him after that. I blame him for the change in her that led her down that dark path to addiction, but I know I'm just as responsible. Her death was my fault, there's no denying that. I couldn't bring up her daughters with that sort of guilt weighing on me. They deserved better than that.

I never thought they wouldn't get adopted. Two young children, even siblings, had a decent chance of success in the care system, or so I thought. Why didn't I check up on them? Why didn't I make it a priority to keep in touch with their social worker and ask to be updated on how they were doing? Now I see these two beautiful young women, but they're obviously so damaged. One hates the whole world, but focuses it on her sister because of the life they had, even though I'm sure she knows inside that it's not Emily's fault, it never was. The other is desperate for her sister's love and affection, the only person who was a constant throughout her childhood, her only link to family and a sense of belonging. I could have prevented all of that hurt, and I need to shoulder the blame.

I had known Lauren for some time, because I volunteered here when she was doing her apprenticeship, then later when she started her current job, but somehow I didn't connect her with the granddaughters I abandoned. It was only when she introduced us to Emily, a sister she'd never spoken of before, that the realisation dawned on me. Their names haven't changed since they were born, but I had never been told Lauren's surname, and it was only when I heard the two names together, along with Emily's deafness, that I knew who they were. Since then, I've been working out the best way to try and speak to them about it, but I've been a coward. It was only Alec's nosiness that forced my hand and made me decide to tell them today, though that plan went out of the window hours ago.

But how can I put that into words, right now? I can't, and it's not fair to foist it onto Lauren. If she suspects the truth, she's never shown any sign of it.

The door bursts open, making both Lauren and I jump. She scrabbles for purchase with her ankles, trying to shuffle further away from the door, and I sit bolt upright on my bench. Dan has snow in his hair, and something long and metallic in his hand. Oh God. It's the shotgun.

He carefully leans the gun against the wall, where it's out of Lauren's reach but still clearly visible to both of us. I know it's a considered move, threatening us without even needing to say a word.

'Where the hell is Emily?' he growls, his voice low. No need for us to imagine the threat anymore.

'How should we know? You're the one who was with her,' Lauren spits, and despite the circumstances I feel a swell of pride that she can still keep up that attitude in the face of someone who murdered her friend.

Dan snarls and looks over at me. 'You were signalling out of the window. I saw the light. Did you get any response?'

I shake my head. 'Nothing.' I had desperately hoped he hadn't seen that, but I suppose now it doesn't make much of a difference. I'm pretty convinced that he wants to kill me, maybe all of us, and he has all the power right now.

'I'm going to wait here,' he says, pulling a bench over to barricade the door. 'Eventually, she'll come looking for one of you. And then I'll have her.'

I look over at Lauren and she has her chin on her chest, as if she's trying to hold back her emotions, and I wonder if she's as scared for Emily as I am.

# Chapter 37

## Ben

Kai and I press ourselves against the wooden exterior of the hide, holding our breath and hoping we blend into the shadows out here and can't be seen. He points into the woods on the other side of the path, and I nod; we can't stay here, right outside, in case we're seen or heard.

Once we both feel comfortable with the amount of tree cover between us and the hide, we turn to look at each other. I can see the same panic and confusion on Kai's face as must be written on mine. How can it have been Dan? And why is he looking for Emily?

'What the fuck is going on?' Kai whispers, and all I can do is shake my head, still battling with disbelief. 'Did Dan kill Alec?'

I shrug. 'He must have done.'

'But why?'

This one I can't answer. I know Alec liked to be manipulative, play games with people, so maybe he picked the wrong person to try and control. I can't imagine someone like Dan would take kindly to the potential blackmail Alec was hinting at. Me, I was just terrified of what Alec was going to say and to whom, but it never crossed my mind to do anything about it.

I squint back through the trees at the hide and wonder what's going on in there now. Kai had managed to give me a boost up so I could look through the open shutter, and I'd seen Lauren sitting against the wall and Morna on a bench. Morna's wrists were tied behind her back, and from the strange position Lauren was sitting in, I'd assumed hers were the same. Dan was standing just inside the door, with a shotgun next to him, asking them where Emily was.

Emily. My heart thuds with the thought of her. Is she lost out in these woods? Is she running, or has she found somewhere to hide? I just hope she's safe.

'I wish we could find out what's happening, what they're saying,' Kai mutters, and I appreciate the irony. Some of the equipment in the boot of my car would be very useful right now, but I can hardly trudge another three or four miles back through the snow, being careful to avoid the poachers hanging around the visitor centre, just to lay my hands on it. By the time I got back everyone else might be dead.

The thought makes me shiver. Is that what Dan wants? Is he planning on killing the rest of us? I don't want to think about it right now, so I turn my mind back to Emily again.

I wasn't lying when I told Kai and Lauren about taking a photo of Emily without her knowledge, but that also isn't the full story. In fact, it's only the beginning. I admit, I became obsessed with that photo pretty quickly. I found

308

myself looking at it countless times a day, until it wasn't enough for me. It was really hard to get through the month, with only the one picture of her, knowing I wouldn't see her again until our next group meet-up. So when the day finally came around, I snuck another couple of pictures, but within a week I was so desperate to see her again that I made a plan.

In hindsight, I know it was completely crazy, and I shouldn't have done it. But I wasn't thinking straight. From the moment I first saw her, I knew she was the one for me, before I'd even spoken to her. She walked in with Lauren, and I knew straight away that I'd do anything for her. My love for Emily sent me mad in the first month, I swear. At first, I had the idea that I could create an 'accidental' meeting, bump into her in the street then get talking to her that way, but I knew that was going to be too far-fetched. She lives in London, so it's not like I could pretend I was just popping to the shops for some milk and happened to find myself near her flat. Besides, I had no idea where she lived. But I did know where she worked. Maybe I couldn't engineer a meeting, but I could at least try to see her, if only from a distance.

The first time, I took the day off and caught the first train down to London that morning. I found the offices for Emily's company, found a convenient coffee shop that had a view of the front door, and I sat and waited. I was rewarded late in the day, when I saw her leaving, but I was so paralysed by a mixture of obsession and fear that I didn't move out of my seat until it was too late, and she'd vanished into a crowd.

I went back a week later, and followed her home. It

sounds creepy, but hand on my heart I didn't have any bad intentions towards her. I love her, all I want to do is spend time with her, so that's all that was going through my mind. That day, I hung around outside her flat for a while, but other than taking a couple of surreptitious photos of her while we were waiting for the tube, that was all I did.

Now I knew where she lived, I could go down at weekends and see where she went, what she did. It would be easier for me to say I was down in London for a reason on a Saturday – to see a friend, go to a show, something like that. The main thing I wanted was more pictures of her, so I could look at them during the week when I was at work, or at home alone, missing her. So I bought some better photographic equipment, including a longer lens and a night vision camera. It's funny, Alec always used to go on about how important decent equipment was, yet he never guessed I had some stuff that would really make a difference to his birdwatching hobby. It didn't occur to me to use it for wildlife, though.

I only did it a few times, going down to Emily's and waiting outside at night. I didn't know which was her flat in the building for a while, until I saw her at the window once, on the phone. I'd been looking in the wrong place half the time, which irritated me. Anyway, I took some photos, got a few images of her. Nothing sleazy; Emily's not the sort of woman to get undressed with the blinds open, however much the darkest part of my mind hoped she would. The photos were all completely innocent, and they could have stayed my secret. Until Alec had to stick his bloody great nose in.

Of course, it was my own fault. I didn't swap out the

memory cards before our next wildlife walk, so the camera I was using was full of pictures of Emily. I was looking through what I'd taken that morning and must have flicked onto one of her by mistake. Alec snatched it off me and got a good look before I could get it back from him, and it was enough for him to put the pieces together. He didn't even say anything that day. It took a few weeks before he even mentioned it, and then it started as sly little digs. Asking me if I'd seen anything of Emily between our meet-ups. I was too scared to go to London again after that, worried that Alec would tell Emily and she'd have me arrested for stalking. I wasn't stalking her, whatever it sounds like. I just wanted to be close to her, and I was too scared and shy to ask her out. That was going to change today, though.

If it wasn't all so bloody awful, I'd find it funny that the others thought I killed Alec. Yes, I was terrified by what he came out with at the pub last week, and I resolved to do something about it – but that resolution wasn't murder. I went home and I deleted nearly every single photo and video I'd taken of Emily over the last few months, except for that one photo that started it all and some others I couldn't bear to get rid of. The one I showed to Lauren and Kai today is one of only a few I have left. Of course I wanted to keep them, but it was too risky. If Alec told anyone about it, I could deny all knowledge and hopefully people would believe me over him. There's a secret folder on my phone with those photos in, but nobody would be looking there without my knowledge.

The photos were never the end goal, though. I want Emily to be mine, to be a part of my life every day. I haven't got around to asking her out yet, but if I can help save her from Dan then perhaps she'll look on me a little more favourably.

Why the hell is Dan after her, though? Is he trying to get everyone together in the hide? But if that's his aim, why didn't he ask about me and Kai? Lauren would be more likely to know where we are than Emily. No, I think it's specifically Emily he wants. But why? And why did he kill Alec? I can't get my head around it.

'Listen, we need to see if that shotgun you found is still there,' Kai whispers to me. 'Where did you hide it?'

I shake my head. 'It won't be there. Dan has a shotgun, so it must be the same one. I didn't hide it very well.' In fact, I didn't hide it at all, really. I threw it down on the ground, not far from the door to the hide, and hoped for the best, so I should have known that there was a good chance someone else would find it. Maybe Dan found it when he went to check Alec's body – he knew full well what he'd find in that hide, so maybe he used the time to find the shotgun that must have slipped out of his hands.

Kai pulls a face, but he knows I'm right. That weapon isn't an option for us anymore.

'Maybe we could rush the door and overpower him?' he suggests next, but I actually laugh at this suggestion.

'Really? I know you're pretty buff, mate, but have you seen the size of him? I don't think we'll be much of a match for Dan, especially as we're both injured.'

'There are two of us, though,' Kai insists.

'And he's the one with a shotgun. If we can't get it off him, we're fucked. And if something goes wrong, if it goes off while we're fighting or whatever, then someone else could get hurt. I don't want that on my conscience.'

'Fuck,' he mutters, then gives a resigned sigh. 'I'm going to have to go and find us a gun.'

The casual way he says it makes me think he's joking, but I can see from his face that he's serious.

'What? Where the hell . . .?' My voice tails off as I realise what he and Lauren must have been arguing about earlier. 'The poachers? You're one of them?'

He holds up his hands defensively. 'Wait, no. I'm not one of them. But . . . my cousin is, and he makes me help him. I don't have any choice.'

'You always have a choice,' I snap, but he steps forward, his face right in mine.

'Don't make assumptions about anyone else's life.'

We stand nose to nose until he shakes his head and backs off. 'Look, I can get us a gun. That way, we can go in there and we're a match for Dan. We can't do anything useful right now, so we need a weapon to even the score a bit.'

I nod, accepting the truth of what he's saying. 'Fine. But you're going to have to find them pretty damn quickly. I don't know how long Dan is going to stay put in there before he decides to go off hunting Emily again.'

I think Kai can hear the fear in my voice because he reaches over and gives my shoulder a squeeze. 'I'll do what I can. You stay put, alright?'

That's not a promise I'm going to make, but I nod anyway. I watch him leave, running through the snow along the path, slipping a couple of times. Once he's out of sight, I take stock of my surroundings. I need to find Emily before Dan does, but how the hell am I going to do that in these woods?

# Chapter 38

## Emily

Where is he? Is he still looking for me? Holding the panic at bay has been such a mammoth task that I can barely think about anything else. When he grabbed me I honestly thought that was it, he was going to kill me there and then.

I don't know why Dan killed Alec, but I'm certain that's what happened. He's the newest member of the group, we should have known to trust him less than everyone else. I don't care why he did it. All I care about is surviving tonight and getting as far away from here as I can. I'll never complain about the noise and crowds in London ever again.

I'm curled up on the ground with my back to a tree, clutching a branch I found. It's the best I can do right now, so I'm clinging to it as if it will protect me. I don't know how long I've been here, but it's long enough for cramp to set in. I've stopped shivering, at least, though isn't that actually a bad sign? The situation I'm in seems to have divorced me from some of my emotions, so I can think perfectly dispassionately about the fact that I might be developing hypothermia. I'd better move, I think, get myself a bit warmer, but the idea of exposing myself again paralyses me with terror.

I saw a light, a while ago, coming from the large hide. It looked like someone flashing a torch, like they were trying to send a message, but I wasn't prepared to go any closer to find out who it was. For all I know, it's a trap. No, I'm going to stay where I am, even if I have to sit here for the rest of the night. In daylight, I might feel a bit safer, because at least I'll be able to see anyone coming.

There's a large bush over to my right that I've only just noticed, and I think it will provide some cover. Time to move. Getting up is painful, as the blood rushes to fill my slightly numb legs, and a shooting pain runs through my right foot. Eventually I'm able to hobble over to the bush, my muscles stiff and uncooperative. I tuck myself in behind it, using the branches for cover, though there's no comfortable way for me to sit down.

I'm considering my options when I suddenly see another light appear through the woods, and I freeze. I don't dare move; not being able to hear means the only way I can avoid alerting them to my presence is by staying as still as possible, not knowing which movements might make a sound. Is it Dan? Is he still looking for me? I don't know if I can run any more. What do I do? I can't give up, and let him find me, but I know I don't have the strength left to save myself.

The light comes nearer. It's moving slowly from side to side, so I think it's someone sweeping the area with a torch. They're looking for someone, and I know it's me. I take slow, deep breaths to try and stay calm. If I run now, they'll definitely see me, and hear me, so my best option is to stay concealed in this bush and hope that I'm hidden well enough. I'm wearing dark clothes, so they won't see me easily, but if they shine the torch directly at me, I'll be obvious.

They've stopped. Have they seen me? The torch beam swings upward to illuminate the person's face, but I can't see them clearly through the branches. I shuffle sideways slightly, worried that I'm making a lot of noise as I feel the brush of leaves against my arms, and the person turns in my direction. It's Ben! Not Dan, but Ben. I'm flooded with relief, and all I want to do is step into his arms, but something holds me back. Dan was chasing me, so I know I'm not safe with him, but does that mean I can trust everyone else in the group? I battle with myself for a moment, but then Ben steps towards me and I realise he's seen me. I move out of the bush and I can see he's smiling, his mouth is moving but I have no idea what he's saying. His arms are outstretched and I step into them, burying my face in his shoulder, feeling his warmth envelop me. I want to sag to my knees, to cry, but I can't. We're still not safe.

'I can't hear anything,' I tell him, trying to feel the volume of my voice and keep it as quiet as possible. 'I lost my processor.'

He nods, then says something, then rolls his eyes at himself. A moment later, he pulls out his phone and opens up a notes app.

*R u ok? Hurt?*

I take the phone off him and type a reply. I know I could speak to him, but I'm too self-conscious of how I sound without any hearing. *I'm ok. Dan tried to grab me but I got away.*

*He's in the big hide with M and L. K gone to find a gun.*

I read this line twice, wondering what the hell I've missed, but there isn't time to ask him to explain.

*Was it D? Did he kill Alec?* I ask, searching his face for clues as he reads my question.

He grimaces. *Think so. Must be him. He has a shotgun.*

*What's he doing?*

*He tied up M and L, he keeps asking them where you are.*

A shiver of horror runs down my spine. *Why does he want me?*

*I don't know.*

Ben and I look at each other for a moment, and I can tell he's wondering what secrets I might be hiding, why Dan could be hunting me down. The truth is, I have no idea. I don't have any big secrets, nothing to hide, except for the fact that Morna is my biological grandmother, and I can't see why that would bother Dan.

*I haven't done anything to him. I wasn't even worried about Alec and his secrets.*

Ben reads my message and nods, and I can see from his face that he's happy enough with my answer. Maybe part of him still isn't sure, but he's chosen to believe me right now and that's all that matters.

*Do you think he's going to hurt Morna and Lauren?*

He takes the phone back from me, and thinks carefully before he types a reply. *I don't know. He might do. He looked very stressed. There's no way of knowing what he's going to do next.*

He starts typing a long message, telling me how he and Kai approached the hide and watched through the window, as well as listening to what was said inside. As I read it, my fear shifts slightly, and I realise I'm no longer scared for myself, but more so for Lauren and Morna. Yes, Lauren and I have had our issues, and we don't seem to be any closer to solving them, but we're sisters. She's the only family I've ever known. And I want Morna to be okay in order to be allowed the opportunity to get to know her, and ask her the questions that have been burning their way through my mind for the last few months.

*We have to go and help them*, I type, then hand the phone back before starting to stretch my arms and legs. I've stiffened up again, standing here with Ben, and if I'm going to be of any use to anyone I need to keep going, keep moving, however hard it gets.

*No.*

I read the message on the screen, expecting him to add something else, but that's it.

*What do you mean, no?*

*We can't go back there, it's too dangerous.*

I stare at him, incredulous. *We're talking about my sister.* I don't think this is the time to tell him about Morna, about the complexities of my family background.

*A sister who probably wouldn't do the same for you.*

I'm stung by this comment, however true it might be. Even if Lauren wouldn't help me if our roles were reversed, I don't care. The way I treat someone isn't dictated by the way they treat me, it's dictated by what I believe to be right or wrong. And I can't, in all good conscience, walk out of here leaving two people in a hide with someone who means them harm.

*I don't care what you think*, I type, then shove the

phone at his chest. There's no point continuing this conversation if he's going to disagree with me, because he's not going to change my mind.

It's true, we're well placed to escape. Now I know where Dan is, and with Ben helping me, listening out for the danger I can't hear, we could make for the visitor centre and get out of here. Maybe I'll regret making this decision, but I'm going back to that hide, with or without him.

I set off through the woods in the direction Ben came from. I can't see the path from here, but I'm pretty certain I'm going the right way. I could use my torch now that I know where Dan is, but I don't want to be seen emerging from the woods if he happens to be looking out of the window.

A moment later, there's a hand on my shoulder, and Ben thrusts his phone into my face.

*Ok, you win. But we need to be careful.*

I don't want to admit to the relief I feel knowing he decided to come with me. Ben's been injured, I remember with a jolt. He's in pain and maybe my priority should have been to help him, find him some medical attention. I wouldn't have blamed him if he'd left me here and chosen to go on, to look after himself.

I nod my thanks and hand the phone back. Ben points in a direction slightly to my left, so I adjust my course and we continue walking together, him slightly in front so I can follow his lead. We continue walking for several minutes with no sign of the trees thinning out; I hadn't realised just how far back into the woods I'd run.

320

Eventually, Ben slows down, then puts his arm out to stop me.

*We're nearly there*, he types. *I think we should wait for Kai.*

*How do you know he's coming back?*

I see Ben thinking about my question before typing his response. *I've learnt a lot about him tonight. I trust him. If he can, he'll come back.*

I think this is the best I'm going to get, but if I'm going to trust Ben then I also have to trust his judgement.

*Okay. What's the plan?*

*Right now, we have to wait. When Kai gets back, we'll go in.* The confidence in his words isn't mirrored by his facial expression. I can see that this is the last thing he wants to be doing, and my heart swells at the thought that he's doing it for me.

*Do you think we can look through the windows again, see what he's doing? I want to check Morna and Lauren are okay.*

Ben grimaces. *I don't think it's a good idea. There's too much chance we'll be seen. You definitely can't do it, Dan's looking for you.* He looks around, as if he's willing Kai to appear around the bend in the path. *I shouldn't have let you come back here, it's too dangerous.*

*No, I need to know why he wants to hurt me*, I reply. *And I can't leave the others in there.*

He sighs, then creeps forward slightly, to the edge of the trees.

*We'll wait here, until we see Kai coming back, then we'll make a plan. Okay?*

I agree, knowing this is the best compromise we'll

manage to reach. Kai could be ages, in fact might not come back at all, but for now we each choose a tree to lean on, and we wait.

A moment later, a thought occurs to me and I reach for his phone. As I take it from him, my thumb slides across the screen accidentally, and I close the notes app, the display flicking to something else. I glance at it and I'm about to close it when I realise what I'm seeing. It's a photo of me, going into the block of flats where I live. Why has Ben got a photo of me in London? The only time I've seen him is when we've met up with this group.

Ben hasn't noticed that I'm not typing a message, and I swipe the screen to see if there are more photos. I press my lips tightly together when I see other shots of myself: in a bar with a couple of friends; walking by the side of the river, engrossed in something on my phone; even one of me standing in the window of my flat. There's quite a close-up one of me on the tube, and I realise the top I was wearing shows a lot of cleavage, especially from the angle the photo was taken.

Has Ben been stalking me? I thought I'd got to know him over the last six or seven months, that we were getting on well and he liked me, but I had no idea he was capable of something like this. Looking at the photos, the invasion into my privacy makes me feel sick, and I have to turn away from him. I told myself I could trust him, but it looks like he's not someone I can feel safe with.

He turns to look at me, a quizzical expression on his face, so I hastily close the folder and pass the phone back to him.

'Doesn't matter,' I say, doing my best to keep my voice

quiet. He watches me for a moment, and I wonder if he can see the change in me that's occurred in the last couple of minutes, but then he smiles and turns back to watch the path.

Come on Kai, I think. I desperately need you to come back. I know if I run, Ben will come after me. Could he and Dan be in on this together? Is he only pretending to help me, all the while intending to deliver me to someone who wants to hurt me? Though judging by the photos, Ben has had ample opportunity to hurt me in the last few months. Still, the thought of him following me, watching me, makes me shiver.

All I know now is that I can't run. I can't hear anything, and if Ben doesn't catch me, Dan will. Until I can finally trust someone, I'm stuck.

# Chapter 39

## Dan

I sit with my back to the door, feeling the grain of the wood against my scalp. Lauren seems immune to me staring at her, but Morna looks away uncomfortably every time my gaze rests on her for more than a couple of seconds. Good. I want her to feel uncomfortable. I want her to find it difficult to look at me. Why should I be the only person suffering? I've been hurting every single day for the last six months.

I still remember the day I was pulled aside and told there'd been an accident. That's all they said, an accident. I'm hundreds of miles away from my pregnant wife and I don't get any more detail than that for several hours. How did I even get through those hours? Now, I can't remember. But what I didn't know at the time was that I should have held onto them, cherished those hours when I was in limbo, when I still had the capacity to hope that everything might be okay.

But everything wasn't okay. Nothing will ever be okay,

ever again. Rachel went out one evening and never came home, died in the middle of the road, my son with her. We didn't find out the gender beforehand. I was happy to know, but Rachel said it wasn't fair because I couldn't come to any of the scans, she wanted to keep that as something we'd discover together when the baby was born. But the doctors told me, afterwards. We're sorry we weren't able to save your son, they said. Just like that. My son. My baby boy, who should have grown up to be a pain in the arse teenager, then a decent adult. I've pictured him every day since I found out, what he might have looked like, what he would have enjoyed doing.

It makes it all more real, thinking of him as a person, even though he never even had the chance to be born. These two are sitting here, not even daring to look at me. Maybe they know that they're helping to keep me from getting my revenge. Maybe they don't care, and they only want to save their own skins. I don't give a shit about them, though.

'Emily killed my wife.'

Lauren looks up at me, her eyes wide, and Morna gasps. Good, I want them to be horrified, to understand why I've done what I've done.

'My wife was killed six months ago. It was a hit and run, but the police weren't able to get enough information about the car to find the driver. They knew the make, model and colour, but even though it wasn't a common car, they couldn't track them down. They couldn't do that one thing to get some sort of justice for Rachel.'

I take a deep breath, pushing down the rage that's rising in my chest. The two women are looking at me in disbe-

326

lief, but I know I'm finally speaking the truth, after keeping my silence for this long.

'I decided I was going to find them. It's been difficult, tracking down the different owners of these cars, but I have a couple of friends who can help with getting into databases, things like that. But there was one detail that a witness swore by that I couldn't match to any car – a sticker in the back window. A blue and white sticker. I assumed it was a charity one, maybe something like the RSPCA, but none of the cars I tracked down had a sticker like that. After they hit Rachel and left her for dead in the middle of the road, whoever it was probably had to get their car fixed, but I didn't expect them to think about the stickers in the window, the one thing that could iden-tify their car.'

Morna lets out a long breath. 'Emily's sticker is to let the emergency services know she's deaf, if she's in an accident.' I think she's talking to herself rather than to me. Lauren turns to glare at Morna, to tell her to shut up, but I don't mind her talking. She's realised that I'm talking about Emily's car, which I had the opportunity to look over in the car park earlier today. It looks like it's never had a mark on it, but I know that's not the case. I turn to Lauren.

'You're the one who helped, you know. You helped me find out who killed Rachel.'

Lauren's expression is a mixture of confusion and fear.

'You told me about the morning you woke up to see your sister's car damaged, do you remember?'

It was only a couple of weeks ago. I was getting frus-trated, because I'd exhausted all the cars in the local area that matched the witness description. I was starting to think they'd got some detail wrong, which was why I'd had no luck. Either that, or they weren't local, which would make my task so much harder.

I'd been walking, as usual, and Lauren had seen me. I stopped to talk to her, and we both got out flasks and had a cup of tea together. It was all very companionable, and she helped to relax me a little. Something about Lauren seemed to invite confidence; I told her about Rachel, when I hadn't told anyone else. I don't use social media, never have, but after it happened one of my friends took the responsibility of telling people we knew, all the friends she'd accumulated over the years. I didn't know most of them, and certainly didn't want their messages of condolence that were thinly disguised attempts to get some gossip and find out exactly what happened. So I had never talked about it, not in person and not online. I was offered counselling, of course, and strongly encouraged to attend. Instead, I quit my job offshore – they allowed me to leave immediately on account of the circumstances – and retreated into myself.

How had Lauren and I even got onto the subject of Emily's car? I think we were talking about Christmas, about how she had no idea what she was supposed to buy for a sister she hadn't seen in ten years, especially when Emily had enough money to buy herself anything she liked. She'd told me all about Emily's car, and then said something that made me sit up.

'Someone smashed into it in the summer. We woke up one morning and it was damaged, so we assume someone backed into it in the middle of the night when it was parked on the road outside my flat. She had to drive it back to London with a big dent in the bumper, because she wanted to take it to her own garage with someone she trusted.'

When Lauren told me this, I got the feeling she was smirking a bit at the damage, that this symbol of wealth and status was somehow tarnished. I tried to be casual when I asked her about the date, trying to pinpoint exactly when it happened, but I know it must have seemed strange that I was asking. Still, now she knows why it was important to me. When Lauren told me that story, I knew I'd finally found the car that killed Rachel.

I admit, my plan wasn't the best one, but right now I don't care. I've been waiting for my revenge, and I'm going to have it sooner or later. The others probably think I'm going to try and escape, but I won't. Once I kill Emily, my intention is to kill myself. I don't care what happens to me afterwards. I'm nothing without Rachel.

'Emily wouldn't do something like that.' Morna's voice is little more than a whisper, but it fans the flames of my anger anyway and I cover the distance between us in no time at all. Grabbing a handful of her clothing, I pull her close to me.

'What the fuck would you know about it? Do you know how much I've been longing for revenge, to get justice for Rachel? I don't care what you think about your precious Emily. She did this, and she's going to pay for it.'

I find it quite telling that Lauren's not the one protesting her sister's innocence. She must know it's true, must have realised something wasn't right with her story about how the car got damaged. Good. I'm not in the mood to argue about it.

329

'But why did you kill Alec?' Lauren narrows her eyes at me as she asks the question, and I feel my heart sink.

'That was a mistake, and I truly regret it. Nobody else was supposed to get hurt.'

'He saw you, didn't he?' Morna says. 'He saw you on the reserve earlier today. Did you put the gun in the hide before we all arrived, so nobody would see it? But you didn't expect him to be there so early, did you?'

I nod, remembering how easy it had been to climb over the side gate near the visitor centre. 'I hid the gun earlier today, yes, in the large hide. And it's possible that Alec saw me, but he didn't say anything if he did. That's not why I killed him. Like I say, it wasn't intentional.'

Lauren had told me she expected us all to watch the murmuration from the largest hide, the one we're currently in, so I picked this one to stash my shotgun in. I thought I could pull it out, kill Emily, then immediately give myself up, although my plan has changed now I've killed an innocent man. But then we'd split up, which was something I wasn't expecting. I'd already announced my intention to stay in this hide, and I thought the others would follow me in, and I knew it would sound suspicious if I suddenly changed my mind. Plus, I needed to get my gun. I tried to watch where the others went, but I couldn't see the door to that hide from here. I saw Emily go into a small hide alone, and I got them mixed up. When it was Alec on the other side of the door, not Emily, I panicked. Alec wasn't supposed to die.

I assumed that Ben must have seen my face when I ran away and barged into him, but if he did, he didn't say anything. Perhaps he was just protecting himself, but I

330

think he genuinely didn't know it was me. I could have left it there, got us all out of here and made plans to kill Emily another day, but I couldn't bring myself to give up. It would have meant letting this opportunity slip through my fingers.

'Why today?' Lauren asks, and I can see she's weary of this now. She wants it to be over, wants to get home, and doesn't have the energy left to fight. Good, then she won't stop me.

'Because it was the first opportunity I had to see Emily in an environment where I could kill her without endangering other people.'

Morna snorts. 'That worked out well, didn't it?' She sounds hysterical, and I wonder why this has affected her so much. Doesn't she care that I'm trying to make sure justice is done? Doesn't she understand that Emily's a murderer?

'Look, I could have easily killed both of you, couldn't I?' I nod to the shotgun that's leaning against the wall, and pull my knife out of my bag. I should have opted to use the knife, I realise that now, but I didn't think I could bring myself to kill someone that up close and personal. Ironic, really, because I killed Alec at close range.

Morna shrinks back as I brandish the knife, so I put it away again to show her I mean it, I don't intend to kill her. Only Emily.

'You could have just followed her home, killed her there,' Lauren snaps. 'Why did you have to do it here, with all of us?'

'That would have taken more time, more planning. I want my revenge. I've waited too long for this!'

331

She snorts and turns her head away in disgust, but I don't care what she thinks. Her opinion of me isn't important. Nothing matters anymore, nothing other than justice, can't she see that?

Suddenly, there's a glint at the window. I've left the shutter up, so I can see if anyone is approaching, and now I can see a light. It's just a brief flash, but I know it's there. Finally, I hope I can finish this.

# Chapter 40

## Kai

The gun bumps off my thigh as I run, but I have no idea how to hold the damn thing. I'm breathing deeply, having run all the way through the woods to the spot where I knew my cousin would be. I crashed out from between the trees and then froze, as he turned his gun on me.

'Kai? The fuck you doing?'

'I need a gun,' I told him. No beating around the bush. He'd know if I was bullshitting him.

'Explain.'

So I did, as quickly as I could, about someone in my group killing another member, then tying up two women in one of the hides.

'We need to take him down, and I can't do that without a weapon.' Even I was impressed at how ballsy I sounded, and my cousin barely paused before he nodded, then handed over the rifle he was holding. I took it from him, but then I realised the major problem. I had absolutely no idea how to hold it, load it, or fire it.

My cousin rolled his eyes at me, and gave me the quickest tutorial anyone has ever been given on how to use a firearm. Point it in the right direction, that's the most important thing, I keep reminding myself. Try not to waste any bullets, then I don't have to worry about reloading. Only fire when there's nobody in the way who could get hurt, other than Dan, of course. My head is spinning with everything that could possibly go wrong.

When I'm close to the largest hide, I step off the path and back into the woods.

'Ben?' I whisper, not knowing where he might be waiting. 'Ben?' There's no response.

Taking a huge gamble, I pull out my torch and flash it on and off a couple of times. Not enough to attract attention from Dan, I hope, but enough to let Ben know I'm here. Where the hell is he? I hope he hasn't gone looking for Emily, or I might never find him.

A few seconds later, there's an answering flash from a little further into the woods, along the path. I make my way round there, and there he is – and he has Emily with him too.

'Hey,' I say, nodding at her, then grabbing Ben's arm. 'What the hell are you thinking? It's not safe for her, she needs to get away.'

'I told her that, but she wouldn't leave, not until she knows Lauren and Morna are safe.'

I turn to look at her, and she gives me a blank smile.

'She can't hear anything,' Ben says, which explains why she hasn't stepped in to defend herself.

'Can she read lips?'

'No, there's not enough light.'

'Good point. Okay, but how are we going to explain the plan to her?'

'Do we have a plan yet?' he asks, and I want to hit him.

'Not yet, but now I've managed to get us a means of defending ourselves, maybe we can come up with something.' I know I need to dial back the sarcasm, but I'm tired and scared and my ankle is in absolute agony, so I don't have a lot of patience left.

Ben pulls out his phone and types something, then hands it to Emily, who nods, then types something in reply.

'She says hurry up, we need to find out what's happening.'

'It's not safe for you,' I tell her. 'I don't want you coming in with us.'

Ben relays this, and she rolls her eyes.

*Dan wants me, so I can distract him. It'll give you two an opportunity to get his gun, then once he's disarmed, we can make sure the others are safe.*

I read this, and all I can see are the flaws in her plan. I'm pleased to see she's not scared, that she's prepared to go in and do this, but I also think she doesn't truly understand the level of danger she's in. If Dan sees her, there won't be time for us to get his gun, because he'll just shoot her the moment she shows her face.

'Does she have any idea why Dan's after her?' I ask Ben, and he shakes his head.

'She says there's nothing.'

'Should we be worried about that?'

Ben looks confused. 'What do you mean?'

'Is she lying to us? Are we doing the right thing, including her in the plan?'

Ben bristles, and I realise I shouldn't have suggested Emily was anything other than an angel from heaven. 'She's telling the truth. Drop it.'

I nod. No way am I prepared to drop it, but I think we can formulate a plan that will still work even if it turns out Emily has her own agenda. One thing's for certain, I'm not letting go of this gun.

We spend a few minutes discussing different options for how we're going to do this, and eventually we agree on a plan of action. I'm still unsure if it's going to work, especially as Emily can't hear anything. What if something goes wrong? How are we going to alert her to danger, or tell her to change the plan? I'm nervous about it, honestly.

I hold back for a minute. 'What if Dan isn't in there?'

Ben turns and I can see the same thing dawning on him, then he shakes his head. 'I'm sure he's still there. We've been watching the hide, he hasn't left.'

'He could have left while you were off looking for Emily.'

Ben pauses. He knows I'm right.

'We need to see inside.'

'I'll go and look,' he volunteers. I agree, not completely happy with it but knowing it's the best option. I'd rather see for myself, but in order to do that I'd need to put the gun down – Ben needed both hands to pull himself up and peer through the window earlier – and that's not going to happen. I'm not going to hand it over to Ben, either. Maybe I don't feel confident handling it, but I'm much happier this way than with it in anyone else's hands.

We move through the trees and get closer to the hide. Emily hangs back and I see her looking at me as if there's something she wants to say, but the moment passes. I briefly wonder if she knows something, but a thump from inside the hide pulls my attention back to what we're doing. The door is still closed, and I hope Dan hasn't found a way to barricade it from the inside. Luckily for us, it opens outward, so it's not simply a matter of dragging a couple of the benches in front of it. He'd have to find a way to secure it. Then, a thought strikes me.

'Shit. The hide has a lock, doesn't it?'

'Yeah,' Ben whispers. 'Why?'

'Lauren has her keys. What if Dan's got them off her and has locked the door?'

Ben thinks about this for a moment. 'I don't think he'll have done that. If he sees Emily, he won't want to mess about trying to unlock the door, giving her time to get away. She's escaped from him once already this evening, he's not going to let that happen again.'

I raise my eyebrows in surprise. My opinion of Emily keeps going up, and if it wasn't for the fact she can't hear anything I'd be happy that she was backing us up on this.

'Right, are you going off to have a look through the window?' I ask him, giving him a gentle prod. Emily is looking confused.

'Tell me what you're saying,' she insists, her voice sounding strange. Ben types something for her on his phone again, and I try to hold back my frustration. As bad as it is for me, it must be worse for her, having to communicate this way. She reads, then nods her agreement and wishes Ben good luck as he goes off towards the hide. The two of us wait; I'm tensed, ready for whatever comes next, but Emily seems to relax slightly as Ben moves away from us.

My hand is trembling as I clutch the gun, trying to keep my finger away from the trigger. It has a safety catch, but my cousin told me I'd be better leaving it off, just in case I need to defend myself in a hurry. I protested, but he said it was less likely that I'd shoot someone accidentally, and more likely that I'd find myself in a dangerous situation with a gun I couldn't fire. I bowed to his experience and judgement again, though reluctantly. I mean, he's less concerned about accidentally hurting someone than I am. I dread to think how many people he's deliberately hurt in his life.

Ben is at the side of the hide now, pressing himself against the wall, creeping slowly sideways. Come on, hurry up, I think. We don't have time now. They've been in there for so long, what the hell is Dan waiting for? Does he really think Emily is going to come to him? I look at her, and realise that's exactly what she's doing. Maybe his plan is a bit more thought out than I gave him credit for.

There's a shout, and I look up. Ben is running back to us, shouting at me to come on, waving his arm. What happened?

'Dan saw me, quick!'

I don't wait for any further explanation, but tighten my grip on the gun and run out of the woods towards the hide. By the time I get there, Ben has passed me in the opposite direction and he has his arm around Emily, though she's flinching away from him. Is he trying to get her away from here? I hope so, but I don't think she's cooperating. The door to the hide flies open, and Dan is standing there. He flips a switch and the interior blazes with light, catching me off guard and blinding me for a moment.

'Emily. Come here, then we can finish this.' Dan's

looking past me, and his voice sounds strange. It's less threatening than I'm expecting, and wearier. What the hell does he mean?

Emily steps up next to me, but I put an arm out to hold her back and shake my head. She dodges me and moves past.

'Let Lauren and Morna go.'

Dan cocks his head to one side as if he's thinking about it, then shakes his head. I raise the gun to my shoulder, conscious of Emily between me and Dan, but wanting to be prepared if he makes a move towards his own gun. Ben is next to me and I can see him dithering – too scared to go closer, but desperate to get Emily away from Dan.

I step closer. 'Let them go, Dan. Nobody else has to get hurt.'

'I don't want to hurt them, only her,' he replies, giving me a withering look. 'Put that bloody thing down.'

'No!' Ben runs forward, putting himself between Emily and Dan, forcing her to move back and away from him. She tries to get past him, slapping him as he grabs hold of her arms, but he doesn't let go. Dan makes an exasperated noise and walks back into the hide, leaving the three of us outside, confused.

I follow him, only going as far as the door, but what I see makes me catch my breath. Dan is standing over Morna, with a knife to her throat. Her eyes are on me, pleading. What can I do? I'm not a good enough shot to hit Dan and guarantee not hurting Morna.

'Let me explain this in a way you might understand. I don't want to hurt Morna. But if it's the only way I can get Emily to give herself up to me, then I will.'

'You bastard,' Ben spits. He's holding tight to Emily, who is struggling in his arms. I'm surprised he has the strength to hold her, and a moment later she goes limp, so Ben makes the mistake of relaxing. The instant he does, she kicks back and gets him right in the crotch, making him release her. As Ben crumples to the floor, Emily dashes forward. I'm expecting her to go to Lauren, or even Morna, but she rams into me and tries to get the gun out of my hands.

'What the hell? Emily, stop!' But of course, she can't hear me.

I keep my fingers curled back into my palm to avoid them going near the trigger, but that makes it harder for me to grip with that hand, and a moment later she's wrestled it off me.

'Bitch!' Dan snarls, his face a terrifying mask of fury and pain. 'You killed my wife!' He lunges forward, the knife still in his hand, and at the same time Ben makes a grab for the gun.

The gunshot that rings out is deafening in the small space. I step back, feeling like I've been punched. There's blood, and screaming. Whose blood is it? Dan is on the floor, with Ben on top of him; Morna is leaning over me, but I can't tell what she's saying. What happened?

Then I realise, the blood's mine.

# Chapter 41

## Emily

The five of us huddle around a table in the café, waiting for the police and an ambulance to arrive. Occasionally, a couple of the others say something, but I don't bother trying to find out what they're talking about. My head is reeling with everything that's happened this evening, and my head and body ache so much I can't think past it.

I know I shouldn't have tried to get the gun off Kai, but I saw red. My intention was never to kill Dan; I didn't want him dead, I wanted him arrested and convicted of Alec's murder. I'm not like him.

I'm not entirely sure what happened. I don't know if any of us is. Dan went for me, Ben went for Dan, or maybe he was trying to get the gun, and one of us pulled the trigger. I look at Kai now, his arm bandaged, looking dazed. He's lucky it was only a graze really, rather than a deep wound, so Lauren's first aid skills should be enough to keep him going until he can be seen by a paramedic. I hope he doesn't blame me, but it would be no surprise

341

if he did. It's my fault he was shot, whoever actually pulled the trigger.

I didn't realise what had happened at first, though of course I felt the gunshot in my entire body, and saw Kai fall to the floor in front of me. I still had Dan to worry about, but Ben had him pinned to the floor, too. It was only when Ben got up that I realised Dan was no longer struggling. The knife sticking out of his neck glinted in the light, and I couldn't focus on anything else. The others were moving around, checking on Kai, trying to see what had happened to Dan, taking me by the arms and leading me to a bench, but I wasn't really aware of any of it. I dropped the gun as soon as Kai fell, and I assume nobody else wanted to pick it up. Then they hustled me out of the hide and we were all moving. It wasn't until we were a lot further along the path that anyone confirmed what I already knew, that Dan was dead.

We all walked back to the visitor centre together, staying as close as we could while still being able to move. As we went, I clung to Morna's arm, and we used the same method of communication that Ben had thought of earlier. I could see him constantly looking at me, wanting to come and check on me, but I was focused on Morna.

I told her while we were walking that I knew she was my grandmother – *our* grandmother. We passed my phone back and forth between us as we walked, telling our secrets. She was full of apologies, and to my own surprise I believe her. We've agreed that now isn't the time to talk about it, but we'll have plenty of opportunities. I'm not sure what we'll say to Lauren, but we'll think of something, when the time is right.

The thing I can't get my head around is what she told me next. Dan was convinced that I killed his wife. Morna told me the whole story, about how she'd been run over by a car just like mine. I'm horrified, and feel sick even thinking about someone doing that, let alone to a pregnant woman, and despite what he did I find myself pitying Dan. I can't imagine what it must be like to experience losing someone in that way. But it wasn't me.

Apparently, Lauren told him about my car being damaged during the summer. It was weird, I'll be the first to admit, but I have no idea how it happened. We'd been on one of our walks one Saturday and I stayed over at Lauren's flat, then the following morning we woke up to find my car had been damaged during the night. It was parked on the road, so we both assumed someone had backed into it in the dark, possibly someone who'd had a bit too much to drink and either didn't realise they'd done it or couldn't be bothered to stop and leave a note. I took it to my usual garage and they sorted it out, then to be honest I didn't think much of it. If it happened on the same day as the hit and run, then I can only think it was a terrible coincidence.

My main concern is what the police will think if they hear Dan's story from someone else. Will they treat me as a suspect in his wife's death? Will they want to look at my car? I snort at the idea. There'll be little chance of that happening now: when we got back to the visitor centre, Ben went to check on the car park, to see if we could get out, with the amount of snow that's fallen. He looked nervous when he walked back in, because he'd discovered my car was missing. Kai put his head in his

343

hands when they were talking about it, but I haven't asked him what he knows. I think we've all been through enough tonight, and after all, it's only a car. I was never that keen on it. I probably won't even replace it – I don't need a car in London, it was an extravagance I thought I needed to prove something to myself.

Ben managed to get through to the emergency services about fifteen minutes ago, so I'm hoping they'll be here soon, if they can make it through the snow. I rub my eyes, fighting to stay awake. Next to me, Morna pulls out her phone and types something.

*I won't say anything to the police about why Dan did it. I won't tell them about the hit and run.*

I feel a surge of gratitude, knowing she wants to protect me, but it's swiftly followed by a feeling of panic.

*I didn't do it, Morna. I promise. I don't know anything about it.*

She hesitates before she replies.

*I believe you.*

But I don't think she does. I appreciate the gesture of keeping it quiet, but it means nothing to me if she is now second-guessing whether or not I have killed someone. Not the best start to us trying to build a relationship, but I don't know how to convince her that it wasn't me. Besides, Dan shouted something at me at the end, so I think the others know what he was accusing me of, too. I won't ask anyone to lie for me. I'll just have to prove my innocence.

Ben comes over and sits next to me, then gives Morna a tight smile. She gets the hint and stands up, but as she moves away, I feel like I want to grab her hand and pull her back. I don't want to be alone with Ben right now, though I don't want to tell her why. Without any hearing, I feel intensely vulnerable, and it almost feels like Ben is enjoying it. But I'm not a woman who needs or wants a man to protect her, and if that's what he's hoping for then he's going to be sorely disappointed.

*I'm sorry I left you alone, earlier. I wanted to talk to Alec about something, and I thought it was a good opportunity.*

I read what he's written and nod. *Thank you for the apology.* I don't know what else to say right now. If he hadn't done it, Alec would still be dead, and it wouldn't have changed Dan's behaviour. The only person it hurt was Ben himself, with his injured head.

*Do you think we could go for a drink one day next week?*

If he'd asked me this twenty-four hours ago I would have answered straight away – of course. I'd been waiting for him to ask me out for weeks. But now, there's no way I'll ever feel safe alone with him, after seeing those photos. It hasn't even sunk in properly, that he's followed me at least once, and been outside my home, watching me. How could I have been so wrong about him? I feel like I've seen everyone here in a different light this evening, and that has changed my opinion of all of them, some for better, others for worse.

*I don't know if it's a good idea*, I reply. *After everything that happened tonight.*

The emotion that flashes across his face when he reads my reply shocks me – I'm sure I see anger before his expression settles into one of disappointment. I'm not ready to confront him about the photos, and I don't know if I ever will be, given this reaction. I'd rather be safe and let him think he hasn't been found out, than risk the alternative.

*Ok, I understand. Maybe in a few weeks.*

I give him a brief smile, knowing my answer will always be no, but I can solve that problem when it arises. After tonight, I doubt I'll be meeting up with this group again, anyway.

Needing to move, I stand up and wander over in the direction of the toilets, locking myself in the first cubicle and splashing some water on my face. As I stand there in front of the mirror, all the horror and fear of the evening rushes in, and I vomit into the sink. My body convulses, and I only straighten up again when I'm sure it's over, and there's nothing left to come up. My eyes are streaming and I'm shaking, my legs feeling so weak I need to sit down on the toilet lid. I want to sob and scream all at the same time, but I keep holding it back. I don't want to show any more weakness than I already have.

I give myself a few more minutes alone, then I rinse out my mouth, splash cold water on my face, and go back to rejoin the others. Nothing seems to have happened since I left; they're all sitting in the same places, mostly looking despondent. Lauren has her back to the room, and is staring out of the large window at the pond and the woods beyond. Well, at the moment all she can really see is the room behind her, reflected in the glass, overlaid on the dark landscape beyond.

Even though part of me doesn't want to talk to her, I think this might be an opportunity to say things we would never normally say. I take out my phone, so I can communicate with her, and I see the trepidation on her face reflected in the window as I approach.

*Are you okay?*

She nods. *You?*

*Sort of.*

She gives me a wry smile of understanding, then we stand together for a minute, looking out at the reserve.

*This hasn't really worked, has it?* she types.

*What do you mean?*

*Us getting to know each other again.*

*Not really.*

I pause for a minute, wondering what else to say.

*I think it could work, though,* I tell her. *But we both need to change our mindsets.*

She frowns at me. *What do you mean?*

*We need to move on, forget about what life was like when we were kids. We went through a lot, and we're still blaming it on each other.*

It feels like she stares at me for a long time without blinking, then she finally replies.

*You're right.*

*I can forgive you for the way you treated me. You were a kid, and that was the only way you knew how to deal with the situation we were in. But you need to forgive me for being deaf. Because I know you've always thought that was the reason we weren't adopted.*

Lauren looks away, and I know I've hit a nerve. I want to reach out and hug my sister, but I don't think it would be welcomed. Hopefully we can move on, but I'm not ready to address the other elephant in the room, yet: Lauren knows why Dan wanted to kill me, and I don't know if she'll pass that on to the police. I can't ask her not to, because that makes me look guilty. But if she tells them about it, and Morna doesn't, that will also raise a red flag. I'm trapped, and I don't know which way to move.

She turns to me and nods, but doesn't type anything else. I think this is as close as I'm going to get to any sort of truce with her, but it's a start. Leaving her to her thoughts, I go back to the table and sit down next to Kai, leaving no space for Ben to move up and join me.

He gives me a gentle nudge with his shoulder, the one I didn't injure.

*Self-defence. It'll be fine.*

I nod. I hadn't even thought about that. Once Dan was dead, I thought it was all over, but really the nightmare might just be beginning. I assume he means the injury to his own arm, but then I realise he's probably talking about Dan.

*I didn't kill Dan*, I type.

*Who did, then?*

I shrug. I didn't see what happened, in the panic. I assumed it was Ben, jumping in to defend me, but I can't be certain.

Suddenly, the other four all look round.

*What is it?* I ask Kai.

*Sirens. The police are here.*

# Chapter 42

## Lauren

### Seven months later

'Hey.'

I look up from my rucksack and see Kai striding into the room. The change in him recently has been interesting to see. He's starting a college course in wildlife conservation in September, and he's been volunteering with us in order to get some experience. Well, it started as community service. Ben helped him get a decent lawyer, and they managed to show he'd been coerced into his involvement with the poachers, which meant he received a much lighter punishment than his cousin and his mates.

At first, I was sceptical. I thought he was feigning an interest in what we do here in order to make himself look better in our eyes, but in the last few months he's proved himself to me. He works harder, and puts in longer hours, than any of our other volunteers. He's more dedicated than some of my employed staff, too. When he applied for the course, he asked me for a reference, and I could tell he was really nervous just broaching the subject, but I was happy to do it. Besides, we all owe him. If he hadn't got hold of the rifle, I don't know how that night would have ended.

'All set for today?' he asks, and I can see through the forced joviality. He's nervous, which actually helps to calm my own nerves. At least we're all in this together.

'Yep, equipment's ready to go.' I point out a bag of night vision scopes that Ben donated to the reserve a few months ago. I never did find out exactly why he had them, as he'd never used them for any of our group meetings, but then again, maybe it's best if I don't know.

'I've never seen a badger in the wild,' he says, and the nerves are now replaced by that boyish excitement he can't hide whenever he's anticipating a new experience.

I smile. 'You won't be disappointed.'

The five of us have met a few times since Boxing Day – the night that Alec and Dan died – but only ever in daylight, sticking to the paths we know. This is the first time we're going to be doing anything after dark. A family of badgers has set up home within the reserve, and a new hide has been built in order to allow us to watch them without disturbing them. The cubs first emerged at the start of May, and they're getting quite big now. I've been out to watch them a couple of times with colleagues, and I've watched the live feed from the cameras we've set up.

As a group, we decided it was time to conquer our fears and get out there in the dark again. I'm not sure Emily was particularly keen, but Morna and Kai talked her into it. I think if it were up to my sister, she wouldn't go anywhere without streetlights ever again. She's a city person now we're adults, and I don't think that will ever change. Still, she wants to impress Morna, desperate as she is for family. Personally, I'm not inclined to acknowledge that we're related. She did nothing for us as kids, so I don't see her as family now. Emily and I are very different. And I have my reasons for not wanting Emily to get too close to Morna.

Ben is the next to arrive, and I can see he's a bit disappointed that Emily isn't here yet. I don't know what went on between them, but they never did get together. Maybe something changed that night, when they were out in the woods. He's had the sense not to push it, though. In fact, I have my suspicions that something might be going on between Emily and Kai, but if there is, they're keeping it under wraps.

Emily and Morna arrive together. My sister has chosen to stay in a hotel the last few times she's visited, rather than with me, which I've tried not to take personally. I think it's her way of taking a step back from me. We both agreed that we'd taken things too fast, trying to develop a relationship, so now she's giving me space.

Morna's smile is a nervous one, as it always is when she looks at me now. We had it out a few weeks into the year, when she and Emily finally got together to tell me the truth. I was more pissed off that they'd both kept it from me than anything. Emily had known about Morna for ages, but didn't think she should tell me. What gave her the right to keep that information from me? I know, I could have asked for our files and found out for myself, but I'd never thought it would tell me anything useful.

'This is nice, all of us back together,' Morna says, her voice strained.

'Yeah, nice,' I say, trying to bite back the sarcastic comment I can feel forming in my brain. Hopefully nicer than the last time we were all here in the dark. Let's not kill anyone tonight, yeah?

All our statements about that night matched up, that Dan wanted Emily dead and was determined to make that happen. Emily didn't face any charges for injuring Kai, and the investigation into who stabbed Dan was inconclusive. I know Emily thinks it was Ben, but he denies it. Morna didn't say anything about the hit and run; by then she already knew who Emily was and wanted to protect her. I didn't mention it either, beyond Dan's insistence that Emily killed his wife, because the last thing I want is the police looking into what happened that night. Without her car, they couldn't really look any further into it, and that part of the investigation petered out pretty quickly.

We'd been out that weekend, but not on this reserve. We'd been to another one, further north, which backed onto the Humber estuary. It had been a really good day and I'd been feeling really positive, until I was sitting up late after she went to bed, and I read an article about Emily's company. The article included estimates of how much each employee was worth, and my jaw nearly hit the ground. How had my sister become so rich? I admit, I was jealous. So I took her car.

I wanted to drive it, to feel what it might be like to be the type of person who could afford one. But as I drove, I just felt my anger building, the sense of injustice that I'd spent my whole adult life struggling with nobody to offer me any support, yet my sister managed to land on her feet and earn the sort of money I could only ever dream of. I was jealous, and bitter, and the more I thought about it, the faster I drove.

I'm not proud of what I did. I didn't see the woman until it was too late, and then I panicked. I don't even remember driving back to my flat. It's a good job I parked it in the same spot, or Emily would have been more suspicious about how it came to be damaged. As it was, she bought my suggestion that someone had backed into it in the night, and never questioned anything else. She went home that day, and probably never saw the local news about the woman killed in a hit and run.

There's no way I can atone for what I did that night, I know that. That guilt will live with me for the rest of my life. It was only when I met Dan and I realised who he was, how we were connected, that I realised I could do some good. I could help him to heal, which might go some way towards assuaging my guilt.

Of course, by then my hatred of my sister had started to fester. I think I kept it pretty well hidden, because she kept visiting and didn't seem to have any reservations about seeing me. I tried out a few plans in my head, but everything seemed too risky. This wasn't something that I could rush. If I wanted to get my hands on her money, and finally experience the lifestyle she had access to, I would have to be smart about it.

It was when I understood that Dan was hell bent on revenge that I realised I had the perfect opportunity in front of me. I could drip feed him enough information to convince him that Emily was the person who killed his wife. Once he knew that, I was certain it was only a matter of time until he did something about it, and I knew it wouldn't be reporting her to the police. He was more of a man of action. Of course, I didn't bank on the fact that he wanted to kill her as soon as possible, regardless of who else was there; I didn't think any of the rest of us would be at risk.

When Alec was shot, it took me a long time to realise it must have been Dan. I didn't link it to my plan at all, which was quite naive of me. For the first few hours it simply didn't occur to me that it was him and that he'd killed Alec by accident. I don't know if Morna told the police about Dan's remorse over killing Alec, but I certainly didn't. No need to create any sympathy for him. They knew he was after Emily and died while trying to attack her. While they were fighting, I managed to work my hands free from the rope Dan had used to tie me up. Luckily, none of the others saw me pick up the knife and stab him swiftly in the neck. I couldn't risk him telling the police that I was the one who pointed him in Emily's direction, of course.

But now I'm back to square one. Dan didn't succeed in doing my dirty work for me, so I'm going to have to find another way, and I want to do it quickly, before she makes a will and leaves everything to bloody Morna. When she stays with me, I've noticed she takes a few different supplements every day, so I've researched ways of replacing them with different capsules. I don't have access to her pills at the moment, so I've filed the idea in case it becomes useful in the future. No, for now I'm just going to have to find another way to kill my sister.

Who knows, maybe an opportunity will present itself tonight . . .

# Acknowledgements

Writing my first standalone novel has been an adventure, and one that I certainly couldn't have undertaken without a huge amount of support.

Thank you to my amazing agent, Juliet Mushens, who is always around to answer questions and offer encouragement, even at short notice. I think there must actually be three of her, to get everything done!

I'm really grateful to Tilda McDonald and Beth Wickington for their enthusiasm when I first brought them the idea for *Nowhere to Hide*, and for convincing me to make certain changes that have ultimately made it a better story.

The team at Avon are fantastic, and I always feel lucky to be working with them. Huge thanks to Lucy Frederick for picking up the editing reins and knowing exactly when I needed an ego boost! Also to Ellie Pilcher, El Slater and Becci Mansell for marketing and publicity, as well as Sarah Whittaker for another cracking cover to add to my bookshelf. There are all sorts of important things that go on in a publishing house that even we authors don't always know about (or understand, frankly!) so thanks to Elisha Lundin, Sammy Luton, Hannah Avery, Charlotte Brown and Catriona Beamish for everything you do in the way of editorial, sales, audio and production, as well as Fran Fabriczki for copyediting and Anne Rieley for proof-reading.

Special mention to Mel and Nick Webb, who run my local independent bookshop, The Rabbit Hole in Brigg. I've never met two people more enthusiastic and energetic in the face of hardship than these two, and the spirit with which they support local authors and engage with the community is indefatigable. I'm looking forward to more events in the shop in the future!

Second special mention goes to Nick Quantrill, Nick Triplow and the Hull Noir team. I love being part of the Humber crime writing scene, even if I am on the other side of the bridge!

To Morna Watts, friend of over twenty years (impossible, surely?): I promised to name a character after you, I just didn't promise you'd like her . . .

Thanks to my writer friends for always answering weird queries and either cheerleading or commiserating when required: David Bishop, Philippa East, Liz King and Mette Thobro.

I wouldn't have made it to my fourth book without the support and backing of a huge variety of friends and family. I'm going to miss someone off this list, I'm sure, but I'll give it a go anyway: Hannah Bowman, Faye Robertson, Kate Davie, Becky Page, Kayleigh Christopher,

Lizzie Monaghan, Monica Warren, Ruth Cheesley, Jen Clapp, Amy McKenzie, John McKenzie, Hazel McEwan, Wendy Stabler, Amy Bidmead, Vicki Appleyard, Katie Philpott, Ange Robinson, Suzy Barrett, Sam Barrett, Lynsey Lowry, Gemma Hall, Shane Kilbee, Kirsty Holmes, Morna Watts, Jillian Cranmer and Emma Rowson. Thanks for always being excited for me, talking about my books, helping with toddler-wrangling and generally helping me feel like I can cope!

My immediate family have done so much for me in the last year, despite the limitations we've all had on our lives. I'm eternally grateful to my parents, Mark and Glynis Hutchinson, and my in-laws, Gary and Edna Pattison, for everything you do for me. Huge thanks also to William and Michelle Hutchinson for your support from afar, and Julia Pattison and Patrick Cousen closer to home.

Stuart and Bertie, you make it all worthwhile. I hope you forgive the time I spend away from you with my laptop, because I do it all for you.

If someone was in your house, you'd know . . .
Wouldn't you?

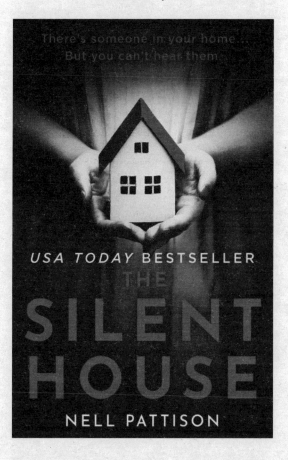

The first gripping Paige Northwood mystery.
Available in paperback and eBook now.

Read on for an exclusive preview now...

# Prologue

There was someone else in the room.

Jaxon rubbed his eyes groggily. Light from the lamppost outside was spilling through the gap in the curtains, and he could see the shape of a grown-up standing by the door. Who was it? He couldn't tell, his eyes blurred with sleep.

Only half awake, he rolled out of bed and patted his little sister Lexi in the bed next to his. He poked her to see if she was awake, but she didn't move. His other sister, Kasey, was asleep on the other side of the room, her chest rising and falling.

*Go back to sleep,* the grown-up signed.

Jaxon looked down at his hands, which glistened with something dark and sticky. He saw the same dark stuff on his sister.

*Why won't Lexi wake up?* Jaxon signed, his confusion over Lexi's lack of response eclipsing his concern about who was in his room.

The grown-up turned to look at the little girl in the bed. They stood over Lexi for a moment, and Jaxon saw their hands moving frantically over her body. They stepped back, one hand raised to their face, then bent over as if they were about to be sick.

Jaxon was too sleepy to resist when the grown-up pulled him out of the room and into the bathroom. They didn't turn the light on, but used a torch to check none of the red had got on his pyjamas, before carefully washing his hands. The light blinded him, keeping the grown-up in shadow.

*Did I do something wrong?* he asked.

*Back to bed now. Don't tell anyone. It's a secret, okay?* Their hands shook as they signed to him.

He nodded again, allowed himself to be led back to his bed. Lexi still had stuff all over her, but maybe they would clean her up next. As he drifted off to sleep, wondering who had been in his room, he didn't notice the adult was still standing by his bed, head bowed and shoulders shaking.

They let out a howl of anguish, but nobody in the house heard.

# Chapter 1

## Saturday 3rd February

'I'm the interpreter,' I said clearly, as I leant over the police tape. My breath fogged in the cold morning air as I spoke. I pulled out my ID badge and waved it at the nearest uniformed officer, a luckless PC who was clearly having a hard time keeping the nosy neighbours back. He only looked about twenty, his eyes bloodshot from tiredness. The card I handed him was my expired ID from the last agency I worked for, the photo an old one. My face had rounded out in the years since it had been taken, but the brown eyes and long dark hair hadn't changed. I hadn't got around to having something new made when I went freelance. I'd been putting it off, out of a fear it'd jinx my fledgling business. The main thing was that it still opened the doors I needed it to.

Those three words were usually met with a look of relief on emergency call-outs, and this time was no different. The PC waved me over to the edge of the crowd and lifted the tape for me to slip under. I could feel the eyes of the onlookers on my back, wondering why I'd been allowed passage. I assumed they were neighbours, their attention drawn by the lights of the emergency vehicles; few people would be passing through this area of Scunthorpe on a Saturday morning, and if they saw police here they wouldn't be inclined to stop.

'Wait here, please,' he instructed me, leaving me on the pavement as he approached the house.

There were officers in white paper suits milling around in the doorway. Other uniformed men and women moved amongst the crowd, notebooks in hand. It was seven on a Saturday morning, didn't these people have better things to do, instead of gawping? A shiver ran through me as a memory surfaced, but I pushed it back down again.

I hovered halfway along the path, unsure if I should go up to the house or stay where I was. The street was typical for that part of Scunthorpe. Rows of identical council houses squashed together, the gardens and exterior walls in varying stages of disrepair. There were neat gardens, clearly loved and tended; there were front yards that were more like the municipal tip in miniature form. How could people cope, living in such disarray?

Past the houses to my left, the road sloped downwards to meet a large patch of waste ground, which stretched away towards the imposing silhouette of the steelworks, jagged against the dark sky. Much of Scunthorpe had been built on the garden city model, but nothing grew amongst the rubble. The street lights enhanced the shadows and for a moment I thought I saw movement. Probably a fox.

In full daylight, the houses on this street looked shabby and rundown, but in the gloom of the winter morning they were bathed in the eerie blue glow of the police car

4

lights. Three cars, lit up but with their sirens off; an ambulance, paramedics moving around inside it but with an air of despondency rather than urgency. It was serious, then.

A phone call first thing in the morning never brings good news. Within an hour of my mobile buzzing me awake, I was pulling up six houses down from the address I'd been directed to. I couldn't get any closer because of the police cordon holding back the gaggle of inquisitive neighbours, pyjamas and slippers visible under their coats. I glanced at the windows nearest to me and saw signs of more observers – corners of curtains pulled back, silhouettes at dark windows. None of them would have known what was happening. Even I had been given the barest of detail, and I wouldn't know more until I went inside.

I ran a hand through my bed hair. I had been on call for the emergency services for six months, and in that time I'd learnt that the people who needed me at short notice would prefer me to be quick rather than smart. If I turned up to a regular job in the afternoon looking like that I probably wouldn't get much repeat business, but when it was an emergency call-out for the police, all bets were off. Still, my professional life was dogged by that little voice in the back of my mind saying that nobody would take me seriously, and my dishevelled state did nothing to quieten it. I grabbed a brush from my bag and tried to sort my hair out while I waited.

The white-suited officers in the entrance to the house had dispersed, leaving a couple with their arms around each other, and I felt a jolt of concern as I recognised them. Alan Hunter, and Elisha . . . I couldn't remember her surname. So, if it was their house, what had happened there? As I watched, the pair separated. There was blood on Elisha's clothes, but she didn't look hurt and the paramedics weren't with her. Alan's eighteen-month-old daughter, Lexi, was my sister's goddaughter. As I pictured her, a horrible thought struck me. Where were the children?

I'd waited for long enough. I needed to know what had happened in that house, and I looked around for a police officer to ask. At that moment, a dark-haired woman came out of the house and marched straight up to me, her hand outstretched.

'DI Forest. You're the British Sign Language interpreter?' Her suit beneath her white overalls was rumpled, but her eyes were sharp.

I nodded. 'Paige Northwood.' At least she gave my job its correct title. Most people called me 'the signer', or worse, 'the signing lady'.

'Come with me. We need to collect some clothing and the woman isn't cooperating.'

'What's happened here? I need context,' I told her as she hurried away from me back towards the house.

DI Forest waved a hand dismissively. 'We don't have the full information. That's why you're here. Right now we need to collect this evidence then get this couple to the station.'

Gritting my teeth in frustration, I followed her. At the door, Forest handed me my own protective paper suit to put over my clothes. After I spent a minute wrestling with it, she ushered me inside. The front door led into the living room, and I could hear voices and footsteps overhead. DI Forest took me straight through a door opposite, into a rear hallway. A door to my right led to the kitchen, and the stairs were to my left. Alan and Elisha were now

6

standing at the foot of the stairs, clinging to each other once again.

The hallway was sparsely decorated – laminate floor, magnolia walls. It reminded me of the house I'd grown up in, another one with the drab decoration of the local housing association. No photographs, no artwork, just a small mirror halfway along the passageway. At the foot of the stairs, by the back door, was a scooter. It looked about the right size for a five- or six-year-old – probably Jaxon's, Alan's oldest child. There was a strange smell in the air – a fuggy mixture of cigarette smoke, marijuana and something else, something more organic. At the top of the stairs I could see figures moving around, but the landing was in darkness, hiding their features.

The phone call that morning had been very curt, simply saying that there had been an incident with a deaf family and the police needed a British Sign Language interpreter immediately. They gave me the address, but no information about what had happened or who was involved. I realised I was shaking as the potential seriousness of the situation hit home: from the amount of blood I could see on Elisha's clothes, someone must have been seriously injured. It was mostly on her sleeves and chest, but I could see smudges on her pyjama bottoms too, probably where she'd wiped her hands.

One of the paper-suited officers was trying to explain something to Elisha, waving a large brown evidence bag in front of her and pointing to her clothes. The woman pleaded with her, but Elisha shrank away; the officer looked at DI Forest and shrugged. I recognised Elisha from the Deaf club, and I spotted a flicker of recognition on her face when she saw me. She was only in her early twenties, as far as I knew, but at that moment she looked much older. There were dark circles under her eyes, which darted back and forth between the two police officers.

'Please could you explain to Miss Barron that we need to take her clothes for evidence? She is allowed to go and get changed, but we need to take those clothes with us. She and Mr Hunter then need to come with us to the station so we can take their statements and their fingerprints.'

'Whose blood is it?' I asked Forest, but she frowned at me and jerked her head in Elisha's direction, as if to say get on with your job. I gave Elisha what I hoped was a supportive smile, trying to keep the fear from my face, and signed the detective inspector's request. Alan had his arm around her, protectively, and looked unwilling to let go. Whenever I'd seen Elisha in the past, she'd been well turned out – not overly dressed up, but neat, as if she looked after herself. This Elisha looked like a different woman. Her brown hair was a mess, half of it falling out of her ponytail. She was wearing an old pair of pyjamas with a couple of holes in. She had probably just got out of bed when it happened, but still, I was surprised by her appearance. Whatever had happened must have been traumatic, to have wrought such a change in her.

As I signed, Alan's knuckles whitened and Elisha grimaced. She shook her head in answer to the request and hugged herself tightly.

'She's refusing,' I told them.

Forest frowned at me again, as if I were the one saying no. 'That's not an option. Her clothes are evidence and we need to get them from her, one way or another. I don't have time for this,' she added with a hiss.

Elisha was surrounded by hearing people making

demands she didn't understand because they weren't using her language, not because she wasn't capable of carrying out their requests. I felt for her, and wasn't surprised she was shutting down. Looking at the exasperation on the officers' faces, I decided it would be best to take the firm approach and get this over with quickly.

*You need to give those clothes to the police, now. Doesn't matter that you don't want to, you have to. Go upstairs, get changed and give those clothes to the police. Now.*

I was rewarded with a long stare then finally a shrug. Alan narrowed his eyes at me, but his grip on Elisha's shoulder loosened and his arm dropped to his side.

'You come upstairs with me?' Elisha asked. Her speech was soft, and the detectives looked surprised to hear her reply.

I checked it was okay with the officers, then nodded.

'Wilson, take her upstairs to get changed, then send the interpreter back down to me,' Forest snapped as she moved back towards the living room.

When her back was turned, I rolled my eyes, but followed the officer and Elisha upstairs to her bedroom.

There was a flurry of activity on the landing as we climbed the stairs, and a door slammed, so by the time we reached the top there was nobody there. My unease grew.

'Please could you take your clothes off and put them in this bag,' the officer asked Elisha, clearly relieved to have me interpreting.

Elisha nodded and pulled a clean t-shirt out of a drawer. I averted my eyes while she changed, but the officer continued to watch her.

9

'I need to know – what happened here?' I muttered to the officer as Elisha changed, but she shook her head.

'DI Forest will fill you in on anything you need to know. I can't discuss it.'

I decided not to push it. The officer took photographs of Elisha's clothing before bagging each item separately. Once I had heard the two paper bags rustle, I turned around, swallowing hard when I realised that Elisha still had a smear of blood across her forehead, going up into her hairline.

'Thank you,' the officer said, and nodded to me. 'DI Forest would like you to return to the living room. Elisha, you can go back and join Alan.'

'Sure,' I replied, quickly translating this for Elisha.

We stepped out onto the landing and were descending the stairs when I heard a door open behind me. I leapt in fright as Elisha let out an unearthly wail, and I realised she was saying a name.

'Lexi! Lexi!'

I turned around on the stairs, expecting to see the little girl. Instead, I saw the open door to the other bedroom and, beyond the officer in the doorway, a toddler bed. My legs went from under me and I fell onto the step. Lexi was lying on the bloodstained mattress, her lifeless eyes open and staring.

I gasped and covered my mouth to stop myself retching, and the officer in the doorway turned, noticing us.

'Shit, get that door shut,' I heard someone say, then our view was obscured once more.

The officer who took us upstairs muttered something under her breath, then guided Elisha towards the stairs, but I was in the way. I wasn't sure if my legs could hold me, so I swivelled around on the step and squashed myself against the wall so they could get past.

I clasped my shaking hands around my knees and swallowed several times to get rid of the bile in my throat. Lexi was dead. Lexi had been killed. How was I going to tell Anna? My sister doted on her little goddaughter.

Elisha ran down the stairs and flung herself at Alan, sobbing as she pressed her face into his chest and clung to him. Alan just stood there, his face blank, not even putting his arms around her. He looked up the stairs and our eyes met, but I looked away quickly. I felt another stab of fear when I thought about his other two children – where were Jaxon and Kasey? Were they dead too?

I needed fresh air, so I forced myself to move. As I stood, someone came out of the smaller bedroom and walked past me on the stairs. It was a different female police officer also dressed in a white paper body suit. She had a large evidence bag in her hand, and she shielded it with her body as she squeezed past me. When she turned, I got a clear view of the bag and its contents: a teddy bear. I remembered taking Anna shopping to buy it when Lexi was born. Its fur was so soft.

I followed her down the stairs, and as she moved into the light in the hallway I saw a dark stain on the bear's foot. Blood. There was blood on Lexi's teddy and they were taking it away for evidence. The room lurched and I stumbled towards the open back door in my haste to get outside, where the rush of cold air precipitated a violent reaction and I vomited onto the cracked patio. Shaking, I sank down onto the doorstep, spitting out the last of the bile in my mouth. What the hell happened in that house?

The officer I knew only as Wilson appeared next to me

11

and handed me a bottle of water. I gave her a grateful smile and rinsed my mouth out, then took a big gulp.

'Sorry, you shouldn't have seen that.'

I made a strangled noise that was somewhere between a laugh and a sob. 'This isn't the sort of job I normally do.'

'Are you okay? Do you know the family?'

I glanced up and saw a wary look in her eyes. I knew there was a potential conflict of interest, but I nodded anyway. 'I know them vaguely from the Deaf club. I know Alan's ex, Laura. Lexi and Jaxon's mum.'

Laura was good friends with my sister, Anna, and I'd known her since I was eighteen. I'd occasionally spent time with Lexi in the last eighteen months, and another wave of horror hit me as I thought about her.

I swallowed and took a deep breath. 'My job can involve working with people I know, in sensitive situations. The Deaf community is small, and you won't find a local interpreter who doesn't know them. I just hadn't expected to arrive here to find out a child is dead.' I swallowed the bile that yet again rushed to the back of my throat, and continued: 'When I'm on call it's usually hospital work, telling doctors what happened and where it hurts. Nothing like this.' I did my best to keep my voice steady, professional, but it cracked a little at the end. I held back the information that Lexi was my sister's goddaughter. Even in my shocked state, I knew I wanted this job; I had to know what had happened. I didn't want the officer knowing the full truth of how close I was to this, in case she told the detectives and they called a different interpreter.

Wilson flashed me a brief smile. 'I understand. Are you okay to continue?'

12

I nodded. There was no way I'd let them replace me. I needed to be there.

She led me back into the house and through to the living room. As we entered, DI Forest frowned, but the man with her smiled warmly and introduced himself as DC Singh. Alan and Elisha had disappeared, either into the kitchen or outside with another officer, I assumed.

'We need to get back to the station and take statements,' Forest said.

'I'm ready,' I said.

'Normally we would have asked you to meet us there, but the communication barrier has slowed things down. Now you're here, hopefully we can get on with things.'

Forest turned on her heel and walked out of the front door, leaving Singh looking a little awkward. He gestured for me to follow, then directed me to where Alan and Elisha were waiting.

I explained the situation to them, and once I was sure they were going to cooperate, I ducked under the police tape and walked back to my car. There were still some onlookers milling around, and I could feel their eyes on my back as I walked away. As I unlocked my car door, I realised my hands were shaking, and I rested my head on the steering wheel before I set off for the police station, taking deep breaths. What the hell could have happened to that poor little girl? And how was I going to tell my sister?

What happened while they were sleeping . . . ?

No one
saw them.

No one
heard them.

No one can find them...

# SILENT NIGHT

NELL PATTISON

*USA TODAY* BESTSELLING AUTHOR

The second in the unmissable Paige Northwood series.
Available in paperback and eBook now.

On a quiet street, one house
is burning to the ground . . .

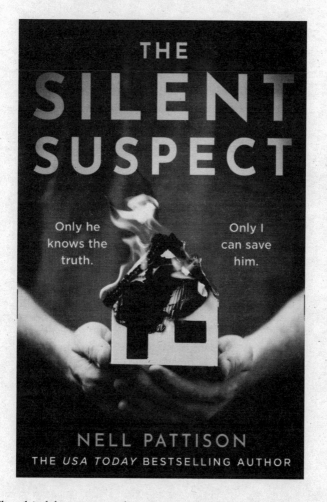

THE
SILENT
SUSPECT

Only he
knows the
truth.

Only I
can save
him.

NELL PATTISON

THE *USA TODAY* BESTSELLING AUTHOR

The third heart-pounding Paige Northwood instalment.
Available in paperback and eBook now.